CRITICAL PRAISE FOR
JACK KEROUAC

"With prose set in the middle of his mind, he reveals consciousness itself on all its syntactic elaboration, detailing the humorous emptiness of his elaboration, detailing the luminous emptiness of his own paranoiac confusion."

—Allen Ginsberg

"Kerouac is extreme, but he is genuine, he is alive, and he is native."

—*Library Journal*

"Life is great, and few can put the zest and candor and sadness and humor of it on paper more interestingly than Kerouac."

—Luther Nichols, *San Francisco Examiner*

"[Kerouac] gives us an excellent and compassionate picture of that segment of the generation which was left to fend for itself after WWII in the absence of goals, and therefore, direction . . ."

—*Kirkus Reviews*

"The first clear development of the American Romantic prose since Hemingway, [Kerouac's writing] is full of mad sex, comedy, leer, wide-screen travel writing, and long lyrical evocation of American childhood and adolescent memories."

—Richard Holmes, *The Times* (London)

BY JACK KEROUAC

DESOLATION ANGELS

JACK KEROUAC

RIVERHEAD BOOKS

NEW YORK

RIVERHEAD BOOKS
Published by The Berkley Publishing Group
200 Madison Avenue
New York, NY 10016

First Riverhead edition: September 1995

A brief excerpt from this novel appeared in *Evergreen Review* under the title "Seattle
Burlesque," later reprinted in *The Moderns: An Anthology of New Writing in America*
and in *Holiday* magazine. The lyrics appearing on page 90 are from "I'm Glad There
Is You" by Paul Madeira and Jimmy Dorsey. Used by permission of the Copyright
Owner, Morley Music Co., Inc. The lyrics appearing on page 91 are from "The
Touch of Your Lips," words and music by Ray Noble. Copyright © 1936 by Santly
Bros.—Joy, Inc., and assigned to Joy Music, Inc. Copyright renewed 1963 and as-
signed to Joy Music, Inc., New York, NY.

Library of Congress Cataloging-in-Publication Data

Kerouac, Jack, 1922–1969.
    Desolation angels / Jack Kerouac. — 1st Riverhead ed.
      p. cm.
    ISBN 1-57322-505-3
    1. Beat generation—Fiction. I. Title.
PS3521.E735D46 1995
813'.54—dc20   95-21092
                          CIP

Printed in the United States of America

10 9 8 7 6 5 4

CONTENTS

INTRODUCTION
BY JOYCE JOHNSON

When I met Jack Kerouac on a cold January night in 1957, I entered Part Two of this novel, which Kerouac originally planned to publish as a separate book under the title *Passing Through*. He had just been in Mexico City and was passing through New York for a couple of months on his way to Tangiers. He was a man without a home, stopping off in different places, then moving on. I think he always fantasized that in some new destination he might find a balance between his craving for novelty and companionship and the reclusive side of his nature.

The night I met him—nine months before the publication of *On the Road*—Jack had no inkling that he was going to become famous or that his Dharma bum life would not continue. He was, as usual, down on his luck, having been short-changed on his last twenty dollars by a clerk in a grocery store. Allen Ginsberg had asked me to rescue him. I was twenty-one and had recently been through some hard times myself. My philosophy back then was: Nothing to lose. I walked into the Howard Johnson's on Eighth Street in Greenwich Village and there at the counter was Jack Kerouac in a red-and-black-checked lumberjack shirt. Though his eyes were a startling light blue, he too seemed all red and black, with his ruddy, sunburned complexion and his gleaming dark hair.

I had never met a man who appeared more vibrant. But as we shyly talked to each other, I began to see how haggard and tired he was. He told me he had recently spent sixty-three days as a fire lookout on a mountain called Desolation Peak and that he wished he were back there now. During the two months we lived together before Jack sailed to Tangiers to join William Burroughs, he said nothing to me about how difficult his weeks of solitude had actually been for him.

Perhaps Kerouac's mind was already converting those sixty-three days into fiction, beginning to give them a retrospective glow. Yet *Desolation Angels*, which he would not complete until 1964, would turn out to be far less a work of the imagination than any of the nine other autobiographical novels comprising what he called his Duluoz Legend. According to Kerouac's biographer Ann Charters, it was the only one that would be drawn so directly from his journals, passage by passage, rather than being written from the transforming distance of memory. Shaped largely through omissions, it is a compelling, often harrowing document of a year in Kerouac's life rather than a recreation. Perhaps just the day after I bought him frankfurters in Howard Johnson's, Kerouac took the black notebook he had bought in Mexico City out of his pocket and wrote about "the blonde in the red coat who seemed to be 'looking for something.'" He would later call me Alyce Newman in *Desolation Angels*.

For Kerouac, writing was the defense against the feelings of emptiness and despair that overcame him whenever his life seemed to be standing still. He told me once that he would never be bored in his old age because he would then be able to read about all his past adventures. When he had nothing more to add to the Duluoz Legend, he planned to conform all the names in the various novels, so that they could be read like one huge book, comparable to *The Remembrance of Things Past*. In fact, Jack thought of himself as "a running Proust." But old age was not in the cards for Kerouac, though his last stop was a tract house in St. Petersburg, Florida, the old-age capital of America. With his literary reputation in eclipse and out of touch with most of his friends, he died there in 1969 at the age of forty-seven.

"It seems to me now that my life is writing, be it only words without meaning,"[1] Kerouac wrote his boyhood friend Sebastien Sampas in 1943. Only twenty-one, he already understood the most important thing about himself. The same letter contained a disturbing, oddly prescient statement: "When I am 33 I shall put a bullet straight through me."[2]

"I feel that I have completely reached my peak maturity now and am blowing such mad poetry and literature that I'll look back years later with amazement and chagrin that I can't do it anymore,"[3] Kerouc would tell John Clellon Holmes nine years later. Although he would survive his thirty-third and thirty-fourth years, there were signs during 1955–56 that his most creative period was indeed drawing to a close. He had completed seven novels, one after another, during a half-dozen remarkable years. But as many far less prolific writers have discovered, autobiography is not an endlessly replenishable source. Even before his summer on Desolation Peak, Kerouac had begun to wonder whether he would just be repeating himself if he continued. For a man who equated life with writing, the idea of stopping was equivalent to a death sentence.

---

1. Jack Kerouac, *Selected Letters, 1940–1956*, edited by Ann Charters (Viking, 1955), p. 38.
2. Ibid., p. 41.
3. Ibid., p. 354.

To compound Kerouac's self-doubts, none of his work had been published since 1950, when Harcourt Brace brought out his first novel, *The Town and the City*. He had believed at first that he had finally redeemed his prodigal son behavior, but the novel did not find many readers and the one-thousand-dollar advance was soon spent. Since 1953, the critic Malcolm Cowley, who was then a consulting editor at Viking Press, had expressed continuing interest in *On the Road*, which Kerouac had written in three nonstop weeks in the spring of 1951. But Viking was fearful about publishing such a daring, sexually explicit work and by June 1955, Kerouac was feeling quite desperate. When Cowley and his associate Keith Jennison took Jack to lunch, he asked the two editors whether Viking would consider paying him twenty-five dollars a month, so that he could live in a hut on a rooftop in Mexico City and finish the book he was working on. For Jack this was a deadly serious proposition, but the two editors seemed to think he was joking. One of them laughed and said, "You certainly aren't holding us up, boy." It would not be until late in 1956, after another year and a half of agonizing uncertainty, that Cowley would be able to make Jack a firm commitment about publishing *On the Road* the following fall. (During the three-year period while Viking was making up its mind, Cowley had rejected a series of newer manuscripts.)

Ironically, Kerouac regarded *On the Road* as a transitional work—less important to his *oeuvre* than some of the more radically experimental novels he wrote soon afterwards, especially *Visions of Neal* (posthumously published in 1972 as *Visions of Cody*), *Dr. Sax*, and *Visions of Gerard*. These were the books in which he felt he had achieved the true voice of the Duluoz Legend, which he described to Malcolm Cowley in 1955 as "a unified spontaneous language lulling out the report forever so

that in my sleep-bed the uproar continues—and the uproar like
the uproar of *Finnegans Wake*, has no beginning and no end."[4]

Kerouac's transformation from the poetic young novelist of
the late 1940s who wrote *The Town and the City* under the spell
of Thomas Wolfe into the daring Bop prosodist of the 1950s
might not have come about if he hadn't encountered an extraordinary group of independent-minded young writers who were
living in and around the Columbia University campus in 1944.
This closely bonded "gang" of male friends, which included
Allen Ginsberg, William Burroughs, and Lucien Carr (the
Irwin Garden, Bull Hubbard, and Julien of *Desolation Angels*),
told each other what to read (Celine, Nietzsche, Blake, Rimbaud) critiqued each other's work, explored Times Square together, experimented with drugs and sex. Untroubled by their
absorption in Kerouac's fiction, they eventually became the cast
of characters who traveled from book to book under different
pseudonyms.

Kerouac always acknowledged his profound spiritual and intellectual attraction to these men. He would listen to them talk
like someone soaking up music, his imagination stimulated by
the rhythms and cadences of their words. With his unerring ear
and exceptional auditory memory, he was able to weave their
voices into his own prose.

The greatest talker of them all, in Kerouac's view, was Neal
Cassady (the Dean Moriarty of *On the Road* and the Cody
Pomeray of *Desolation Angels*), a brilliant autodidact who had
done three stretches in Colorado reform schools for stealing
cars. In 1947, Cassady boarded a Greyhound bus for New York,

4. Ibid., p. 514.

coming to the door naked the day Kerouac first met him in an East Harlem cold-water flat.

With his powerful sexual charisma and boundless physical and verbal energy, this twenty-one-year-old "jailkid" who had grown up in the flophouses and poolrooms of Denver was unlike anyone in Kerouac's New York circle of university-educated friends. Neal reminded Kerouac of the working-class boys he had known in Lowell, Massachusetts, the factory town he left behind at eighteen when he came to a New York prep school on a football scholarship. It was Cassady who inspired in Kerouac the desire to leave "the effete East" and go on the road. Between 1947 and 1950, as the two made a series of marathon cross-country trips together with Cassady at the wheel, Kerouac discovered his great subject: postwar America, seen from the perspective of young men who had opted out of the American dream and who, in order to "know time," exposed themselves to the risks, hardships, and ecstacies of life with no safety net. Kerouac called himself and his brethren of the road "Beat"—a term that had its root in the word *beatitude* and thus a hidden meaning: not only beaten down but blessed.

"Don't think of me as a simple character—" he would later warn his readers in *Desolation Angels*. "A lecher, a ship-jumper, a loafer, a conner of older women, even of queers, an idiot, nay a drunken baby Indian when drinking. . . . In any case, a wondrous mess of contradictions (good enough, said Whitman) but more fit for Holy Russia of 19th Century than for this modern America of crew cuts and sullen faces in Pontiacs—"

When Kerouac and Cassady were apart, they would correspond with each other. Kerouac predicted that Cassady would become a great writer because of "the muscular rush" of his narrative style, the freedom that allowed him to hold nothing

back. "Don't undervalue your poolhall musings, your excruci-
ating details about streets, appointment times, hotel rooms, bar
locations, window measurements, smells, heights of trees, etc."[5]
he wrote his friend on December 23, 1950, giving Cassady the
advice he would shortly act upon himself. (Kerouac was re-
sponding to an extraordinary 13,000-word letter composed on
benzedrine in which Cassady had recounted his relationship
with a woman named Joan Anderson during Christmas 1946.)

Five days later, he sat down to write a "full confession" of
his own life to Cassady, announcing "I hereby renounce all
fiction." It was a turning point for Kerouac. He had suddenly
found a new spontaneous voice for himself that seemed pure
music set free. In order to become the medium for what Kerouac
now called "wild prose," written without stopping or second
thoughts, he would sacrifice everything—health, sanity, marriage and fatherhood, any vestige of comfort or security. "The
voice is all"[6] would become Kerouac's credo, though he would
seldom touch upon this in his fiction. How could he bear to
admit that words were more important to him than human rela-
tionships? Because Kerouac never made his central motivation
manifest, his "true life" novels often seem defiantly plotless.

Did he sacrifice too much? One has only to read the letters
Kerouac wrote between the late 1940s and the mid 1950s to
realize that the writer who spent nearly a decade "on the road,"
crashing in flophouses or in friends' pads, hopping freight
trains, hitching rides the length and breadth of America, was
also a man who suffered from the humiliation and chaos of
homelessness.

In 1951 shortly after his stylistic breakthrough and the com-

5. Ibid., p. 244.
6. Ibid., p. 253.

pletion of *On the Road*, Kerouac abruptly terminated his marriage of six months, telling his pregnant wife, Joan Haverty, to get herself an abortion. When she pursued him for child support payments for their daughter, Jan, Kerouac fled to Mexico and the Coast, always fearful of being hounded by the police and being forced to abandon writing for menial jobs. For the next seven years, he had no place of his own—only a bed and a desk wherever his mother, Gabrielle Kerouac, happened to be living. He would visit Memere to type up his manuscripts, file away his journals and letters and quietly recuperate until boredom and loneliness made him move on.

Kerouac was always most at risk between books, when his reentry into the hectic lives of his Beat gang in New York, San Francisco, and Mexico City would culminate in epic binges. As he began using increasing amounts of alcohol and drugs to evoke his "wild prose," he became angry, bitter, and suspicious, falling out with friends like Allen Ginsberg who expressed criticism of his work.

During his twenties, Kerouac had come up with a recipe for communal living that might actually have suited him. For a couple of years he had an elaborate fantasy about sharing a "homestead" ranch with Neal Cassady and other Beats. (Jack's mother as well as the perfect Kerouac wife—"wild and crazy yet a sunny housekeeper,"[7]—would have been included in this "tumultuous" setup, where something would always be happening.) "To be alone in a house or home is the last unhappiness,"[8] Jack wrote Cassady in 1949. But when his friends entered their thirties, they became less emotionally available to Kerouac as their own existences became more stable: Lucien

7. Ibid., p. 158.
8. Ibid., p. 155.

Carr and Neal Cassady had wives, children, family responsibilities; by 1955 even Allen Ginsberg was settling down with his new lover, Peter Orlovsky. Only Kerouac was still rootless and alone, feeling that "loss and tedium" were driving him insane. "A quiet life" became his stated goal, but he couldn't imagine how to achieve it.

He began to study Buddhism in 1954, hoping that it would provide some answers. With penetrating insight into the roots of Jack's despair, William Burroughs warned him: "A man who uses Buddhism or any other instrument to remove love from his being in order to avoid suffering, has committed, in my mind, a sacrilege comparable to castration."[9]

Although Kerouac would achieve a deep intellectual understanding of Buddhism and would learn to practice meditation, his pursuit of peace had a frantic quality that was self-defeating. Through Buddhism, he could rationalize the void he had discovered within himself, but he could never really accept it. "That nothin' means nothin' is the saddest thing I know,"[10] he once confessed to Neal Cassady the year before his sixty-three days on Desolation Peak.

"My life is a vast inconsequential epic," Kerouac wrote in his notebook up there, not even trying to work on a novel—despite the fact that, for once, he had all the time in the world. He could only stare at Mount Hozomeen and set down his feelings from day to day—which he did cold sober and with ruthless honesty. "The trouble with Desolation is," he wrote, "no characters, alone, isolated." Although Kerouac soon realized that he needed to immerse himself in life again—to "live, travel, adventure, bless and don't be sorry"—there are no sad-

9. Ibid., p. 439.
10. Ibid., p. 474.

der or more self-revealing words in *Desolation Angels* than "no characters." Characters, if he had been able to evoke them through a fusion of memory and inspiration, would indeed have kept Kerouac company in his solitude. But "no characters" was also an indication of the growing distance Kerouac felt between himself and other people. He could still observe them brilliantly but could no longer connect.

Kerouac's deliberate confrontation with the Void in the summer of 1956 was the act of a man who did not fully recognize how worn down he was, but who had not yet lost the courage or the freedom to go wherever his imagination led him. His stint as a fire lookout was to be one of Kerouac's last "on the road" adventures; in 1957 his unwanted notoriety as "the avatar of the Beat Generation" would end his anonymity forever.

In *Desolation Angels*, Jack Duluoz, like Kerouac, comes down from the mountain into the excitement of the San Francisco Renaissance that will set the stage for his long-deferred fame. But as he uproariously wanders the streets of Berkeley and San Francisco with Irwin Garden (Ginsberg), Cody Pomeray (Cassady), and Raphael Urso (Gregory Corso), there is the sense of impending losses, which will ultimately culminate in the moment, a year later, when the first copies of *Road* finally arrive and Cody turns away from Jack Duluoz "shifty-like." "I foresaw a new dreariness in all this literary success," Jack Duluoz tells the reader of *Desolation Angels*.

If there is a fictional moment in this novel—a white lie to provide a sense of closure—it comes at the very end. After revealing that he's now living with his mother "in a house of her own miles from the city," Jack Duluoz describes the sorrow he's feeling as "peaceful": "A peaceful sorrow at home is the best I'll ever be able to offer the world."

* * *

I could always sense the shadowy presence of Jack's spiritual pain during the months we spent together before and after the publication of *On the Road*. But I remember feeling innately resistant to his view that there was no difference between birth and death (an argument that seemed to justify his rejection of fatherhood and his distrust of women). I hated being reminded that Everything is emptiness, though I never hurt Jack's feelings by saying so explicitly. The Beat Generation writers had kicked off my own generation's revolution. How could I believe in the Void at a time when life seemed so full? For a while I thought I could save Jack Kerouac through loving him. But no one could.

Years later, in 1982, my sixteen-year-old son became curious about a small book with a black and yellow binding that he noticed on my shelves—Alan Watts's *Zen Flesh, Zen Bones*. I must have bought it soon after I met Jack, hoping to please him by attempting to understand Buddhism. When my son opened it, a piece of folded green paper fell out. It was part of a label for Eagle Typewriter Paper. On the back of it was a fragment of conversation Jack had jotted down in pencil. It reflected his awareness of our basic philosophical conflict:

> Somebody told me
> that W.C. Handy had
> just died—I said
> "He was never even
> born" — "Oh you,"
> she said.

DESOLATION ANGELS

BOOK ONE

DESOLATION
ANGELS

PART ONE

DESOLATION
IN SOLITUDE

1 THOSE AFTERNOONS, those lazy afternoons, when I used to sit, or lie down, on Desolation Peak, sometimes on the alpine grass, hundreds of miles of snowcovered rock all around, looming Mount Hozomeen on my north, vast snowy Jack to the south, the encharmed picture of the lake below to the west and the snowy hump of Mt. Baker beyond, and to the east the rilled and ridged monstrosities humping to the Cascade Ridge, and after that first time suddenly realizing "It's me that's changed and done all this and come and gone and complained and hurt and joyed and yelled, not the Void" and so that every time I thought of the void I'd be looking at Mt. Hozomeen (because chair and bed and meadowgrass faced north) until I realized "Hozomeen is the Void—at least Hozomeen means the void to my eyes"— Stark naked rock, pinnacles and thousand feet high protruding from hunch-muscles another thousand feet high protruding from immense timbered shoulders, and the green pointy-fir snake of my own (Starvation) ridge wriggling to it, to its awful vaulty blue smokebody

rock, and the "clouds of hope" lazing in Canada beyond with their tittlefaces and parallel lumps and sneers and grins and lamby blanks and puffs of snout and mews of crack saying "Hoi! hoil earth!"—the very top tittermost peak abominables of Hozomeen made of black rock and only when storms blow I dont see them and all they do is return tooth for tooth to storm an imperturbable surl for cloudburst mist—Hozomeen that does not crack like cabin rigging in the winds, that when seen from upsidedown (when I'd do my headstand in the yard) is just a hanging bubble in the illimitable ocean of space—

Hozomeen, Hozomeen, most beautiful mountain I ever seen, like a tiger sometimes with stripes, sunwashed rills and shadow crags wriggling lines in the Bright Daylight, vertical furrows and bumps and Boo! crevasses, boom, sheer magnificent Prudential mountain, nobody's even heard of it, and it's only 8,000 feet high, but what a horror when I first saw that void the first night of my staying on Desolation Peak waking up from deep fogs of 20 hours to a starlit night suddenly loomed by Hozomeen with his two sharp points, right in my window black—the Void, every time I'd think of the Void I'd see Hozomeen and understand— Over 70 days I had to stare it.

2 YES, FOR I'D THOUGHT, in June, hitch hiking up there to the Skagit Valley in northwest Washington for my fire lookout job "When I get to the top of Desolation Peak and everybody leaves on mules and I'm alone I will come face to face with God or Tathagata and find out once and for all what is the meaning of all this existence and suffering and going to and fro in vain" but instead I'd come face to face with myself, no liquor, no drugs, no chance of faking it but face to face with ole Hateful Duluoz Me and many's the time I thought I die, suspire of boredom, or jump off the mountain, but the days, nay the hours dragged and I had no guts for such a leap, I had to *wait* and get to see the face of reality—and it finally comes

that afternoon of August 8 as I'm pacing in the high alpine yard
on the little wellworn path I'd beaten, in dust and rain, on many
a night, with my oil lamp banked low inside the cabin with the
four-way windows and peaked pagoda roof and lightning rod
point, it finally comes to me, after even tears, and gnashing,
and the killing of a mouse and attempted murder of another,
something I'd never done in my life (killing animals even ro-
dents), it comes in these words: "The void is not disturbed by
any kind of ups or downs, my God look at Hozomeen, is he
worried or tearful? Does he bend before storms or snarl when
the sun shines or sigh in the late day drowse? Does he smile?
Was he not born out of madbrained turmoils and upheavals of
raining fire and now's Hozomeen and nothing else? Why
should I choose to be bitter or sweet, he does neither?—Why
cant I be like Hozomeen and O Platitude O hoary old platitude
of the bourgeois mind "take life as it comes"—Twas that alcoholic biographer, W. E. Woodward, said, "There's nothing to
life but just the living of it"— But O God I'm bored! But is
Hozomeen bored? And I'm sick of words and explanations. Is
Hozomeen?

> Aurora Borealis
> over Hozomeen—
> The void is stiller

—Even Hozomeen'll crack and fall apart, nothing lasts, it
is only a faring-in-that-which-everything-is, a passing-through,
that's what's going on, why ask questions or tear hair or weep,
the burble blear purple Lear on his moor of woes he is only a
gnashy old flap with winged whiskers beminded by a fool—to
be *and* not to be, that's what we are— Does the Void take any
part in life and death? does it have funerals? or birth cakes?
why not I be like the Void, inexhaustibly fertile, beyond seren-
ity, beyond even gladness, just Old Jack (and not even that)
and conduct my life from this moment on (though winds blow
through my windpipe), this ungraspable image in a crystal ball

is not the Void, the Void is the crystal ball itself and all my woes the Lankavatara Scripture hairnet of fools, "Look sirs, a marvelous sad hairnet"— Hold together, Jack, pass through everything, and everything is one dream, one appearance, one flash, one sad eye, one crystal lucid mystery, one word— Hold still, man, regain your love of life and go down from this mountain and simply *be*—*be*—be the infinite fertilities of the one mind of infinity, make no comments, complaints, criticisms, appraisals, avowals, sayings, shooting stars of thought, just *flow, flow,* be you all, be you what it is, it is only what it always is— Hope is a word like a snow-drift— This is the Great Knowing, this is the Awakening, this is Voidness— So shut up, live, travel, adventure, bless and dont be sorry— Prunes, prune, eat your prunes— And you have been forever, and will be forever, and all the worrisome smashings of your foot on innocent cupboard doors it was only the Void pretending to be a man pretending not to know the Void—

I come back into the house a new man.

All I have to do is wait 30 long days to get down from the rock and see sweet life again—knowing it's neither sweet nor bitter but just what it is, and so it is—

So long afternoons I sit in my easy (canvas) chair facing Void Hozomeen, the silence hushes in my little shack, my stove is still, my dishes glitter, my firewood (old sticks that are the form of water and welp, that I light small Indian fires with in my stove, to make quick meals) my firewood lies piled and snaky in the corner, my canned goods wait to be opened, my old cracked shoes weep, my pans lean, my dish rags hang, my various things sit silent around the room, my eyes ache, the wind wallows and belts at the window and upped shutters, the light in late afternoon shades and bluedarks Hozomeen (revealing his streak of middle red) and there's nothing for me to do but wait—and breathe (and breathing is difficult in the thin high air, with West Coast sinus wheezings)—wait, breathe, eat, sleep, cook, wash, pace, watch, never any forest fires—and daydream, "What will I do when I get to Frisco? Why first thing I'll get a room in Chinatown"—but even nearer and sweeter I daydream what I'll do Leaving Day, some hallowed day in early September, "I'll walk down the trail, two hours, meet Phil in the boat, ride to the Ross Float, sleep there a night, chat in the kitchen, start early in the morning on the Diablo Boat, go right from that little pier (say hello to Walt), hitch right to Marblemount, collect my pay, pay my debts, buy a bottle of wine and drink it by the Skagit in the afternoon, and leave next morning for Seattle"—and on, down to Frisco, then L.A., then Nogales, then Guadalajara, then Mexico City— And still the Void is still and'll never move—

But I will be the Void, moving without having moved.

3   AW, AND I REMEMBER SWEET DAYS OF HOME that I didn't appreciate when I had them—afternoons then, when I was 15, 16, it meant Ritz Brothers crackers and peanut butter and milk, at the old round kitchen table, and my chess problems or self-invented baseball games, as the orange sun of Lowell October'd slant thru the porch and kitchen curtains and make a lazy dusty shaft and in it my cat'd be licking his forepaw laplap with tiger tongue and cue tooth, all undergone and dust betided, Lord—so now in my dirty torn clothes I'm a bum in the High Cascades and all I've got for a kitchen is this crazy battered stove with cracked stovepipe rust—stuffed, yea, at the ceiling, with old burlap, to keep the rats of night out—days long ago when I could have simply walked up and kissed either my mother or my father and say "I like you because someday I'll be an old bum in desolation and I'll be alone and sad"— O Hozomeen, the rocks of it gleam in the downgo sun, the inaccessible fortress parapets stand like Shakespeare in the world and for miles around not a thing knows the name of Shakespeare, Hozomeen or me—

Late afternoon long ago home, and even recently in North

Carolina when, to recall childhood, I did eat Ritz and peanut butter and milk at four, and played the baseball game at my desk, and it was schoolboys in scuffed shoes coming home just like me hungry (and I'd make them special Jack Bananasplits, only a measly six months ago)— But here on Desolation the wind whirls, desolate of song, shaking rafters of the earth, progenitating night— Giant bat shadows of cloud hover on the mountain.

Soon dark, soon my day's dishes done, meal eaten, waiting for September, waiting for the descent to the world again.

4   MEANWHILE THE SUNSETS ARE MAD ORANGE FOOLS raging in the gloom, whilst far in the south in the direction of my intended loving arms of señoritas, snowpink piles wait at the foot of the world, in general silver ray cities—the lake is a hard pan, gray, blue, waiting at the mist bottoms for when I ride her in Phil's boat—Jack Mountain as always receives his meed of little cloud at highbrow base, his thousand football fields of snow all raveled and pink, that one unimaginable abominable snowman still squatted petrified on the ridge— Golden Horn far off is yet golden in a gray southeast— Sourdough's monster hump overlooks the lake— Surly clouds blacken to make fire rims at that forge where the night's being hammered, crazed mountains march to the sunset like drunken cavaliers in Messina when Ursula was fair, I would swear that Hozomeen would move if we could induce him but he spends the night with me and soon when stars rain down the snowfields he'll be in the pink of pride all black and yaw-y to the north where (just above him every night) North Star flashes pastel orange, pastel green, iron orange, iron blue, azurite indicative constellative auguries of her makeup up there that you could weigh on the scales of the golden world—

The wind, the wind—

And there's my poor endeavoring human desk at which I sit

so often during the day, facing south, the papers and pencils and the coffee cup with sprigs of alpine fir and a weird orchid of the heights wiltable in one day— My Beechnut gum, my tobacco pouch, dusts, pitiful pulp magazines I have to read, view south to all those snowy majesties— The waiting is long.

> On Starvation Ridge
> little sticks
> Are trying to grow.

5 ONLY THE NIGHT BEFORE my decision to live loving, I had been degraded, insulted, and made mournful by this dream:

"And get a good tenderloin steak!" says Ma handing Deni Bleu the money, she's sending us to the store to get a good supper, also she's suddenly decided to put all her confidence in Deni these later years now that I've become such a vague ephemeral undeciding being who curses the gods in his bed sleep and wanders around bareheaded and stupid in the gray darkness— It's in the kitchen, it's all agreed, I dont say anything, we go off— In the front bedroom by the stairs Pa is dying, is in his death bed and practically dead already, it's in spite of *that* that Ma wants a good steak, wants to plank her last human hope on Deni, on some kind of decisive solidarity— Pa is thin, pale, his bed sheets white, it seems to me he's dead already— We go down in the gloom and negotiate our way somehow to the butcher store in Brooklyn in the downtown main streets around Flatbush— Bob Donnelly is there and the rest of the gang, bareheaded and bummy in the street— A gleam has now come in Deni's eyes as he sees his chance to turn tail and become a con man with all Ma's money in his hand, in the store he orders the meat but I see him pulling shortchange tricks and stuffing money in his pocket and making some kind of arrangement to renege on *her* agreement, her *last* agreement— She had pinned her hopes on him, I was of no more avail— Somehow we wander from there and dont go back to Ma's house and wind up in the River Army which is dispatched, after watching a speedboat race, to swim downstream in the cold swirling dangerous waters— The speedboat, if it had been a "long" one could have dived right under the flotilla'd crowd and come up the other side and completed its time but because of faulty short design the racer (Mr. Darling) complains that that was the reason his boat just ducked under the crowd and got stuck there and couldnt go on—big official floats took note.

Me in the lead gang, the Army starts swimming downstream, we are going to the bridges and cities below. The water is cold and the current extremely bad but I swim and struggle on. "How'd I get here?" I think. "What about Ma's steak? What did Deni Bleu do with her money? Where is he now? O I have no time to think!" Suddenly from a lawn by the St. Louis de France church on the shore I hear kids shouting a message at me, "Hey your mother's in the insane asylum! Your mother's gone to the insane asylum! Your father's dead!" and I realize what's happened and still, swimming and in the Army, I'm stuck struggling in the cold water, and all I can do is grieve, grieve, in the hoar necessitous horror of the morning, bitterly I hate myself, bitterly it's too late yet while I feel better I still feel ephemeral and unreal and unable to straighten my thoughts or even really grieve, in fact I feel too stupid to be really bitter, in short I dont know what I'm doing and I'm being told what to do by the Army and Deni Bleu has played a wood on me too, at last, to get his sweet revenge but mostly it's just that he's decided to become an out-and-out crook and this was his chance—

 . . . And even though the saffron freezing message may come from the sunny ice caps of this world, O haunted fools we are, I add an appendage to a long loving letter I'd been writing to my mother for weeks:

Dont despair, Ma, I'll take care of you whenever you need me—just yell. . . . I'm right there, swimming the river of hardships but I know how to swim— Dont ever think for one minute that you are left alone.

She is 3,000 miles away living in bondage to ill kin. Desolation, desolation, how shall I ever repay thee?

6 I COULD GO MAD IN THIS— O carryall menaya but the weel may track the rattle-burr, poniac the avoid devoidity runabout, minavoid the crail— Song of my all the vouring me the part de rail-ing carry all the pone—part you too may green and fly—welkin moon wrung salt upon the tides of come-on night, swing on the meadow shoulder, roll the boulder of Buddha over the pink partitioned west Pacific fog mow— O tiny tiny tiny human hope, O molded cracking thee mirror thee shook pa t n a watalaka—and more to go—
Ping.

7 EVERY NIGHT AT 8 the lookouts on all the different mountaintops in the Mount Baker National Forest have a bull session over their radios—I have my own Packmaster set and turn it on, and listen.
It's a big event in the loneliness—
"He asked if you was goin to sleep, Chuck."
"You know what he does Chuck when he goes out on patrol?—he finds a nice shady spot and just goes to sleep."
"Did you say Louise?"
"—I doant knaow—"
"—Well I only got three weeks to wait—"
"—right on 99—"
"Say Ted?"
"Yeah?"

"How do you keep your oven hot for makin those, ah, muffins?"

"Oh just keep the fire hot—"

"They only got one road that ah zigzags all over creation—"

"Yeh well I hope so—I'll be there waitin anyway."

Bzzzzz bzgg radio—long silence of pensive young lookouts—

"Well is your buddy gonna come up here and pick you up?"

"Hey Dick— Hey Studebaker—"

"Just keep pourin wood in it, that's all, it stays hot—"

"Are you still gonna pay him the same thing as you did ah pay him comin out?"

"—Yeah but ah three four trips in three hours?"

My life is a vast and insane legend reaching everywhere without beginning or ending, like the Void—like Samsara— A thousand memories come like tics all day perturbing my vital mind with almost muscular spasms of clarity and recall— Singing in a false limey accent to *Loch Lomond* as I heat my evening coffee in cold rose dusk, I immediately think of that time in 1942 in Nova Scotia when our seedy ship put in from Greenland for a night's shore leave, Fall, pines, cold dusk and then dawn sun, over the radio from wartime America the faint voice of Dinah Shore singing, and how we got drunk, how we slipped and fell, how the joy welled up in my heart and exploded fuming into the night that I was back to my beloved America almost—the cold dog dawn—

Almost simultaneously, just because I'm changing my pants, or that is putting on an extra pair for the howling night, I think of the marvelous sex fantasy of earlier in the day when I'm reading a cowboy story about the outlaw kidnapping the girl and having her all alone on the train (except for one old woman) who (the old woman now in my daydream sleeps on the bench while ole hard hombre me outlaw pushes the blonde into the men's compartment, at gun point, and she wont respond but scratch) (natch) (she loves an honest killer and I'm old Erdaway Molière the murderous sneering Texan who slit bulls in El Paso and held up the stage to shoot holes in people only)—I get her on the seat and kneel and start to work, French postcard style, till I've got her eyes closed and mouth open until she cant stand it and loves this lovin outlaw so she by her own wild willin volition jumps to kneel and works, then when I'm ready turns while the old lady sleeps and the train rattles on— "Most delightful my dear" I'm saying to myself in Desolation Peak and as if to Bull Hubbard, using his way of speech, and as if to amuse him, as if he's here, and I hear Bull saying "Dont act effeminate Jack" as he seriously told me in 1953 when I had started joking with him in *his* effeminate manner routine "On *you* it dont look good Jack" and here I am wishing I could be in London with Bull tonight—

And the new moon, brown, sinks early yonder by Baker River dark.

My life is a vast inconsequential epic with a thousand and a million characters—here they all come, as swiftly we roll east, as swiftly the earth rolls east.

8 FOR SMOKING all I have is Air Force paper to roll my tobacco in, an eager sergeant had lectured us on the importance of the Ground Observer Corps and handed out fat books of blank paper to record whole armadas apparently of enemy bombers in some paranoiac Conelrad of his brain— He was from New York and talked fast and was Jewish and made me homesick—"Aircraft Flash Message Record," with lines and numbers, I take my little aluminum scissors and cut a square and roll a butt and when airplanes pass I mind my own business although he (the Sgt) did say "If you see a flying saucer report the flying saucer"— It says on the blank: "Number of aircraft, one, two, three, four, many, unknown," reminds me of the dream I had of me and W. H. Auden standing at a bar on the Mississippi River joking elegantly about "women's

urine"—"Type of aircraft," it goes on, "single—, bi—, multi—, jet, unknown"— Naturally I love that unknown, got nothin else to do up there on Desolation—"Altitude of aircraft" (and dig this) "Very low, low, high, very high, unknown"—then SPECIAL REMARKS: EXAMPLES: "Hostile aircraft, blimp" (bloop), "helicopter balloon, aircraft in combat or distress, etc." (or whale)— O distressed rose unknown sorrow plane, come!

My cigarette paper is so sad.

"When will Andy and Fred get here!" I yell, when they come up that trail on mules and horses I'll have real cigarette paper and my dear mail from my millions of characters—

For the trouble with Desolation, is, no characters, alone, isolated, but is Hozomeen isolate?

9 MY EYES IN MY HAND, welded to wheel to welded to whang.

10 TO WHILE AWAY THE TIME I play my solitaire card baseball game Lionel and I invented in 1942 when he visited Lowell and the pipes froze for Christmas—the game is between the Pittsburgh Plymouths (my oldest team, and now barely on top of the 2nd division) and the New York Chevvies rising from the cellar ignominiously since they were world champions last year—I shuffle my deck, write out the lineups, and lay out the teams— For hundreds of miles around, black night, the lamps of Desolation are lit, to a childish sport, but the Void is a child too—and here's how the game goes:—what happens:—how it's won, and by whom:—

The opposing pitchers are, for the Chevvies, Joe McCann, old vet of 20 years in my leagues since first at 13 age I'd belt iron rollerbearings with a nail in the appleblossoms of the Sarah backyard, Ah sad—Joe McCann, with a record of 1–2, (this is the 14th game of the season for both clubs), and an earned run average of 4.86, the Chevvies naturally heavily favored and especially as McCann is a star pitcher and Gavin a secondrater in my official effectiveness rulings—and the Chevvies are hot anyway, comin up, and took the opener of this series 11–5 . . .

The Chevvies jump right out ahead in their half of the first inning as Frank Kelly the manager belts a long single into center bringing home Stan Orsowski from second where he'd gone on a bingle and walk to Duffy—yag, yag, you can hear those Chevvies (in my mind) talking it up and whistling and clapping the game on— The poor greenclad Plymouths come on for their half of the opening inning, it's just like real life, real baseball, I cant tell the difference between this and that howling wind and hundreds of miles of Arctic Rock without—

But Tommy Turner with his great speed converts a triple into an inside-the-park homerun and anyway Sim Kelly has no arm out there and it's Tommy's sixth homerun, he is the "magnificent one" all right—and his 15th run batted in and he's only been playin six games because he was injured, a regular Mickey Mantle—

Followed immediately back to back by a line drive homerun over the rightfield fence from the black bat of old Pie Tibbs and the Plyms jump out ahead 2–1 . . . wow . . .

(the fans go wild in the mountain, I hear the rumble of celestial racing cars in the glacial crevasses)

—Then Lew Badgurst singles to right and Joe McCann is really getting belted (and him with his fancy earned run average) (pah, goes to show)—

In fact McCann is almost batted out of the box as he further gives up a walk to Tod Gavin but Ole Reliable Henry Pray ends up the inning grounding out to Frank Kelly at third—it will be a slugfest.

Then suddenly the two pitchers become locked in an unexpected brilliant pitching duel, racking up goose egg after goose egg, neither one of them giving up a hit except one single (Ned

Gavin the pitcher got it) in the second inning, right on brilliantly up to the uttermost eighth when Zagg Parker of the Chevs finally breaks the ice with a single to right which (he too for great super runner speed) unopposed stretches into a double (the throw is made but he makes it, sliding)—and a new tone comes in the game you'd think but no!—Ned Gavin makes Clyde Castleman fly out to center then calmly strikes out Stan the Man Orsowski and stalks off the mound chewing his tobacco unperturbed, the very void— Still, a 2–1 ballgame favor of his team—

McCann yields a single to big bad Lew Badgurst (with big arms southpawing that bat) in *his* half of the eighth, and there's a base stolen on him by pinch runner Allen Wayne, but no danger as he gets Tod Gavin on a grounder—

Going into the final inning, still the same score, the same situation.

All Ned Gavin has to do is hold the Chevvies for 3 long outs. The fans gulp and tense. He has to face Byrd Duffy (batting .346 up to this game), Frank Kelly, and pinch hitter Tex Davidson—

He hitches up his belt, sighs, and faces the chubby Duffy— and winds up— Low, one ball.

Outside, ball two.

Long fly to center field but right in the hands of Tommy Turner.

Only two to go.

"Come on Neddy!" yells manager Cy Locke from the 3rd base box, Cy Locke who was the greatest shortstop of all time in his time in my appleblossom time when Pa was young and laughed in the summernight kitchen with beer and Shammy and pinochle—

Frank Kelly up, dangerous, menacing, the manager, hungry for money and pennants, a whiplash, a firebrand—

Neddy winds up: delivers: inside.

Ball one.

Delivers.

Kelly belts it to right, off the flagpole, Tod Gavin chases, it's a standup double, the tying run is on second, the crowd is wild. Whistles, whistles, whistles—

Speedboy Selman Piva is sent out to run for Kelly.

Tex Davidson is a big veteran chaw-chawin old outfielder of the old wars, he drinks at night, he doesnt care— He strikes out with a big wheeling whackaround of the empty bat.

Ned Gavin has thrun him 3 curves. Frank Kelly curses in the dugout, Piva, the tying run, is still on second. *One more to go!*

The batter: Sam Dane, Chevvy catcher, old veteran chawidrinkbuddy in fact of Tex Davidson's, only difference is Sam bats lefty—same height, lean, old, dont care—

Ned pitches a call strike across the letters—

And there it comes:—a booming homerun over the center-field barrier, Piva comes home, Sam comes loping around chewing his tobacco, still doesnt care, at the plate he is mobbed by the Kellies and the crazies—

Bottom of the 9th, all Joe McCann has to do is hold the Plymouths—Pray gets on on an error, Gucwa singles, they hold at second and first, and up steps little Neddy Gavin and doubles home the tying run and sends the winning run to third, pitcher eat pitcher—Leo Sawyer pops up, it looks like McCann'll hold out, but Tommy Turner simply slaps a sacrifice grounder and in comes the winning run, Jake Gucwa who'd singled so unobtrusively, and the Plymouths rush out and carry Ned Gavin to the showers atop their shoulders.

Tell me Lionel and I didnt invent a good game!

11 GREAT DAY IN THE MORNING, he's committed another murder, in fact the same one, only this time the victim sits happily in my father's chair just about on Sarah Avenue location and I'm just sitting at my desk writing on, unconcerned, when I heard of the new murder I go on writing (pre-

sumably about it, he he)— All the ladies have gone to the lawns but what horror when they come back just to sense murder in that room, what will Ma say, but he has cut up the body and washed it down the toilet— Dark brewing face bends over us in the gloomdream.

I wake up in the morning at seven and my mop is still drying on the rock, like a woman's head of hair, like Hecuba forlorn, and the lake is a misty mirror a mile below out of which soon the ladies of the lake shall rise in wrath and all night long I hardly slept (I hear faint thunder in my eardrums) because the mice, the rat, and the two fawns befawdledawdled all over my place, the fawns unreal, too skinny, too strange to be deer, but new kinds of mystery mountain mammals— They cleaned out utterly the plate of cold boiled potatoes I laid out for them— My sleepingbag is flat for another day—I sing at the stove: "How coffee, you sure look good when you brewin"—

"How how lady, you sure look good when you lovin"

(the ladies of the North Pole Snow I heard sing in Greenland)

12 MY TOILET is a little peaked wood outhouse on the edge of a beautiful Zen precipice with boulders and rock slate and old gnarled enlightened trees, remnants of trees, stumps, torn, tortured, hung, ready to fall, unconscious, Ta Ta Ta—the door I keep jammed open with a rock, faces vast triangular mountain walls across Lightning Gorge to the east, at 8:30 A.M. the haze is sweet and pure—and dreamy—Lightning Creek mores and mores her roar—Three Fools joins in, and Shull and Cinammon feed him, and beyond, Trouble Creek, and beyond, other forests, other primitive areas, other gnarled rock, straight east to Montana— On foggy days the view from my toilet seat is like a Chinese Zen drawing in ink on silk of gray voids, I half expect to see two giggling old dharma bums,

or one in rags, by the goat-horned stump, one with a broom, the other with a pen quill, writing poems about the Giggling Lings in the Fog—saying, "Hanshan, what is the meaning of the void?"

"Shihte, did you mop your kitchen floor this morning?"

"Hanshan, what is the meaning of the void?"

"Shihte, did you mop—Shihte, did you mop?"

"He he he he."

"Why do you laugh, Shihte?"

"Because my floor is mopped."

"Then what is the meaning of the void?"

Shihte picks up his broom and sweeps empty space, like I once saw Irwin Garden do—they wander off, giggling, in the fog, and all's left are the few near rocks and gnarls I can see and above, the Void goes into the Great Truth Cloud of upper fogs, not even one black sash, it is a giant vertical drawing, showing 2 little masters and then space endlessly above them—"Hanshan, where is your mop?"

"Drying on a rock."

A thousand years ago Hanshan wrote poems on cliffs like these, on foggy days like these, and Shihte swept out the monastery kitchen with a broom and they giggled together, and King's Men came from far and wide to find them and they only ran, hiding, into crevasses and caves— Suddenly I see Hanshan now appearing before my Window pointing to the east, I look that way, it's only Three Fools Creek in the morning haze, I look back, Hanshan has vanished, I look back at what he showed me, it's only Three Fools Creek in the morning haze.

What else?

13 THEN COME THE LONG DAYDREAMS of what I'll do when I get out of there, that mountaintop trap. Just to drift and roam down that road, on 99, fast, mebbe a filet mignon on hot coals in a riverbottom some night, with good

wine, and on in the morning—to Sacramento, Berkeley, go up
to Ben Fagan's cottage and say first off this Haiku:

> Hitch hiked a thousand
> miles and brought
> You wine

—mebbe sleep in his grass yard that night, at least one night in
a Chinatown hotel, one long walk around Frisco, one big Chinese two big Chinese dinners, see Cody, see Mal, look for Bob
Donnely and the others—few things here and there, a present
for Ma—why plan? I'll just drift down the road looking at
unexpected events and I wont stop till Mexico City

14 I HAVE A BOOK UP THERE, confessions of ex communists who quit when they recognized its totalitarian
beastliness, *The God That Failed* the title (including one dull
O awfully dull account of André Gide's that old postmortem
bore)—all I have, for reading—and become depressed by the
thought of a world (O what a world is this, that friendships
cancel enmity of the heart, people fighting for something to
fight, everywhere) a world of GPU's and spies and dictators
and purges and midnight murders and marijuana revolutions
with guns and gangs in the desert—suddenly, just by tuning in
on America via the lookout radio listening to the other boys in
the bull session, I hear football scores, talk of so-and-so "Bo
Pelligrini!—what a bruiser!! I dont talk to anybody from Mary-
land"—and the jokes and the laconic stay, I realize, "America
is as free as that wild wind, out there, still free, free as when
there was no name to that border to call it Canada and on
Friday nights when Canadian Fishermen come in old cars on
the old road beyond the lake tarn" (that I can see, the little
lights of Friday night, thinking then immediately of their hats
and gear and flies and lines) "on Friday nights it was the name-
less Indian came, the Skagit, and a few log forts were up there,

and down here a ways, and winds blew on free feet and free antlers, and still do, on free radio waves, on free wild youngtalk of America on the radio, college boys, fearless free boys, a million miles from Siberia this is and Amerikay is a good old country yet—"

For the whole blighted darkness-woe of thinking about Russias and plots to assassinate whole peoples' souls, is lifted just by hearing "My God, the score is 26–0 already—they couldn't gain anything thru the line"—"Just like the All Stars"—"Hey Ed when you comin down off your lookout?"—"He's goin steady, he'll be wantin to go home straight"—"We might take a look at Glacier National Park"—"We're goin home thru the Badlands of North Dakota"—"You mean the Black Hills"—"I don't talk to anybody from Syracuse"—"Anybody know a good bedtime story?"—"Hey it's eight thirty, we better knock off— How 33 ten-seven till tomorrow morning. Good night"—"Ho! How 32 ten-seven till tomorrow morning— Sleep tight"—"Did you say you had Honkgonk on your portable radio?"—"Sure, listen, hingya hingya hingya"—"That does it, good night"—

And I know that America is too vast with people too vast to ever be degraded to the low level of a slave nation, and I can go hitch hiking down that road and on into the remaining years of my life knowing that outside of a couple fights in bars started by drunks I'll have not a hair of my head (and I need a haircut) harmed by Totalitarian cruelty—

Indian scalp say this, and prophesy:

"From these walls, laughter will run over the world, infecting with courage the bent laborious peon of antiquity."

15 AND I BUY BUDDHA, who said, that what he said was neither true nor untrue, and there's the only true thing or good thing I ever heard and it rings a cloudy bell, a mighty supramundane gong— He said, "Your trip was long,

illimitable, you came to this raindrop called your life, and call it *yours*—we have purposed that you vow to be awakened—whether in a million lifetimes you disregard this Kingly Heeding, it's still a raindrop in the sea and who's disturbed and what is time—? This Bright Ocean of Infinitude sails many fish afar, that come and go like the sparkle on your lake, mind, but dive into the rectangular white blaze of this thought now: You have been assigned to wake up, this is the golden eternity, which knowledge will do you no earthly good for earth's not pith, a crystal myth—face the A-H truth, awakener, be you not knuckled under the wile of cold or heat, comfort or unrepose, be you mindful, moth, of eternity—be you loving, lad, lord, of infinite variety—be you one of us, Great Knowers Without Knowing, Great Lovers Beyond Love, whole hosts and unnumberable angels with form or desire, supernatural corridors of heat—we heat to hold you woke—open your arms embrace the world, it and we rush in, we'll lay a silver meeting brand of golden hands on your milky embowered brow, power, to make you freeze in love forever— Believe! and ye shall live forever— Believe, that ye have lived forever—overrule the fortresses and penances of dark isolate suffering life on earth, there's more to life than earth, there's Light Everywhere, look—"

In these strange words I hear every night, in many other words, varieties and threads of discourse pouring in from that evermindful rich—

Take my word for it, something will come of it, and it will wear the face of sweet nothingness, flappy leaf—

The bullnecks of strong raft drivers the color of purple gold and kirtles of silk will carry us uncarried uncrossing crossable no-cross voids to the ulum light, where Ragamita the lidded golden eye opes to hold the gaze— Mice skitter in the mountain night with little feet of ice and diamonds, but's not my time yet (mortal hero) to know what I know I know, so, come in

Words . . .
The stars are words . . .
Who succeeded? Who failed?

16 AH YAIR, and when
I gets to Third and
Townsend,
    I'll ketch me
the Midnight Ghost—
We'll roll right down
        to San Jose
As quick as you can boast—
—Ah ha, Midnight,
    midnight ghost,
Ole Zipper rollin
    down the line—
Ah ha, Midnight,
    midnight ghost,
Rollin
        down
                the
                    line
We'll come a blazing
To Watson-ville,
And whang on through
        the line—
Salinas Valley
        in the night,
On down to Apaline—
Whoo Whoo
    Whoo ee
Midnight Ghost
Clear t'Obispo Bump
—Take on a helper
and make that mountain,

and come on down the town,
—We'll rail on through
to Surf and Tangair
and on down by the sea—
The moon she shines
    the midnight ocean
goin down the line—
Gavioty, Gavioty,
O Gavi-oty,
Singin and drinkin wine—
Camarilla, Camarilla,
Where Charley Parker
        went mad
We'll roll on to L.A.
—O Midnight
        midnight,
    midnight ghost,
rollin down the line.
Sainte Teresa
Sainte Teresa, dont you worry,
We'll make it on time,
down that midnight
        line

And that's how I figure I'll make San Francisco to L.A. in 12 hours, ridin the Midnight Ghost, under a lashed truck, the First-class Zipper freight train, zooam, zom, right down, sleepingbag and wine—a daydream in the form of a song.

17 GETTING TIRED OF LOOKING AT ALL THE ANGLES OF my lookout, as for instance, looking at my sleeping-bag in the morning from the point of view of opening it again at night, or at my stove with high supper heat of midafternoon from the point of view of midnight when the mouse'll be

scratching in it cold, I turn my thoughts to Frisco and I see it like a movie what'll be there when I get there, I see myself in my new (to-be-bought-in-Seattle-I-plan) black large-sized leather jacket that hangs and ties over my waist low (mebbe hangs over my hands) and my new gray Chino pants and new wool sports shirt (orange and yellow and blue!) and my new haircut, there I go bleakfaced Decembering the steps of my Skid Row Chinatown hotel; or else I'm at Simon Darlovsky's pad at 5 Turner Terrace in the crazy Negro housing project at Third & 22nd where you see the giant gastanks of eternity and a whole vista of the smoky industrial Frisco including the bay and the railroad mainline and factories—I see myself, rucksack on one shoulder, coming in the ever-unlocked backdoor to Lazarus' bedroom (Lazarus is Simon's strange $15\frac{1}{2}$ year old mystic brother who never says anything but "D'ja have any dreams?") (last night in your sleep?) (he means), I come in, it's October, they're at school, I go out and buy ice cream, beer, canned peaches, steaks and milk and stock the icebox and when they come home at late afternoon and in the courtyard the little kids have started screaming for Fall Dusk Joy, I've been at that kitchen table all day drinking wine and reading the papers, Simon with his bony hawk nose and crazy glittering green eyes and glasses looks at me and says through his ever-sinus nostrils "*Jack! You!* When'd you get here, hnf!" as he sniffs (horribly the torment of his sniff, I hear it now, cant tell how he breathes)—"Just today—look, the icebox is full of food—Mind if I stay here a few days?"—"Plenty room"—Lazarus is behind him, wearing his new suit and all combed to make the junior highschool lovelies, he just nods and smiles and then we're having a big feast and Lazarus finally says "Where dja sleep last night?" and I say "In a yard in Berkeley" so he says "Djav any dreams?"—So tell him a long dream. And at midnight when Simon and I have gone out walking all the way up Third Street drinking wine and talking about girls and talking to the spade whores across from the Cameo Hotel and going to

North Beach to look for Cody and the gang, Lazarus all alone in the kitchen fries himself three steaks for a midnight snack, he's a big goodlooking crazy kid, one of many Darlovsky brothers, in the madhouse most of them, for some reason, and Simon hitch hiked all the way to New York to rescue Laz and brought him back to live with him, on relief, two Russian brothers, in the city, in the void, Irwin's protégés, Simon a Kafka writer—Lazarus a mystic who stares at pictures of monsters on weird magazines, for hours, and wanders around the city zombie like, and when he was 15 claimed he would weigh 300 pounds before the year was out and also had set himself a deadline to make a million dollars by New Year's Eve—to this crazy pad Cody ofttimes goes in his shabby blue brakeman's uniform and sits at the kitchen table then leaps out and jumps in his car yelling "Short on time!" and races off to North Beach to look for the gang or to work to catch his train, and girls everywhere in the streets and in our bars and the whole Frisco scene one insane movie—I see myself arriving on the scene, across that screen, looking around, all done with desolation—White masts of ships at the foot of streets.

I see myself wandering among the wholesale markets—down past the deserted MCS union hall where I'd tried so hard to get a ship, for years— There I go, chewing on a Mister Goodbar—

I wander by Gump's department store and look in the art-frame shop where Psyche, who always wears jeans and turtle-neck sweater with a little white collar falling over, works, whose pants I would like to remove and just leave the turtle-neck sweater and the little collar and the rest is all for me and all too sweet for me—I stand in the street staring in at her—I sneak by our bar several times (The Place) and peek in—

18

I WAKE UP AND I'M ON DESOLATION PEAK and the firs are motionless in the blue morning— Two butterflies comport, with worlds of mountains as their backdrop— My clock ticks the slow day— While I slept and traveled in dreams all night, the mountains didnt move at all and I doubt they dreamed—

I go out to fetch a pail of snow to put in my old tin washtub that reminds me of my grandfather's in Nashua and I find that my shovel has disappeared from the snowbank on the precipice, I look down and figure it will be a long climb down and up but I can't see it— Then I do see it, right in the mud at the foot of the snow, on a ledge, I go down very carefully, slipping in the mud, for fun yank out a big boulder from the mud and kick it down, it goes booming and crashes on a rock and splits in two and thunders 1500 feet down to where I see the final rock of it rolling in long snowfields and coming to rest against boulders with a knock that I only hear 2 seconds later— Silence, the beautiful gorge shows no sign of animal life, just firs and alpine heather and rocks, the snow beside me blinds whitely in the sun, I loose down at the cerulean neutral lake a look of woe, little pink or almost brown clouds hover in its mirror, I look up and there's mighty Hozomeen redbrown pinnacles high in the sky—I get the shovel and come up carefully in the mud, slipping—fill the pail with clean snow, cover the stash of carrots and cabbage in a new deep snowhole, and go back, dumping the lump in the tin tub and splashing water over the sides onto my dusty floor—- Then I get an old pail and like the old Japanese woman go down among beautiful heather meadows and gather sticks for my stove. It's Saturday afternoon all over the world.

19 "IF I WERE IN FRISCO NOW," I think in my chair in the late aftersolitudes, "I'd buy a great big quart of Christian Brothers Port or some other excellent special brand and go up to my Chinatown room and empty half its contents in an empty pint, stick that in my pocket, and take off, around the little streets of Chinatown watching the children, the little Chinese children so happy with their little hands in their parents' wrapt, I'd look in grocery stores and see the noncommittal Zen butchers cutting the necks of chickens, I'd gaze water mouthed at the beautiful glazed cured roasted ducks in the window, I'd wander around, stand on the corner of Italian Broadway too, to get the feel of life, blue skies and white clouds above, I'd go back and into the Chinese movie with my pint and sit there drinking it (from now, 5 P.M.) three hours digging the weird scenes and unheard-of dialogs and developments and maybe some of the Chinese would see me drink-a-pint and they'd think "Ah, a drunken white man in the Chinese movie"—at 8 I'd come out to a blue dusk with sparkling lights of San Francisco on all the magic hills around, now I'd refill my pint in the hotel room and really take off for a long hike around the city, to work up an appetite for my midnight feast in a booth in Sun Heung Hung's marvelous old restaurant—I'd strike over the hill, over Telegraph, and right down to the rail spur where I know a place in a narrow alley where I can sit and drink and wallgaze a vast black cliff that has magic vibratory properties that send back messages of swarming holy light in the night, I know I tried it—then, drinking, sipping, re-capping the bottle, I walk the lonely way along the Embarcadero through Fisherman's Wharf restaurant areas where the seals break my heart with their coughing cries of love, I go, past shrimp counters, out, past the masts of the last docked ships, and then up Van Ness and over and down into the Tenderloin—the winking marquees and bars with cocktail cherry-

sticks, the sallow characters the old alcoholic blondes stumbling to the liquor store in slacks—then I go (wine almost gone and me high and glad) down main arterial Market Street and the honkytonk of sailors, movies, and sodafountains, across the alley and into Skid Row (finishing my wine there, among scabrous old doorways chalked and be-pissed and glass-crashed by a hundred thousand grieving souls in Goodwill rags) (the same old boys who roam the freights and cling to little bits of paper on which you always find some kind of prayer or philosophy)— Wine finished, I go singing and handclapping quietly to the beat of my feet all the way up Kearney back to Chinatown, almost midnight now, and I sit in the Chinatown park on a dark bench and take the air, drinking in the sight of the foody delicious neons of my restaurant blinking in the little street, occasionally crazy drunks go by in the dark looking for half finished bottles on the ground, or, butts, and across Kearney there you see the blue cops goin in and out of the big gray jailhouse— Then I go in my restaurant, order from the Chinese menu, and instantly they bring me smoked fish, curried chicken, fabulous duck cakes, unbelievably delicious and delicate silver platters (on stems) containing steaming marvels, that you raise the cover off and look and sniff—with tea pot, cup, ah I eat— and eat—till midnight—maybe then over tea write a letter to beloved Ma, telling her—then, done, I either go to bed or to our bar, The Place, to find the gang and get drunk . . .

20 ON A SOFT AUGUST EVENING I scramble down the slope of the mountain and find a steep place to sit crosslegged near firs and blasted old tree stumps, facing the moon, the yellow halfmoon that's sinking into the mountains to the southwest— In the western sky, warm rose— About 8:30— The wind over the mile-down lake is balmy and reminiscent of all the ideas you've ever had about enchanted lakes—I pray and ask Awakener Avalokitesvara to lay his dia-

mond hand on my brow and give me the immortal understanding— He is the Hearer and Answerer of Prayer, I know that this business is self hallucination and crazy business but after all it is only the awakeners (the Buddhas) who have said they do not exist— In about twenty seconds comes this understanding to my mind and heart: "When a baby is born he falls asleep and dreams the dream of life, when he dies and is buried in his grave he wakes up again to the Eternal Ecstasy"—"And when all is said and done, it doesnt matter"—

Yea, Avalokitesvara did lay his diamond hand . . .

And then the question of why, why, it's only the Power, the one mental nature exuding its infinite potentialities— What a strange feeling reading that in Vienna in February of 1922 (month before I was born) such and such was going on in the streets, how could there have been a Vienna, nay even the conception of a Vienna before I was born?!—It's because the one mental nature goes on, has nothing to do with individual arrivers and departers that bear it and fare in it and that are fared in by it— So that 2500 years ago was Gotama Buddha, who thought up the greatest thought in Mankind, a drop in the bucket those years in that Mental Nature which is the Universal Mind—I see in my mountainside contentment that the Power delights and joys in both ignorance and enlightenment, else there wouldnt be ignorant existence alongside enlightened inexistence, why should the Power limit itself to one or the other— whether as the form of pain, or as impalpable ethers of formlessness and painlessness, what matters it?—And I see the yellow moon a-sinkin as the earth rolls away, I twist my neck around to see upsidedown and the mountains of the earth are just those same old hanging bubbles hanging into an unlimited sea of space— Ah, if there was another sight besides *eye* sight what atomic other levels wouldnt we see?—but here we see moons, mountains, lakes, trees and sentient beings only, with our eyesight— The Power delights in all of it— It is reminding itself that it is the Power, that's why, for it, The Power, is really only ecstasy, and its manifestations dream, it is the Golden Eternity, ever peaceful, this bleary dream of existence is just a blear in its—I run out of words— The warm rose in the west becomes a hushed pastel park of gray, the soft evening sighs, little animals rustle in the heather and holes, I shift my cramped feet, the moon yellows and mellows and finally begins to hit the topmost crag and as always you see silhouetted in its magic charm some snag or stump that looks like the legendary Coyotl, God of the Indians, about to howl to the Power—

O what peace and content I feel, coming back to my shack knowing that the world is a babe's dream and the ecstasy of the golden eternity is all we're going back to, to the essence of the Power—and the Primordial Rapture, *we all know it*—I lie on my back in the dark, hands joined, glad, as the northern lights shine like a Hollywood premiere and at that too I look upside-down and see that it's just big pieces of ice on earth reflecting the other-side sun in some far daylight, in fact, too, the curve of the earth silhouetted is also seen arching over and around— Northern lights, bright enough to light my room, like ice moons.

What content to know that when all is said and done it doesnt matter— Woes? the piteousnesses I feel when I think of my mother?—but it all has to be roused and remembered, it isnt there by itself, and that's because the mental nature is by nature free of the dream and free of everything— It's like those pipesmoking Deist philosophers who say "O mark the marvelous creation of God, the moon, the stars etc., would you trade it for anything?" not realizing they wouldnt be saying this at all if it wasnt for some primordial memory of when, of what, of how nothing was— "It's only recent," I realize, looking at the world, some recent cycle of creation by The Power to joy in its reminder to its selfless self that it is The Power—and all of it in its essence swarming tender mystery, that you can see by closing your eyes and letting the eternal silence in your ears—that blessedness and bliss surely to be believed, my dears—

The awakeners, if they choose, are born as babes— This is my first awakening— There are no awakeners and no awakening.

In my shack I lie, remembering the violets in our backyard on Phebe Avenue when I was eleven, on June nights, the blear dream of it, ephemeral, haunted, long gone, going further out, till it shall be all gone out.

21   I WAKE UP IN THE MIDDLE OF THE NIGHT and remember Maggie Cassidy and how I might have married her and been old Finnegan to her Irish Lass Plurabelle, how I might have got a cottage, a little ramshackle Irish rose cottage among the reeds and old trees on the banks of the Concord and woulda worked as a grim bejacketed gloved and bebaseballhatted brakeman in the cold New England night, for her and her Irish ivory thighs, her and her marshmallow lips, her and her brogue and "God's Green Earth" and her two daughters— How I would of laid her across the bed at night all mine and laborious sought her rose, her mine of a thing, that emerald dark and hero thing I want—remember her silk thighs in tight jeans, the way she folded back one thigh under her hands and sighed as we watched Television together—in her mother's parlor that last haunted 1954 trip I took to October Lowell— Ah, the rose vines, the river mud, the run of her, the eyes— A woman for old Duluoz? Unbelievable by my stove in desolation midnight that it should be true—Maggie Adventure—

The claws of black trees by moonlit rosy dusk mayhap and by chance hold me much love too, and I can always leave them and roam along—but when I'm old by my final stove, and the bird fritters on his branch of dust in O Lowell, what'll I think, willow?—when winds creep inside my sack and give me bareback blues and I go bent about my meritorious duties in the

sod-cover earth, what lovesongs then for old bedawdler bog
bent foggy Jack O—?—no new poets will bring laurels like
honey to my milk, sneers— Sneers of love woman were better
I guess—I'd fall down ladders, brabac, and wash me river underwear—gossip me washlines—air me Mondays—fantasm me
Africas of housewives— Lear me daughters—panhandle me
marble heart—but it might have been better than what it may
be, lonesome unkissed Duluoz lips surling in a tomb

22   EARLY SUNDAY MORNINGS I always remember home
in Ma's house in Long Island, recent years, when
she's reading the Sunday papers and I get up, shower, drink a
cup of wine, read the scores and then eat the charming little
breakfast she'll lay out for me, just all I have to do is ask her,
her special way of crisping bacon and the way she sunnysides
the eggs—The TV not turned because there's nothing much of
note on Sunday mornings—I grieve to think that her hair is
turning gray and she's 62 and will be 70 when I'm in my owlish
40's—soon it will be my "old mother"—in the bunk I try to
think of how I'll take care of her—

Then as day lengthens and Sunday drags and the mountains
wear the pious dullish aspect Sabbathini I always begin to think
instead of earlier days in Lowell when the redbrick mills were
so haunted by the riverside about 4 in the afternoon, the kids
coming home from the Sunday movies, but O the sad redbrick
and everywhere in America you see it, in the reddening sun,
and clouds beyond, and people in their best clothes in all that—
We all stand on the sad earth throwing long shadows, breath
cut with flesh.

Even the skitter of the mouse in my shack attic on Sundays
has a Sunday halidom about it, as though churchgoing, church-
ment, preachments— We'll have a whack at it around.

Mostly Sundays I'm bored. And all my memories are bored.
The sun is too golden bright. I shudder to think what people

are doing in North Carolina. In Mexico City they wander around eating vast planks of fried porkskin, among parks, even their Sunday is a Blight— It must be the Sabbath was invented to soften joy.

For normal peasants Sunday is a smile, but us black poets, ahg—I guess Sunday is God's lookingglass.

Compare the churchyards of Friday night, with the pulpits of Sunday morn—

In Bavaria, men with bare knees walk around with hands behind their backs— Flies drowse behind a lace curtain, in Calais, and out the window see the sailboats— On Sunday Céline yawns and Genêt dies— In Moscow there's no pomp— Only in Benares on Sundays peddlers scream and snakecharmers open baskets with a lute— On Desolation Peak in the High Cascades, on Sundays, ahg—

I think in particular of that redbrick wall of the Sheffield Milk Company by the mainline of the Long Island Railroad in Richmond Hill, the mud tracks of workers' cars left in the lot during the week, one or two forlorn Sundayworker cars parked there now, the clouds passing in the pools of brown puddlewater, the sticks and cans and rags of debris, the commute local passing by with pale blank faces of Sunday Travelers— presaging the ghostly day when industrial America shall be abandoned and left to rust in one long Sunday Afternoon of oblivion.

23 WITH HIS UGLY MANY BUD LEGS the green alpine caterpillar comports in his heather world, a head like a pale dewdrop, his fat body reaching up straight to climb, hanging upsidedown like a South American ant eater to fiddle and fish and sway around in search, then cromming up like a boy making a limb he aligns himself hidden under heather limbs and plucks and monsters at the innocent green—the part of the green, he is, that was given moving juice—he twists and peers

and intrudes his head everywhere—he is in a jungle of dappled shady old lastyear's gray heather pins—sometimes motionless like the picture of a boa constrictor he yaws to heaven a song-less gaze, sleeps snakeheaded, then turns in like a busted-out tube when I blow on him, swift to duck, quick to retire, meek to obey the level injunction of lie still that's meant by the sky whatever may chance from it— He is very sad now as I blow again, puts head in shoulder mourning, I'll let him free to roam unobserved, playing possum as he wists—there he goes, disappearing, making little jiggles in the jungle, eye level to his world I perceive that he too is overtopped by a few fruits and then infinity, he too's upsidedown and clinging to his sphere—we are all mad.

I sit there wondering if my own travels down the Coast to Frisco and Mexico wont be just as sad and mad—but by bejesus j Christ it'll be bettern hangin around *this* rock—

24 SOME OF THE DAYS ON THE MOUNT, tho hot, are permeated with a pure cool beauty that presages October and my freedom in the Indian Plateau of Mexico which will be even purer and cooler— O old dreams I've had of the mountains on the plateau of Mexico when the skies are filled with clouds like the beards of patriarchs and indeed I'm the Patriarch himself standing in a flowing robe on the green hill of gold— In the Cascades summer may heat in August but you get the Fall hint, especially on the eastern slope of my hill in the afternoons, away from the burn of the sun, where the air is sharp and mountainlike and the trees have well withered to a beginning of the end— Then I think of the World Series, the coming of football across America (the cries of a keen Middle-western voice on the scratchy radio)—I think of shelves of wine in stores along the mainline of the California Railroad, I think of the pebbles in the ground of the West under vast Fall-

booming skies, I think of the long horizons and plains and the ultimate desert with his cactus and dry mesquites stretching to red tablelands far away where my traveler's old hope always wends and wends and only void-returns from nowhere, the long dream of the Western hitch hiker and hobo, the harvest tramps who sleep in their cottonpickin bags and rest content under the flashy star— At night, Fall hints in the Cascade Summer where you see Venus red on her hill and think "Who will be my lady?"—It will all, the haze shimmer and the beezing bugs, be wiped off the slate of summer and hurled to the east by that eager sea west wind and that's when hairflying me'll be stomping down the trail for the last time, rucksack and all, singing to the snows and jackpines, en route for further adventures, further yearnings for adventures—and all behind me (and you) the ocean of tears which has been this life on earth, so old, that when I look at my panoramic photographs of the Desolation area and see the old mules and wiry roans of 1935 (in the picture) hackled at a no-more corral fence, I marvel that the mountains lookt the same in 1935 (Old Jack Mountain to an exact degree with the same snow arrangement) as they do in 1956 so that the oldness of the earth strikes me recalling primordially that it was the same, they (the mountains) looked the same too in 584 B.C.—and all that but a sea spray drop— We live to long, so long I will, and jounce down that mountain highest perfect knowing or no highest perfect knowing full of glorious ignorant looking to sparkle elsewhere—

Later in the afternoon the west wind picks up, comes from smileless wests, invisible, and sends clean messages thru my cracks and screens— More, more, let the firs wither more, I want to see the white marvels south—

25 NOUMENA IS WHAT YOU SEE WITH YOUR EYES CLOSED, that immaterial golden ash, Ta the Golden Angel— Phenomena is what you see with your eyes open, in my case the debris of one thousand hours of the living-conception in a mountain shack— There, on top of the woodpile, a discarded cowboy book, ugh, awful, it is full of sentimentality and long-winded comments, silly dialog, sixteen heroes with double guns to one ineffectual villain whom I'd rather like for his irascibility and clomping boots—the only book that I have thrown away— Above it, sitting on corner of window, a can of Macmillan Ring Free Oil that I use to keep my kerosene in and to stoke fires, to fire fires, wizard like, vast dull explosions in my stove that get the coffee boiling— My frying pan hangs from a nail over another (castiron) pan too big to use but my used pan keeps dripping dribbles of fat down its back reminds of streamers of sperm, that I scrape off and flut into the wood, who cares— Then the old stove with the water pan, the perpetual coffee potpan with long handle, the tea pot seldom used—Then on a little table the great greasy dishpan with its surroundant accoutrements of steel scrubber, rags, stove rags, washwhirl stick, one mess, with a perpetual puddle of black scummy water under it that I wipe out once a week— Then the shelf of canned goods diminishing slowly, and other foods, Tide soap box with the pretty housewife holding up a Tide box saying "Just made for each other"— Box of Bisquick left here by the other lookout I never opened, jar of syrup I dont like—give to an ant colony down the yard—old jar of peanutbutter left here by some lookout presumably when Truman was President apparently from the old peanut rot of it— Jar I keep pickled onions in, that turns to smell like hard cider as the afternoon sun works it, to rancid wine—little bottle of Kitchen Bouquet gravy juice, good in stews, awful to wash off your fingers— Box of Chef Boyardee's Spaghetti Dinner, what

a joyous name, I picture the Queen Mary docked in New York
and Chefs going out to hit the town with little berets, towards
the sparkling lights, or else I picture some sham chef with mus-
tachio singin Italian arias in the kitchen on television cook
shows— Pile of enveloped green pea powder soup, good with
bacon, good as the Waldorf-Astoria and that Jarry Wagner first
introduced me to that time we hiked and camped at Potrero
Meadows and he dumped frying bacon into the whole soup pot
and it was thick and rich in the smoky night air by the creek—
Then a half-used cellophane bag of blackeyed peas, and a bag
of Rye Flour for my muffins and to glue together Johnny-
cakes— Then a jar of pickles left in 1952 and froze in the winter
so that the pickles are just spicy water husks looking like Mexican greenpeppers in a jar— My box of cornmeal, unopened can
of Calumet Baking Powder with the full-headed Chief—new
unopened can of black pepper— Boxes of Lipton soup left by
Ole Ed the previous lonely fucker up here— Then my jar of
pickled beets, ruby dark and red with a few choice onions whit-
ening against the glass—then my jar of honey, half gone, for
hot-milk-and-honey on cold nights when I feel bad or sick—
Unopened can of Maxwell House coffee, the last one— Jar of
red wine vinegar I'll never use and which I wish was wine and
looks like wine so red and deep— Behind that, new jar of molasses, that I drink from the bottle sometimes, mouthfuls of
iron— The box of Ry-Krisp, which is dry sad concentrated
bread for dry sad mountains— And a row of cans left years
ago, with frozen and dehydrated asparagrass that is so ephemeral to eat it's like sucking water, and paler— Canned whole
boiled potatoes like shrunk heads and useless— (that only the
deer eat) —the last two cans of Argentine roastbeef, of an original 15, very good, when I arrived in the lookout on that cold
storming day with Andy and Marty on the horses I found $30
worth of canned meat and tuna, all good, which in my tightness
I'd never have thought to buy— Lumberjack syrup, a big tall
can, also a leftover gift, for my delicious flapjacks— Spinach,

which, so iron like, never lost its flavor in its seasons on the shelf— My box full of potatoes and onions, O sigh! I wish I had an ice cream soda and a sirloin steak!

La Vie Parisienne, I picture it, a restaurant in Mexico City, I go in and sit at the rich tablecloth, order good white Bordeaux, and a filet mignon, for dessert pastries and strong coffee and a cigar, Ah, and stroll down the boulevard Reforma to interesting darknesses of the French movie with the Spanish titles and the sudden booming Mexico Newsreel—

Hozomeen, rock, never eats, never stores up debris, never sighs, never dreams of distant cities, never waits for Fall, never lies, maybe though he dies— Bah.

Every night I still ask the Lord, "Why?" and havent heard a decent answer yet

26 REMEMBERING, REMEMBERING, that sweet world so bitter to taste—the time when I played Sarah Vaughan's "Our Father" on my little box in Rocky Mount and the colored maid Lula wept in the kitchen so I gave it to her so on Sunday mornings in the meadows and pine barrens of North Carolina now, emerging from her man's old bare house with the pickaninny porch, you hear the Divine Sarah—"for Thine is the Kingdom, and the Power, and the Glory, forever, a men"—the way her voice breaks into a bell on the "a" of amen, quivering, like a voice should— Bitter? because bugs thrash in mortal agony even on the table as you'd think, death-less fools that get up and walk off and are reborn, like us, "hooman beens"—like winged ants, the males, who are cast off by the females and go die, how utterly futile they are the way they climb windowpanes and just fall off when they get to the top, and do it again, till they exhausted die— And the one I saw one afternoon on my shack floor just thrashing and thrashing in the filthy dust from some kind of fatal hopeless seizure—oi, the way we do, whether we can see it now or not— Sweet? just as

sweet, tho, as when dinner is bubbling in the pot and my mouth is watering, the marvelous pot of turnip greens, carrots, roast-beef, noodles and spices I made one night and ate barechested on the knoll, sitting crosslegged, in a little bowl, with chop-sticks, singing— Then the warm moonlit nights with still the red flare in the west—sweet enough, the breeze, the songs, the dense pine timber down in the valleys of the cracks— A cup of coffee and a cigarette, why zazen? and somewhere men are fighting with frighting carbines, their chests crisscrossed with ammo, their belts weighed down with grenades, thirsty, tired, hungry, scared, insaned— It must be that when the Lord thought forth the world he intended for it to include both me and my sad disinclined pain-heart A N D Bull Hubbard rolling on the floor in laughter at the foolishness of men—

At night at my desk in the shack I see the reflection of myself in the black window, a rugged faced man in a dirty ragged shirt, need-a-shave, frowny, lipped, eyed, haired, nosed, eared, handed, necked, adamsappled, eyebrowed, a reflection just with all behind it the void of 7000000000000 light years of infinite darkness riddled by arbitrary limited-idea light, and yet there's a twinkle in me eye and I sing bawdy songs about the moon in the alleys of Dublin, about vodka hoy hoy, and then sad Mexico sundown-over-rocks songs about amor, corazón, and tequila— My desk is littered with papers, beautiful to look at thru half closed eyes the delicate milky litter of papers piled, like some old dream of a picture of papers, like papers piled on a desk in a cartoon, like a realistic scene from an old Russian film, and the oil lamp shadowing some in half— And looking at my face closer in the tin mirror, I see the blue eyes and sun red face and red lips and weekly beard and think: "Courage it takes to live and face all this iron impasse of die-you-fool? Nah, when all is said and done it doesnt matter"— It must be, it *is*, the Golden Eternity enjoying itself with movies— Torture me in tanks, what else can I believe?— Cut me limbs off with a sword, what must I do, hate Kalinga to the bitter death and beyond?—Pra, it's the mind. "Sleep in Heavenly Peace."—

27 ALL OF A SUDDEN ON AN INNOCENT MOONLIT TUES-DAY NIGHT I turn on the radio for the bull session and hear all the excitement about lightning, the Ranger has left a message with Pat on Crater Mountain for me to call at once, I do, he says "How is the lightning up there?"—I say "It's a clear moonlit night up here, with a north wind blowing"— "Well," he says a little nervous and harassed, "I guess you live right"— Just then I see a flash to the south— He wants me to call the trail crew at Big Beaver, which I do, no answer— Suddenly the night and the radio is charged with excitement, the flashes on the horizon are like the second-to-the-last stanza of the Diamond Sutra (the Diamondcutter of the Wise Vow), a sinister sound comes out of the heather, the wind in the cabin rigging takes on a hypersuspicious air, it seems as though the six weeks of lonely bored solitude on Desolation Peak has come to an end and I'm *down* again, just because of distant lightning and distant voices and the rare distant mumble of thunder— The moon shines on, Jack Mountain is lost behind clouds, but Desolation is not, I can just make out the Jack Snowfields surling in their gloom—a vast batwing 30 miles or 60 miles wide advances slowly, soon t'obliterate the moon, which ends sorrowing in her cradle thru the mist—I pace in the windy yard feeling strange and glad—the lightning yellowdances over ridges, two fires are already started in the Pasayten Forest according to excited Pat on Crater who says "I'm having fun here noting down the lightning strikes" which he doesnt have to do it's so far away from him and from me 30 miles— Pacing, I think of Jarry Wagner and Ben Fagan who wrote poems on these lookouts (on Sourdough and Crater) and I wish I could see them to get that strange feeling that I'm down off the mountain and the whole bloody mess of boredom done— Somehow,

because of the excitement, the door of my shack is more exciting as I open and close it, it seems to be *peopled,* poems written
about it, washtubs and Friday night and men in the world,
something, something to do, or be— It is no longer Tuesday
Night August 14 in Desolation but the Night of the World and
the Lightning Flash and there I pace thinking the lines from the
Diamond Sutra (in case lightning should come and curl me up
inside my sleeping bag with the fear of God or a heart attack,
thunder crashing right on my lightning rod)—: "If a follower
should cherish any limited judgment of the realness of the feeling of his own selfhood, the realness of the feeling of the self-
ness of others, the realness of the feeling of living beings, or
the realness of the feeling of a universal self, he would be cher-
ishing something that is non-existent" (my own paraphrase)
and now tonight more than ever I see these words to be true—
For all this phenomena, that which shows, and all noumena,
that which shows not, is the loss of the Heavenly Kingdom
(and not even that)— "A dream, a phantasm, a bubble, a
shadow, the lightning's flash . . ."

"I'll find out and let you know—woop, one more—so I'll
find out and let you know, aw, how things are," Pat is saying
on the radio as he stands at his firefinder marking X's where he
judges the lightning strikes, he says "Woop" every 4 seconds,
I realize how funny he really is with his "woops" like Irwin
and I with our "Captain Oops" who was Captain of a Crazy
Ship up the gangplank of which on sailing day all kinds of
vampires, zombies, mysterious travelers and harlequin clowns
in disguise did troop on board, and when, en route sur le voyage, the ship reaches the end of the world and's gonna plop
over, the Captain says "Oops"

A bubble, a shadow—
woop—
The lightning flash

"Woop," say people spilling soup— It really is dreadful, but
the passer-through-everything must really feel good about ev-

erything that happens, the lucky exuberant bastard— (cancer's exuberant) —so if a lightning bolt disintegrates Jack Duluoz in his Desolation, smile, Ole Tathagata enjoyed it like an orgasm and not even that

28   HISS, HISS, SAYS THE WIND bringing dust and lightning nearer— Tick, says the lightning rod receiving a strand of electricity from the strike on Skagit Peak, great power silently and unobtrusively slithers through my protective rods and cables and vanishes into the earth of desolation— No thunderbolts, only death— Hiss, tick, and in my bed I feel the earth move— Fifteen miles to the south just east of Ruby Mountain and somewhere near Panther Creek I'd guess a large fire rages, huge orange spot, at 10 o'clock electricity which is attracted to heat hits it again and it flares up disastrously, a distant disaster that makes me say "Oo wow"— Who burns eyes crying there?

> Thunder in the mountains—
>   the iron
> Of my mother's love

And in the dense electrical air I sense the remembrance of Lakeview Avenue near Lupine Road where I was born, some thunderstorm night in the summer of 1922 with grit in the wet pavement, trolley tracks electrified and shiny, wet woods beyond, my apocloptatical paratomanotial babycarriage yeeurking on the porch of blues, wet, under fruited lightglobe as all Tathagata sings in horizoning flash and rumble bumble thunder from the bottom of the womb, the Castle in the night—

Round about midnight I've been staring so intently out the window dark I get hallucinations of fires everywhere and near, three of them right in Lightning Creek, phosphorescent orange faint verticals of ghost fire that come and go in my swarming electrified eyeballs— The storm keeps lulling then sweeping

around somewhere in the void and hitting my mount again, so
finally I fall asleep— Wake to the patter of rain, gray, with
hope silver-holes in the skies to my south—there at 177° 16'
where I saw the big fire I see a strange brown patch in the
general snowy rock showing where the fire raged and spitted
out in the allnight rain— Around Lightning and Cinammon no
sign of lastnight ghost-fires— Fog seeps, rain falls, the day is
thrilling and exciting and finally at noon I feel the raw white
winter of the North sweeping from a Hozomeen wind, the feel
of Snow in the air, iron gray and steel blue everywhere the
rocks—"*My*, but she was yar!" I keep yelling as I wash my
dishes after a good a delicious pancake breakfast with black
coffee.

> The days go—
>   they cant stay—
> I dont realize

I think this as I draw a ring around August 15 on the calendar
and look, it's already 11:30 on the clock and so the day half
over— With a wet rag in the yard I wipe the summer's dust
off my ruined shoes, and pace and think— The hinge of the
outhouse door is loose, the chimney piece is knocked over, I'll
have to wait a month for a decent bath, and I dont care— The
rain returns, all the fire's'll lose their tinder— In my dreams I
dream that I have controverted some wish of Cody's wife Evelyn concerning their daughter, on some sunny barge house in
sunny Frisco, and she gives me the dirtiest look in the history
of hate and sends me an electrical bolt that sends a wave of
shock into my gut but I'm determined not to be afraid of her
and stick by my ideas and go on calmly talking from my
chair— It's the same barge where my mother'd entertained the
Admirals in an old dream— Poor Evelyn, she hears me agree
with Cody that it was silly of her to give the only floor lamp to
the Bishop, over her dishes her heart pounds— Poor human
hearts pounding everywhere.

29 THAT RAINY AFTERNOON, according to a promise I made myself owing to the memory of a wonderful Chinese rice dish Jarry'd cooked up for us in the Mill Valley shack in April, I make a crazy Chinese sweet and sour sauce on the hot stove, compounded of turnip greens, sauerkraut, honey, molasses, red wine vinegar, pickled beet juice, sauce concentrate (very dark and bitter) and as it boils on the stove and the little rice pot makes the lid dance I pace in the yard and say ¡"Chinee dinner alway velly good!" and remember in a rush my father and Chin Lee in Lowell, I see the redbrick wall outside the windows of the booths of the restaurant, scent rain, rain of redbrick and Chinese dinners unto San Francisco across the lonesome rains of the plains and mountains, I remember raincoats and smiling teeth, it's a vast inevitable vision with poor misguided hand of—of fog—sidewalks, or cities, of cigar smoke and paying at the counter, of the way Chinese Chefs always scoop up a round ladleful of rice from the big pot and bring the little China bowl up to the inverted ladle and dump in leaving a round globe of steaming rice that is brought to you in your booth along with those insanely fragrant sauces— "Chinee dinner alway velly good"—and I see generations of rain, generations of white rice, generations of redbrick walls with the old-fashioned red neon flashing on it like warm compost of brick-dust fire, ah the sweet indescribable verdurous paradise of pale cockatoos and yocking mongrels and old Zen Nuts with staffs, and flamingos of Cathay, that you see on their marvelous Ming Vases and those of other duller dynasties— Rice, steaming, the smell of it so rich and woody, the look of it as pure as driven lakevalley clouds on a day like this one of the Chinee dinner when wind pusheth them rilling and milkying over stands of young fir, towards raw wet rock—

30 I DREAM OF WOMEN, women in slips and in slip-shod garments, one sitting next to me coyly moving my limp hand from her spot in the soft roll of flesh but even tho I make no effort one way or the other the hand stays there, other women and even aunts are watching— At one point that awful haughty bitch who was my wife is walking away from me to the toilet, sniffy, saying something nasty, I look at her slim ass—I'm a regular fool in pale houses enslaved to lust for women who hate me, they lay their bartering flesh all over the divans, it's one fleshpot—insanity all of it, I should forswear and chew em all out and go hit the clean rail—I wake up glad to find myself saved in the wilderness mountains— For that lumpy roll flesh with the juicy hole I'd sit through eternities of horror in gray rooms illuminated by a gray sun, with cops and alimoners, at the door and the jail beyond?—It's a bleeding comedy—The Great Wise Stages of pathetic understanding that characterize the Greater Religion elude me when it comes to harems— Harem-scarem, it's all in heaven now—bless their all their bleating hearts— Some lambs are female, some angels have woman-wings, it's all mothers in the end and forgive me for my sardony—excuse me for my rut.

(Hor hor hor)

31 AUGUST 22 is such a funny date in my life, it was (for several years) the climactic (for some reason) day on which my biggest handicaps and derbies were run in the Turf I conducted as a child in Lowell, the racing marbles— It was also the Augustcool end of summer, when trees of starry nights swished with a special richness outside my screen window and when the sand of the bank got cool to the touch and little clamshells glistened therein and across the face of the moon the Shadow of Doctor Sax flew—Mohican Springs race-

track was a special raw western Massachusetts misty track with cheaper purses and older railbirds and hardboots and seasoned horses and grooms from East Texas and Wyoming and old Arkansas— In the Spring it ran the Mohican Derby which was for plugs of age three usually but the big 'Cap of August was a hoi polloi event that had the best society of Boston and New York flocking and it was then Ah then that the summer being over, the results of the race, the name of the winner, would have an Autumn flavor like the flavor of the apples now begathered in baskets of the Valley and the flavor of cider and of tragic finality, with the sun going down over the old stalls of Mohican on the last warm night and now the moon's shining sadfaced through the first iron and massed concentrates of Fall cloud and soon it will be cold and all done—.

Dreams of a kid, and this whole world is nothing but a big sleep made of reawakened material (soon to reawake)— What could be more beautiful—

To complete, cap, and tragedize my August 22, it was upon that date, the day Paris was liberated in 1944, that I was let out of jail for 10 hours to marry my first wife in a hot New York afternoon around Chambers Street, complete with bestman detective with holstered gun—how far the cry from sad-side-pensive Ti Pousse with his migs, his carefully printed Mohican Springs entries, his innocent room, to the rugged evil-looking seaman in tow of a policeman being married in a judge's chamber (because the D.A. thought the fiancée to be pregnant)— Far cry, I was so degraded in level in that time, that August month, my father wouldnt even talk to me let alone bail me out— Now the August moon shines through ragged new clouds that are not August*cool* but August*cold* and Fall is in the look of the firs as they silhouette to the far-down lake at after-dusk, the sky all snow silver and ice and breathing fog of frost, it will soon be over— Fall in the Skagit Valley, but how can I ever forget even madder Fall in the Merrimac Valley where it would whip the silver ooing moon with slavers of cold mist, smelling of orchards, and tar rooftops with night-ink colors that smelled as rich as frankincense, woodsmoke, leafsmoke, river rain, the smell of the cold on your kneepants, the smell of doors opening, the door of Summer's opened and let in brief glee-y fall with his apple smile, behind him old sparkly winter hobbles— The tremendous secrecy of alleys between houses in Lowell on the first Fall nights, as though amens were falling by the sisters in there—Indians in the mouths of trees, Indians in the sole of earth, Indians in the roots of trees, Indians in the clay, Indians in there— Something shoots by fast, no bird— Canoe paddles, moonlit lake, wolf on the hill, flower, loss— Woodpile, barn, horse, rail, fence, boy, ground— Oil lamp, kitchen, farm, apples, pears, haunted houses, pines, wind, midnight, old blankets, attic, dust— Fence, grass, tree trunk, path, old withered flowers, old corn husks, moon, colorated clouts of cloud, lights, stores, road, feet, shoes, voices, windows of stores, doors opening and closing, clothes, heat, candy, chill, thrill, mystery—

32 AS FAR AS I CAN SEE and as I am concerned, this so-called Forest Service is nothing but a front, on the one hand a vague Totalitarian governmental effort to restrict the use of the forest to people, telling them they cant camp here or piss there, it's illegal to do this and you're allowed to do that, in the Immemorial Wilderness of Tao and the Golden Age and the Millenniums of Man—secondly it's a front for the lumber interests, the net result of the whole thing being, what with Scott Paper Tissue and such companies logging out these woods year after year with the "cooperataion" of the Forest Service which boasts so proudly of the number of board feet in the whole Forest (as if I owned an inch of a board altho I cant piss here nor camp there) result, net, is people all over the world are wiping their ass with the beautiful trees— As for lightning and fires, who, what American individual loses, when

a forest burns, and what did Nature do about it for a million years here up to now?—And in that mood I lie on my bunk in the moonlit night on my stomach and contemplate the bottomless horror of the world, from that worst of all spots in the world, a set of streets in Richmond Hill beyond Jamaica Avenue just northwest of Richmond Hill Center I'd guess where one hot summer-night when Ma (1953) was visiting Nin in the south I was walking and suddenly because completely depressed almost to match the depression-walk I had the night before my father died, and in those streets one winter night I called Madeleine Watson on the phone to make a date with her to see if she was going to marry me, a kind of fit of madness like I'm subject to, I really am a "madman bum and angel"—realizing that there is no place on earth where that bottomless horror can be dispelled (Madeleine was surprised, scared, said she had a steady boy friend, must still be wondering these years later why I called or what's the matter with me) (or maybe she secretly loves me) (I just saw her face in a vision, in the bed beside me, those tragic beautiful dark Italian lines of her face so streakable of tears, so kissable, firm, lovely, like I like)—thinking, even if I lived in New York, bottomless horror of palefaced pockmarked television actors in smorgasbords wearing thin silver ties and the utterest dismality of all the windswept apartments of Riverside Drive and the Eighties where they always live or cold January dawn on Fifth Avenue with the garbage cans all neatly lined near the incinerators in the courtyard, cold hopeless in fact malicious-minded rose in the skies above clawy trees of Central Park, no place to rest or warm up because you aint a millionaire and even if you were nobody'd care— Bottomless horror of the moon shining on Ross Lake, the firs that cant help you—Bottomless horror of Mexico City in the pine trees of the hospital grounds and the overworked Indian children at the market stalls Saturday night awfully late— Bottomless horror of Lowell with the Gypsies in empty stores on Middlesex Street and the hopelessness stretch-

ing over that to the mainline rail of the B & M Railroad cut by
Princeton Boulevard where trees that dont care for you grow
by a river of no-concern— Bottomless horror of Frisco, the
streets of North Beach on a foggy Monday morning and the
dontcare Italians buying cigars on the corner or just staring
or old paranoiac Negroes who take you to be insulting them or
even nutty intellectuals taking you to be an FBI man and avoiding you in the gruesome wind—the white houses with empty
big windows, the telephones of hypocrites— Bottomless horror
of North Carolina, the little redbrick alleys after the movie on
a winter night, the small towns of the South in January—agh,
in June—June Evans dead after a lifetime of irony, is right, her
unknown grave leers at me in the moonlight telling that all is
right, right damnable, right got rid of— Bottomless horror of
Chinatown at dawn when they slam garbage pails and you pass
drunk and disgusted and shamed— Bottomless horror everywhere, I can picture Paris almost, the Poujadists pissing off the
quai— Sad understanding is what compassion means—I resign
from the attempt to be happy. It's all discrimination anyway,
you value this and devalue that and go up and down but if you
were like the void you'd only stare into space and in that space
though you'd see stiffnecked people in their favorite various
displaytory furs and armors sniffing and miffed on benches of
this one-same ferryboat to the other shore you'd still be staring
into space for form is emptiness, and emptiness is form— O
golden eternity, these simperers in your show of things, take
them and slave them to your truth that is forever true forever—
forgive me my human floppings—I think therefore I die—I
think therefore I am born— Let me be void still— Like a
happy child lost in a sudden dream and when his buddy addresses him he doesnt hear, his buddy nudges him he doesnt
move; finally seeing the purity and truth of his trance the buddy
watches in wonder—you can never be that pure again, and
jump out of such trances with a happy gleam of love, being an
angel in the dream

33   A LITTLE INTERPLAY ON THE LOOKOUT RADIO one morning brings a laugh and a memory—it's clean early sunlight, 7 A.M., and you hear: "How 30 ten eight for the day. How 30 clear." Meaning station number 30 is on the air for the day. Then:—"How 32 also ten-eight for the day," right after it. Then:—"How 34, ten eight." Then:—"How 33, ten seven for ten minutes." (Off the air for ten minutes.) "Afternoon, men."

And said in that bright early morning wry voice of college boys, I see them on campuses in the mornings of September with their fresh cashmere sweaters and fresh books crossing dewy swards and making jokes just like that, their pearly faces and pristine teeth and smooth hair, you'd think youth were nothing but this kind of lark and nowhere in the world any grubby bearded youths grumbling in wood shacks and hauling water with a flatulent comment—no, just fresh sweet youngsters with fathers who are dentists and successful retired professors walking longstrided and light and glad across primordial lawns towards interesting dark shelves of college libraries—aw hell who cares, when I was a college boy myself I slept till 3 P.M. and set a new record at Columbia for cutting classes in one semester and am still haunted by dreams of it where finally I've forgotten what classes they were and the identities of the professors and instead I wander forlornly like a tourist among the ruins of the Colosseum or the Pyramid of the Moon among vast 100-foot-high shelled haunted abandoned buildings that are too ornate and too ghostly to contain classes— Well, little alpine firs at 7 A.M. dont care about such things, they just exude dew.

34

OCTOBER IS ALWAYS A GREAT TIME FOR ME (knock on wood), 's why I always talk about it so much— The October of 1954 was a wild quiet one, I remember the old corncob I started smoking that month (living in Richmond Hill with Ma) staying up late-a-nights writing one of my careful prose (deliberate prose) attempts to delineate Lowell in its entirety, brewing café-au-lait in the midnights with hot milk and Nescafé, finally taking a bus trip to Lowell, with my fragrant pipe, the way I strolled around those haunted streets of birth and boyhood puffing on it, eating red firm MacIntosh apples, wearing my Japanese-made plaid shirt with the white and deep brown and deep orange designs, under a pale blue jacket, with my white crepesole shoes (black foamsole) making all the Siberian-drab residents of Centerville stare at me making me realize that what was an ordinary outfit in New York was dazzling and even effeminate in Lowell, tho my pants were just dumpy old brown corduroys— Yes, brown corduroys and red apples, and my corncob pipe and big sack of tobacco stuffed in pocket, not inhaling then but just puffing, walking and kicking the gutter-deep leaves as of yore as I'd done at four, October in Lowell, and those perfect nights in my Skid Row hotel room there (Depot Chambers near the old depot) with my complete Buddhist or rather reawakened understanding of this dream this world—a nice October, ending with the ride back to New York through leafy towns with white steeples and the old sere brown New England earth and young luscious college girls in front of the bus, arriving Manhattan at 10 P.M. on a glittery Broadway and I buy a pint of cheap wine (port) and walk and drink and sing (slugging in excavations on 52nd Street and in doors) till on Third Avenue who do I pass on the sidewalk but Estella my old flame with a party of people including her new husband Harvey Marker (author of *Naked and the Doomed*) so I just dont even look but downstreet I turn just as they turn, curious

lookings, and I dig the wildness of the New York streets, thinking: "Gloomy old Lowell, just as well we left it, look how the
people in New York are on a perpetual carnival and holiday
and Saturday Night of revel—what else do in this hopeless
void?" And I stride to Greenwich Village and go in the Montmartre (hepcat) bar high and order a beer in the dim light full of
Negro intellectuals and hipsters and junkies and musicians
(Allen Eager) and next to me is a Negro kid with a beret who
says to me "What do you do?"

"I am the greatest writer in America."

"I am the greatest jazz pianist in America," says he, and we
shake on it, drink to it, and at the piano he whangs me strange
new chords, crazy atonal new chords, to old jazz tunes— Little
Al the waiter pronounces him great— Outside it's October
night in Manhattan and on the waterfront wholesale markets
there are barrels with fires left burning in them by the longshoremen where I stop and warm my hands and take a nip two
nips from the bottle and hear the *bvoom* of ships in the channel
and I look up and there, the same stars as over Lowell, October,
old melancholy October, tender and loving and sad, and it will
all tie up eventually into a perfect posy of love I think and I
shall present it to Tathagata my Lord, to God, saying "Lord
Thou didst exult—and praised be You for showing me how
You did it—Lord now I'm ready for more— And this time I
wont whine— This time I'll keep my mind clear on the fact
that it is Thy Empty Forms."

. . . This world, the palpable thought of God . . .

35 UP UNTIL THAT LIGHTNING STORM which was a dry
one, the bolts hitting dry timber, followed only afterwards by rain that banked the fires awhile, fires start popping
up all over the wilderness— One on Baker River sends a big
cloud of hazy smoke down Little Beaver Creek just below me
making me mistakenly assume a fire there but they calculate the

way the valleys run and how the smoke drifted— Then, when
during the lightning storm I'd seen a red glow behind Skagit
Peak on my east, then no more, four days later the airplane
spots a burned-out acre but it is mostly dead making a haze in
Three Fools Creek— But then comes the big fire on Thunder
Creek which I can see 22 miles south of me billowing smoke
out of Ruby Ridge— A high southwest wind makes it rage
from a two-acre fire at 3 to an eighteen-acre fire at 5, the radio
is wild, my own gentle district ranger Gene O'Hara keeps sighing over the radio at every new report— In Bellingham they
assemble eight smokejumpers to fly in and drop on the steep
ridge— Our own Skagit crews are shifted from Big Beaver to
the lake, a boat, and the long high trail to the big smoke— It's
a sunny day with a high wind and lowest humidity of the
year— This fire was at first mistakenly assumed by excitable
Pat Garton on Crater to be closer to him than where it is, near
Hoot Owl pass, but sneering Jesuit Ned Gowdy on Sourdough
verifies with the airplane the exact location and so it is "his"
fire—these guys being forestry careerists they are very reli-
giously jealous of "his" and "my" fire, as tho—"Gene are you
there?" says Howard on Lookout Mountain, relaying a message
from the Skagit crew foreman who is standing under the fire
with a walkie-talkie and the men staring at the steep inaccessible
slide it's on—"almost perpendicular— Ah How 4, he says that
you might get down from the top, it would probably be a rope
job and couldnt pack in what you needed—"—"Okay," sighs
O'Hara, "tell him to stand by— How 33 from 4"—"33"—
"Has McCarthy got out the airport yet?" (McCarthy and the
bigwig Forest Supervisor are flying over the fire), 33 has to call
the airport to see— "How one from 33"—repeats four times—
"Back to How four, I cant seem to get a hold of the airport"—
"Okay, thank you"— But turns out McCarthy is in the Bellingham office or at home, apparently not much concerned yet
because it isnt his fire— Sighing O'Hara, a sweet man, never a
harsh word (unlike bossy cold-eyed Gehrke), I think if I should

find a fire in this crucial hour I should have to preamble my
announcement with "Hate to pile sorrows on you—" Meanwhile nature innocently burns, it's only nature burning nature— Myself I sit eating my Kraft Cheese Noodle dinner and
drinking strong black coffee and watching the smoke 22 miles
away and listening to the radio— Only got three weeks to go
and I'm off to Mexico— At six o'clock in the still hot sun but
high wind the plane sneaks up on me, calling me, "We're about
to drop your batteries," I go out and wave, they wave back like
Lindbergh in their monoplane and turn around and make a run
over my ridge dropping a miraculous bundle from heaven
which whips out in a burlap parachute and goes sailing sailing
far over the target (high wind) and as I watch it gulping I see
it's going to go clear over the ridge and down the 1500-foot
Lightning Gorge but a lordly little fir captures the shrouds and
the heavy bundle hangs on the cliff side—I put on my empty
rucksack after finishing the dishes and hike down, find the stuff,
very heavy, put it in my rucksack, cutting shrouds and tapes
and sweating and slipping in the pebbles, and with the rolled-
up parachute under my arm lugubriously I labor on back up the
ridge to my lovely little shack—in two minutes my sweat's
gone and it's done—I look at the distant fires in distant mountains and see the little imaginary blossoms of sight discussed in
the Surangama Sutra whereby I know it's all an ephemeral
dream of sensation— What earthly use to know this? What
earthly use is anything?

36   AND THAT IS PRECISELY WHAT MAYA MEANS, it means
       we're being fooled into believing in the reality of
the feeling of the show of things—Maya in Sanskrit, it means
wile— And why do we go on being fooled even when we know
it?— Because of the energy of our habit and we hand it down
from chromosome to chromosome to our children but even
when the last living thing on earth is sucking at the last drop of

water at the base of equatorial ice fields the energy of the habit
of Maya will be in the world, embued right in rock and scale—
What rock and scale? There are none there, none now, none
ever were— The simplest truth in the world is beyond our
reach because of its complete simplicity, *i.e.*, its pure nothingness—There are no awakeners and no meanings— Even if suddenly 400 naked Nagas came solemn tromping over the ridge
here and say to me "We have been told the Buddha was to be
found on this mountaintop—we have walked many countries,
many years, to get here—are you alone here?"—"Yes"—
"Then you are the Buddha" and all 400 of em prostrate and
adore, and I sit suddenly perfectly in diamond silence—even
then, and I wouldn't be surprised (why be surprised?) even then
I would realize that there are, there is no Buddha, no awakener,
and there is no Meaning, no Dharma, and it is all only the wile
of Maya

37   FOR MORNING IN LIGHTNING GORGE IS ONLY A BEAU-
TIFUL DREAM—the wick wicky wick of a bird, the
long blue-brown shadow of primal mist dews falling sun wise
across the firs, the hush of the creek ever-constant, the burlying
bum trees with smoke heads around a dewdrop central pew
pool, and all the phantasmagoria of orange golden imaginary
heaven light-blossoms in my eyeball apparatus that connects in
Wile to see it, the porches of the ear that balance liquidly to
purify hearings into sounds, the ever busy gnat of mind that
discriminates and vexes differences, the old dry turds of mammals in the shed, the bizong bizong of morning flies, the few
wisps of cloud, Amida's silent East, the hill bump heavy matter-
knock balled, it's all one rare liquid dream imprinting (*imprinting?*) on my end plates of nerves and as I say not even that, my
God why do we live to be fooled?— Why do we fool to be
alive—holes in the wood wurl, wiss water from sky to jean
kidney, pulp from park to paper stall, dirt from dry to reening

receive, soak, in, up, twirl, green worm leaves wrung out of toil of constant—eeeeing little bug dingly lingers whinging sings morning void devoid of *loi*— Enough I've said at it all, and there's not even a Desolation in Solitude, not even this page, not even words, but the prejudiced show of things impinging on your habit energy— O Ignorant brothers, O Ignorant sisters, O Ignorant me! there's nothing to write about, everything is nothing, there's everything to write about!— Time! Time! Things! Things! Why? Why? Fools! Fools! Three Fools Twelve Fools Eight and Sixty Five Million Swirls of Innumerable Epochs of Fools!— Whatyawamme do, rail?— It was the same for our forefathers, who are long dead, long of dirt compounded they, fooled, fooled, no transmission of Great Knowing to us from their chromosome worms— It will be the same for our great grandchildren, long unborn, of space compounded they, and dirt and space, whether as dirt or whether as space what matters it?—come, now, children, wake up—come, now is the time, wake up—look closely, you're being fooled—look close, you're dreaming—come, now, look—being and not being, what's the difference?— Prides, animosities, fears, contempts, slights, personalities, suspicions, sinister forebodings, lightning storms, death, rock, WHO TOLD YOU THAT RADAMANTHUS WAS ALL THERE? WHO WRITES WRONG ON THE WHO THE WHY THE WHAT WAIT O THING I I I I I I I I I I I I I O MODIIGRAGA NA PA RA TO MA NI CO SA PA RI MA TO MA NA PA SHOOOOOOO BIZA RIIII - - - - - - - I O O O O— M M M—S O–S O–S O–S O–S O–S O—SO–S O S O— SO—S O

WHO WHAT WHY WHEN ITIBTO RAT

          After that there never was
That's all there is to what there's not—
Boom

   Up in the valley
      and down by the mountain,
   The bird—
Wake up! Wake up! Wake up! Wake
Wake Wake Wake A W A K E N
   A W A K E N   A W A K E N
      A W A K E N
         N O W
            This is the wisdom
               of the millennial rat
               —Theriomorphous, highest perfect
               Rat

Black black black black bling bling bling
bling black black black black
   bling bling bling bling
   black black black black
   bling bling bling

38 SWORD ETC., flat part of an oar or calamity, sudden vio-dashing young fellow, lent gust of wind;
forcible stream of leaf, air, blare of a trumpet or horn, blamable
deserving of Explosion as of gunpowder, blame, find fault with
Blight; censure, Imputation of a blatant Brawling noisy, Speak

ill, blaze, Burn with a blameful meriting flame, send forth a flaming light, less without blame innocent, torch, firebrand, stream of blamelessly blameless flame of light, bursting out, actness, worthy of blame, cul-blaze, Mark trees by pable, paring off part of the bark, mark blanch, whiten, par-out a way or path in this manner, boil, parboil and skin, as almonds, mark made by parking bark from grow white, a tree, white spot on the face of white, a horse or cow, pale, blancmange, blazon, publish or Jelly like preparation of sea-moss, proclaim extensively, herald, em-arrowroot, corn-starch or the like, blazon, embellish, adorn, eat art of accurately describing coats of bland, mild, balmy suave arms, blazonry art smooth of delineating or of explaining coats, blandishment of arms, coat of arms, art of expressing fondness, artful bleach, make pale or white caress, amenity pleasure, grow pale, flatter bleak, unsheltered deso-blank, white or pale late, cheerless cold cutting, not written or printed upon or keen, bleakly bleakness marked, void empty vacant pale, confused unqualified complete blear, make the eyes unrhymed, paper un-sore and watery, becloud bedim written upon, form not filled in observe, inflamed and watery lottery ticket which draws no prize dim or blurred, with inflammation empty space, mental vacancy modification of blur, white bleat cry as a sheep, blanket woolen cor-cry of a sheep, bleatering for beds, covering for horses bleed, bleeding bled bled broad wrapping or covering or draw blood from shed

> Anykind blanket dim of blood
> Blare sound loudly as a blemish impair tar
> Trumpet blast nigh that which tarnishes
> Blarney smooth wheed-flaw defect soil
> Ling speech cajole wheedle stain fault
> > speak de
> From Castle Blarney in Ireland

> > Blast and rend praise or glorify
> > Part of a bridle which is placed

            in a fidence
        Tattle telltale

                        Vain boast—
            box, blow on the head or er boastful

    Combining of persons to have nobles
        and rich gravy,
    And slow baking commercial dealings
        with a person afterward,
    Meat so cooked

                    See?

39 THE MOON—she come peekin over the hill like she
            was sneakin into the world, with big sad eyes, then
she take a good big look and show her no-nose and then her
ocean cheeks and then her blemish jaw, and O what a round
old moon lugu face it is, OO, and a lil twisted pathetic understanding smile for me, you—she got a swirl surl like a woman's
been dustin all day and didnt wash her face—she got tongue-
a-cheek—and say "Is dis wort me comin?"—She say, "OO la
la," and got creases in her eye sides, and looketh over ridges of
rocks, as yellow as a blind lemon, and O she sad— She let Old
Sun go first cause he's after her this month, now cat-mouse-
play moon come, late— She got a rougey twooty mouth like
little girls who dont know how to smear on lipstick— She got
a bump in her forehead from a fire rock— She is bursting at
the seams with moon goodness and moon fat and moon golden
fire and over her Golden Eternal angels sprinkle imaginary
flowers— She is Lord and Master Lesbian King of all the blue
and purple survey of her ink kingdom— Though the sun's left
his ravage glow she looks on't content and convinced in a minute his fire'll bank as always then she'll ensilver the night whole,
rise higher too, her triumph is in our east-rolling kneel of

earth— From her big pocky face I see (and planetary rims) epithalamial roses— Potpourri seas mark her smoothskin sailing, her character features that's dry dust and hairy rock— The big mosquitoes of straw that smile on the moon are going bzzz— She wears a light fire-latent lavender veil, prettiest hat since rose was wove and garland made, and the hat bedazzles on an angle and now'll drop like fair fire hair and soon be dim veil for brow of round hard woe—hack wow what a roll skull bowed bone sorrow that moon can hold in her roily poily joints—she is tendered on an insect's leg— Violent black purple is the west as her veil spreads, face-covers, wisps, ineffates, mmm— Pretty soon now she blears in her veil of blurs—now mystery marks where oft you've seen expressive sadness— Now is just level sneer of moon conveying her round respects to us moon men mad— All right, I buy— It's just a old dut ball burling into view because we're rolling upside bulky down around in planetary arrangements and it's just to come, what's all the pose and posy about?— Finally she is abandoning her veil for cleaner pastures, she heads for higher stores, her veil drops off in little strips of silk as soft as a baby's eyes and softer than what he sees in dreams of lambs and fairies— Blimps of clouds dimple her chin— She has a twisted round mustache tootered up and puckywucked and so the moon looks like Charley Chaplin— Not a breath of wind attend her rising, and the west is a still coal—the south is mauve and majesties and heroes— The north: white strips and lavender silks of ice and Arctic steadfast voids—

The moon is a piece of me

40 ONE MORNING I FIND BEAR STOOL and signs of where the unseen monster has taken cans of frozen hardened can-milk and squeezed it in his apocalyptical paws and bit with one insane sharp tooth in, trying to suck out

the sour paste— Never seen, and in the foggy dusk I sit and look down the mysterious Ridge of Starvation with its fog-lost firs and humping-into-invisibility hills, and the fog-wind blowing by like a faint blizzard, and somewhere in that Zen Mystery Fog stalks the Bear, the Primordial Bear—all of it, his house, his yard, his domain, King Bear who could crush my head in his paws and crack my spines like a stick—King Bear with his big mysterious black horseshit by my garbage pit— Tho Charley may be in the bunkhouse reading a magazine, and I sing in the fog, Bear can come and take us all— How vast that power must be— He is a tender silent thing crawling towards me with interested eyes, from the mist unknowns of Lightning Gorge— The Sign of the Bear is in the gray wind of Autumn— The Bear will carry me to my cradle— He wears on his might the seal of blood and reawakening— His toes are webbed and mighty—they say you can smell him downwind at a hundred yards— His eyes glint in the moonlight— He and the buck deer avoid each other— He will not show himself in the mystery of those silent foggy shapes, tho I look all day, as tho he were the inscrutable Bear that cant be looked into— He owns all the Northwest and all the Snow and commands all mountains— He prowls among unknown lakes, and at early morning the pearl pure light that shadows mountainsides of fir make him blink with respect— He has millenniums of thus-prowling here behind him— He has seen Indians and Redcoats come and go, and will see it again— He continually hears the reassuring rapturous rush of silence, except near creeks, he continually is aware of the light material the world is made of, and never discourses, nor makes signs for meaning, nor complains a breath, but nibbles and paws, and lumbers along snags paying no attention to inanimate things or animate— His big mouth chew-chews in the night, I can hear it across the mountain in the starlight. Soon he will come out of the fog, huge, and come and stare in my window with big burning eyes— He is Avalo-kitesvara the Bear

I am waiting for him

41 IN MY MIDNIGHT SLEEP SUDDENLY the rainy season begins and rain pours heavily on the entire forest including the great fire on McAllister and Thunder Creeks, while men shiver in the woods I lie in my warm-as-toast sleepingbag and dream—I do dream of a cold gray pool I'm swimming in, it presumably belongs to Cody and Evelyn, it's raining in my dream head all right, I come out of the pool proudly and go fish in the icebox, Cody's "two sons" (actually Tommy & Brucie Palmer) are in bed playing, they see me poking for butter—"Listen—now you hear the noises" (meaning the noises of my foraging) (like noises of a rat) —I pay no attention, sit down and start eating raisin toast with butter and Evelyn comes home and sees me and I proudly boast how I've been swimming— It seems to me she eyes my toast begrudgingly but she says "Couldnt you get something bettern that to eat?"— Passing through what everything is, like the Tathagata, I reappear in Frisco walking along toward Skid Row Street which is like Howard Street but not Howard Street like West 17th in old Kansas City and full of swingin door honkytonk bars, as I go along I see shelves of cheap wine in stores and the big bar where all the men and bums go, Dilby's, on the corner, and simultaneously I see a newspaper story about the wild boys of the Washington D.C. reformatory (redheads, rough looking blackhaired car thieves, tough and young) they're sitting on a park bench in front of the State House and just out of stir and the news photo shows a brunette in jeans going by sucking on a coke bottle and the story tells how she is the famous troublemaking temptress who has had dozens of guys sent to reform school for trying to make her tho she flaunts in front of them (as picture shows) on purpose, you see the boys lounging on the bench staring at her, smiling for the photo, in the dream I'm mad at her for being a bitch but when I wake up I realize all this is just pathetic tricks of her own invention to get one of these boys to impregnate her so she can turn soft and mother

lovey with a little infant at her breast, a Madonna Suddenly—I
see that same gang of boys now going into Dilby's, I dont think
I'll go there— Up around Broadway and Chinatown I roam
around looking to amuse myself but it's that bleak Frisco of
Dreams with nothing but wooden houses and wooden bars and
cellars and underground caves, like Frisco in 1849 the look of
it, except for Seattle-like dismal neoned bars, and rain—I wake
up from these dreams to a cold rainy north wind marking the
end of the fire season— In trying to remember the details of
the dreams I recall the words of Tathagata to Mahamati: "What
think you, Mahamati, would such a person" (seeking to recall
details of a dream, since it's only dreams) "would such a person
be considered wise or foolish?"—O Lord, I see it all—

> Mist boiling from the
> ridge—the mountains
> Are clean

> Mist before the peak
> —the dream
> Goes one

42   AS PROFOUND A MAN AS YOU'LL FIND ANYWHERE is
old Blacky Blake whom I'd met at the week of fire
school where all of us walked around with tin helmets and
learned how to dig progressive fire lines and put out fires till
they were dead out (run our hands over the cold embers) and
how to read azimuths and vertical angles on the firefinders
which turn and point to all directions of the compass so you
can sight the location of a seen fire—Blacky Blake, who is a
ranger of the Glacier District, who'd been recommended to me
as a great old-timer by Jarry Wagner—Jarry because of Com-
munist accusals at Reed College (he probably sat in on leftist
meetings and talked about his always anarchy talk) was banned
from this government fire work after an FBI Snoop (ridiculous,

as tho he had affiliations with Moscow and should run out there and light fires at night and run back to his lookout or jam the radio communications with a gleam in his eyes pressing the transmitter up and down) —Old Blacky said: "Damn silly to me to see that boy blackballed outa here—he was a damn good little firefighter and a good lookout and *good boy*— It seems like nowadays nobody can say anything any more the FBI'll investigate em— Me I'm gonna say my mind and I do say my mind— Now the *ting* that gets me, is how they kin blackball a boy like Jarry dere" (the way Blacky talks)— Old Blacky, years in the forest, an oldtime loggin boomer himself and was around in the days of the IWW Wobblies and the Everett Massacre so celebrate in Dos Passos and leftwing annals— What I like about Blacky is his sincerity, above all the Beethoven Sorrow of him, he has large sad black eyes, he's sixty, big, strong, big gut, strong arms, stands erect—everybody loves him— "Whatever Jarry's gonna do I tink he'll always have a good time—you know he had one a dem lil Chinese girls down in Seattle dere, O he had a time—" Blacky sees young Blacky in Jarry, for Jarry was also brought up in the Northwest, on a harsh wilderness farm in eastern Oregon, and spent his youth climbing around these rocks and camping in inaccessible gorges and praying to Tathagata on mountaintops and climbing monstrosities whole like Mt. Olympus and Mt. Baker—I can see Jarry scale Hozomeen like a goat— "And all dem books he reads," says Blacky, "about Buddha n all dat, he's the smart one all right dat Jarry"— Next year Blacky retires, I cant imagine what he'll do but I have a vision of him going on a long lonely fishing trip and I see him sitting by the creek, pole down, staring the ground at his feet, sad, huge, like Beethoven, wondering what is Blacky Blake after all and all this forest, bareheaded in the woods the highest perfect knowing he will surely come to pass through— On the day the rainy season comes I can hear Blacky on the radio talking to his Glacier District lookouts: "Now what I want ya to do is make an inventory of *every ting you got* up there and bring the list down wit ya to the station—" He says: "Take care of messages for me, there's a horse loose on the trail here and I better go out and chase im" but I understand that Blacky just wants to be on the trail, outdoors, away from the radio, among horses, the woods are *ave* of him— So there goes Old Blacky, huge, going after a horse in the wet mountain woods, and 8000 miles away on a templed hill in Japan his young admirer and semi-disciple of knowing and full disciple of the woods, Jarry, sits meditating under the teahouse pines repeating, with shaved head and clasped hands, "Namu Amida Butsu"— The fog Japan is the same as the fog northwest Washington, the sensing being is the same, and Buddha's just as old and true anywhere you go— The sun sets dully on Bombay and Hongkong like it sets dully on Chelmsford Mass.—I called Han Shan in the fog—there was no answer—

> The sound of silence
>   is all the instruction
> You'll get

   —In the talk I'd had with Blacky his earnestness had sent a shiver thru my chest—it is ever so, and men are men— And is Blacky less a man because he never married and had children and did not obey nature's injunction to multiply corpses of himself? With his brooding dark face and pout by the stove and lowered pious eyes, on some rainy night next winter, there will come diamond and lotus hands to ring a rose around his forehead (or I bust) (to miss my guess) —

> Desolation, Desolation,
>   wherefore have you
> Earned your name?

43 ON SUNDAY, just because it's Sunday, I remember, that is to say, a spasm takes place in my memory chamber of the brain (O hollow moon!) Sundays at Aunt Jeanne's in Lynn, I guess when Uncle Christophe was alive, just as I sip delicious and very hot black coffee after a good meal of spaghetti with super-rich sauce (3 cans tomato paste, 12 garlic cloves, half teaspoon oregano and all the basil in the paste, and onions) and a dessert of three little delightful bites of peanut butter mixed with raisins and dried prunes (as lordlike a dessert!) I guess I think of Aunt Jeanne's because of the after-dinner satisfaction when in their shirtsleeves they'd smoke and sip coffee and talk— Just because it's Sunday I also remember the blizzard Sundays when Pa and me and Billy Artaud play the Jim Hamilton Football Game put out by Parker Game Company, also again white shirtsleeves of Pa and his cigar smoke and the human happy satisfaction there a moment— including finally because I pace in the yard (the foggy wind-cold) to get an appetite while my spaghets cooks, reminding tic-ly the brain spasm of when I'd take long blizzard hikes Sundays before dinner, the mind being choked with cabinets with memories in them overflowing, some mystery makes the tic, the spasm, out it comes and it's so sweetly pure to be human I think— The bole of my flower is that my heart aches from human—Sunday—the Sundays in Proust, aye the Sundays in Neal Cassady's writings (hidden away), the Sundays in all our hearts, the Sundays of long-dead Mexican Grandees who re-membered Orizaba Plaza and the churchbells thronging in the air like flowers.

44 WHAT DID I LEARN ON GWADDAWACKAMBLACK? I
learned that I hate myself because by myself I am
only myself and not even that and how monotonous it is to be
monostonos—ponos—purt—pi tariant—hor por por—I
learned to disappreciate things themselves and hanshan man
mad me mop I dont want it—I learned learn learned no learning nothing—A I K—I go mad one afternoon thinking like
this, only one week to go and I dont know what to do with
myself, five straight days of heavy rain and cold, I want to
come down RIGHT AWAY because the smell of onions on
my hand as I bring blueberries to my lips on the mountainside
suddenly reminds me of the smell of hamburgers and raw onions and coffee and dishwater in lunchcarts of the World to
which I want to return at once, sitting at a stool with a hamburger, lighting a butt with coffee, let there be rain on redbrick
walls and I got a place to go and poems to write about hearts
not just rocks—Desolation Adventure finds me finding at the
bottom of myself abysmal nothingness worse than that no illu-
sion even—my mind's in rags—

45 THEN COMES THE LAST DAY OF DESOLATION—
"With wings as swift as meditation" the world
pops back into place as I wake up (or "as swift as thoughts of
love") —The old bacon rind is still out in the yard where the
chipmunkies have been pecking and pippling at it all week
showing their sweet little white bellies and sometimes standing
stiff in trance— Weird yawking birds and pigeons have come
and rifled my blueberries clean off the grass—creatures of the
air feeding from fruits of the grass, as's foretold—*my* blueberries, it's their blueberries—every bite I took was a watermelon
less in their larder—I b'reaved them of twelve trainloads—the
last day on Desolation, it'll be easy enough to crack and

crack— Now I go to Abomination and whores yelling for hot water— It all goes back to Jarry Wagner, my being here, showing me how to climb mountains (Matterhorn in the crazy Fall of 1955 when everybody on North Beach was wailing with tense religious beat and beatific excitement culminating dismally in Rosemarie's suicide, a story already told in this Legend)— Jarry, as I say, showing me how to buy a rucksack, poncho, down sleepingbag, camp cook kit and take off for the hills with trail rations of raisins and peanuts in a bag—my bag with the inside rubber and so the second to last night in Desolation as I take a few bites out of it for meager dessert it, the rubbery peanut raisin taste, brings back the whole flood of reasons that took me to Desolation and the Mountains, the whole idea we worked out together on long hikes concerning a "rucksack revolution" with all over America "millions of Dharma Bums" going up to the hills to meditate and ignore society O Ya Yoi Yar give me society, give me the beauteous-faced whores with lumpy-muscle shoulders full of rich fat and thick pearly cheeks their hands down between their skirts and bare feet (ah the dimpled knees and yea the dimples in the ankle) yelling "A g u a C a l i e n t e" to the madame, their dress straps falling over clear halfway down their arms so's one pressed breast shows almost out, the lunge power of nature, and you see the little fleshy corner of the thigh where't meets the under-knee and you see the darkness going under— Not that Jarry would deny this, but enough! enough of rocks and trees and yalloping y-birds! I wanta go where there's lamps and telephones and rumpled couches with women on them, where there're rich thick rugs for toes, where the drama rages all unthinking for after all would That-Which-Passes-Through-Everything ask for one or the other?— What'm I gonna do with snow? I mean real snow, that gets like ice in September so's I can no longer crunch it in my pails—I'd rather undo the back straps of redheads dear God and roam the redbrick walls of perfidious samsara than this rash rugged ridge full of bugs that sing in harmony and mysterious earth rumbles— Ah sweet enough the afternoon naps I took i' the grass, in Silence, listening to the radar mystery—and sweet enough the last sunsets when at last I knew they were the last, dropping like perfect red seas behind the jagged rocks— No, Mexico City on a Saturday night, yea in my room with chocolates in a box and Boswell's Johnson and a bed-lamp, or Paris on a Fall afternoon watching the children and the nurses in the windblown park with the iron fence and old rimed monument—yea, Balzac's grave— In Desolation, Desolation is learned, and 't's no desolation there beneath the fury of the world where 'all is secretly well—

46 FLIGHTS OF GRAY BIRDS COME MERRYING to the rocks of the yard, look around awhile, then start pecking at little things—the baby chipmunk runs among them unconcerned— The birds look up quickly at a fluttering yellow butterfly—I have the urge to run to the door and yell "Y a a a h" but that would be a frightful imposition on their little beating hearts—I closed down all my shutters to all four points of the compass and so I sit in the darkened house with just the door, open, admitting bright warm sunlight and air and it seems that the darkness is trying to squeeze me out that last orifice to the world— It is my last afternoon, I sit thinking that, wondering what prisoners have felt like on their last afternoons after 20-year imprisonments— All I can do is sit and wait for the proper gloat— The anemometer and pole are down, everything is down, all I have to do is cover the garbage pit and wash the pots and goodbye, leaving the radio wrapped and antenna under house and toilet limed liberally— How sad my great bronzed face in the windows with their dark backdrop, the lines in my face indicating halfway in life, middle age almost, the decay and the strife all come to the sweet victory of the golden eternity— Absolute silence, a windless afternoon,

the little firs are dry and brown and their summer christmas is over and not long from now hoar storms'll blizzard the area down— No clock will tick, no man yearn, and silent will be the snow and the rocks underneath and as ever Hozomeen'll loom and mourn without sadness evermore— Farewell, Desolation, thou hast seen me well— May angels of the unborn and angels of the dead hover over thee like a cloud and sprinkle offerings of golden eternal flowers— That which passes through everything has passed through me and always through my pencil and there is nothing to say— The little firs will be big firs soon—I throw my last can down the steep draw and hear it clammering all the way 1500 feet and again reminding me (because of the great dump of cans down there of 15 years of Lookouts) of the great dump of Lowell on Saturdays when we'd play among the rusty fenders and stinking piles and think it great, all of it including old cars of hope with gaunt rutted clutches all underneath the new sleek superhighway that runs from clear around the boulevard to Lawrence—the last lonesome clang of my Desolation cans in the void valley, to which I listen, naked, with satisfaction— Way far back in the beginning of the world was the whirlwind warning that we would all be blown away like chips and cry— Men with tired eyes realize it now, and wait to deform and decay—with maybe they have the power of love yet in their hearts just the same, I just don't know what that word means anymore— All I want is an ice cream cone.

47 IN 63 DAYS I LEFT A COLUMN OF FECES about the height and size of a baby—that's where women excel men—Hozomeen doesnt even raise an eyebrow—Venus rises like blood in the east and it's the last night and it's a warm tho chill Fall night with mysteries of blue rock and blue space—24 hours from said time I expect to be sitting by the Skagit River crosslegged on my sawdust stump-hole with a bot-

tle of port wine— All hail stars— Now I know what the mystery of the mountain flow was—

Okay, that's enough—

That which passes through everything passes through little bits of insulation plastic that I see lying discarded nay more than discarded in the yard and which was once a big important insulation for men but is now just what it is, that which passes through everything so exultantly I take it and yell and in my heart Ho-Ho and throw it out west in the gathered dusk hush and it sails a little black thing awhile then thuds in the earth and that's that— That shiny little piece of brown plastic, when I said it was a shiny little piece of brown plastic did I assert that it truly was "a shiny little piece of brown plastic?"—

The same with this and me and you—

Gathering all the immensities about me in a shroud I glide off "with Tarquin's ravishing strides" into the gloom of the foreknown globe, the vision of the freedom of eternity is like a bulb that's suddenly come on in my brain—enlightenment—reawakening—adventures of raw plasticity made of material of light regonijate and rigamarolerate ahead, I see through it all, ur, arg, oig, ello—

Wait for me Charley I'll be down with the rain man— All of you can see that this was never— Ring the black new fraon— Da fa la bara, gee meria—hear?— Ah fuck, man, I'm tired of trying to figure out what to say; it doesnt matter anyway— *Eh maudit Christ de batême que s'am'fend!*—How can anything ever *end?*

PART TWO

DESOLATION IN THE WORLD

48 BUT NOW THE STORY, the confession . . . What I'd learned on the solitary mountain all summer, the Vision on Desolation Peak, I tried to bring down to the world and to my friends in San Francisco, but they, involved in the strictures of time and life, rather than the eternity and solitude of mountain snowy rocks, had a lesson to teach me themselves— Besides, the vision of the freedom of eternity which I saw and which all wilderness hermitage saints have seen, is of little use in cities and warring societies such as we have— What a world is this, not only that friendship cancels enmity, but enmity doth cancel friendship and the grave and the urn cancel all— Time enough to die in ignorance, but now that we live what shall we celebrate, what shall we say? What to do? What, boidened flesh in Brooklyn and everywhere, and sick stomachs, and suspicious hearts, and hard streets, and clash of ideas, all humanity on fire with hate & *odio*— The very first thing I noticed as I arrived in S.F. with my pack and messages was that everybody was goofing—

wasting time—not being serious—trivial in rivalries—timid before God—even the angels fighting—I only know one thing: everybody in the world is an angel, Charley Chaplin and I have seen their wings, you dont have to be a seraphic little girl with a wistful smile of sadness to be an angel, you can be broadstriped Bigparty Butch sneering in a cave, in a sewer, you can be monstrous itchy Wallace Beery in a dirty undershirt, you can be an Indian woman squatting in the gutter crazy, you can even be a bright beaming believing American Executive with bright eyes, you can even be a nasty intellectual in the capitals of Europe but I see the big sad invisible wings on all the shoulders and I feel bad they're invisible and of no earthly use and never were and all we're doing is fighting to our deaths—

Why?

In fact why do I fight myself? Let me begin with a confession of my first murder and go on with the story and you, wings and all, judge for yourself— This is the Inferno— Here I sit upside-down on the surface of the planet earth, held by gravity, scribbling a story and I know there's no need to tell a story and yet I know there's not even need for silence—but there's an aching mystery—

Why else should we live but to discuss (at least) the horror and the terror of all this life, God how old we get and some of us go mad and everything changes viciously—it's that vicious *change* that hurts, as soon as something is cool and complete it fall apart and burns—

Above all, I'm sorry—but my sorriness wont help you, or me—

In the mountain shack I murdered a mouse which was— agh—it had little eyes looking at me pleadfully, it was already viciously wounded by my stabbing it with a stick through its protective hidingplace of Lipton's Green Pea Soup packages, it was all covered with green dust, thrashing, I put the flashlight right on it, removed the packages, it looked at me with "human" fearful eyes ("All living things tremble from the fear of punishment"), little angel wings and all I just let her have it, right on the head, a sharp crack, that killed it, eyes popped out covered with green pea dust— As I hit it I almost sobbed yelling "Poor little thing!" as though it wasn't me doin it?— Then I went out and dumped it over the precipice, salvaging first those packages of soup which were not crushed open, soup I later enjoyed too—I dumped, and then put the dishpan (in which I'd stashed destroyable food and hung it from the ceiling, nevertheless the clever mouse somehow jumped into it) put the dishpan in the snow with a pailful of water in it and when I looked in the morning there was a dead mouse floating in the water—I went to the precipice and looked and found a dead mouse—I thought "Its mate committed suicide in the pan of its death, from grief!"—Something sinister was happening, I was being punished by little humble martyrs— Then I realized it was the same mouse, it had stuck to the bottom of the pan (blood?) when I dumped in the dark, and the dead mouse in the ravine of the precipice was simply an earlier mouse that had drowned in the ingenious water trap invented by the previous fellow in my shack and which I'd halfheartedly set (a can with a rod, with bait on top, mouse steps to nibble and can turns over, dumping mouse, I was reading in the afternoon when I heard the fatal little splash in the attic right over my bed and the first preliminary thrashings of the swimmer, I had to go out in the yard not to hear it, almost crying, when I came back, *silence*) (and the next day, drowned mouse elongated like a ghost worldward reaching scrawny neck to death, the tail hairs streaming)— Ah, murdered 2 mouses, and attempted murder on a third, which, when finally I caught it standing on little hind legs behind the cupboard with a fearful upward look and its little white neck I said "Enough," and went to bed and let it live and romp in my room—later it was killed by the rat anyway— Less than a handful of meat and flesh, and the hateful bubonic tail, and I had prepared for myself future sojourns in the hell of murderers and all because of fear of rats—I thought

of gentle Buddha who wouldnt fear a tiny rat, or Jesus, or even
John Barrymore who had pet mice in his room in childhood
Philadelphia— Expressions like "Are you a man or a mouse?"
and "the best laid plans of mice and men" and "wouldnt kill a
mouse" began to hurt me and also "scared of a mouse"—I
asked forgiveness, tried to repent and pray, but felt that because
I had abdicated my position as a holy angel from heaven who
never killed, the world might now go fires— Methinks it has—
As a kid I'd break up gangs of squirrel murderers, at risk of my
own hurt— Now this— And I realize we are all of us murderers, in previous lifetimes we murdered and we had to come
back to work out our punishment, by punishment-under-death
which is life, that in this lifetime we must *stop murdering* or be
forced to come back because of our inherent God natures and
divine magic power to manifest anything we want—I remembered my father's pity when he drowned baby mice himself one
morning long ago, and my mother saying "Poor little
things"— But now I had joined the ranks of the murderers and
so I had no more reason to be pious and superior, for for a
while there (prior to the mice) I had somewhat considered myself divine and impeccable— Now I'm just a dirty murdering
human being like everybody else and now I cant take refuge in
heaven anymore and here I am, with angel's wings dripping
with blood of my victims, small or otherwise, trying to tell
what to do and I dont know any more than you do—

Dont laugh—a mouse has a little beating heart, that little
mouse I let live behind the cupboard was really "humanly"
scared, it was being stalked by a big beast with a stick and *it
didn't know why it was chosen to die*—it looked up, around, both
ways, little paws up, on hind legs, breathing heavily—*hunted*—

When big cow-y deer grazed in my moonlight yard still I
stared at their flanks as with a rifle sight—tho I would never
kill a deer, which dies a big death—nevertheless the flank
meant bullet, the flank meant arrow-penetrating, there is nothing but murder in the hearts of men—St. Francis must have

known this— And supposing someone had gone to St. Francis
in his cave and told him some of the things that are said about
him today by nasty intellectuals and Communists and Existen-
tialists all over the world, supposing: "Francis, you're nothing
but a scared stupid beast hiding from the sorrowing world,
camping and pretending to be so saintly and loving animals,
hiding from the real world with your formal seraphic cherubim
tendencies, while people cry and old women sit in the street
weeping and the Lizard of Time mourns forever on a hot rock,
you, *you*, think yourself so holy, farting in secret in caves, stink
as much as anybody, are you trying to show you're better than
man?" Francis might have killed the man— Who knows?—I
love St. Francis of Assisi as well as anybody in the world but
how do I know what he woulda done?—maybe murdered his
tormentor— Because whether you murder or not, that's the
trouble, it makes no difference in the maddening void which
doesn't care what we do— All we know is that everything is
alive otherwise it wouldnt be here— The rest is speculation,
mental judgments of the reality of the *feeling* of a good or bad,
this or that, nobody knows the holy white truth because it is
invisible—

All the saints have gone to the grave with the same pout as
the murderer and the hater, the dirt doesnt discriminate, it'll eat
all lips no matter what they did and that's because nothing matters and we all know it—

But what we gonna do?

Pretty soon there'll be a new kind of murderer, who will kill
without any reason at all, just to prove that it doesnt matter,
and his accomplishment will be worth no more and no less than
Beethoven's last quartets and Boito's Requiem— Churches will
fall, Mongolian hordes will piss on the map of the West, idiot
kings wil burp at bones, nobody'll care then the earth itself'll
disintegrate into atomic dust (as it was in the beginning) and
the void still the void wont care, the void'll just go on with that
maddening little smile of its that I see everywhere, I look at a

tree, a rock, a house, a street, I see that little smile— That "secret God-grin" but what a God is this who didn't invent justice?—So they'll light candles and make speeches and the angels rage. Ah but "I dont know, I dont care, and it doesnt matter" will be the final human prayer—

Meanwhile in all directions, in and out, of the universe, outward to the neverending planets in never ending space (more numerous than the sands in the ocean) and inward into the illimitable vastnesses of your own body which is also never ending space and "planets" (atoms) (all an electromagnetic crazy arrangement of bored eternal power) meanwhile the murder and the useless activity goes on, and has been going on since beginningless time, and will go on never endingly, and all we can know, we with our justified hearts, is that it is just what it is and no more than what it is and has no name and is but beastly power—

For those who believe in a personal God who cares about good and bad are hallucinating themselves beyond the shadow of a doubt, tho God bless them, he blankly blesses blanks anyway—

It's just nothing but Infinity infinitely variously amusing itself with a movie, empty space and matter both, it doesnt limit itself to either one, infinitude wants all—

But I did think on the mountain, "Well" (and passing the little mound where I'd buried the mouse every day as I went to my filthy defecations) "let us keep the mind neutral, let us *be* like the void"—but as soon as I get bored and come down the mountain I cant for the life of me be anything but enraged, lost, partial, critical, mixed-up, scared, foolish, proud, sneering, shit shit shit—

> The candle burns
> And when that's done
> the wax lies in cold artistic piles
> ——s about all I know

49

SO I START TRUDGIN DOWN THAT MOUNTAIN TRAIL with full pack on my back and think from the thap and steady whap of my shoes on stone and ground that all I need in this world to keep me goin is my feet—my legs—of which I'm so proud, and there they start giving way not 3 minutes after I've taken one final look at the shuttered (goodbye strange) cabin and even made a little kneel to it (as one would kneel to the monument of the angels of the dead and the angels of the unborn, the shack where everything had been promised to me by Visions on lightning nights) (and the time I was afraid to do my pushups from the ground, face down, hands, because meseems Hozomeen'll take bear or abominable form and bend down on me as I lay) (fog)— You get used to the dark, you realize the ghosts are all friendly—(Hanshan says "Cold Mountain has many hidden wonders, people who climb here are always getting scared")—you get used to all that, you learn that all the myths are true but empty and mythlike aint even there, but there are worse things to fear on the (upsidedown) surface of this earth than darkness and tears— There's people, your legs giving way, and finally your pockets get rifled, and finally you convulse and die— Little time and no point and too happy to think of that when it's Autumn and you're clomping down the mountain to the wondrous cities boiling in the distance—

Funny how, now the time (in timelessness) has come to leave that hated rock-top trap I have no emotions, instead of making a humble prayer to my sanctuary as I twist it out of sight behind my heaving back all I do is say "Bah—humbug" (knowing the mountain will understand, the void) but where was the joy?— the joy I prophesied, of bright new snow rocks, and new strange holy trees and lovely hidden flowers by the down-go happy-o trail? Instead of all that I muse and chew anxiously, and the end of Starvation Ridge, just out of sight of house, I'm already quite tired in the thighs and sit down to rest and

smoke— Well, and I look, and there's the Lake still as far
below and almost the same view, but O, my heart twists to see
something— God has made some little thin cerulean haze to
penetrate like unnamable dust the spectacle of a pinkish late-
morning northern cloud reflected in the lake-body-blue, and it
comes out rose-tint, but so ephemeral as almost not worth talking about and thus so evanescent as to tug at my heart's mind
and make me think "But God made that little pretty mystery
for me to see" (and no one else's there to see)— The fact, that
it's a heartbreaking mystery makes me realize it's a God-game
(for me) and I see the movie of reality as a vanishment of sight
in a pool of liquid understanding and I almost feel like crying
to realize "I love God"—the affair I've had with Him on the
Hill—I've fallen in love with God— Whatever happens to me
down that trail to the world is all right with me because I am
God and I'm doing it all myself, who else?

> While meditating,
> I am Buddha—
> Who else?

50 AND MEANWHILE THERE I'M SITTING IN THE HIGH
ALPINE, leaning in my straps against the pack
against a hump of grassy knob— Flowers everywhere— Jack
Mountain same place, Golden Horn— Hozomeen now out of
sight behind the peak Desolation— And far off at the head of
the lake no sign yet of Fred and the boat, which would be a
little bug-funnel in the circular watery void of the lake—
"Time to go down"— No time to waste—I have two hours to
make five miles down— My shoes have no more soles so I have
thick cardboard slip-ins but already the rocks have cut into that
and already the cardboard slip't so I've already tread on rocks
(with 70 pounds on back) in my stockinged feet— What a
laugh, for champeen mountain singer and King of Desolation

cant even get down his own peak—I heave up, ugh, sweating and start again, down, down the dusty rocky trail, around switchbacks, steep, some switchbacks I cut and just sliver down the slope and slide to ski on my feet to next level—filling my shoes with pebbles—

But what a joy, the world! I go!— But the aching feet wont enjoy and rejoice— The aching thighs that quiver and dont feel like carrying down anymore from the top but have to, step by step—

Then I see the boat's mark coming 7 miles away, it's Fred comin to meet me at the foot of the trail where two months before the mules'd clambered full-packed and slipslided up rocks to the trail, off the tug-pushed barge, in the rain— "I'll be there right on the button with him"—"meet the boat"— laughing— But the trail gets worse, from high meadow swing-along switchbacks it comes to bushes that tug at my pack and boulders in the trail that murder the pinched squeezed feet— Sometimes a knee-deep weed trail full of invisible hurts— Sweat—I keep hitching my thumbs through the packstrap to hunch it high on my back— It's much harder than I thought—I can see the guys laughing now. "Old Jack thought he'd make it down the trail in two hours with his pack! He couldnt even make it halfway down! Fred waited with the boat an hour, went to look for him, and had to wait all night till he come in by moonlight cryin 'O Mama why'd dyever do this to me?' "— I appreciate suddenly the great labor of those smokefighters at the big Thunder Creek burn— Not only to stumble and sweat with firepacks but only to get to a burning blaze and work even harder and hotter, and no hope anywhere in rocks and stones— Me who'd et Chinee dinners watching the smoke 22 miles away, hah—I was getting my come-on-down

51 THE BEST WAY TO COME DOWN A MOUNTAIN is like
running, swing your arms free and fall as you come,
your feet will hold you up for the rest—but O I had no feet
because no shoes, I was "barefooted" (as the saying goes) and
far from stomping down on big trail-singin steps as I bash along
tra la tra la I could hardly even mincingly place them the soles
were so thin and the rocks so sudden some of them with a sharp
bruise— A John Bunyan morning, it was all I could do to keep
my mind on other things—I tried to sing, think, daydream, do
as I did by the desolation stove— But Karma your trail is laid
out for you— Could have no more escaped that morning of
bruised torn feet and burning-ache thighs (and eventual searing
blisters like needles) and the gasping sweats, the attack of in-
sects, than I can escape and than you can escape being eternally
around to go through the emptiness of form (including the
emptiness of the form of your complaining personality)—I had
to do it, not rest, my only concern was keeping the boat or
even losing the boat, O what sleep on that trail that night would
have been, full moon, but full moon was shining down on the
valley too—and there you could hear music over the waters,
and smell cigarette smoke, and listen to the radio— Here, all
was, thirsty little creeks of September no widern my hand, giving out water with water, where I splashed and drank and mud-
dled to go on—Lord— How sweet is life? As sweet

                    as cold
                        water in a dell
                            on a dusty tired trail—

—on a rusty tired trail—bestrewn with the kickings of the
mules last June when they were forced at stickpoint to jump
over a badly hacked pathway around a fallen snag that was too
big to climb, and Lord I had to bring up the mare among the
frightened mules and Andy was cursing "I cant do this all by

myself goddamit, bring up that mare!" and like in an old dream
of other lifetimes when I handled the horses I came up, leading
her, and Andy grabbed the reins and heaved at her neck, poor
soul, while Marty stabbed her in the ass with a stick, deep—to
lead the frightened mule—and stabbed the mule—and rain and
snow—now all the mark of that fury is dry in September dust
as I sit there and puff— A lot of little edible weeds all around—
A man could do it, hide in these hills, boil weeds, bring a little
fat with him, boil weeds over small Indian fires and live forever— "Happy with a stone underhead let heaven and earth go
about their changes!" sang old Chinese Poet Hanshan— No
maps, packs, firefinders, batteries, airplanes, warnings on radios, just mosquitoes humming in harmony, and the trickle of
the streamlet— But no, Lord has made this movie in his mind
and I'm a part of it (the part of it known as me) and it's for me
to understand this world and so go among it preaching the
Diamond Steadfastness that says: "You're here and you're not
here, both, for the same reason,"—"it's Eternal Power mung-
ing along"— So I up I get and lunge along with pack, thumbed,
and wince on ankled pains and turn the trail faster and faster
under my growing trot and pretty soon I'm running, bent, like
a Chinese woman with a pack of faggots on her neck, jingle
jingle drunning and pumping stiff knees thru rock underbrush
and around corners, sometimes I crash off the trail and bellow
back on't, somehow, never lose, the way was made to be followed— Down the hill I'll meet thin young boy starting out
on his climb, I'm fat with hugepack, I'm going to get drunk
in the cities with butchers, and it's Springtime in the Void—
Sometimes I fall, on haunches, slipt, the pack is my back
bumper, I burnst right along bumbing for fair, what words to
describe hoopely tootely pumling down a parpity trail, pra-
pooty— Swish, sweat— Every time I hit my bruised football
toe I cry "Almost!" but it never gets it straight so's to lame
me— The toe, bruised in Columbia College scrimmages under
lights in Harlem dusks, some big bum from Sandusky trod on

it with his spikes and big boned calf all down— Toe never recovered—bottom and top both busted and sore, when a rock prods in there my whole ankle will turn to protect it—yet, turning an ankle is a Pavlovian *fait accompli*, Airapetianz couldnt show me any better how not to believe I've strained a needed ankle, or even sprained—it's a dance, dance from rock to rock, hurt to hurt, wince down the mountain, the poetry's all there— And the world that awaits me!

52   SEATTLES IN THE FOG, burlesque shows, cigars and wines and papers in a room, fogs, ferries, bacon and eggs and toast in the morning—sweet cities below.

Down about where the heavy timber begins, big Ponderosas and russet all-trees, the air hits me nice, green Northwest, blue pine needles, fresh, the boat is cutting a swath in the nearer lake, it's going to beat me, but just keep on swinging, Marcus Magee— You've had falls before and Joyce made a word two lines long to describe it—brabarackotawackomanashtopatarata-wackomanac!

We'll light three candles to three souls when we get there.

The trail, last halfmile, is worse, than above, the rocks, big, small, twisted ravines for your feet— Now I begin sobbing for myself, cursing of course— "It never ends!" is my big complaint, just like I'd thought in the door, "How can anything ever end? But this is only a Samsara-World-of-Suffering trail, subject to time and space, therefore must end, but my God it will never end!" and I come running and thwapping finally no more— For the first time I fall exhausted without planning.

And the boat is coming right in.

"Cant make it."

I sit there a long time, moody faced and finished— Wont do it— But the boat gets coming closer, it's like timeclock civilization, gotta get to work on time, like on the railroad, tho you cant make it you'll make it— It was blasted in the forges with iron vulcan might, by Poseidon and his heroes, by Zen Saints with swords of intelligence, by Master Frenchgod—I push myself up and try on— Every step wont do, it wont work, that my thighs hold it up's'mystery to me—plah—

Finally I'm loading my steps on ahead of me, like placing topheavy things on a platform with outstretched arms, the kind of strain you cant keep up—other than the bare feet (now battered with torn skin and blisters and blood) I could just plow and push down the hill, like a falling drunk almost falling never quite falling and if so would it hurt as much as my feet?—nu— gotta push and place each up-knee and down with the barbfoot on scissors of Blakean Perfidy with worms and howlings everywhere—dust—I fall on my knees.

Rest that way awhile and go on.

"Eh damn Eh maudit" I'm crying last 100 yards—now the boat's stopped and Fred whistles sharply, no a hoot, an Indian Hooo! which I answer with a whistle, with fingers in mouth— He settles back to read a cowboy book while I finish that trail— Now I dont want him to hear me cry, but he does he must hear my slow sick steps—plawrp, plawrp—timble tinker of pebbles plopping off a rock round precipice, the wild flowers dont interest me no more—

"I cant make it" is my only thought as I keep going, which thought is like phosphorescent negative red glow imprinting the film of my brain "Gotta make it"—

> Desolation, Desolation
> so hard
> To come down off of

53 BUT THAT WAS OKAY, the water was shrill and close and lapping on dry driftwood when I rounded the final little shelf-trail to the boat— This I plodded and waved with a smile, letting the feet go by, blister in left shoe that I thought was a sharp pebble ground into my skin—

In all the excitement, dont realize I am back in the world at last—

And no sweeter man in the world to meet me at the bottom of it.

Fred is an oldtime woodsman and ranger liked by all the old fellows and the young— Gloomily in bunkhouses he presents to you a completely saddened and almost disappointed face staring off into the void, sometimes he wont answer questions, he lets you drink in his trance— You learn from his eyes, which look far, that there's nothing further to see— A great silent Bodhisattva of a man, these woodsmen have it— Ole Blacky Blake loves him, Andy loves him, his son Howard loves him— Instead of good old soul Phil in the boat, whose day-off, it's Fred, wearing incredibly long visor, crazyhat, golf link hat he uses to shade in the sun while prorping the boat around the lake— "There comes the fire warden" say the buttonhatted fishermen from Bellingham and Otay—from Squohomish and Squonalmish and Vancouver and pine towns and residential suburbs of Seattle— They ease up and down the lake casting their lines for secret joyful fish who once were birds but fell— They were angels and fell, the fisherman, loss of wings meant need of food— But they fish for the joy of the joyous dead fish—I've seen it—I understand the gaping mouth of a fish on a hook— "When a lion claws ya, let him claw . . . that kind of courage wont help ya"———— Fish submit,

fishermen sit
And cast the line.

Old Fred, all's he gotta do is see no fisherman campfire runs wild and burns up the timber scene— Big binoculars, he looks the far shore over— Illegal campers— Parties of drinkers on little islands, with sleepingbags and cans of beans— Women sometimes, some of them beautiful— Great floating harems in putput boats, legs, show all, awful them Samsara-World-of-

Suffering women with they show you their legs for to turn the wheel along—

What makes the world
go around?
Between the stems

Fred sees me and starts up the motor to edge up closer, make it easier for easy-to-see-dejectable me— First thing he does is ask me a question which I dont hear and I say "Huh?" and he looks surprised but us ghosts that spend summer in the solitude wilds we lose all our touch, get ephemeral and not there— A lookout coming down the mountain is like a boy that was drowned reappearing in ghost form, I know— But he's only asked "How's the weather up there, hot?"

"No, a big wind's blowin up there, from the west, from the Sea, it's not hot, only down here"

"Gimme your pack"

"It's heavy"

But he reaches over the gunwale and hauls it in anyway, arms outstretched and strained, and lays it on the bilgey boards, and I clamber on and point to my shoes—"No shoes, look"—

Starts up the motor as we leave, and I put on Band-Aids after soaking my feet in the rush by the starboards— Wow, the water comes up and slams up my legs, so I wash them too, clear to the knee, and soak my tortured woolsocks too and wring em and lay em out to dry on the poop—oop—

And here we go putputtin back to the world, in a bright sunny and beautiful morning, and I sit in the front seat and smoke the new Lucky Strikes Camels he's brought me, and we talk— We yell—the engine is loud—

We yell like everywhere in the world of No-Desolation (?) people are yelling in telling rooms, or whispering, the noise of their converse is melded into one vast white compound of holy hushing silence which eventually you'll hear forever when you

learn (and learn to remember to hear)— So why not? go ahead
and yell, do what you want—

And we talk about deer

54   HAPPY, HAPPY, THE LITTLE GASOLINE FUMES ON THE
      LAKE—happy, the cowboy book he has, which I
glance at, the first rough dusty chapter with sneering hombres
in dust hats pow-wowing murders in a canyon crack—hatred
steeling in their faces all blue—woe, gaunt, worn, weathered
horses and rough chaparral— And I think "O pooey it's all a
dream, who care? Come on, that which passes through everything, pass through everything, I'm with you"—"Pass through
dear Fred, make him feel the ecstasy of you, God"—"Pass
through it all"— How can the universe be anything but a
Womb? And the Womb of God or the Womb of Tathagata, it's
two languages not two Gods— And anyway the truth is relative, the world is relative— Everything is relative— Fire is
fire and isnt fire— "Dont disturb the sleeping Einstein in his
bliss"—"So it's only a dream so shut up and enjoy—lake of
the mind"—

Only seldom Fred talks, especially with old loquacious Andy
the muleskinner from Wyoming, but his loquaciousness only
takes a fill-in role— Today though as I sit smoking my first
package cigarette, he talks to me, thinking I need talkin after 63
days in solitary—and talking to a human being is like flying
with angels.

"Bucks, two bucks—does—one night two fawns ate in my
yard"—(I'm shouting over the engine)——"Bear, signs of a
bear—blueberries—" "Strange birds," I add to think, and chip-
munks with little oatsies in their paws they'd pick up from old
corral fence rack— Ponies and horses of old 1935

where
Are they now?

"There's coyotes up on Crater!"

55 DESOLATE ADVENTURE—we go slowly three miles an hour down the lake, I settle back on the backboard and just take in the sun and rest, no need shouting—no sense— And soon he's got that lake whipped and turned Sourdough on our upright and left Cat Island way behind and the mouth of the Big Beaver, and we're turning in to the little white flag rag that's hoiked on booms (logs) that the boat passes through but a congestion of other logs that majestically took all August to idle on down from the tarn of Hozomeen—there they are and we have to maneuver and push them around and slip thru—after which Fred returns to his hour-long perusal of Insurance forms with little cartoons and advertising showing anxious American heroes worrying about what will happen to their kin when they pass on—good enough—and up ahead, flat on the lakebottom scene, the houses and floats of Ross Lake Resort— Ephesus, the mother of cities to me—we aim right straight for there.

And there's the bankside where I'd spent a whole day digging in the rocky soil, four feet down, for the Forest Ranger Garbage Pit and had talked with Zeal the quarter Indian kid who'd quit running down the dam trail and was never seen again, usta split cedar shakes with his brothers for independent pay— "Don't like to work for the government, damn I'm goin to L.A."—and there's the waterside where, finished with the pit dug and the trail yawrked out of brush, twisty, to the latrine hole Zeal'd dug, I'd gone down and thrun rocks at little sailing can ships and Admiral me Nelson if they didnt get away and sail off and make it to the Golden Eternity—me resorting finally to huge plaps of wood and great boulders, to swamp the ship-can, but wouldnt sink, Ah Valor— And the long long booms I thought I'd make it back to the Ranger Station Float without a boat but when I got out to the middle boom and had to jump three feet over choppy water to half submerged log I knew I'd get wet and I quit and went back—there it all is, all in June, and now's September and I'm going four thousand miles down the cities of the rib of America—

"We'll eat lunch on the float then go get Pat."

Pat has also same morning left Crater Lookout and started down a 15-mile trail, at dawn, 3 A.M., and will be waiting 2 P.M. at foot of Thunder Arm—

"Okay—but I'll take a nap while you do that," I say—

Tsokay with old Tokay—

We ease into the float and I get out and tie the line to the bit and he heaves my pack out, now I'm barefooted and feel good— And O the vast white kitchen full of food and a radio on the shelf, and letters waiting for me— But we're not hungry anyway, a little coffee, I turn on the radio and he goes off to get Pat, 2-hour trip, and suddenly I'm alone with the radio, coffee, cigarettes, and strange pocketbook about a used-car hero salesman in San Diego who sees a girl on a drugstore stool and thinks "She has a neat can"— Wow, back to America.— And on the radio suddenly it's Vic Damone singing a tune I had completely forgotten on the mountain to sing, an old standard, hadnt completely forgotten it but no work over, here he goes with full orchestra (O the genius of American Music!) on "In This World,

> Of ordinary people,
> Ex-tra-ordinary people,
> I'm glad there is you,"

—holding the "you," breath, "In this world, of overrated pleasures, and underrated treasures," hum, "I'm glad there is You"— Twas me told Pauline Cole to tell Sarah Vaughan to sing that in 1947— Oh the beautiful American music across the lake now, and then, after choice amusing charming words from the announcer in Seattle, Oi, Vic sings

"The Touch of your hand
Upon my brow,"

at middle tempo, and a gorgeous trumpet comes in, "Clark Terry!" I recognize him, playing sweet, and the old float moans gently on her booms, mid brightlight day— The same old float that on choppy nights blams and booms and the moonlight ululates the water a splashing sheen, O hoar sorrow of the Last Northwest and now I have no borders more to go and— The world out there is just a piece of cheese, and I'm the movie, and there's the pretty singing trap—

56 RAPPLE TRAP ME, if it aint them old mountains stickin clear up from the lappylap lapis lazuli lakeshore, with still old Spring snow on em, tops, and those woe moreful ole summery clouds pinkmopping the Emily Dickinson afternoon of peace and ah butterflies— Twitting in the brush is bugs— On the float, no bugs, just the lily lap of the water on the underslaps of booms, and the constant pour of the kitchen tap which they had plumbed to an endless mountain stream, so let it run cold all day, so when you need a glass of water there it is, tune in—Sunshine—hot sun drying my socks on the hot warped deck—and Fred's already given me a new old pair of shoes to get down on, at least to a store in Concrete to buy new shoes—I've hangled their nailpoints back in to the leather with big Forest Service tools in the toolhouse barge, and they'll be comfortable with the big socks— It's always a triumph to get your socks dried, to have a fresh pair, in mountains and war

Angels in Desolation—
Visions of Angels—
Visions of Desolation—
Desolation Angels

And by and by here he comes, old Fred and the boat and I see the little puppet figure beside him a mile away, Pat Garton the

Crater Mountain lookout, back, gasping, glad, just like me—
Boy from Portland Oregon and all summer long on the radio
we've exchanged consolements— "Don't worry, it'll soon be
over" it'll even be October soon— "Yeah, but when that day
comes I'm going to *fly* down that mountain!" Pat'd yelled—
But unfortunately his pack was too heavy, almost twice as
heavy as mine, and he'd almost not made it and had a logger
(kind man) carry his pack for him the last mile down to the
creek arm—

They bring the boat up and tie the little rope bit, which I
like to do because I used to do it with vast hemp cables around
freighter bits as big as my body, the big rhythmic swing of
loops, with a little bit it's fun too— Besides I wanta look useful,
still getting paid today— They get out and from listening to
his voice all summer I look at Pat and he looks like somebody
else— Not only that but soon as we're in the kitchen and he's
walking beside me suddenly I get the eerie feeling he's not there
and I take a good look to check— For just an instant this angel
had faded away— Two months in desolation'll do it, no matter
what mountain's your name— He'd been on Crater, which I
could see, right on the hem of an extinct volcano apparently,
snowbound, and subject to all the storms and shifts of wind
flowing from any direction down there along the groove of
Ruby Mountain and Sourdough, and from the east, and from
my north, he'd had more snow than me— And coyotes howling at night he said— And was afraid to go out of his shack at
night— If he'd ever feared the green face in the window of his
Portland suburban boyhood, he had plenty masks up here to
mince in the mirror of his night-hooling eyes— Especially
foggy nights, when you might as well be in Blake's Howling
Void or just an oldtime Thirties Airplane lost in the ceiling-
zero fog— "Are ya there Pat?" I say for a joke—

"I'll say I'm here and I'm ready to go, too—you?"

"All set—we got another stretcha trail to make down the
dam tho, damn—"

"I dont know if I can make it," he says honestly, and he's limping. "Fifteen miles since sunup before sunup—my legs are dead."

I lift his pack and it weighs 100 pounds— He hasn't even bothered to discard the 5 pounds of Forest Service literature with pictures and ads, tsall stuck in his pack, and on top of that a sleeping bag under his arm— Thank God his shoes had bottoms.

We eat a jolly lunch of old porkchops re-heated, wailing at butter and jam and things we didn't have, and cup after cup of strong coffee I made, and Fred talks about the McAllister Fire— Seems so many hundred tons of equipment were dropt in by plane and's all strewn over the mountainside right now— "Oughta tell the Indians to go up there and eat," I think to say, but where are the Indians?

"I'm never gonna be a lookout again," announces Pat, and I repeat it—for then—Pat has an old crew cut that's all over-grown from summer and I'm surprised to see how young he is, 19 or so, and I'm so *old*, 34— It doesn't disturb me, it pleases— After all and old Fred is 50 and he doesnt care and we fare as we fare and part forever as we part— Only to come back again in some other form, as form, the essence of our 3 respective beings has certainly not taken 3 forms, it just passes through— So it's all God and we the mind-angels, so bless and sit down—

"Boy," I say, "tonight I'm gettin me a few beers"—or a bottle of wine—"and sit by the river"—I dont tell them all this—Pat doesnt drink or smoke—Fred has a snort every now and then, on the way up in the truck two months before old Andy'd uncorked his quart of Marblemount-bought blackberry 12 percent wine and we'd all slupped it under before Newhalem at least— At that time I'd promised Andy I'd buy him a great quart of whisky, in gratitude, but now I see he's somewhere else, up on Big Beaver with the pack, I sneakily realize I can sneak out of all this without buying Andy that fourdollar bot-tle— We get our things together, after long talk at table—Fred putputs the boat down past the Resort floats (gasoline pumps, boats, rooms for rent, tackle and gear) —down to the big white wall of Ross Dam—"I'll carry your pack Pat," I offer, figuring I'm strong enough to do it and I wont give it a second thought because it says in the Diamondcutter of the Wise Vow (my bible, the *Vajra-chedika-prajna-paramita* which was supposed to've been spoken orally—how else?—by Sakyamuni himself) "practice generosity but think of generosity as being but a word and nothing but a word," to that effect—Pat is grateful, hoiks my rucksack up, I take his immense topheavy packboard and sling on and try to get up and cant make it, I have to push Atlas away to make it—Fred's in the boat smiling, actually hates to see us leave— "See ya later, Fred."

"Take it easy now"

We start off but right away there's a nail in my flesh so we stop at the dam trail and I find a little piece of fisherman cigarettepack and make a bulge in my shoe, and we go on— Tremble, I cant make it, my thighs are gone again— It's a steep downgoing trail winding around the cliff by the dam— At one point it goes up again— That's a relief on the thighs, I just bend and upsweat— But we stop several times, both exhausted—"We'll never make it," I keep saying and babbling on all kinds of talk—"You learn pure things on the mountain, dont you?—dont you feel that you appreciate life more?"

"I sure do," says Pat, "and I'll be glad when we get outa here."

"Ah tonight we'll sleep in the bunkhouse and tomorrow go home—" He has a ride for me to Mount Vernon on Highway 99 at five P.M. but I'll just hitch hike out in the morning, not wait— "I'll be in Portland afore you," I say.

Finally the trail levels off down at the water level and we come thwapping and sweating thru sitting groups of City Electric dam employees—run the gauntlet— "Where's the boat land?"

His sleepingbag under my arm has slipped and unrolled and

I just carry it that way, dont care— We come to the boat land-
ing and there's a little wood walk we clomp right on, woman
and dog sitting on it have to move, we wont stop, we slap the
gear on the planks and presto I lie down on my back, pack
underhead, and light a cigarette— Done. No more trail. The
boat'll take us to Diablo, to a road, a short walk, a giant Pittsburgh lift, and our truck waiting for us at the bottom with
Charley drivin—

57 THEN DOWN THE TRAIL we'd just sweatingly completed, racing to make the boat, here come two
mad fishermen with gear and a whole outboard motor slung on
a 2-wheel contraption which they roll and bounce along—
They make it just in time, the boat comes, we've all got on—I
stretch out on a seat and start to meditate and rest—Pat's in the
back talking to tourists about his summer— The boat goes
churning down the narrow lake between boulder-cliffs—I just
lie on back, arms folded, eyes closed, and meditate the scene
away—I know there's more than meets the eye, as well as what
does meet the eye— You know it too— The trip takes 20 minutes and soon I can feel the boat slow up and bump into dock—
Up, at the packs, I'm still luggin Pat's big pack, generosity right
down to the end?—Even then we have a painful quartermile
dirt road to walk, turning at a cliff, and lo! there's a big lift
platform ready to ease us down a thousand feet to little neat
houses and lawns below and a thousand cranes and wires con-
necting the Power Dam, Diablo Dam, Devil Dam—the devil
of the dullest place in the world to live, one store and no beer
in it— People watering their prison lawns, children with dogs,
mid-Industrial America in the afternoon— Little bashful girl at
her mother's dress, men talking, all on the lift, and soon it starts
grinding down and slowly we descend to the earth valley—
Still I'm countin: "Goin one mile an hour towards Mexico City
on her High Valley Plateau four thousand miles away"—snap

of a finger, who care?— Up comes the big weight of unsol-
dered iron that's holding us poised precarious downcoming, a
majestical ton upon ton of black mass, Pat points it out (with
comments) (he's going to be an engineer) —Pat has a slight
speech defect, a slight stutter and excitement and burbling-up,
choke, sometimes, and his lips hang a little, but his brain is
sharp—and he has manly dignity—I know that on the radio all
summer he's said some very funny boners, his "oopses" and
excitement, but nothing on that radio was madder than serious
evangelical Jesuit student Ned Gowdy who, when visited by a
gang of our climbers and firefighters, screamed a crazy tittrous
laugh, the wildest I've ever heard, his voice hoarse, all from
talking so suddenly with unexpected visitors— As for me, all
my record on radio was "Hozomeen Camp from forty-two,"
beautiful poem every day, to talk to Old Scotty, about nothing,
and a few curt exchanges with Pat and a few charmed talks with
Gowdy and a few early concessions of what I was cooking,
how I felt, and why—Pat was the one who made me laugh
most— Somebody called "John Trotter" was referred to, at a
fire, and Pat made these two announcements: "John Trot Scoop
will be in with the next drop load, John Twist did not make it
in the first plane load," actual fact he said that—a completely
mad mind—

At lift bottom no sign of our truck, we sit and wait and drink
water and talk to a little boy who has a big beautiful Collie-
Lassie dog with him in the perfect afternoon—

Finally the truck comes, there's old Charley driving it, the
clerk at Marblemount, 60, lives in a little trailer right there,
cooks, smiles, types, measures logger wood—reads in his
bunk—his son's in Germany—washes the dishes for everybody
in the big kitchen— Glasses—white hair—one weekend when
I'd come down for my butts he'd gone off into the woods with
a Geiger counter and a fishing rod—"Charley," I say, "there's
lots of uranium in the dry mountains of Chihuahua I bet"

"Where's that?"

"South of New Mexico and Texas, boy—dintya ever see *Treasure of the Sierra Madre* that picture about the old coot prospector who outwalk'd the boys and found gold, a reglar mountain goat of gold and they first met him in Skidrow Flophouse in his pee-jamas, old Walter Huston?"

But I dont talk too much seeing as how Charley's a little embarrassed and for all I know they cant understand a word of my speech with its French-Canadian and New York and Boston and Okie accents all mixed up and even Español and even Finnegans Wake— They stop awhile to talk to a Ranger, I lay on the grass then I see children digging horses at a fence under a tree, I go over— What a beautiful moment in Diablo Dulltown! Pat's on the grass over there (at my suggestion) (us old winos all know the secret of the grass), Charley's talkin to the Forest Service old boy, and here's this big beautiful stallion nuzzling his golden nose at my fingertips and snuffling, and a littler mare beside him— The children giggle as we communicate with the horse little tendernesses— One's a 3-year-old boy, who cant reach up—

They wave me over and off we go, packs in back, to the Marblemount bunkhouse— Talking— And already the woes of the non-mountain world are pressing in, big sideswipey rock-bearing trucks are lumbering in the narrow dust, we have to park aside and let em pass— Meanwhile to our right is what's left of the Skagit River after all those dams and the backing up of her waters in Ross (cerulean neutral) Lake (of my love-God) —a boiling roily old madstream yet, wide, washing gold to the night, to the arterial Skwohawlwish Kwakiutl Pacific out there a few miles west— My pure little favorite river of the Northwest, by which I'd sat, with wine, on sawdust stumps, at night, drinking to the sizzle of the stars and watching the moving mountain send and pass that snow— Clear, green water, tugging at snags, and Ah all the rivers of America I've seen and you've seen—the flow without end, the Thomas Wolfe vision of American bleeding herself out in the night in rivers that run to the maw sea but then comes upswirls and newbirths, thundrous the mouth of the Mississippi the night we turned into it and I was sleeping on a deck cot, splash, rain, flash, lightning, smell of the delta, where Gulf of Mexico middens her stars and opes up for shrouds of water that will divide as they please in dividable unapproachable passes of mountains where lonely Americans live in little lights—always the rose that flows, thrown by lost but intrepid lovers off fairy bridges, to bleed to the sea, and moisten up sun's works and come back again, come back again— The rivers of America and all the trees on all those shores and all the leaves on all those trees and all the green worlds in all those leaves and all the chlorofic molecules in all those green worlds and all the atoms in all those molecules, and all the infinite universes within all those atoms, and all our hearts and all our tissue and all our thoughts and all our brain cells and all the molecules and atoms in every cell, and all the infinite universes in every thought—bubbles and balloons—and all the starlights dancing on all the wavelets of rivers without end and everywhere in the world never mind America, your Obis and Amazons and Urs I believe and Congoal appurtenant Lake Dam Niles of blackest Africa, and Ganges of Dravidia, and Yangtzes, and Orinocos, and Plates, and Avons and Merrimacs and Skagits—

> Mayonnaise—
> Mayonnaise comes in cans
> Down the river

58 WE DRIVE DOWN THE VALLEY IN GATHERING DARK about 15 miles, and come to that right hand turn that's a mile straightaway blacktar road among trees and little innested farmhouses to the Ranger Station at the dead end, such a perfect road for speeding that the car who had been my last hitch hike ride two months before, a little high on beer, and

aimed me 90 miles an hour at that Ranger Station, turned into the gravel driveway at 50, kicked up dust, goodbye, and had swiveled and roared and hotrodded off, so's Marty the Assistant Ranger meeting me for the first time "You John Duluoz?" hand outstretched then added too: "S' that a friend of yours?"

"No"

"I'd like to teach him a few things about speeding on government property"— Here we come in again now, but slow. Old Charley's got the wheel in his grip and our summer's work is done—

The bunkhouse under big trees (Lazy 6 painted on it) is deserted, we throw our things on bunks, the place is littered with girlie books and towels from recent vast gangs of McAllister-Fire-bound firefighters— Tin helmets on nails, the old radio that wont play—I start right off by lighting a big fire in the shower woodstove, for a hot shower—I'm diddling with matches and sticks, Charley comes over and says "Make a big fire" and picks up an ax (that he's sharpened himself) and surprises the hell out of me with sudden sharp chops of the ax (in the half dark) splitting logs clean open and shaking that down, 60 years old and I couldn't whap at wood that way—dead aim—"My God Charley, I didn't know you could handle an ax like that!"

"Oh yeah."

Because of a little redness on his nose I'd assumed he was a sedentary wino—no—when he did drink he did drink, but not on work— Meanwhile Pat's in the kitchen heating up an old beefstew— It's so soft and delightful to be down in a valley again, warm, no wind, a few leaves of autumn yellow in the grass, warm lights of homes (Ranger O'Hara's home, with three kids, Gehrke's too)— And for the first time I realize it's really Autumn and another year is dead— And that faint not-painful nostalgia of Autumn hangs like smoke in the evening air, and you know "O Well, O Well, O Well"— In the kitchen I load up on chocolate pudding and milk and a whole can apri-

cots with evaporated milk and polish all off with a huge plate
of ice cream—I write my name down on the meal list, meaning
to be charged 60¢ for the meal—

"Is that all you're going to eat—how about beefstew?"

"No, this is what I felt like eatin—I'm satisfied"

Charley eats too— My checks for several hundred dollars
are in the night-closed office, Charley offers to get em for me—
"Naw, I'll only end up spending three bucks on beer at the
bar."—I'll make a quiet evening of it, take a shower, sleep—

We go to Charley's trailer for a brief sitting visit, it's like
folks visitin in some Midwest farm kitchen, I cant stand the
boredom of it, I go take my shower—

Pat's immediately snoring but I cant sleep—I go out and sit
on a log in the Indian Summer night and smoke— Think about
the world—Charley's asleep in his trailer— All's well with the
world—

Ahead of me are adventures with other far madder angels,
and dangers, tho I cant foresee I'm determined to be neutral—
"I'll just pass through everything, like that which passes
through everything—"

And tomorrow is Friday.

Finally I do get to sleep, half out of my sleepingbag it's so
warm and muggy low altitude—

In the morning I shave, forego breakfast for a big lunch, go
to the office to collect my checks.

> Bright morning on morning desks
> Where we face the delicate music

59 THE BOSS IS THERE, big kind tender O'Hara with a
beaming face, who nods and says pleasant, Charley's at the desk befuddling over forms as forever, and here
comes Assistant Ranger Gehrke wearing (since the fire, when
he had his comeuppance) logger overalls with the traditional

suspenders, and a blue washable shirt, and cigarette in mouth, coming to office morning work, and eyeglasses neat and trim, and just left his young wife at breakfast table— Says to us: "Well, it didnt do you no harm"— Meaning we look all right even tho we thought we're dead, Pat and I— And they shovel me out big checks to go roam the world with, I hobble down a mile and a half to town in shoes stuffed with wrapping paper, and pay my $51.17 store bill (for all summer's eats), and then Post Office, where I mail debts— Ice cream cone and latest baseball news on a green chair by the grass, but the paper is so new and clean and print-fresh I can smell the print and it makes my ice cream sour, and I keep thinking of eating the paper, which makes me sick— All that paper, America makes one sick, I cant eat paper—all the drinks they serve are paper, and the supermarket doors open automatically to ballooned bellies of pregnant shoppers—the paper is too dry— A jolly salesman goes by and says "Can you find any news in there?"

Seattle *Times*—

"Yeh, baseball news," I say—licking on my cream cone— ready to start hitch hiking down across America—

Hobble back to bunkhouse, past barking dogs and Northwest characters sitting in doorways of little cottages talking about cars and fishing—I go in the kitchen and heat me a 5-egg lunch, five eggs and bread and butter, that's all— For gyzm for the road— And suddenly in come O'Hara and Marty saying there's just been a report from Lookout Mountain of a fire, and will I go?—No, I cant go. I show them my shoes, even Fred's shoes are pitiful answers and I say "My muscles couldnt take it, in my feet"—"over small rocks"—to go lookin for what probably was not a fire at all but just a smoke reported by reportingest Howard on Lookout Mountain and it's just industrial smoke— In any case, I cant feature it— They really urge me to change my mind, I cant—and I'm sorry when they leave— and I go limping to my bunkhouse to take off, and Charley yells from the office door "Hey Jack, what ya limpin about?"

60 WHICH KICKS ME OFF, and Charley rides me to the crossroads, and we exchange pleasant farewells, and I go around the car with my pack and say "Here I go" and thumb the first car passes, which doesnt stop— To Pat, to whom I'd just at lunchtime said "The world's upsidedown and funny and it's a crazy movie" I say "So long Pat, see you sometime, hasta la vista," and to both of them "Adios," and Charley says:

"Drop me a card"

"A *picture* card?"

"Yeh, anything" (because I've arranged to have final checks forwarded by mail to Mexico) (so later at the bottom of the world I did send him an Aztec red headdress postcard)—(that I can see being criticized and laughed at by all three, Gehrke, O'Hara and Charley, "They got them down there too," meaning the Indian faces)— "So long Charley," and I never found out his last name.

61 I'M ON THE ROAD, after they go, I walk a half-mile to go round the bend and be out of sight when they come back— Here comes a car going wrong way but stops, in it's Phil Carter the regular man on the boat on the lake, good old Okie soul, as sincere and as wide as the ranges to east, with him's riding a 80-year-old man who glares and stares at me with lighted eyes— "Jack, good to see ya— Here's Mr. Winter the man that built the cabin on Desolation Peak"

"That's a good cabin, Mr. Winter, you're a mighty carpenter," and I mean it, remembering the winds that hit that rigging on the roof while the house, sunk in concrete in steel rods, never budged—except when thunder shook the earth and another Buddha was born 900 miles south down in Mill Valley— Mr. Winter glares and stares at me with illuminated eyes, and a grin so wide—like Old Connie Mack—like Frank Lloyd Wright— We shake hands and farewell. Phil, he was the old boy who'd read the boys' letters over the radio, you never heard anything so sad and so sincere as the way he'd read "—and Mama wants you to know that J-j—j—Jilcey was born on the 23rd of August, what a cute little boy— And here it says" (breaks in Phil) "something that wasn't writ right, I think yore Mama judged wrong on that wra-tin"—Old Phil from Oklahoma, where Cherokee Prophets roar— He drives off in his Hawaiian sports shirt, with Mr. Winter (Ah Anthony Trollope), and I never see him again— About 38—or 40—sat by television—drank beer—burped—went to bed—woke with the Lord. Kissed his wife. Bought her little gifts. Went to bed. Sleep. Drove the boat. Didnt care. Never commented. Or criticized. Never said nothin that wasn't plain ordinary talk of Tao.

I walk that halfmile around the hot glary bend, sun, haze, it's going to be a sun-scorched day hitch hiking with a heavy pack.

Dogs that bark at me from farmhouses dont bother me— Old Navajoa Jacko the Yaqui Walkin Champeen and Saint of the Self-Forgiven Night goes clompin down to the dark.

62 SAFE AROUND THE BEND SO Pat and Charley wont laugh at me, and even maybe O'Hara and Gehrke driving somewhere, to see me there, their all-summer's lookout, standing desolate on an empty road waiting for a 4000-mile ride— It's a bright September day with hazish heat, a little too hot, I wipe my brow with big red bandana and wait— Here comes a car, I thumb it, three old men, whoop it stops down a ways and I take off after it with my pack on one shoulder— "Where ya goin, son?" asks the kindly hawknosed old driver with his pipe in mouth— The other two are keenly interested—

"Seattle," I say, "99, Mount Vernon, San Francisco, all the way"—

"Well we can take you a ways"

Turns out they're going to Bellingham on 99 but that's north of my route and I figure I'll get off where they turn off the Skagit Valley Rt. 17— Then I sling my pack in the backseat and get in the front seat crowding the two old boys up there, without thinking, without realizing the one next to me wont like it—I can feel him stiffen up in interest after a while, and meanwhile I'm talking to beat the band answering all questions about the back country— How strange these three old buddies! The driver is the stolid, fair-hearted, willing one, who has de- cided to abide by God, and they know it—next to him's his oldest pardner, also God-straight, but not so keen on kindness and gentleness, a little suspicious of the all around motive— S'all these angels in the void— Backseat is a two-time regular card, meaning he's all right, but he's taken the backseat in life, to watch and be interested (like me) and so like me he's got a little bit of the Fool in him and little bit of the Moon Goddess too— Finally when I say "There's a nice breeze blowin up there," to cap a long talk, as Hawknose veers the curves, none of them reply, dead silence, and I young Witchdoctor have been instructed by the Three Old Witchdoctors to keep silent, for nothing matters, we're all Immortal Buddhas Who Know Silence, so I clam up, and there's a long silence as the good car zings along and I am being ferried to the other shore by Nirmanakaya, Smaboghakaya and Dharmakaya Buddhas all Three, really One, with my arm draped over the right hand door and the wind blowing in my face (and from sensitation- excitement of seeing the *Road* after months among rocks) I dig every little cottage and tree and meadow along the way, the cute little world God's whupped up for us to see and travel and movie-in, the selfsame harsh world that will wring our breath from our chests and lay us in deadened tombs at last, and us no complain (or better not)—Chekhov's angel of silence and sad- ness flies over our car— Here we come into old Concrete and cross a narrow bridge and there's all the Kafkaean gray cement factories and lifts for concrete buckets a mile long into the concrete mountain—then the little American parked cars aslant of monastic countryfied Main Street, with hot flashing windows of dull stores, Five & Tens, women in cotton dresses buying packages, old farmers pitting on their haunches at the feed store, the hardware store, people in dark glasses in the Post Office, scenes I'll see clear down to the borders of Fellaheen Mexico—scenes I'll have to hitch hike through and protect my pack through (in Grant's Pass Oregon two months before fat old cowboy driving a gravel truck deliberately tried to run over my rucksack in the road, I pulled it back just in time, he just grinned) (I waved at him to come back, with my fist, thank God he didn't see me, twoulda been "He's in the jailhouse now, fellow called Ramblin Bob, usta drink and gamble and rob, he's in the jailhouse now") (and me no escapee with broadbrimmed cowboy desolate Mexicano hat, rolling cigarettes in the honkytonk saloon, then fork a hoss and head for Old Mexico) (Monterey, Mazatlán preferably)— The three old geezers ball me down to outside Sedro-Woolley where I get off to hitch to 99— Thank them—

I walk across the hot road towards the town, I'm going to buy a new pair of shoes— First I comb my hair in a gas station and come out and there's a goodlooking woman busy at her work on the sidewalk (arranging cans) and her pet raccoon comes up to me at's squattin there rolling a cigarette a minute, brings long strange delicate nose to my fingertips and wants to eat—

Then I start off—across the curving road is a factory plant, a guy on duty in there keeps watching me with great interest— "Look at that guy with a rucksack on his back thumbin down the road, where the hell's he goin? where's he comin from?" He looks at me so much I keep moving, t'duck into bushes for a quick leak, and out across tarns and oil-meadow ditches between superhighway macadams, and come out and lope with the big nail-split cracking shoes into Sedro-Woolley proper— My first stop will be the bank, there's a bank, a few people stare as I burden by— Yeah, the career of Jack the Great Walking Saint is only begun, holily he goes into banks and cashes government checks into traveler's checks—

I choose a pretty schoolmarm redhead delicate girl with blue believing eyes and tell her I want trav-checks and where I'm going and where I've been and she evinces interest, so much so when I say "I gotta get a haircut" (meaning all summer mountains) she says "You dont look like you need a haircut" and appraises me, and I know she loves me, and I love her, and I know tonight I can walk hand in hand with her to the starlit banks of the Skagit and she wont care what I do, sweet—she'll let me violate her everywhichway, that's what she wants, the women of America need mates and lovers, they stand in marble banks all day and deal with paper and paper they're served at the Drive-In after Paper Movies, they want kissing lips and rivers and grass, as of old—I get so engrossed in her pretty body and sweet eyes and gentle brow under gentle red bangs, and little freckles, and gentle wrists, I dont notice that behind me a line of six people has amassed, old angry jealous women and young guys in a hurry, I pull out fast, with my checks, pick up my bag and sling out— Take one look back, she's busy with next customer—

Here's the time anyway for my first beer in ten weeks.

There's the saloon . . . next door.

It's hot afternoon.

63   I GET A BEER AT THE BIG SHINY BAR and sit at a table, back to the bar, and roll a smoke, and here comes an old doddering man of 80 with a cane, sits at table next to me and waits with bleary eyes— O Gauguin! O Proust! had I been your kind of painter or writer, I'd give a description of that eaten and mungy face, prophecy of all men's sorrow, no rivers no lips no starlit cunts for that sweet old loser, and all is ephemeral, all is lost anyway— Takes him five minutes to dig

out his little dollar— Holds it trembling— Still staring at the bar— The bartender is busy— "Why doesnt he get up and go get his beer?"—Aw, it's a prideful story in the afternoon in the bar in Sedro-Woolley in northwest Washington in the world in the void that's desolation upsidedown— Finally he starts to rattle his cane and knock for service—I drink my beer, get another— I think of getting his beer for him— Why interfere? Black Jack's liable to walk in with all guns blazing and I'll be famous throughout the West for shooting Slade Hickox in the back? The Chihuahua Kid, I say nothing—

The two beers dont hit me right, I realize there's no need for alcohol whatever in your soul—

I go out to buy my shoes—

Main Street, stores, sporting goods, basketballs, footballs for coming Autumn—Elmer the happy kid's about to swim in the air above the football field and eat big steaks at school banquets and get his letter, I know—I go in a store and clomp to the back and take off the clod-hoppers and the kid gives me blue canvas shoes with thick soft soles, I put em on and stroll, it's like walking in heaven—I buy em, leave the old shoes there, and walk out—

Squat against a wall and light a cigarette and dig the little afternoon city, there's the hay and grain feed silo outside town, the railroad, the lumberyard, just like in Mark Twain, that's where Sam Grant got a million of em for the graves of the Civil War—this sleepy atmosphere's what gave birth to the fire in Stonewall Jackson's Virginian soul, whittle—

Okay, I cut off—back down to the highway, over the tracks, and out on the bend getting traffic three ways—

Wait about fifteen minutes.

"In hitch hiking," I think now, to steadfast up my soul, "you get good Karma and bad Karma, the good makes up for the bad, somewhere down that road" (I look and there it is, haze-ends, hopeless no-name nothing of us) "is the guy who'll take you clear to Seattle for your newspapers and wine tonight, be kind and wait"—

Who does stop is a blond kid with ulcers who cant play on the Sedro-Woolley High football team because of that, but was a rising star (my hunch is, he was the best), but's allowed to wrestle on the wrestling team, he has big thighs and arms, 17, I was a wrestler too (Blackmask Champeen of the block) so we talk about wrestling— "That's official wrestling where you get on all fours, and the guy behind you, and go?"

"That's right, none of this TV bullshit stuff—the real"

"How do they count points?"

That long complicated answer gets me clear to Mount Vernon but I suddenly feel sorry for him, that I cant stay wrestle with him, and even toss footballs, he's really a lonely American kid, like the girl, looking for uncomplicated friendship, purity of angels, I shudder to think of the claques and cliques in high school tearing him apart and his parents and his doctor's warnings and all he's got is pie at night, no moon— We shake hands, and I get off, and here I am in the 4 P.M. hot sun with cars coming home from work in a steady stream, on a corner, in front of a gas station, everybody so concerned about wheeling the corner they cant examine me so I hang there almost an hour.

Funny, eerie, a man in a Cadillac is parked there waiting for someone, at first when he pulls off I thumb him, he smirks and does a U-turn and parks across the street, then he starts up and U-turns again and passes me again (by this time I'm mum) and parks again, harried nervous face, O America what have you done to your children machine! Yet the stores are full of the best food in the world, delicious goodies, the new peach crop, melons, all the butterfat fruit of the Skagit rich with slugs and damp earth— Then here comes an MG and my God it's Red Coan driving it, with a girl, he said he'd be in Washington this summer, he does a violent U-turn in the garage driveway as I yell "Hey Red!" and just as I yell it I see it's not Red and my the smirk of I-dont-know-you he puts on, not even a smirk, a snarl, snarling at his clutch and wheel, zip, around he goes and roars off farting fumes in my face, some Red Coan—and even then I'm not sure if it wasn't really him, changed and mad—and mad at *me*—

Bleak.
Blook.
Void.

But here comes a 90- or 80-year-old octogenarian poctogenarian patriarchtirian aryan with white hair sitting low and old behind a high wheel, stops for me, I run up, ope the door, he winks. "Get in, young feller—I can take you some ways up the road."

"How far?"

"Oh—few miles."

It'll be just like Kansas again (1952) when I was taken few miles up the road and ended up in the sunset on an open plains stretch everybody balls by at 80 aiming for Denver and nothing else— But I shrug, "Karma-karma," and get in—

He talks a little bit, not much, I can see he's real old, he's funny too— He goes palootzing his old heap along, passes everybody, gets out on the straightaway and starts battin 80 miles an hour across the farmlands— "My God, what if he has a heart attack!"—"Nothing slow about you, is there?" I say, keeping my eye on him and the wheel—

"No sirree"

He goes even faster . . .

Now I'm being ferried to ole Hotsapho Buddhaland across the river of No-Rivers by a mad old Bodhisattva Saint—who'll either get me there fast or not at all— There's your Karma, ripe as peaches.

I hang on— After all he aint drunk, like the fat guy in Georgia (1955) who did 80 in soft shoulders and kept looking at me not the road and was reeking with moonshine, from him I got

off ahead of my schedule and took a bus to Birmingham I was
so shook up—

No, it's Pappy deposits me all right at a farm gate in the
open, there's his tree-elm porch, his pigs, we shake hand and
he goes off to supper—

I'm out there with cars flying by, I know I'm stuck for a
time— Getting late too—

But equipment truck slurs up and slows down and plows
balloons of dust for me in the shoulder, I run and jump on—
Fancy your Heroes! This is a big Two-Tone Butch Champeen
I.W.W. bigfist tarp of a sailorman aint afraid of no man and
more than that can talk and more than that builds bridges and
behind him's his bridge building concretes and crowbars
and tools— And when I tell him I'm going to Mexico he says:
"Yeah, Mexico, me and the wife put the kids in the trailer and
took off—went all the way to Central America— Slept and ate
in the trailer—I let my wife do the Spanish talkin—I had me a
few tequilas in bars here and there— Good education for the
kids— Just come back last week from a smaller trip around
Montana and down to East Texas and back"—And I can picture
any banditos trying to get tough with him, he's 230 pounds of
proud bone and muscle—what he could do with a wrench or a
crowbar I'd hate to Orozco in spaghetti-sauce paint— He
drives me to Everett, and lets me off in the hot late sun of a
dismal semi-Main Drag with suddenly a dismal redbrick fire-
house and clock and I feel awful— The vibrations in Everett
are low—Angry workers stream by in cars stinking exhaust—
Nobody deigns to look at me but to sneer— It's awful, it's
hell—I begin to realize I should be back in my mountain sack
on a cold moonlit night. (The Everett Massacre!)

But no! The adventure parade goes Karma-ing down—I'm
in it to the end, dead—I'll have to wash my teeth and spend
money until the ends of time, until at least that day I'm the last
old woman on the earth gnawing on the last bone in the final
cave and I cackle my last prayer on the last night before I dont

wake up no more— Then it'll be bartering with the angels in
heaven but with that special astral speed and ecstasy so maybe
we wont mind at all then, seems— But O Everett! Tall stacks
of sawmill yards and distant bridges, and heat no-hope in the
pavement—

In desperation after a half hour I go in a luncheonette and
order a hamburger and milkshake—for while hitch hiking I
allow my food budget to go up— The girl in there is so stud-
iedly cold I fall even deeper in despair, she's well shaped and
neat but bleak and has feelingless blue eyes and in fact she's all
interested in some middleaged guy in there who's just then taking off for Las Vegas to gamble, his car's parked outside, and
when he leaves she calls "Take me for a ride in your car sometime" and he's so sure of himself it amazes and enrages me, "O
I'll think about it," or some such airy reply, and I look at him
and he's got a crew cut and glasses and looks mean— He gets
in his car and drives off to Las Vegas through all that—I can
barely eat—I pay the bill and hurry out— Go across the road
with fullpack—ugh, oy—I've finally hit bottom (of the mountain).

64 I'M STANDING THERE IN THE SUN and dont notice
the football scrimmage going on in the sun-glare
behind me to the west, until a hitch hiking sailor walks by and
says "Signals, hip hip" and I look and see him and the game of
kids simultaneously and even then simultaneously a car driven
by an interested face stops, and I run to get on, looking my last
look at the football game where just then a kid is carrying the
ball through tackle and is smothered—

I jump in the car and see it's some kind of secret fag, which
means good hearted anyway, so I speak up for the sailor, "He's
hitch hiking too," and we pick him up too, and three in the
front seat light fresh cigarettes and drive to Seattle, just like
that.

Desultory talk about the Navy—how dreary, "I was stationed at Bremerton and I used to come over on Sadday nights but it was much better when I was transferred to—" and I close my eyes— Evincing some interest in the driver's school, Washington U., he offers to drop me off on the campus, I bring it up myself, so we drop the sailor on the way (lackadaisical dont-care sailor hitch hiking with his girl's underwear in a paper bag which I thought was full of peaches, he shows me the silk slip on top)—

The University of Washington campus is all right and pretty Eternal with big new million-windowed dorms and long late walks leading from traffic frenzies and O the whole college-in-the-city scene, it's like Chinaman to me, I cant make it out, my pack's too heavy anyway, I take the first bus into downtown Seattle and soon as we're flying by old slips of sea water with ancient scows in em, and red sun sinks behind the masts and shedrooves, that's better, I understand that, it's old Seattle of the fog, old Seattle the City in the shroud, old Seattle I'd read about as a kid in phantom detective books and I'd read about in Blue Books for Men all about the old days a hundred men breaking into the embalmer's cellar and drinking embalming fluid and all dying, and all being Shanghaied to China that way, and mud flats— Little shacks with seagulls.

> Girls' footprints
> in the sand
> —Old mossy pile

The Seattle of ships—ramps—docks—totem poles—old locomotives switching on the waterfront—steam, smoke—Skid Row, bars—Indians—the Seattle of my boyhood vision I see there in the rusted old junkyard with old non color fence leaning in a general maze—

> Wooden house
> raw gray—
> Pink light in the window

I tell the busdriver to let me off downtown, I jump off and go klomping past City Halls and pigeons down to the general direction of the water where I know I'll find a good clean Skid Row room with bed and hot bath down the hall—

I go all the way down to First Avenue and turn left, leaving the shoppers and the Seattleites behind, and lo! here's all humanity hep and weird wandering on the evening sidewalk amazing me outa my eyeballs—Indian girls in slacks, with Indian boys with Tony Curtis haircuts—twisted—arm in arm—families of old Okie fame just parked their car in the lot, going down to the market for bread and meat— Drunks— The doors of bars I fly by incredible with crowded sad waiting humanity, fingering drinks and looking up at the Johnny Saxton-Carmen Basilio fight on TV— And bang! I realize it's Friday Night all over America, in New York it's just ten o'clock and the fight's started in the Garden and longshoremen in North River bars are all watching the fight and drinking 20 beers apiece, and Sams are sitting in the front row of the fight betting, you can see them on the screen, handpainted neckties from Miami— In fact all over America it's Friday Fight Night and it's a Big Fight— Even in Arkansas they're watching it in the poolhall and out in the cotton patch house on TV—everywhere— Chicago—Denver—cigar smoke all over—and Ah the sad faces, now I'd forgotten and I see and remember, while I spent all summer pacing and praying in mountaintops, of rock and snow, of lost birds and bears, these people've been sucking on cigarettes and drinks and pacing and praying in their souls too, in their own way— And it's all writ on the scars of their faces—I must go in that bar.

I turn back and go in.

Throw my pack on the floor, get a beer at the crowded bar, sit down at a table, occupied by another old man facing the other way out the street, and I roll a joint and watch the fight and the faces— It's *warm*, humanity is warm, and it's got potential love in it, I can see it—I'm a pure fresh daisy, I know—I could deliver them a speech and remind them and reawake them— Even then I see in their faces the boredom of "Oh we know, we've heard all that, and we've been down here all this time waitin and prayin and watching the fights on Friday nights—and *drinkin"*— My God they ben drinkin! Every one is a lush, I can see it—Seattle!

I have nothing to offer them but my stupid face, which I avert anyway— The bartender's busy and has to step over my pack, I move it aside, he says "Thanks"— Meanwhile Basilio's not hurt by Saxton's light punches, he steps in and wallops him all over—it's guts against brains and guts'll win— Everybody in the bar is Basilio guts, I'm just brains—I have to hurry out of there— At midnight they'll put on a fight of their own, the young toughs in the booth— You gotta be a nutty wild masochistic Johnny O New York to go to Seattle and take up fist-fighting in bars! You gotta have scars! Backgrounds of pain! Suddenly I'm writing like Céline—

I get out of there and go get my Skid Row hotel room for the night.

A night in Seattle.

Tomorrow, the road to Frisco.

65 HOTEL STEVENS IS AN OLD CLEAN HOTEL, you look in the big windows and see a clean tile floor and spittoons and old leather chairs and a clock talkin and a silver-rimmed clerk in the cage—$1.75 for one night, steep for Skid Row, but no bed bugs, that's important—I buy my room and go up in the elevator with the gent, second floor, and get my room— Throw my pack in the rocking chair, lay on the bed— Soft bed, clean sheets, reprieve and retreat till 1 P.M. checkout time tomorrow—

Ah Seattle, sad faces of the human bars, and you dont realize you're upsidedown—Your sad heads, people, hang down in the unlimited void, you go skipplering around the surface of streets and even in rooms, upsidedown, your furniture is upsidedown and held by gravity, the only thing prevents it from all flying off is the laws of the mind of the universe, God— Waiting for God? And because he is not limited he can not exist. Waiting for Lefty? Same, sweet Bronx-singer. Nothing there but mind-matter essence primordial and strange with form and names you have for it just as good—agh, I get up and go out to buy my wine and paper.

A drinking and eating place is still showing the fight but also what attracts me (on the rosy blue neon-coming-on street) is a fellow in a vest carefully chalking out the day's baseball scores on a huge scoreboard, like old days—I stand there watching.

In the paper store my God a thousand girlie books showing all the fulsome breasts and thighs in eternity—I realize "America's going sex-mad, they cant get enough, something's wrong, somewhere, pretty soon these girlie books'll be impossibly tight, they'll show you every crease and fold except the hole and nipple, they're crazy"— Of course I look too, at the rack, with the other sexfiends.

Finally I buy a St. Louis *Sporting News* to catch up on the baseball news, and a *Time* Magazine, to catch up on world news and read all about Eisenhower waving from trains, and a bottle of Italian Swiss Colony port wine, expensive one of the best—I thought— With that I go cutting back down the drag and there's a burlesque house, "I'll go to the burlesque tonight!" I giggle (remembering the Old Howard in Boston) (and recently I'd read how Phil Silvers had put on an oldtime burlesque act in some burlesque somewhere and what a delicate art it was)— Yes—and is—

For after an hour and a half in my room sipping that wine (sitting with stockinged feet on the bed, pillow back), reading about Mickey Mantle and the Three-I League and the Southern Association and the West Texas League and the latest trades and stars and kids upcoming and even reading the Little League news to see the names of the 10-year-old prodigy pitchers and glancing at *Time* Magazine (not so interesting after all when you're full of juice and the street's outside), I go out, carefully pouring wine in my polybdinum canteen (used earlier for trail thirsts, with red bandana around my head), stick it in my pocket of jacket, and down into night—

> Neons, Chinese restaurants
>   coming on—
> Girls come by shades

Eyes—strange Negro kid who was afraid I would criticize him with my eyes because of the segregation issue down South, I almost do criticize him, for being so square, but I dont want to attract his attention so I look away—Filipino nobodies going by, with hands hanging, their mysterious poolhalls and bars and barrels of ships— A Surrealistic street, with cop at a bar counter stiffens when he sees me walk in, as tho I'd's about to steal his drink— Alleys— Views of old water between older rooftops— Moon, rising on downtown, coming up to be unnoticed by Grant's Drug Store lights shining white near Thom McAns, also shining, open, near marquee of *Love Is a Many-Splendored Thing* movie with pretty girls waiting in line— Curbstones, dark back alleys where hotrodders do the screaming turn—racing the motor on their tires, skeek!—hear it everywhere in America, it's tireless Joe Champion biding his time—America is so vast—I love it so— And its bestness melts down and does leak into honkytonk areas, or Skid Row, or Times Squarey—the faces the lights the eyes—

I go into seaward backalleys, where's nobody, and sit on curbs against garbage cans and drink wine, watching the old men in the Old Polsky Club across the way playing pinochle by brown bulb light, with green slick walls and timeclocks— Zooo! goes an oceangoing freighter in the bay, *Port of Seattle*, the ferry's nosing her say from Bremerton and plowing into the piles at bottom's otay, they leave whole pints of vodka on the white painted deck, wrapt in *Life* Magazine, for me to drink (two months earlier) in the rain, as we nose in— Trees all around, Puget Sound— Tugs hoot in the harbor—I drink my wine, warm night, and mosey on back to the burlesque—

I walk in just in time, to see the first dancer.

66 AW, THEY'VE GOT LITTLE SIS MERRIDAY UP THERE, girl from across the bay, she oughtnt be dancing in no burlesque, when she shows her breasts (which are perfect) nobody's interested because she aint thrown out no otay hip-work—she's too clean—the audience in the dark theater, upsidedown, want a dirty girl— And dirty girl's in back getting upsidedown ready before her stagedoor mirror—

The drapes fade back, Essie the dancer goes, I take a sip of wine in the dark theater, and out come the two clowns in a sudden bright light of the stage.

The show is on.

Abe has a hat, long suspenders, keeps pulling at them, a crazy face, you can see he likes girls, and he keeps smacking at his lips and he's an old Seattle ghost— Slim, his straight man, is handsome curlyhaired pornographic hero type you see in dirty postcards giving it to the girl—

ABE Where the hell you been?
SLIM Back there countin the money.
ABE What the hell d'you mean, money—

*   *   *   *

SLIM I've been down at the graveyard
ABE What were you doin there?
SLIM Burying a stiff

*   *   *   *

and such jokes— They go through immense routines on the stage before everybody, the curtains are simple, it's simple theater— Everybody gets engrossed in their troubles— Here comes a girl walking across the stage—Abe's been drinkin out of the bottle meanwhile, he's been tricking Slim into emptying the bottle— Everybody, actors and audience, stare at the girl that comes out and strolls— The stroll is a work of art— And her answers better be juicy—

They bring her out, the Spanish dancing girl, Lolita from Spain, long black hair and dark eyes and wild castanets and she starts stripping, casting her garments aside with an "Olé!" and a shake of her head and showing teeth, everybody eats in her cream shoulders and cream legs and she whirls around the castanet and comes down with her fingers slowly to her cinch and undoes the whole skirt, underneath's a pretty sequined virginity-belt, with spangles, she jams around and dances and stomps and lowers her haid-hair to the floor and the organist (Slim) (who jumps in the pit for the dancers) is wailing tremendous Wild Bill jazz—I'm beating with my feet and hands, it's jazz and great!—That Lolita goes slumming around then ends up at the side-drape revealing her breast-bras but wont take them off, she vanishes offstage Spanish— She's my favorite girl so far—I drink her a toast in the dark.

The lights go bright again and out come Abe and Slim again.

"What ya been doin out in the graveyard?" says the Judge, Slim, behind his desk, with gavel, and Abe's on trial—

"I've been out there burying a stiff."

"You know that's against the law."

"Not in Seattle," says Abe, pointing at Lolita—

And Lolita, with a charming Spanish accent, says "He was the stiff and I was the under-taker" and the way she says that, with a little whip of her ass, it kills everybody and the theater is plunged into dark with everybody laughing, including me and a big Negro man behind me who yells enthusiastically and claps at everything great—

Out comes a middleaged Negro dancer to do us a hotfoot tap dance, hoof, but he's so old and so puffing he cant finish up and the music tries to ride him (Slim on the Organ) but the big

Negro man behind me yells out "Oh ya, Oh ya" (as if to say, "Awright go home")— But the dancer makes a desperate dancing panting speech and I pray for him to make good, I feel sympathetic here he is just in from Frisco with a new job and he's gotta make good somehow, I applaud enthusiastically when he goes off—

It's a great human drama being presented before my all-knowing desolation eyes—upsidedown—

Let the drapes open more—

"And now," announces Slim at the mike, "presenting Seattle's own redhead KITTY O'GRADY" and here she comes, Slim leaps to the Organ, and she's tall and got green eyes and red hair and minces around—

(O Everett Massacres, where was I?)

67   PRETTY MISS O'GRADY, I can see her bassinets— Have seen them and will see her someday in Baltimore leaning in a redbrick window, by a flowerpot, with mascara and her hair masqueraded in shampoo permanent—I'll see her, have seen her, the beauty spot on her cheek, my father's seen the Ziegfeld Beauties come down the line, "Aint you an old Follies girl?" asks W. C. Fields of the big 300-pound waitress in the Thirties Luncheonette—and she says, looking at his nose, "There's something awfully big about you," and turns away, and he looks at her behind, says, "Something awfully big about you too"—I'll have seen her, in the window, by the roses, beauty spot and dust, and old stage diplomas, and backdoors, in the scene that the world was made out to present— Old Playbills, alleys, Shubert's in the dust, poems about graveyard Corso— Me'n old, Filipino'll pee in that alley, and Porto Rico New York will fall down, at night—Jesus will appear on July 20 1957 2:30 P.M.— I'll have seen pretty pert Miss O'Grady mincing dainty on a stage, to amuse the paying customers, as obedient as a kitty. I think "There she is, Slim's

broad— That's his girl—he brings her flowers to the dressing-room, he serves her"—

No, she tries as hard to be naughty but caint, goes off showing her breasts (that take up a whistle) and then Abe and Slim, in bright light, put on a little play with her.

Abe is the judge, desk, gavel, bang! They've arrested Slim for being indecent. They bring him in with Miss O'Grady.

"What's he done indecent?"

"Aint what he's done, he *is* indecent."

"Why?"

"Show him, Slim"

Slim, in bathrobe, turns his back to the audience and opens his flaps—

Abe stares and leans almost falling from the judge desk—"Great day in the morning, it cant be! Who ever saw a thing like that? Mister, are you sure that's all yours? It's not only indecent it aint *right!*" And so on, guffaws, music, darkness, spotlight, Slim says triumphant:

"And *now*—the Naughty Girl—S A R I N A !"

And jumps to the organ, ragdown jazz drag, and here comes naughty Sarina— There's a furor of excitement throughout the theater— She has slanted cat's eyes and a wicked face—cute like cat's mustache—like a little witch—no broom—she comes slinking and bumping out to the beat.

Sarina the fair-haired
bright
Bedawnzing girl

68 SHE IMMEDIATELY GETS DOWN ON THE FLOOR in the coitus position and starts throwing a fit at heaven with her loinsies— She twists in pain, her face is distorted, teeth, hair falls, shoulders squirm and snake— She stays on the floor on her two hands supporting and knocking her works right at the audience of dark men, some of em college boys— Whistles! The organ music is lowdown get-down-there what-you-doin down there blues— How really naughty she is with her eyes, slant blank, and the way she goes to the righthand box and does secret dirty things for the dignitaries and producers in there, showing some little portion of her body and saying "Yes? No?"—and sweeping away and coming around again and now her hand-tip sneaks to her belt and she slowly undoes her skirt with tantalizing fingers that snake and hesitate, then she presents a thigh, a higher thigh, a pelvic corner, a belly corner, she turns and reveals a buttock corner, she lolls her tongue out—she's sweating juice at every pore—I cant help thinking what Slim does to her in the dressingroom—

By this time I'm drunk, drank too much wine, I'm dizzy and the whole dark theater of the world swirls around, it's all insane and I remember vaguely from the mountains it's upsidedown and wow, sneer, sleer, snake, slake of sex, what are people doing in audience seats in this crashing magician's void hand-clapping and howling to music and a girl?—What are all those curtains and drapes for, and masques? and lights of different intensity playing everywhere from everywhere, rose, pink, heart-sad, boy-blue, girl-green, Spanish-cape black and black-black? Ugh, ow, I dont know what to do, Sarina the Naughty One is now on her back on the stage slowly moving her sweet loins at some imaginary God-man in the sky giving her the eternal works—and pretty soon we'll have pregnant balloons and castoff rubbers in the alley and sperm in the stars and broken bottles in the stars, and soon walls'll be built to hold her *protect* inside some castle Spain Madkinghouse and the walls will be cemented in with broken beer glasses and nobody can climb to her snatch except the Sultan organ who'll bear witness to her juices then go to his juiceless grave and her grave be juiceless too in time, after the first black juices the worms love so, then dust, atoms of dust, whether as atoms of dust or as great universes of thighs and vaginas and penises what will it matter, it's all a Heaven Ship— The whole world is roaring right there in that theater and just beyond I see files of sorrowing humanity wailing by candlelight and Jesus on the Cross and Buddha sitting neath the Bo Tree and Mohammed in a cave and the serpent and the sun held high and all Akkadian-Sumerian antiquities and early sea-boats carrying courtesan Helens away to the bash final war and broken glass of tiny infinity till nothing's there but white snowy light permeating everywhere throughout the darkness and sun—pling, and electromagnetic gravitational ecstasy passing through without a word or sign and not even passing through and not even being—

But O Sarina come with me to my bed of woes, let me love you gently in the night, long time, we got all night, till dawn, till Juliet's rising sun and Romeo's vial sink, till I have slaked my thirst of Samsara at your portal rosy petal lips and left saviour juice in your rosy flesh garden to melt and dry and ululate another baby for the void, come sweet Sarina in my naughty arms, be dirty in my clean milk, and I'll detest the defecate I leave in your milky empowered cyst-and-vulva chamber, your cloacan clara file-hool through which slowly drool the hallgyzm, to castles in your hassel flesh and I'll protect your trembling thighs against my heart and kiss your lips and cheeks and Lair and love you everywhere and that'll be that—

At the drape she parts her bra and shows the naughty teats and vanishes inside and show's over—lights come on—everybody leaves—I sit there sipping my last possible shot, dizzy and crazy.

It dont make no sense, the world is too magical, I better go back to my rock.

In the toilet I yell at a Filipino cook, "Aint those beautiful girls, hey? Aint they?" and he loath to admit it admits it to the yelling bum at the urinal—I go back, upstairs, to sit out the movie for the next show, maybe next time Sarina'll fly everything off and we'll see and feel the infinite love— But my God the movies they show! Sawmills, dust, smoke, gray pictures of logs splashing in water, men with tin hats wandering in a gray rainy void and the announcer: "The proud tradition of the Northwest—" then followed by color pictures of water skiers, I cant make it, I leave the show by the side left exit, drunk—

Just as I hit the outside night air of Seattle, on a hill, by redbrick neons of the stagedoor, here come Abe and Slim and the colored tapdancer hurrying and sweating up the street for the next show, even on an ordinary street the tapdancer cant make it without puffing—I realize he has asthma or some serious heart defect, shouldnt be dancing and hustling—Slim looks strange and ordinary on the street and I realize it's not him's making it with Sarina, it's some producer in the box, some sugar candy— Poor Slim— And Abe the Clown of Eternity Drapes, there he is talking as ever and yakking with big interested face in the actual streets of life, and I see all three of them as *troupers*, vaudevillians, sad, sad— Around the corner for a quick drink or maybe gulp a meal and hurry back for the next show— Making a living— Just like my father, your father, all fathers, working and making a living in the dark sad earth—

I look up, there are the stars, just the same, desolation, and the angels below who dont know they're angels—

And Sarina will die—

And I will die, and you will die, and we all will die, and even the stars will fade out one after another in time.

69 IN A CHINESE RESTAURANT IN A BOOTH I order pan fried chow mein and dig the Chinese waitress and the younger beautifuller Filipino waitress and they watch me and I watch them but I lose myself in my chow mein and pay the bill and leave, dizzy— No possible way in the world for me to get a girl tonight, the hotel wouldnt let her in and she wouldnt come anyway, I realize I'm just an old fuck of 34 and nobody wants to go to bed with me anyway, a Skid Row bum with wine on his teeth and jeans and dirty old clothes, who cares? Everywhere up and down the street other characters like me— But as I go in my hotel here comes a neat crippled man with a woman, they go up the elevator, and an hour later after I've had my hot bath and rested and got ready to sleep I hear them creak the bed in the next room in real sexual ecstasy— "It must all depend on the way," I think, and go to sleep girl-less with girls dancing in my dreams— Ah Paradise! bring me a wife!

And already in my life I've had two wives and sent one away and ran away from the other, and hundreds of lover-girls everyone of em betrayed or screwed in some way by me, when I was young and open-faced and not ashamed to ask— Now I look at my mirror face scowl and it's disgusting— We have sex in our loins and wander beneath the stars on hard sidewalks, pavement and broken glass cant receive our gentle thrust, our gentle thrust— Everywhere bleak faces, homeless, loveless, around the world, sordid, alleys of night, masturbation (the old man of 60 I once saw masturbating for two hours straight in his cell in the Mills Hotel in New York)—(Nothing was there but paper—and pain—)

Ah, I think, but somewhere ahead in the night waits a sweet beauty for me, who will come up and take my hand, maybe Tuesday—and I'll sing to her and be pure again and be like young arrow-slinging Gotama vying for her prize— Too late! All my friends growing old and ugly and fat, and me too, and nothing there but expectations that dont pan out—and the Void'll Have Its Way.

Praise Lord, if you can't have fun turn to religion.

Till they re-establish paradise on earth, the Days of Perfect Nature, and we'll wander around naked and kissing in gardens, and attend dedicatory ceremonies to the Love God at the Great Love Meeting Park, at the World Shrine of Love— Until then, bums—

Bums—

Nothing but bums—

I fall asleep, and it's not the sleep in the mountaintop shack, it's in a room, traffic's outside, the crazy silly city, dawn, Saturday morning comes in gray and desolate—I wake up and wash and go out to eat.

The streets are empty, I go down the wrong way, among warehouses, nobody works on Saturdays, a few dismal Filipinos walk in the street pass me— Where is my breakfast?

And I realize too that my blisters (from the mountain) have grown so bad now I cant hitch hike, I cant take that pack on my back and walk two miles out—south—I decide to take a bus to San Francisco and git it over with.

Maybe a lover there for me.

I have plenty of money and money is only money.

And what will *Cody* be doing when I get to Frisco? And Irwin and Simon and Lazarus and Kevin? And the girls? No more summer daydreams, I'll go see what "reality" has in store for "me"—

"To hell with Skid Row." I go up the hill and out and immediately find a splendid serve-yourself restaurant where you pour your own coffee as many time's you want and pay that on an honor basis and get your bacon and eggs at the counter and eat at tables, where stray newspapers feed me the news—

The man at the counter is so kind! "How you want your eggs, sir?"

"Sunny side up"

"Yes *sir,* coming right up," and all his stuff and griddles and spatulas as clean as a pin, here's a real believing man who wont let the night discourage him—the awful brokenbottle sexless gut night—but'll awake in the morning and sing and go to his job and prepare food for people and honor them with the title "sir" to boot— And exquisite and delicate come out the eggs and the little shoe-string potatoes, and the toast crisp and well buttered with melted butter and a brush, Ah, I sit and eat and drink coffee by the big plateglass windows, looking out on an empty bleak street— Empty but for one man in a nice tweed coat and nice shoes going somewhere, "Ah, there's a happy man, he dresses well, goes believingly down the morning street—"

I take my little paper cup of grape jelly and spread it on my toast, squeezing it out, and drink another cup of hot coffee— Everything'll be all right, desolation is desolation everywhere and desolation is all we got and desolation aint so bad—

In the papers I see where Mickey Mantle aint gonna beat Babe Ruth's homerun record, O well, Willie Mays'll do it next year.

And I read about Eisenhower waving from trains on campaign speeches, and Adlai Stevenson so elegant so snide so proud—I read about riots in Egypt, riots in North Africa, riots in Hong Kong, riots in prisons, riots in hell everywhere, riots in desolation— Angels rioting against nothing.

Eat your eggs
and
Shut up

70 EVERYTHING IS SO KEEN WHEN YOU COME DOWN FROM SOLITUDE, I notice all Seattle with every step I take—I'm going down the sunny main drag now with pack on back and room rent paid and lotsa pretty girls eating ice cream cones and shopping in the 5 & 10— On one corner I see an eccentric paperseller with a wagon-bike loaded with ancient issues of magazines and bits of string and thread, an oldtime Seattle character—"The *Reader's Digest* should write about him," I think, and go to the bus station and buy my ticket to Frisco.

The station is loaded with people, I stash my rucksack in the baggage room and wander around unencumbered looking everywhere, I sit in the station and roll a cigarette and smoke, I go down the street for hot chocolate at a soda fountain.

A pretty blonde woman is running the fountain, I come in there and order a thick milkshake first, move down to the end of the counter and drink it there— Soon the counter begins to fill up and I see she's overworked— She cant keep up with all the orders—I even order hot chocolate myself finally and she does a little "Hmf O my"— Two teenage hepcats come in and order hamburgers and catsup, she cant find the catsup, has to go in the backroom and look while even then fresh further people sit at the counter hungry, I look around to see if any-body'll help her, the drug clerk is a completely unconcerned type with glasses who in fact comes over and sits and orders something himself, free, a *steak sandwich*—

"I cant find the catsup!" she almost weeps—

He turns over a page of the newspaper, "Is that a fact"—

I study him—the cold neat white-collar nihilistic clerk who doesnt care about anything but does believe that women should wait on him!—She I study, a typical West Coast type, probable ex-showgirl, maybe even (sob) ex-burlesque dancer who didnt make it because she wasnt naughty enough, like O'Grady last night— But she lives in Frisco too, she always lives in the Tenderloin, she is completely respectable, very attractive, works very hard, very good hearted, but somehow something's wrong and life deals her a complete martyr deck I dont know why—something like my mother— Why some man doesnt come and latch on her I dont know— The blonde is 38, ful-some, beautiful Venus body, a beautiful and perfect cameo face, with big sad Italianized eyelids, and high cheekbones creamy soft and full, but nobody notices her, nobody wants her, her man hasnt come yet, her man will never come and she'll age with all that beauty in that selfsame rockingchair by the potted-flower window (O West Coast!)—and she'll complain, she'll say her story: "All my life I've tried to do the best I could"— But the two teenagers insist they want catsup and finally, when she has to admit she's out they get surly and start to eat— One, an ugly kid, takes his straw and to pop it out of its paper wrapper stabs viciously at the counter, as tho stabbing someone to death, a real hard fast death-stab that frightens me— His buddy is very beautiful but for some reason he likes this ugly murderer and they pal around together and probably stab old men at night— Meanwhile she's all fuddled in a dozen different orders, hot dogs, hamburgers (myself I want a hamburger now), coffee, milk, lime-ades for children, and cold clerk sits reading his paper and chewing his steak sandwich— He notices nothing— Her hair is falling over one eye, she's almost *weeping*— Nobody cares because nobody notices— And tonight she'll go to her little clean room with the kitchenette and feed the cat and go to bed with a sigh, as pretty a woman as you'll ever see— No Lochinvar at the door— An angel of a woman— And yet a bum like me, with no one to love her tonight— That's the way it goes, there's your world— Stab! Kill!—Dont care!— There's your Actual Void Face—exactly what this empty universe holds in store for us, the Blank—Blank Blank Blank!

When I leave I'm surprised that, instead of treating me contemptuously for watching her sweat a whole hour, she actually sympathetically counts up my change, with a little harried look from tender blue eyes—I picture myself in her room that night listening first to her list of legitimate complaints.

But my bus is going—

71   THE BUS PULLS OUT OF SEATTLE and goes barreling south to Portland on swish-swish 99—I'm comfortable in the back seat with cigarettes and paper and near me is a young Indonesian-looking student of some intelligence who says he's from the Philippines and finally (learning I speak Spanish) confesses that white women are shit—

"Las mujeres blancas son la mierda"

I shudder to hear it, whole hordes of invading Mongolians shall overrun the Western world saying that and they're only talking about the poor little blonde woman in the drugstore who's doing her best— By God, if I were Sultan! I wouldnt allow it! I'd arrange for something better! But it's only a dream! Why fret?

The world wouldnt exist if it didnt have the power to liberate itself.

Suck! suck! suck at the teat of Heaven!

Dog is God spelled backwards.

72

AND I HAD RAGED PURELY AMONG ROCKS AND SNOW, rocks to sit on and snow to drink, rocks to start avalankies with and snow to throw snowballs at my house— raged among gnats and dying male ants, raged at a mouse and killed it, raged at the hundred mile cyclorama of snow-capped mountains under the blue sky of day and the starry splendor of night— Raged and been a fool, when I shoulda loved and repented—

Now I'm *back* in that goddam movie of the world and *now* what do I do with it?

Sit in fool and be fool,
that's all—

The shades come, night falls, the bus roars downroad— People sleep, people read, people smoke— The busdriver's neck is stiff and alert— Soon we see the lights of Portland all bleak bluff and waters and soon the city alleys and drivearounds flash by— And after that the body of Oregon, the Valley of the Willamette—

At dawn I restless wake to see Mount Shasta and old Black Butte, mountains dont amaze me anymore—I dont even look out the window— It's too late, who cares?

Then the long hot sun of the Sacramento Valley in her Sunday afternoon, and bleak little stop-towns where I chew up popcorn and squat and wait— Bah!— Soon Vallejo, sights of the bay, the beginnings of something new on the cloud-splendrous horizon—San Francisco on her Bay!

Desolation anyway—

73 IT'S THE BRIDGE THAT COUNTS, the coming-into-San Francisco on that Oakland-Bay Bridge, over waters which are faintly ruffled by oceangoing Orient ships and ferries, over waters that are like taking you to some other shore, it had always been like that when I lived in Berkeley—after a night of drinking, or two, in the city, bing, the old F-train'd take me barreling across the waters back to that other shore of peace and contentment— We'd (Irwin and I) discuss the Void as we crossed— It's seeing the rooftops of Frisco that makes you excited and believe, the big downtown hulk of buildings, Standard Oil's flying red horse, Montgomery Street highbuildings, Hotel St. Francis, the hills, magic Telegraph with her Coit-top, magic Russian, magic Nob, and magic Mission beyond with the cross of all sorrows I'd seen long ago in a purple sunset with Cody on a little railroad bridge—San Francisco, North Beach, Chinatown, Market Street, the bars, the Bay-Oom, the Bell Hotel, the wine, the alleys, the poorboys, Third Street, poets, painters, Buddhists, bums, junkies, girls, millionaires, MG's, the whole fabulous movie of San Francisco seen from the bus or train on the Bridge coming in, the tug at your heart like New York—

And they're all there, my friends, somewhere in those little toystreets, and when they see me the angel'll smile— That's not so bad— Desolation aint so bad—

74 WOW, AN ENTIRELY DIFFERENT SCENE, San Francisco always is, it always gives you the courage of your convictions— "This city will see to it that you make it as you wish, with limitations which are obvious, in stone and memory"— Or such—thus—that feeling, of, "Wow O Alley, I'm gonna get me a poorpoy of Tokay and drink it on the way"— The only city I know of where you can drink the open in the street as you walk and nobody cares—everybody avoids you like poison sailor O Joe McCoy just off the Lurline—"one of the bottlewashers there?"—"No, just a old seedy S.I.U. deckhand, and's been to Hongkong and Singapore and back more time's almost he's et that wine in backalleys of Harrison"—

Harrison is the street the bus comes in on, ramping, and we go twaddling seven blocks north to Seventh Street, where he turns into the city traffic of Sunday—and there's all your Joes on the street.

Things happening everywhere. Here comes Longtail Charley Joe from Los Angeles, suitcase, blond hair, sports shirt, big thick wrist watch, with him's Minnie O'Pearl the gay girl who sings in the band at Rooey's—"Whooey?"

There're the Negro baggagehandlers of the Greyhound Company, described by Irwin as Mohammedan Angels I believe—sending precious cargo to Loontown and Moontown and Moonlight in Colorado the bar where they'll be tonight whanging with the chicks among U-turning cars and Otay Spence on the box—down among the Negro housing projects, where we'd gone at morning, with whisky and wine and oolyakoo'd with the sisters from Arkansas who'd seen their father hanged— What notion could they get of this country, this Mississippi— There they are, neat and welldressed, perfect neckties and collars, the cleanest dressers in America, presenting their Negro faces at the employer-judge, who judges harshly on the basis of their otay perfect neckties—some with glasses, rings, polite pipesmokers, college boys, sociologists, the whole we-all-know-the-great-scene-in-otay that I know so well in San Fran—sound—I come dancing through this city with big pack on my back and so I have to hustle not to bump into anybody but nevertheless make time down that Market Street parade—

A little deserted and desolate, Sunday— Tho Third Street be crowded, and great big Pariahs bark a-doors and discuss Wombs of Divinity, it's all houndsapack—I crap along and farty up Kearney, towards Chinatown, watching all stores and all faces to see which way the Angel points this fine and perfect day—

"By God I'm gonna give myself a haircut in my room," I say, "and make it look like sumptin"—"Because first thing I'm gonna do is hit that otay sweet saxophone Cellar." Where I'll immediately go for the Sunday afternoon jam session. O they'll all be there, the girls with dark glasses and blonde hair, the brunettes in pretty coats by the side of their little boy (The Man)—raising beers to their lips, sucking in cigarette smoke, beating to the beat of the beat of Brue Moore the perfect tenor saxophone— Old Brue he'll be high on Brew, and me too— "I'll tap him on the toenail," I think— "We'll hear what the singers gotto say today"— Because all summer I've provided myself my own jazz, singing in the yard or in the house at night, whenever I had to hear some music, see which way the Angel pours the bucket, what stairs down she goes, and otay jazz afternoons in the Maurie O'Tay nightclub okay—music— Because all these serious faces'll only drive you mad, the only truth is music—the only meaning is without meaning— Music blends with the heartbeat universe and we forget the brain beat.

75

I'M IN SAN FRANCISCO AND I'M GONNA TAKE IT ALL IN. Incredible the things I saw.

I get out of the way for two Filipino gentlemen crossing California. I pass through to the Bell Hotel, by the Chinese playground, and go in get my room.

The attendant is immediately succinctly anxious to please me, and there are women in the hall gossiping Malay. I shudder to think the sounds will come in through the courtyard window, all Chinese and melodious. I hear even choruses of French talk, from the owners. A medley of a hotel of rooms in dark carpeted halls, and old creaky night steps and blinking wallclock and 80-year-old bent sage behind the grille, with open doors, and cats— The attendant brings me back my change as I wait with waited door. I take out my little tiny aluminum scissors that cant cut buttons off a sweater, but cut my hair anyway— Then I examine the effect with mirrors— Okay, then I go and shave anyway. I get hot water and I shave and I square away and on the wall is a nude calendar of a Chinese girl. Lot I can do with a calendar. ("Well," said the bum in the burlesque to the other bum, two Limies, "I'm avin er naow.")

In hot little flames.

76   I GO OUT AND HIT THE STREET crossing at Columbus and Kearney, by Barbary Coast, and a bum in a long bum overcoat sings out to me "When we cross streets in New York we cross em!—None a this waitin shit for me!" and both of us barrel across and walk among cars and shoot back and forth about New York— Then I get to the Cellar and jump down, steep wooden steps, in a broad cellar hall, right to the right is the room with the bar and the bandstand otay where now as I come Jack Minger is blowing on trumpet and behind him's Bill the mad blond pianist scholar of music, on the drums that sad kid with the sweating handsome face who has such a desperate beat and strong wrists, and on bass I cant see him bobbing in the dark with beard— Some crazy Wigmo or other—but it's not the session, it's the regular group, too early, I'll come back later, I've heard every one of Jack Minger's ideas alone with the group, but first (as I'd just dropped into the bookstore to look around) (and a girl called Sonya had prettily come up to me, 17, and said "O do you know Raphael? He needs some money, he's waiting at my place") (Raphael being my old New York crony) (and more about Sonya later), I run in there and am about to turn around and swing out, when I

see a cat looks like Raphael, wearing dark glasses, at the foot of the bandstand talking to a chick, so I run over (walking fast) (to avoid goofing the beat as the musicians play on) (some little tune like "All Too Soon") I look right down to see if it's Raphael, almost turning over, looking at him upsidedown, as he notices nothing talking to his girl, and I see it aint Raphael and cut out— So the trumpetplayer who's playing his solo wonders what he sees, knowing me from before as always crazy, running in now to look upsidedown at someone then running out—I go running up to Chinatown to eat and come back to the session. Shrimp! Chicken! Spare ribs! I go down to Sun Heung Hung's and sit there at their new bar drinking cold beers from an incredibly clean bartender who keeps mopping the bar and polishing glasses and even mops under my beer several times and I tell him "This is a nice clean bar" and he says "Brand new"—

Meanwhile I watch for a booth to sit in—none—so I go upstairs and sit in a big curtained booth for families but they throw me outa there ("You cannot sit there, that's for families, big parties") (then they dont come and serve me as I wait) so I slonk back my chair and stomp downstairs fast on quiet feet and get a booth and tell the waiter "Dont let nobody sit with me, I like to eat alone" (in restaurants, naturally)— Shrimp in a brown sauce, curried chicken, and sweet and sour spare ribs, in a Chinese menu dinner, I eat it with another beer, it's a terrific meal I can hardly finish—but I finish it clean, pay and cut out— To the now late afternoon park where the children are playing in sandboxes and swings, and old men are staring on benches—I come over and sit down.

The little Chinese children are waging big dramas with sand— Meanwhile a father gathers up his three different little ones and heads them home— Cops are going into the jailhouse across the street. Sunday in San Francisco.

A bearded point-bearded patriarch nods at me then sits near an old crony and they start talking loudly in Russian. I know olski-dolski when I hear it, nyet?

Then I amble along in the gathering cool and do walk through Chinatown duskstreets like I said I would on Desolation, the wink of pretty neons, the faces in the stores, the festooned bulbs across Grant Street, the Pagodas.

I go to my hotel room and rest awhile on the bed, smoking, listening to the sounds coming in the window from the Bell Hotel court, the noises of dishes and traffic and Chinese— It is all one big wailing world, all over, even in my own room there is sound, the intense roaring silence sound that swishes in my ear and swashes the diamond persepine—I let go and feel my astral body leave, and lay there completely in a trance, seeing through everything. It's all white.

77

IT'S A NORTH BEACH TRADITION, Rob Donnelly had done it in a Broadway hotel and floated away and saw whole worlds and came back and woke up in his room on the bed, all dressed to go out—

Like as not, too, Old Rob, wearing Mal Damlette's sharp cap on the side of his head, would be in the Cellar even right now—

By now the Cellar is waiting for the musicians, not a sound, nobody I know in there, I hang on the sidewalk and here comes Chuck Berman one way, and Bill Slivovitz the other, a poet, and we talk at a fender of a car—Chuck Berman looks tired, his eyes are all puffed, but he's wearing soft smart shoes and looking so cool in the twilight—Bill Slivovitz doesnt care, he's wearing a shabby sports coat and scuffed out shoes and carrying poems in his pocket—Chuck Berman is high, says he's high, lingers a minute looking around, then cuts— He'll be back— Bill Slivovitz the last time I saw him'd said "Where you goin?" and I'd yelled "Ah what's the difference?" so now I apologize and explain I was hungover— We repair to The Place for a beer.

The Place is a brown lovely bar made of wood, with sawdust, barrel beer in glass mugs, an old piano for anybody to bang on, and an upstairs balcony with little wood tables—who care? the cat sleeps on the bench. The bartenders are usually friends of mine except today, now—I let Bill get the beers and we talk at a little round table about Samuel Beckett and prose and poetry. Bill thinks Beckett is the end, he talks about it all over, his glasses glint in my eyesight, he has a long serious face, I cant believe he's serious about death but he must be—"I'm dead," he says, "I wrote some poems about death"—

"Well where are they?"

"They're not finished, man."

"Let's go to the Cellar and hear the jazz," so we cut around the corner and just as we walk in the streetdoor I hear them baying down there, a full group of tenors and altos and trumpets riding in for the first chorus— Boom, we walk in just in time for the break, bang, a tenor is taking the solo, the tune is simply "Georgia Brown"—the tenor rides it big and heavy with a big tone— They've come from Fillmore in cars, with their girls or without, the cool colored cats of Sunday San Fran in incredibly beautiful neat sports attire, to knock your eyes out, shoes, lapels, ties, no-ties, studs— They've brought their horns in taxis and in their own cars, pouring down into the Cellar to really give it some class and jazz now, the Negro people who will be the salvation of America—I can see it because the last time I was in the Cellar it was full of surly whites waiting around a desultory jam session to start a fight and finally they did, with my boy Rainey who was knocked out when he wasn't looking by a big mean brutal 250-pound seaman who was famous for getting drunk with Dylan Thomas and Jimmy the Greek in New York— Now everything is too cool for a fight, now it's jazz, the place is roaring, all beautiful girls in there, one mad brunette at the bar drunk with her boys— One strange chick I remember from somewhere, wearing a simple skirt with pockets, her hands in there, short haircut, slouched, talking to everybody— Up and down the stairs they come—

The bartenders are the regular band of Jack, and the heavenly drummer who looks up in the sky with blue eyes, with a beard, is wailing beer-caps of bottles and jamming on the cash register and everything is going to the beat— It's the beat generation, it's *béat*, it's the beat to keep, it's the beat of the heart, it's being beat and down in the world and like oldtime lowdown and like in ancient civilizations the slave boatmen rowing galleys to a beat and servants spinning pottery to a beat— The faces! There's no face to compare with Jack Minger's who's up on the bandstand now with a colored trumpeter who outblows him wild and Dizzy but Jack's face overlooking all the heads and smoke— He has a face that looks like everybody you've ever known and seen on the street in your generation, a sweet face— Hard to describe—sad eyes, cruel lips, expectant gleam, swaying to the beat, tall, majestical—waiting in front of the drugstore— A face like Huck's in New York (Huck whom you'll see on Times Square, somnolent and alert, sad-sweet, dark, beat, just out of jail, martyred, tortured by sidewalks, starved for sex and companionship, open to anything, ready to introduce new worlds with a shrug)— The colored big tenor with the big tone would like to be blowing Sunny Stitts clear out of Kansas City roadhouses, clear, heavy, somewhat dull and unmusical ideas which nevertheless never leave the music, always there, far out, the harmony too complicated for the motley bums (of music-understanding) in there—but the musicians hear— The drummer is a sensational 12-year-old Negro boy who's not allowed to drink but can play, tremendous, a little lithe childlike Miles Davis kid, like early Fats Navarro fans you used to see in Espan Harlem, hep, small—he thunders at the drums with a beat which is described to me by a near-standing Negro connoisseur with beret as a "fabulous beat"— On piano is Blondey Bill, good enough to drive any group—Jack Minger blows out and over his head with these angels from Fillmore, I dig him— It's terrific—

I just stand in the outside hall against the wall, no beer neces-

sary, with collections of in-and-out listeners, with Sliv, and now
here returns Chuck Berman (who is a colored kid from West
Indies who barged into my party six months earlier high with
Cody and the gang and I had a Chet Baker record on and we
hoofed at each other in the room, tremendous, the perfect grace
of his dancing, casual, like Joe Louis casually hoofing)— He
comes now in dancing like that, glad— Everybody looks
everywhere, it's a jazz-joint and beat generation madtrick, you
see someone, "Hi," then you look away elsewhere, for something someone else, it's all insane, then you look back, you look
away, around, everything is coming in from everywhere in the
sound of the jazz— "Hi"—"Hey"—

Bang, the little drummer takes a solo, reaching his young
hands all over traps and kettles and cymbals and foot-peddle
BOOM in a fantastic crash of sound—12 years old—what will
happen?

Me'n Sliv stand bouncing to the beat and finally the girl in
the skirt comes talk to us, it's Gia Valencia, the daughter of the
mad Spanish anthropologist sage who'd lived with the Pomo
and Pit River Indians of California, famous old man, whom I'd
read and revered only three years ago while working the railroad outa San Luis Obispo— "Bug, give me back my shadow!"
he yelled on a recorded tape before he died, showing how the
Indians made it at brooks in old California pre-history before
San Fran and Clark Gable and Al Jolson and Rose Wise Lazuli
and the jazz of the mixed generations— Out there's all that sun
and shade as same as old doodlebug time, but the Indians are
gone, and old Valencia is gone, and all's left is his charming
erudite daughter with her hands in her pockets digging the
jazz— She's also talking to all the goodlooking men, black and
white, she likes em all— They like her— To me she suddenly
says "Arent you going to call Irwin Garden?"

"Sure I just got into town!"

"You're Jack Duluoz arent you!"

"And yeah, you're—"

"Gia"

"Ah a Latin name"

"Oh you frightening man," she says seriously, suddenly meaning my impenetrable of myself way of talking to a woman, my glare, my eyebrows, my big lined angry yet crazy eye-gleaming bony face— She really means it—I feel it— Often frighten myself in the mirror— But for some tender chicken to look into my mirror of all-the-woes-you-know . . . it's worse!

She talks to Sliv, he doesn't frighten her, he's sympathetic and sad and serious and she stands there I watch her, the little thin body just faintly feminine and the low pitch of her voice, the charm, the veritable elegant oldworld way she comes on, completely out of place in the Cellar— Should be at Katherine Porter's cocktail—should be exchanging duet-os of art talk in Venice and Fiorenza with Truman Capote, Gore Vidal and Compton-Burnett—should be in Hawthorne's novels—I really like her, I feel her charm, I go over and talk some more—

Alternately bang bang the jazz crashes in to my conscious-ness and I forget everything and just close my eyes and listen to the ideas—I feel like yelling "Play A Fool Am I!" which would be a great tune— But now they're on some other jam— whatever they feel like, the downbeat, the piano chord, off—

"How can I call Irwin?" I ask her— Then I remember I've got Raphael's phone number (from sweet Sonya in the book-shop) and I slip into the booth with my dime and dial, typical jazz joint stuff, like the time I'd slipped into the booth at Bird-land in New York and in the comparative silence suddenly heard Stan Getz, who was in the toilet nearby, blowing his saxophone quietly to the music of Lennie Tristano's group out front, when I realized he could do anything—(Warne Marsh me no Warne Marsh! his music said)—I call Raphael who answers "Yes?"

"*Raphael?* This is Jack—Jack Duluoz!"

"Jack! Where are you?"

"The Cellar—come on down!"

"I cant, I have no money!"

"Cant you walk?"

"*Walk?*"

"I'll call and get Irwin and we'll come over get you in a cab— Call you back half hour!"

I try to call Irwin, it wont do, he's nowhere— Everybody in the Cellar is goofing, now the bartenders are beginning to whip at beers themselves and get flushed and high and drunk— The drunken brunette falls off her stool, her cat carries her to the ladies' room— Fresh gangs roam in— It's mad— And finally to cap everything (O Desolation Me Silent Me) here comes Richard de Chili the insane Richard de Chili who wanders around Frisco at night in long fast strides, all alone, examining the examples of architecture, strange hodgepodge notions and bay windows and garden walls, giggling, alone in the night, doesnt drink, hoards funny soapy candy bars and bits of string in his pockets and half out combs and half toothbrushes and when he comes to sleep at any of our pads he'll burn toothbrushes at the stove jet, or stay in the bathroom hours running water, and brush his hair with assorted brushes, completely homeless, always sleeping on someone's couch and yet once a month he goes to the bank (the night watchman vault) and there's his monthly income waiting for him (the daytime bank's embarrassed), just enough money to live on, left to him by some mysterious unknown elegant family he never talks about— No teeth in the front of his mouth whatever— Crazy clothes, like a scarf around his neck and jeans and a silly jacket he found somewhere with paint on it, and offers you a peppermint candy and it tastes like soap—Richard de Chili, the Mysterious, who was for a long time out of sight (six months earlier) and finally as we're driving down the street we see him striding into a supermarket "There's Richard!" and all jump out to follow him and there he is in the store lifting candybars and cans of peanuts on the sly and not only that he's seen by the Okie storeman and we have to pay his way out and he comes with us with his incomprehensible low-spoken remarks, like, "The moon is a piece of tea," looking up at it in the rumble seat— Whom finally I welcomed to my 6-month-earlier shack in Mill Valley to stay a few days and he takes all the sleepingbags and slings them (except mine, hidden in the grass) over the window, where they tear, so the last time I see my Mill Valley shack as I start hitch hiking for Desolation Peak there's Richard de Chili sleeping in a great roomful of duck feathers, an incredible sight—a typical sight—with his under-arm paper bags full of strange esoteric books (one of the most intelligent persons I know in the world) and his soaps and candles and giblets of junk, O my, the catalogue is out of my memory— Who finally took me on a long walk around Frisco one drizzly night to go peek through the street window of an apartment occupied by two homosexual *midgets* (who werent there)—Richard comes in and stands by me and as usual and in the roar I cant hear what he's saying and it doesnt matter anyway— He too goofing nervously, looking around everywhere, everybody reaching for that next kick and there's no next-kick . . .

"What are we gonna do?" I say—

Nobody knows—Sliv, Gia, Richard, the others, they all just stand shuffling around in the Cellar of Time waiting, waiting, like so many Samuel Beckett heroes in the Abyss— Me, I've *got* to do something, go somewhere, establish a rapport, get the talk and the action going, I fidget and shuffle with them—

The beautiful brunette is even worse— Clad so beautifully in a tightfitting black silk dress exhibiting all her perfect dusky charms she comes out of the toilet and falls down again— Crazy characters are milling around— Insane conversations I cant remember anymore, it's too mad!

"I'll give up, I'll go sleep, tomorrow I'll find the gang"

A man and a woman ask us to move over please so they can study the map of San Francisco on the hall wall— "Tourists from Boston, hey?" says Richard, with his witless grin—

I get on the phone again and cant find Irwin so I'll go home to my room in the Bell Hotel and sleep— Like sleep on the mountain, the generations *are* too mad—

Yet Sliv and Richard dont want me to leave, everytime I edge off they follow me, shuffling, we're all shuffling and waiting for nothing, it gets on my nerves— It takes all my willpower and sad regret to say so long to them and cut out into the night—

"Cody'll be at my place at eleven tomorrow," shouts Chuck Berman so I'll make that scene—

At the corner of Broadway and Columbus, in the famous little open eatery, I call Raphael to tell him to meet me in the morning at Chuck's— "Okay—but listen! While I was waiting for you I wrote a poem! A terrific poem! It's all about you! I address it to you! Can I read it to you over the phone?"

"Go ahead"

"*Spit* on Bosatsu!" he yells. "*Spit* on Bosatsu!"

"Oo," I say, "that's beautiful"

"The poem is called 'To Jack Duluoz, Buddha-fish'— Here's the way it goes—" And reads me this long insane poem over the phone as I stand there against the counter of hamburgs, as he yells and reads (and I take in every word, every meaning of this Lower Eastside New York Italian genius reborn from the Renaissance) I think "O God, how sad!—I have poet friends who yell me their poems in cities—it's just as I predicted on the mount, it's celebrating in cities upsidedown—

"Sweet, Raphael, great, you're a greater poet than ever— you're really going now—great—dont stop—remember to write without stopping, without thinking, just go, I wanta hear what's in the bottom of your mind."

"And that's what I'm doing, see?—do you dig it? do you under*stand?*" The way he says "under*stand*," like, "stahnd," like Frank Sinatra, like something New York, like something new in the world, a real down-from-the-bottom city Poet at last, like Christopher Smart and Blake, like Tom O Bedlam, the song of the streets and of the alley cats, the great great Raphael Urso who'd made me so mad in 1953 when he made it with my girl—but whose fault was that? mine as much as theirs—it's all recorded in *The Subterraneans*—

"Great great Raphael I'll see you tomorra— Let's sleep and be silent— Let's dig silence, silence is the end, I've had it all summer, I'll teach you."

"Great, great, I dig that you dig silence," comes his sad enthusiastic voice over the pitiful telephone machine, "it makes me sad to think you dig silence, but I will dig silence, believe it, I *will*"—

I go to my room to sleep.

And lo! There's the old night clerk, an old Frenchman, I dont know his name, when Mal my buddy used to live in the Bell (and we'd drink big toasts of port wine to Omar Khayyam and pretty girls with short haircuts in his bulb-hanging room) this old man used to be angry all the time and screaming at us incoherently, annoyed— Now, two years later, he's completely changed and with it his back has bent all the way, he's 75 and walks completely bent over muttering down the hall to unlock your transient room, he's completely sweetened, death is sooth- ing his eyelids, he's seen the light, he's no longer mad and annoyed— He smiles sweetly even when I come on him (1 A.M.) standing bent on a chair trying to fix the clerk cage clock— Comes down painfully and leads me to my room—

"*Vous êtes francais, monsieur?*" I say. "*Je suis francais moi- même.*"

In his new sweetness is also new Buddha-blankness, he doesnt even answer, he just unlocks my door and smiles sadly, way down bent, and says "Good night, sir—everything all right, sir"—I'm amazed— Crotchety for 73 years and now he'll bide right out of time with a few dewdrop sweet years and they'll bury him all bent in his tomb (I dont know how) and I would bring him flowers— *Will* bring him flowers a million years from now—

In my room invisible eternal golden flowers drop on my head as I sleep, they drop everywhere, they are Ste. Terese's roses showering and pouring everywhere on the heads of the world— Even the shufflers and madcaps, even the snarling winos in alleys, even the bleating mice still in my attic a thousand miles and six thousand feet up in Desolation, even on the least her roses shower, perpetually— We all know that in our sleep.

78

I SLEEP A GOOD SOLID TEN HOURS and wake up roses-refreshed— But I'm late for my meet with Cody and Raphael and Chuck Berman—I jump up and put on my little checkered cotton shortsleeved sportshirt, my canvas jacket over that, and my chino pants, and hurry out into the bright ruffling Monday Morning harbor wind— What a city of whites and blues!—What air!—Great churchbells bonging, the hint of tinkling flutes from Chinatown markets, the incredible Old Italy scene on Broadway where old dark-garmented Wops gather with twisted black little cigarillos and chot the black coffee— It's their dark shadows on the white sidewalk in the clean bell-ringing air, with white ships seen coming in the Golden Gate down below the etched Rimbaud milky rooftops—

It's the wind, the cleanness, great stores like Buon Gusto's with all the hanging salamis and provelones and assortments of wine, and vegetable bins—and the marvelous oldworld pastry shops—then the view of the tangled wood tenement childscreaming daydrowsy Telegraph Hill—

I swing along on my new heavenly softsoled canvas blueshoes ("Oog, like the shoes queers wear!" comments Raphael next day) and lo! there's bearded Irwin Garden coming down the opposite side of the street— Wow!—I yell and whistle and wave, he sees me and throws out his arms with rounded eyes and comes running across the traffic with that peculiar gazotsky run of his, flapping feet—but his face is immense and serious surrounded by a great solemn Abrahamic beard and his eyes are steady in a candlesteady gleam in their ogling sockets, and his sensuous fulsome red mouth shows out thru the beard like the poopoo lips of old prophets about to say something— Long ago I'd dug him as a Jewish prophet wailing at the final wall, now it was official, a big article had just been written about him in the New York *Times* mentioning that— The author of "Howling," a big wild free verse poem about all of us beginning with the lines:—

"I have seen the best minds of my generation destroy'd by madness"—etc.

But I never know what he means by mad, like, he had a vision in a Harlem pad in 1948 one night of a "giant machine descending from the sky," a big ark-dove of his imagination, and keeps saying "But do you realize the state of mind I was in—have you ever really had a real vision?"

"Sure, whattayou mean?"

I never understand what he's driving at and sometimes I suspect he's Jesus of Nazareth reborn, sometimes I get mad and think he's only Dostoevsky's poor devil in poorclothes, giggling in the room— An early idealistic hero of my days, who'd come on the scene of my life at 17—I remember the strangeness of the firmness of his voice-tone even then— He talks low, distinct, excited—but he looks a little pooped with all this San Francisco excitement which for that matter will wear me out in 24 hours—"Guess who's in town?"

"I know, Raphael—I'm going there to meet him and Cody now."

"Cody?—where?"

"Chuck Berman's pad—everybody's there—I'm late—let's hurry"

We talk a million forgettable little things as we race, almost run up the sidewalk—Desolation Jack is now ankling along with a bearded compatriot—my roses wait—"Simon and I are going to Europe!" he announces. "Why dont you come with us! My mother left me a thousand dollars. I've got another thousand saved! We'll all go visit the Old World Strange!"

"Okay with me"—"I've got a few bucks too— Might as well— About time, hey ole buddy?"

For Irwin and I had discussed and dreamed Europe, and of course read everything, even unto the "weeping on the old stones of Europe" of Dostoevsky and the gutters-saturated-with-symbols of early Rimbaud excitements when we wrote poems and ate potato soup together (1944) on the Columbia Campus, even unto Genêt and the Apache heroes—even unto Irwin's own sad dreams of spectral visits to a Europe all drenched with old rain and woe, and standing on the Eiffel Tower feeling silly and effete— Arm over each other's shoulder we hurry up the hill to Chuck Berman's streetdoor, knock and walk in— There's Richard de Chili on the couch, as foretold, turning around to give us a weak grin— A couple other cats with Chuck in the kitchen, one a crazy Indian with black hair who wants change for a poorboy, a French-Canadian like me, I'd talked to him the night before in the Cellar and he'd called out "So long brother!"— Now it's "Good morning brother!" and we're all milling around, no Raphael there yet, Irwin suggests we go down to the hep coffee place and meet everybody there—

"They all go there anyway"

But nobody's there so we head for the bookstore and bang! up Grant here comes Raphael with his John Garfield longstride and swinging arms, talking and yelling as he comes, bursting all over with poems, we're all yelling at the same time— We mill around bumping into one another, across streets, down streets, looking for a place to drink coffee—

We go in the coffee joint (on Broadway) and sit in a booth and out come all the poems and books and bang! here comes a redheaded girl and behind her Cody—

"Jackson me boyyyy" says Cody as usual imitating old
W. C. Fields railroad conductors—

"Cody! Aye! Sit down! Wow! Everything's happening!"

For it comes, it always comes in great vibrating seasons.

79 BUT IT'S ONLY SIMPLE MORNING IN THE WORLD, and
the waitress only brings simple coffee, and all our
excitements are simple and will end.

"Who is the girl?"

"She's a mad girl from Seattle who heard us read poetry up
there last winter and's come down in an MG with another girl,
looking for a ball," Irwin informs me. He knows everything.

She says "Where does that Duluoz get all that vitality?"

Vitality, shmitality, by midnight roaring beers I'll be done
for another year—

"I lost all my poems in Florida!" Raphael is screaming. "In
the Greyhound Bus Terminal in Miami Florida! These new
poems are all the poems I've got! And I lost my other poems in
New York! You were there Jack! What'd that editor do with
my poems? And I lost all my earlier poems in Florida! Imagine
that! Balls on that!" It's the way he talks. "For years after that
I went from Greyhound office to Greyhound office talking to
all kinds of presidents begging them to find my poems! I even
cried! You hear that Cody? I cried! But they werent moved! In
fact they began to call me a nuisance all because I used to go to
this office on 50th Street most every day begging them for my
poems! It's the truth!"—and as someone else is saying something he hears that too and interjects: "I'd never call the police
unless a horse fell and cripples itself or something! *Balls* on
that!" He bangs the table—

He's got a crazy little pixy face of some kind which is actually a great brooding dark face when suddenly he feels sad and
falls silent, the way he stares off—pouting— A little bit like
the pout of Beethoven— A bit of a snubbed, or rubbed, rough

Italian nose, rough features, with soft cheeks and soft eyes and
pixy hair, black, he never combs, coming down from the back
of his square head flat down over his brow, like a boy— He's
only 24— He actually is a boy, the girls are all mad for him—

Whispers Cody in my ear "That guy, that Raff, that cat,
why, shit, he's got more *broads*'n he knows what to do with—
I'm telling you—Jack, listen, everything's set, it's all arranged,
we're going to make a million in the races, it's a sure thing, this
year, THIS YEAR M'BOY" he rises to announce "that second
choice of mine has been coming in and coming in like *mad!*"

"Making up for last year," I say, remembering the day I'd
bet $350 on the second choice for Cody (while he worked) and
he missed every race and I got drunk in a haystack with a 35¢
poorboy before going to the train to tell Cody he'd lost, whom
it didnt disturb because he'd already lost $5,000 net—

"*This* is the year—and *next* year" he insists—

Meanwhile Irwin is reading his own new poems and the table
is mad—I can tell Cody I'd like him (my old bloodbrother) to
drive me to Mill Valley to pick up my old clothes and manuscripts, "Will *do,* we'll all go, we're all together"

We rush out to Cody's crazy little 1933 Chevvy coupe, we
cant fit in, we try it and burst out at the seams—

"You think this little baby cant go?" says Cody.

"But your great car you had when I left?"

"Sugar in the transmission, she's gone"

Irwin says: "Listen, all of you go to Mill Valley and come
back and meet me this afternoon"

"Okay"

The girl squeezes by Cody, Raphael because he's shorter and
lighter than me sits on my lap, and off we go, waving to Irwin
who leaps with his beard and dances to show his sweet concern
in the North Beach street—

Cody bats the little car around unmercifully, he swings
around corners perfect and fast, no squealing, he darts thru
traffic, curses, barely beats lights, jams up hills in grinding sec-

ond, swishes thru intersections, takes the blame, balls out to the Golden Gate bridge where finally (toll paid) we go zooming across the Gate of Dreams in high-above-the-water airs, with Alcatraz on our right ("I weep, I feel sorry for Alcatraz!" yells Raphael)—

"What are they *doon?*"—the tourists on the Marin bluff looking towards white San Fran with cameras and binoculars, their sightseeing bus—

All talking at the same time—

Old Cody again! Old Visions-of-Cody Cody, the maddest one (as you'll see) and as ever on our left the vast blue trackless Maw Pacific, Mother of Seas and Peaces, leading out to Japan—

It's all too much, I feel wonderful and wild, I've found my friends and a great vibration of living Joy and of Poetry is running thru us— Even tho Cody be yakking about this second choice betting system he does it in amazing rhythms of talk— "Why my boy inside *five* years I'll have so much money why I'll just be a pilantro—plilantrop—poff poff."

"Philanthropist"

"Be givin money to all who deserve— Mete ye out as ye shall be received—" He's always quoting Edgar Cayce the Seer, the American Okie healer who never learned medicine but would go into an ailing man's house and undo his old sweaty tie and lay stretched out on his back and sleep into a trance and his wife'd take his answers to her questions down, "Why is so-and-so sick?" Answer: "So and so has thrombo-phlebitis, clotting of the veins and arteries, because in a previ-ous lifetime he drank the blood of the living human sacrifice"— Question: "What is the cure?" Answer: "Stand on his head for three minutes every day— Also general exercise— A little glass of whisky or 100 proof whisky or bourbon every day, for thinning the blood—" Then he'd come out of his trance, and had healed thousands that way (Edgar Cayce Institute, Atlantic Beach, Virginia)— Cody's new God—the God that was mak-

ing even excited-over-girls Cody begin to say: "I'm almost finished with them little things"

"Why?"

He too has his silences, rocky, severe—I can sense too now
as we fly over the Gate of Gold that Cody and Raphael are not
exactly on close terms—I study to know why—I dont want
none of my boys fighting— It's all going to be great— We'll
at least all die in harmony, we'll have great Chinese Wailing
and Howling and screaming funerals of joy because old Cody,
old Jack, old Raphael, old Irwin, or old Simon (Darlovsky,
coming up) is dead and free—

"My head is dead, I dont care!" yells Raphael—

"—why that dog couldnt even come in second and repair
my losses with a measly five bucks, but I'll show ya honey—"
Cody is whispering to Penny (she's just a big happy strange
sad girl drinking this all in, I see now she hangs around my
gang because they, except Cody, pay her no particular sexual
attention) (in fact they're always putting her down and telling
her to go home)—

But I'm amazed to see when we get to Mill Valley she's a
Buddhist, while we're all talking at the same time in the shack
on the horse-hill I turn and as in a dream there she is, like a
solid ruby statue, sitting against the wall crosslegged with her
hands joined and her eyes staring straight ahead, seeing nothing, maybe hearing nothing—a mad world.

Mad above all the shack— It belongs to Kevin McLoch, my
old buddy Kevin also with a beard but a working carpenter with
a wife and two kids, always in sawdust paint pants, barechester
usually, patriarchal, kind, delicate, subtle, extremely serious, intense, also a Buddhist, in back of his good old ramshackle wood
house with the unfinished porch he's building, rises a steep
grassy hill till it becomes upper Deer Parks, real actual ancient
deer parks where on moonlit nights as if from nowhere there
you'll see the deer sitting and munching under the immense
Eucalypti—down from the mountain, the game refuge, as the

Dharma Bums all know, the deer have been coming to this Holy Grove for longer than twelve histories of California— High up, on top, the shack lies hidden in rosebushes— Wood-piles, high grass, wild flowers, bushes, seas of trees swishing everywhere— The shack as I say built by an old man to die in, which he did, and a great carpenter he was—Kevin has it all fixed up with pretty burlap walls and pretty Buddhist pictures and teapots and delicate teacups and fronds in vases, and gaso-line-primer to boil the tea-water, to make it his Buddhist refuge and ceremonial tea-house, for visitors and also long-staying 3-month guests (who must be Buddhists, that is, understand that the Way is not a Way) like I'd been, and so that on Thursdays when he tells his carpenter boss "I'm taking the day off" and the boss says "Who's gonna lift the other end of the board?" "Get someone else" Kevin leaves pretty wife and kiddies downhill and climbs the Deer Park Eucalyptus trail, with Sutras under his arm, and spends that day in meditation and study— Meditates crosslegged, on Prajna—reads Suzuki's commentar-ies and the Surangama Sutra—says, "If every worker in America took a day off to do this, what a wonderful world it would be."

Very serious, beautiful man, 23, with blue eyes, perfect teeth, handsome Irish charm, and a lovely melodious way of speaking—

Here we (Cody, Penny, Raff and I) after short talk with Kevin's wife downstairs, climb that hot trail (leaving car parked by the mailbox) and barge in on Kevin's meditation day— Tho it's Monday, he's not working today anyway— He's on his haunches boiling tea, just like a Zen Master.

He smiles wide and glad to see us—

Penny establishes herself on his beautiful meditation mat and starts to meditate, while Cody and Raphael yak and Kevin and I listen laughing—

It's supremely funny—

"What? What?" is yelling Raphael as Cody, standing,

launches on a speech about the universality of God, "you mean
to tell me all is God? *She's* God, my God?" pointing at Penny.

"Yes, sure," I say, and Cody goes on:—

"As we leave the astral plane—"

"I'm not gonna listen to this guy, I'm not gonna be corrupted by his talk! Is Cody the devil? Is Cody an angel?"

"Cody's an angel," I say.

"Oh no!" Raphael grabs his head because Cody is still
talking:—

"—reaching Saturn where it might not be committable unto
the Saviour's higher graces to change into a rock, tho I know
old Jack here that sonumbitch he'd just as soon turn into a
rock"—

"No! I'm going outside! This man is evil!"

Here it looks like a verbal battle to see who'll talk and hold
the floor, and Penny is sitting there really rosy and radiant,
with little freckles, on face and arms, red heart hair—

"Go out and study the beautiful trees," I advise Raphael,
and he does go out anyway, to dig it, and comes back (during
which time Cody has said: "Try a little a this here tea, boy,"
handing me a cup of hot tea in a Jap cup, "and see if that dont
put the cockles out of your hockles clean—agh!" (coughing,
splurting on the tea) "hem!—"

"The juicy Saviour that was manoralized and reputed on
the gold hill," I say to myself, like often I'll read me a string of
talk from my head and see what it says.

Kevin is just laughing to beat the band, crosslegged, on the
floor, I look and see the little Hindu, I remember now his little
bare feet always made me realize I knew him before in some
temple where I was a priest and he was a dancer making it with
the outer women— And how delicately he's received all that
storm of sound and talk from both Cody and Raphael—
laughing with a choking little hold of his belly, which is lean
and hard like the belly of a young Yogi—

"Why," Cody's saying, "they even have readers who see

auras over people's heads perfectly which ah reflect *exactly* the purposes-of-speaking inner mind of the entity, so *that!*" pounding his hand and leaping ahead to pound it with his voice suddenly breaking with excitement like Old Conny Murphy in the Mill Valley morning, and doing this after a long pause of thought or of word-hangup, "they can see like with a cat, like who was read by an aura reader as to having it under the necessity (and placed there by God, the Almighty) of meeting with his Karma, his earned fate as Jack says, or his just needs, or his deed-upon-done pile, of sins and mistakes—meet that Karma by actually doing what the Aura reader says, *you have an evil spirit* and *a good spirit* vying for your special entity soul, I see them (above their heads, see), you can repel the evil and draw the good by meditating on the white square of your mind which I see above your head and in which the two spirits do dwell—sfact," and he spits a cigarette pip. Gazes at the floor. Now if Raphael's an Italian, a Renascent Italian, Cody's a Greek—a Roman Aryan mixture (claims he's "Atlantean") confined to the athletes of Sparta and having its roots in nomad miocene man.

Then Cody further explains that by a process of osmosis, through our capillary veins and veinlets, comes the actual pulling juicy influence of the stars and especially the moon— "So that when the moon's out the man's mad, to put an example— the *pull* of that Mars, man."

He scares me with his Mars.

"Mars is the *closest!* That's our next journey."

"We're going from Earth to Mars?"

"And then *on,* don't you see" (Kevin is cackling with glee) "to the next and to the others and the really mad ones, dadd"— "on the outer fringe there," he adds. Matter of fact brakeman on the railroad, Cody is, in fact he's wearing his brakeman's blue pants right now, neatly pressed, and starched white shirt under a blue vest, his blue TRAINMAN hat is in the little pathetical gogetter 33 Chevvy, Ah me—many's the time Cody

fed me when I was hungry— A *believing* man— What an anxious and troubled man!—How he'd run out into that dark with
a lamp and go get her, and throw that flower car for Sherman's
Local in the morning— Ah Old Cody, what a man!

I remember the daydreams of desolation and see how it happens all right. Everything is the same emptiness, Cody and I
drive along blankly staring ahead knowing this. Cody just runs
the machine, I sit and meditate Cody and the machine both. But
it's his hard arm has to swack over the pool-wheel and guide
the car off head-on crashes (as he slips in and out of the lane)—
We know it all, we heard the heavenly music one night driving
along in the car, "Did you hear that?" I had just heard clangor
of music suddenly in the motor-humming room of the car—
"Yes" says Cody, "what *is* it?" He'd heard.

80   AMAZING ME AS HE IS, what amazes me even more
is Raphael coming back with his manuscript in
his hand, from the yard, where he silently studied the trees,
and says, "I have a leaf in my pamphlet"— To Cody who deals
and disbelieves, hears him say it, but I see the look he gives
Raphael— But it's two different worlds, Urso and Pomeray,
both their names mean something that may once have been
Casa D'Oro, which would make it no coarser than Corso, but
it's the Italian Sweet Singer vs. the Irish Brabacker—crash—
(it's Keltic, wood cracking in the sea)—Raphael saying "All
Jack has to do is write little insensible ditties and be the nowhere Hamlin's leader"—songs like that from Raphael.

"Well if that's what he wants to do check check check,"
comes from Cody like a machine without music and singing—

Raphael sings: "You! my aunts always warned me about you
Pomeray—they tole me not to go down the Lower East
Side"—

"Burp"

That's the way they fought back and forth—

Meanwhile sweet and gentle Jesus Father Joseph, Kevin with the Joseph beard, smiles and listens and all round and bent on the floor, sitting up.

"What are ya thinkin, Kevin?"

"I'm thinkin what a bad day it'll be tomorrow if I cant find that goddam driver's license."

Cody digs Kevin, of course, has dug him for months, as a fellow Irish father perhaps as well as fellow cat—Cody has been in and out of their house eating a hundred thousand myriads of times, bringing the True Law.—Cody is now called "The Preacher" by the Namer, Mal, who calls Simon Darlovsky "The Mad Russian" (which he is)—

"Where's old Simon these days?"

"O we'll pick him up there this afternoon bout five," says Cody very rapidly matter of factly.

"Simon Darlovsky!" yells Raphael. "What a mad cat!" And the way he says mad, m-a-h-d, real Eastern—real crazy strange from the Baltic alley cats—real fence-talk . . . like you hear little kids talking in gas yards around the used tire lots—"He's insane," bringing his hands to his head, then knocking off and grinning, sheepishly, a strange little humble absence of pride in Raphael, who's also sittin on the floor now crosslegged, but as though he'd collapsed like that.

"Strange strange world," says Cody marching away a little bit then wheeling and coming back to our group— The Chekhovian Angel of Silence falls over all of us and we're all dead quiet, and listen to the hmm of the day and the shh of the silence, and finally Cody coughs, just a little, says "Hnf—haf"—indicating, with his big smokes, the Indian mystery— Which Kevin acknowledges with a typical upward tender look toward Cody of amazement and wonder, out of his mind with blue-eyed clear astonishment— Which Cody also sees, eyes slitted now.

Penny is still sitting there (and has been) in the formal Buddha position for all this half and an hour of talk and thought—

Buncha nuts— We all wait for the next thing to happen. It's happening all over the world only some places they supply prophylactics, and some places they talk business.

We havent got a leg to stand on.

81 IT'S ONLY A STORY OF THE WORLD AND WHAT HAP-
PENED IN IT— We all go down to Kevin's main house and his wife Eva (sweet sisterly greeneyed barefooted longhaired beauty) (who lets little Maya wander around naked if she wants, which Maya does, going "Abra abra" in the high grass) a big lunch spread out but I'm not hungry, in fact announce a little sententiously "I dont eat anymore when I'm not hungry, I learned that on the mountain" so of course Cody and Raphael eat, voraciously, yakking at table— While I listen to records— Then after lunch Kevin is kneeling there on his favored straw-weaved rug unfolding a delicate record from its onion-papered delicatenesces in a white album, the most Hindu-perfect little guy in the world, as Raphael directs him, they're also going to play the Gregorian Chants— It's a bunch of priests and brothers singing beautifully and formally and strangely together to old music older than stones—Raphael is very fond of music especially Renaissance music—and Wagner, the first time I met him in New York in 1952 he'd yelled "Nothing matters but Wagner, I want to drink wine and trample in your hair!" (to girl'd Josephine)—"Balls on that jazz!"—tho he's a regular little hepcat and should like jazz and in fact his rhythm comes from jazz tho he doesnt know it—but there's a little Italian Bird in his makeup has nothing to do with modern cacophonic crashbeats— Judge him for yourself— As for Cody he loves all music and is a great connoisseur, the first time we played him Indian Hindu music he realized right away that the drums ("The most subtle and sophisticated beat in the world!" says Kevin, and Kevin and I even speculated whether Dravidia had contributed anything to Aryan Hindu themes)—Cody'd

realized that the soft gourds, the soft drums, the kettle Blonk bottom soft hand-drums, were simply drums with loose skins— We play the Gregorian Chants and also Indian again, every time Kevin's two little daughters hear it they start chattering happily, they've heard it every night all spring (before) at bed time with the big Hi Fi wall speaker (the back of it) opening and blasting right out on their cribs, the snake flutes, the wood charmers, the softskinned gourds, and the sophisticated old Africa-softened-by-Dravidia drumbeat, and above all the old Hindu who has taken a vow of silence and plays the oldworld Harp with showers of impossible heavengoing ideas that had Cody stupefacted and others (like Rainey) (in the big Dharma Bum season we'd had before I left) stoned outa their heads— All up and down the quiet little tar road, you can hear Kevin's Hi Fi booming soft chants of India and high Gothic priests and lutes and mandolins of Japan, even Chinese incomprehensible records— He'd had those vast parties where big bonfires were built in the yard and several celebrants (Irwin and Simon Darlovsky and Jarry) had stood around it stark naked, among sophisticated women and wives, talking Buddhist philosophy with the head of the Asian Studies himself, Alex Aums, who positively didnt care and sipped his wine only and repeated it to me "Buddhism is getting to know as many people as you can"—

Now it's noon and lunch over, a few records, and we cut out back to the city, with my old manuscripts and clothes which I'd left in a wooden box in Kevin's cellar—I owe him $15 from previous Spring so I sign him two of my Sedro-Woolley traveler's checks and he mistakenly (in the cellar) (and gently with sad eyes) hands me back a crumpled handful of dollar bills, four, one short, which I cant for the life of me bring up— For Kevin is by now stoned (on wine of lunch and all) and saying "Well when do I see you again Jack?" as we'd gone one night six months earlier and sat in the Waterfront railyards with a bottle of tokay and wallgazed (like Bodhidharma the bringer-of-Buddhism-to-China) a vast Cliff that protrudes from the

lower haunches of back Telegraph Hill, at night, and both of us
had seen the waves of electromagnetic-gravitational light coming out of that mass of matter, and how glad Kevin was that
with me he'd spent a good night of wine and wallgazing and
street-prowling instead of the usual beer in The Place—

We get back in the little coupe and U-run and all wave at
Kevin and Eva, and go back across the Bridge to the City—

"Ah Cody, you're the craziest cat I've ever known," concedes Raphael now—

"Listen Raphael, you said you was Raphael Urso the Gambling Poet, come on boy, come on to the racetrack with us
tomorrow," I urge—

"Dammit we could make it today if it wasnt so late—" says
Cody—

"A deal! I'll go with you! Cody you show me how to win!"

"It's in the bag!"

"Tomorrow—we'll pick you up at Sonya's"

Sonya is Raphael's girl but in the earlier year Cody had (naturally) seen her and fallen in love with her ("O man you dont
realize how mad Charles Swann was over those *girls* of his—!"
Cody had once told me . . . "Marcel Proust couldnt possibly
have been a queer and written that book!")—Cody falls in love
with every pretty chick around, he'd chased her and brought
his chess board to play with her husband, one time he'd brought
me and she'd sat there in slacks in the chair with her legs spread
before the chessplayers looking at me and saying "But doesnt
your life as a lonely writer get monotonous, Duluoz?"—I'd
agreed, seeing the slit in her pants, which Cody naturally while
slipping Bishop to Queen's Pawn Four had also seen— But she
finally put Cody down saying "I know what you're after," but
then left her husband anyway (the chess pawn) (now gone from
the scene temporarily) and gone to live with newly-arrived-
from-the-east yakking Raphael— "We'll go pick you up at
Sonya's pad"

Raphael says "Yeah, and I'm having a fight with her leaving this week, Duluoz you can have her"

"Me? Give her to Cody, he's mad—"

"No, no," says Cody—he's got her off his chest—

"We'll all go to my pad tonight and drink beer and read poems," says Raphael, "and I'll start packing"

We come back to the coffee place where Irwin is back waiting, and here simultaneously in the door walk in Simon Darlovsky, alone, done with his day's work as ambulance driver, then Geoffrey Donald and Patrick McLear the two old (old-established) poets of San Fran who hate us all—

And Gia walks in too.

8 2   BY NOW I'VE SLIPPED OUT AND STUCK A POORBOY OF CALIFORNIA ROTGUT WINE in my belt and started to belt at it so everything is blurry and exciting—Gia comes in with her hands in her skirt as ever and says in her low voice "Well it's all over town already, *Mademoiselle* Magazine is going to take all your pictures Friday night—"

"Who?"

"Irwin, Raphael, Duluoz— Then it'll be *Life* Magazine next month."

"Where did you hear this?"

"Count me out," says Cody just as Irwin is grabbing his hand and telling him to come, "Friday I'll be on duty Friday night"

"But *Simon* will have his picture taken with us!" calls Irwin triumphantly, grabbing Darlovsky by the arm, and Darlovsky nods simply—

"Can we have a sex orgy after?" says Simon.

"Count me out," says Gia—

"Well I'd may not be around for that either," says Cody, and everyone is pouring coffee themselves at the urn and sitting at three different tables and other Bohemians and Subterraneans are coming in and out—

"But we'll all make it together!" yells Irwin. "We'll all be famous—Donald and McLear you come with us!"

Donald is 32, plump, fair-faced, sad-eyed, elegant, looks quietly away, and McLear, 20's, young, crew cut, looks blankly at Irwin: "O we're having our pictures taken separately tonight"

"And we're not in it!?" yells Irwin—then he realizes there are plots and intrigues and his eyes darken in thought, there are alliances and rifts and separations in the holy gold—

Simon Darlovsky says to me "Jack I've been looking for you for two days! Where you been? What you doin? Dyav any dreams lately? Anything great? Dany girls loosen your belt? Jack! Look at me! Jack!" He makes me look at him, his intense wild face with that soft hawk nose and his blond hair crew cut now (before a wild shock) and his thick serious lips (like Irwin's) but tall and lean and really only just outa high school— "I've got a million things to tell you! All about love! I've discovered the secret of beauty! It's love! Everybody love! Everywhere! I'll explain it all to you—" And in fact at the forthcoming poetry reading of Raphael (his first introduction to the avid poetry fans of 50's Frisco) he was scheduled (by arrangement and consent of Irwin and Raphael who giggled and didnt care) to stand up after their poems and deliver a big long spontaneous speech about love—

"What will you say?"

"I'll tell them everything—I wont leave nothing out—I'll make them cry— Beautiful brother Jack listen! Here's my hand to you in the world! Take it! Shake! Do you *know* what happened to me the other *day?*" he suddenly cries in a perfect reproduction of Irwin, elsetimes he imitates Cody, he's just 20—"Four P.M. go into library with a rasperry pill—what do you know?—"

"Rasperry?"

"Dextidrene—in my stomach"—patting it— "See?—high

in my stomach I came upon Dostoevsky's *Dream of a Queer Fellow*—I saw the possibility—"

"*Dream of a Ridiculous Man*, you mean?"

"—the possibility of love within the clasel halls of my heart but not outside my heart in real life, see, I got a glimpse of the love life Dostoevsky had in his deep light dungeon, it stirred my tears to move in my heart to swell all over blissful, see, then Dostoevsky has the dream, see he puts in the drawer the gun after he wakes up, was gonna shot himself, BANG!" socks his hands, "he felt a even extra keen desire to love and to preach— yes to *Preach*—that's what he said—'To Live and Preach that Bundle of Truth I know so Well'—so that when the time comes for me to give that speech when Irwin and Raphael read their poems, I'm going to embarrass the group and my self with ideas and words about love, and why people dont love each other as much as they could—I'll even cry in front of them to get my feelings across—Cody! Cody! Hey you crazy youngster!" and he runs over and pummels and pulls Cody, who goes "Ah hem ha ya" and keeps glancing at his old railroad watch, ready to go, as we all mill— "Irwin and I have been long l-o-n-g talks, I want our relationship to build like a Bach fugue see where the all the sources move in between each other see—" Simon stutters, brushes back his hair, really very nervous and crazy, "And we've been taking our clothes off at parties me and Irwin and having big orgies, the other night before you came we had that girl Slivovitz knew and took her in the bed and Irwin made her, the one you broke her mirror, such a night, it took me a half minute to come the first time—I've been having no dreams, in fact a week and a half ago I had a wet dream without remembering the dream, how lonely . . ."

Then he grabs me "Jack sleep read write talk walk fuck and see and sleep again"— He's sincerely advising me and looking me over with worried eyes, "Jack you gotta get laid more, we must get you laid *tonight!*"

"We're going to Sonya's," interjects Irwin who's been listening with glee—

"We'll all take our clothes off and do it— Come you Jack do it!"

"What's he *talkin* about!" shouts Raphael coming over— "Crazy Simon!"

And Raphael pushes Simon kindly and Simon just stands there like a little boy brushing back his crew cut and blinking at us, innocently, "It's the truth!"

Simon wants to be "as perfect as Cody," he says, as a driver, a "talker,"—he adores Cody— You can see why Mal the Namer called him the Mad Russian—but always doing innocent dangerous things, too, like suddenly running up to a perfect stranger (surly Irwin Minko) and kissing him on the cheek out of exuberance, "Hi there," and Minko'd said *You don't know how close you just came to death.*

And Simon, beset on all sides by prophets, couldnt understand—luckily we were all there to protect him, and Minko's kind—Simon a true Russian, wants the whole world to love, a descendant indeed of some of those insane sweet Ippolits and Kirilovs of Dostoevsky's 19th Century Czarist Russia— And looks it too, as the time we'd all eaten peyotl (the musicians and I) and there we are banging out a big jam session at 5 P.M. in a basement apartment with trombone, two drums, Speed on piano and Simon sitting under the all-day-lit red lamp with ancient tassels, his rocky face all gaunt in the unnatural redness, suddenly then I saw: "Simon Darlovsky, the greatest man in San Francisco" and later that night for Irwin's and my amusement as we tromped the streets with my rucksack (yelling "The Great Truth Cloud!" at gangs of Chinese men coming out of card rooms) Simon'd put on a little original pantomime à la Charley Chaplin but peculiar to his own also Russian style which consisted of his running dancing up to a foyer filled with people in easy chairs watching TV and putting on an elaborate mime (astonishments, hands of horror to mouth, looking around, woops, tipping, humbling, sneaking off, as you might expect some of Jean Genêt's boys goofing in Paris streets drunk) (elaborate masques with intelligence)— The Mad Russian, Simon Darlovsky, who always reminds me of my Cousin Noël, as I keep telling him, my cousin of long ago in Massachusetts who had the same face and eyes and used to glide phantomly around the table in dim rooms and go "Muee hee hee ha, I am the Phantom of the Opera" (in French saying it, *je suis le phantome de l'opera-a-a-a*)— And strange too, that Simon's jobs have always been Whitman-like, nursing, he'd shaved old psychopaths in hospitals, nursed the sick and dying, and now as an ambulance driver for a small hospital he was batting around San Fran all day picking up the insulted and injured in stretchers (horrible places where they were found, little back rooms), the blood and the sorrow, Simon not really the Mad Russian but Simon the Nurse— Never could harm a hair of anybody's head if he tried—

"Ah yes, aw well," says Cody finally, and goes off, to work on the railroad, with instructions to me in the street, "We go to the racetrack tomorrow, you wait for me at Simon's"— (Simon's where we all sleep) . . .

"Okay"

Then the poets Donald and McLear offer to drive the rest of us home two miles down Third Street to the Negro Housing Project where even right now Simon's 15½ year old kidbrother Lazarus is frying potatoes in the kitchen and brushing his hair and wondering about the moon-men.

83

THAT'S JUST WHAT HE'S DOING AS WE WALK IN, frying potatoes, tall goodlooking Lazarus who stands up in high school freshman class and says to the teacher "We all want to be free to talk"—and always says "Dyav any dreams?" and wants to know what you dreamed and when you tell him he nods— Wants us to get him a girl too— He has a

perfect profile like John Barrymore, will really be a handsome
man, but here he's living alone with his brother, the mother
and other crazy brothers are back east, it's too much for Simon
to take care of him— So he's being sent back to New York but
he doesnt want to go, in fact he wants to go to the moon— He
eats up all the food Simon buys for the house, at 3 A.M. he'll
get up and fry all the lamb chops, all eight of them, and eat em
without bread— He spends all his time worrying about his long
blond hair, finally I let him use my brush, he even hides it, I
have to recover it— Then he puts on the radio fullblast to
Jumpin George Jazz from Oakland—then he just simply wanders out of the house and walks in the sun and asks the weirdest
questions: "Dyou think the sun'll fall down?"—"Is there monsters where you said you were?"—"Are they goyna have another world?"—"When this one's done?"—"Are you blindfolded?"—"I mean really blindfolded like with a hanky round
your eyes?"—"Are you twenty years old?"

Four weeks previous, on his bike, he'd gone barreling down
the intersection at the foot of the Housing Project hill, right by
the Steel Company office building, near the railroad underpass,
and blammed into a car and fractured leg— He's still limping
a little bit— He looks up to Cody also—Cody had been most
worried about his injury— There are simple commiserations in
even the wildest people— "That poor kid, man, he could
hardly walk—he was in pretty bad shape for a time—I was
really worried about old Lazarus there. That's right, Laz, more
butter," as tall shambly kiddy Laz is serving us at table and
brushing back his hair—very silent, never says much—Simon
addresses his brother by his real first name Emil—"*Emil,* dyou
go to the store?"

"Not yet"

"What time is it?"

Long pause—then Lazarus' deep mature voice—"Four"—

"Well aint you goin to the store?"

"Right now"

Simon brings out insane leaflets that the stores distribute door to door showing the daily bargains, instead of writing out a list of groceries he just arbitrarily rings in some of the bargains, like,

TYDOL SOAP

TODAY ONLY 45¢

—they ring that in, not because they really need soap, but it's there, offered to them, at two cents saving—they bend their pureblood Russian-brother heads together over the leaflet and make additional rings— Then Lazarus goes uphill whistling with the money in his hand and spends hours in the store looking at science fiction bookcovers—comes back late—
"Where ya been?"
"Looking at pitchers"
There's old Lazarus frying his potatoes as we all drive up and walk in— The sun is shining over all San Francisco as seen from the long housing porch in back

84   THE POET GEOFFREY DONALD IS AN ELEGANT SAD-WEARY TYPE who's been in Europe, to Ischia and Capri and such, known the rich elegant writers and types, and had just spoken for me to a New York publisher so I am surprised (first time I meet him) and we go out on that veranda to look at the scene—
It's all South Side San Fran of lower Third Street and gastanks and water tanks and industrial tracks, all smoky, slimy with cement dust, rooftops, beyond which the blue waters go all the way to Oakland and Berkeley, seen plain, even unto the foothills beyond that start their long climb to the Sierra, under cloud tops of divine majestical hugeness of snow-rosy-tinted at dusk— The rest of the city to the left, the whiteness, the sadness— A typical place for Simon and Lazarus, it's all Negro

families living around there and they are of course well liked and even gangs of children come right in the house and shoot play guns and scream and Lazarus instructs them in the arts of quiet, their hero—

I wonder as I lean with sad Donald if he knows all this (type) or cares or what he's thinking—suddenly I notice he's turned fullface around to stare at me a long serious stare, I look away, I cant take it—I dont know how to say or how to thank him— Meanwhile young McLear's in the kitchen, they're all reading poems all scattered among bread and jam—I'm tired, I'm already tired of all this, where will I go? what do? how pass eternity?

Meanwhile the candle soul burns in our "clasel" brows . . .

"I suppose you've been to Italy and all that?—what are you going to do?" I finally say—

"I dont know what I'm going to *do*," he says sadly, with sad-weary humor—

"What does one does when one does," I say listless witless—

"I heard a lot about you from Irwin, and read your work—"

In fact he's too decent for me—all I can understand is franticness—I wish I could tell him—but he knows I know—

"We'll be seeing you around?"

"Oh yes," he says—

Two nights later he arranges a kind of little dinner party for me at Rose Wise Lazuli, the woman who runs the poetry readings (at which I never read, from shame)— On the phone she invites me, Irwin standing by me whispers "Can we come too?" "Rose, can Irwin come too?"—("And Simon")—"And Simon?"—"Why certainly"—("And Raphael")—"And Raphael Urso the poet?" "But of course"—("And Lazarus" whispers Irwin)—"And Lazarus?"—"Surely"—so that my dinner party with Geoffrey Donald there with a pretty elegant intelligent girl, turns into a frantic screaming supper over ham, ice cream and cake—which I describe in its place right ahead—

Donald and McLear go off and we eat some kind of crazy gobble supper of everything there is in the icebox and rush out to Raphael's girl's pad for an evening of beer and talk, where Irwin and Simon immediately take off their clothes (their trademark) and Irwin even plays with Sonya's bellybutton—and naturally Raphael a hepcat from the Lower East Side dont want nobody playing with his chick's belly, or have to sit there looking at naked men— It's a surly evening—I see that I have a big job on my hands patching things up— And in fact Penny is with us again, sitting in the background—it's an old Frisco roominghouse, topfloor, littered with books and clothes—I just sit with a quart of beer and dont look at anyone—the only thing that attracts my attention from out of my thoughts is that beautiful silver crucifix Raphael's been wearing around his neck, and I mention it—

"Then it's *yours!*" and he takes it off and hands it to me— "Really, truly, take it!"

"No no I'll wear it for a few days and give it back to you."

"You can keep it, I *want* to give it to you! You know what I like about you Duluoz, you understand why I'm sore—I dont wanta have to sit here look at naked guys—"

"O what's *wrong?*" says Irwin where he's kneeling at Sonya's stool and touching her bellybutton under the little fold of clothes he's lifted up, and Sonya herself (pretty little thing) is bound to prove nothing will bother her and let's him do it, while Simon watches prayerfully (holding himself)— In fact Irwin and Simon begin to shiver a little, it's night, cold, the windows are open, the beer is cold, Raphael's sitting by the window brooding and wont talk or if so, to call them down— ("How you expect me to let you make it with my chick?")

"Raphael's right, Irwin—you dont understand."

But I have to make Simon understand too, he wants it worse than Irwin, all Simon wants is a continued orgy—

"Ah, you guys," finally sighs Raphael, waving his hand— "Go ahead, Jack, take the cross, keep it, it looks good on you."

It has a little silver chain, I pass it over my head and under my collar and wear the cross—I feel strangely glad— Meantime Raphael has been reading the Diamondcutter of the Wise Vow (Diamond Sutra) that I paraphrased on Desolation, has it on his lap, "Do you understand it Raphael? There you'll find everything there is to know."

"I know what you mean. Yes I understand it."

Finally I read sections of it to the party to take their minds off the girl jealousies—:

"Subhuti, living ones who know, in teaching meaning to others, should first be free themselves from all the frustrating desires aroused by beautiful sights, pleasant sounds, sweet tastes, fragrance, soft tangibles, and tempting thoughts. In their practice of generosity, they should not be blindly influenced by any of these intriguing shows. And why? Because, if in their practice of generosity they are not blindly influenced by such things they will pass through a bliss and merit that is beyond calculation and beyond imagining. What think you, Subhuti? Is it possible to calculate the distance of space in the eastern skies?

No, blissful awakener! It is impossible to calculate the distance of space in the eastern skies.

Subhuti, is it possible to calculate the limits of space in the northern, southern, and western skies? Or to any of the four corners of the universe, or above or below or within?

No, honored of the worlds!

Subhuti, it is equally impossible to calculate the bliss and merit through which the living ones who know will pass, who practice generosity not blindly influenced by any of these judgments of the realness of the feeling of existence. This truth should be taught in the beginning and to everybody". . . .

They all listen intently . . . nevertheless there's something in the room I'm not in on . . . pearls come in clams.

The world will be saved by what I see
Universal perfect courtesy—

Orion in the fresh space of heaven
One, two, three, four, five, six, seven—

It ends up a bad night, we go home leaving Raphael brooding and in fact fighting with Sonya, packing to leave—Irwin
and Simon and I and Penny go back to the pad, where Lazarus
is cooking the stove again, bring more beer and all get drunk—
Finally Penny comes in the kitchen almost crying, she wants to
sleep with Irwin but he's asleep, "Sit on *my* lap baby" I say—
Finally I go to my bed and she crawls into it and puts her arms
around me right away (tho saying at first: "I just want a place
to sleep in this madhouse") and we go to town— Then Irwin
wakes up and then Simon makes her too, there are bumpings
and creakings of beds and old Lazarus is prowling around and
finally the next night Penny kisses Lazarus too, and everybody's happy—

I wake up in the morning with my cross around my neck, I
realize what thicks and thins I'll have to wear this through, and
ask myself "What would Catholics and Christians say about me
wearing the cross to ball and to drink like this?—but what
would Jesus say if I went up to him and said 'May I wear Your
cross in this world as it is'?"

No matter what happens, may I wear your cross?—are there
many kinds of purgatories not?

". . . not blindly influenced . . ."

85 IN THE MORNING PENNY GETS UP BEFORE ANYONE
ELSE and goes out to buy bacon and eggs and orange juice and makes a big breakfast for everybody—I begin
to like her— Now she's cuddling and kissing me all over and
(after Simon and Irwin go off to work, Irwin's merchant ship is
in Oakland, drydocked) Cody walks right in just as we're coo-
ing (or have cooed again) on the bed and he yells out "Ah just
what I like to see in the morning, boys and girls!"

"Can I go with you, can I follow you today?" she says to me—

"Sure"

Cody's whipping out his race entries and lighting cigar and getting all eager at the kitchen table over the new day's racing, just like my father long ago— "Just a little bit sugar in that coffee, Lazarus m'boy," says he—

"Yes sir"

Lazarus is bounding around the kitchen with a thousand breads and eggs and bacons and toothbrushes and hairbrushes and book comics— It's a bright sunny morning in Frisco, Cody and I get high on pot right away at the kitchen table.

Both of us are talking in loud voices suddenly about God again. We want Lazarus to learn. Half the time we address our remarks to him— He just stands there grinning and pushing back his hair.

Cody is at his best but I've got to make him understand, as he goes "And so it's true as you do say that God is us"—poor Cody—"right here now, etcet, we dont have to run to God because we're already there, yet Jack really now and face it ole buddy that sonumbitch trail to Heaven is a *long* trail!" Yelling it, seriously, and Lazarus smiles lazy at the stove, that's why they call him "Laz."

"You dig that, Lazarus?" I say.

Of course he does.

"Words," I say to Cody.

"We start out with our astral bodies man and you know the way a ghost'd go when headin out there to that bright black night, go in a straight line—then as he wanders, just astral born and new to the game, he gets to wigglin and a-goin from side to side, that is, to explore, much as H. G. Wells says about a maid sweeps a hall from side to side, the way migrations advance—astral he'll go migrate out there to the next, or *Martian*, level—where he bumps into all them sentinels you see, but with that special astral interpenetration speed"—

"Words!"

"True, true, but then after—now listen Jack, there was a guy who had such a bad aura of traitorship around him, in fact he was a later entity of Judas, he'd, people'd sense him turn in the street 'Who's that *betrayer* just went by?'—all his life suffering from some curse, people had of him, which was the Karmic debt he had to pay for sellin Jesus for a handful silver—"

"Words"

I keep saying words and really mean it—I'm trying to get Cody to shut up so I can say "God is words—"

But it's still all words—but Cody insists and bashes to prove that it's a physical universe, he really believes the body is physically independent form right there in front of you—that then the astral ghost went out: "And when he gets to Saturn certain conditions there may seek, saught, hot, seet to *foil* him there, he might get to be a rock, or go on—"

"Tell me seriously, doesnt the entity go to God in heaven?"

"That it does, after a long trail and trial, you see," lighting his cigarette suavely.

"Words"

"Words as you will"

"Birds"

He pays no attention to my "Birds."

"Until finally purified and so spotless as to be like the garment that was never rented, the entity does arrive in heaven and back to God. See's why I say, 'we're not there now!' "

"We cant help being there now, we cant avoid our reward."

This blanks Cody a minute, I usually spin words—

"Heaven so sure," I say.

He's wont to shake his head—there's something about Cody wont agree with me, if so we get to be ghosts bumping on the same issues on another plane out there (in the distanceless vasts)— But what's the point?

"WORDS!!!" I yell, like Raphael yelling "Balls on that!"

"Dont you see," says Cody beaming with real gratitude and

joy, "it's all really worked out for us in advance and all we gotta do is pile right on. . . . That's why I wanta go to the racetrack today," Cody goes pilin on, "I got to win that money back and 'sides boy there's something I want you to know, how many times have I gone to that betting window and asked the man for Number Five, because somebody just then says 'Number Five,' and the ticket I'd originally wanted was Number Two?"

"Why dont you just say give me Number Two, instead of Number Five, I made a mistake. Would he give it back to ya, Numbers?"

(Raphael and I had also been amazed in the shack yesterday by Cody's constant talk of numbers, as you'll see at the races.)

Instead of answering me would the ticket taker change the deal, he goes: "Because that was a disincarnate entity telling me 'Number Five'—"

"Sometimes you just hear them in your head?"

"This entity may be trying to have me win or lose, with certainly the foreknowledge of the outcome of that race, old buddy, dont you think I dont know why pshaw boy I got and you know Lazy Willie never said he ever you ever deviate from that second choice—"

"So at least you know the disembodied ghost entities are trying to make you lose—because you say the second choice system cant fail."

"Cant"

"Whaddo they look like?" asks Lazarus from the other room where now he's been brushing his hair, on the edge of the bed, playing a little music on the box.

"All kinds of ways, auras, auras say for instance of that *betrayer* scared everybody down the street, auras showing ogres of the imagination probably—opers anyway." That's where Cody plys the Keltic language.

"Big seedy ghosts amplin down the line—into that endless sky, shit man Cody, wha happens?"

Oh the frou-frous and fifi-sweets he'll demonstrate the eye, to show how, jumping up from the chair to wave and talk—The Preacher—Mal was right—Laz comes in to dig Cody dancing like that. Cody'll lean way down and sock his fist on the floor, and reach up and jump a point about Nijinsky off the floor and come around and bring big muscular Lil Abner's-15½-year-old brother arms to whisk and wave at your nose, he wants you to feel the Lord's wind and heat—

"It's all one essential light beyond which there can be no further division," I essay, and here to add: "Words."

"Jesus Christ comes down and his Karma is to know that he is the Son of God assigned to die for the sake of the eternal safety of mankind—"

"Of all sensing beings."

"No—not ants. Knowing it, he does it, dies on the Cross. That was his Karma as Jesus.—Dig what that means."

Les onges qui mange
dans la terre . . .

86 ALL CODY HAD TO DO TO GET OUTA THAT WAS SAY "But God is beyond words" but what does he care about words he wants to go to the races.

"What we're gonna do now is get in that little car and go see a sweet baby-pussy I want you to see and then we'll go get your boy Raphael Shmashael there, and we're ORF!" Like the announcer at the races. He's banding all his papers and switch keys and cigarettes in the pockets, we're off, Penny who was combing her hair to go out and taking her time about it now has to run right out with us and into the car, Cody wont wait, we leave Lazarus stranded in the doorway free to goof all day long in the apartment alone—we go barreling businesslike down the steep hill, and around to the right, around again, and around left and right into Third Street and wait at the light then on down just before it changes into the city, Cody wont waste a split-hair of time— "It's all TIME, m'boy!" he yells—he goes into his theory of time and how we all gottact *fast*. "There's no end to the things to be done!" he yells (the motor's loud)— "If we only had TIME!" he cries almost moaning.

"Whatinhell do you mean about time?" the girl is yelling. "For krissakes, all I hear is this talk about Time and God and every damn thing!"

"Ah shut up" we both say (in our sneering thoughts) which gets Cody mad and he bats the car outa hell right into Third Street winos stumbling from the bottles you can see empty in the alleys and traffic around, he curses and swivels— "Hey take it easy!" yells Penny as his mad elbows bang her. He looks mad enough to rob a bank or kill a cop. You'd think looking at him he was a wanted outlaw in Oklahoma Panhandle 1892. He'd make Dick Tracy shiver before shoot holes in his head.

But then at Market the pretty girls are in evidence and here goes Cody's description. "There's one. She aint bad. See her cutting in the store there. Nice ass."

"Oh you!"

"Not half so nice that one there—hmm—nice front, nice side—no hippies—flippy dippy."

Flippy dippy, that's when he forgets himself and when there are children around they all go mad laughing and digging it. Never will be clown with adults, though. The shooting star of mercy musta had a bleak face.

"There's another one. O is she a gone cutie, tho aint she?"

"Where where?"

"Oh you men."

"Let's eat!"—we'll go eat in Chinatown, breakfast, I'll have sweet and sour spare ribs and almond duck with my orange juice, ugh.

"And now children I want you to realize that this is the day of days," announces Cody in the restaurant booth, removing his racing forms from one pocket to another, "and by *God*" banging the table "I'm going to recoup my loss-es," like W. C. Fields, and looks up blankly as the waiter comes but doesn't stop (a Chinese cat with trays), "We're bein *ostraci̧zed* here," yells Cody— Then when orders come he gets a regular old ham n eggs breakfast or lunch, like the time we took G. J. to the Old Union Oyster House in Boston and he ordered pork-chops. I get all that almond duck and can hardly finish it.

No room in the car, or some kind of dissuasion use, to drop Penny off at the corner and cut on down to see Cody's favorite new girl who lives out there and we park the car violently and run out and into the room, there she is in a tightfitting little dress fixing her hair before the mirror, and lipsticking, saying "I'm on my way to a Filipino photographer to take nude photos."

"Oh isn't that nice," says Cody with extreme unction. And while she's primping at the mirror even I cant keep my eye off her shape, which is dead perfect, and Cody like a sexfiend in some never-published special pornographic photo is standing right behind her holding himself up to her, close, not touching, as she either does or does not notice, or neither, and he's look-ing at me with a big plea in his mouth, and pointing at her, and shaping and molding her with his free hand, without touching, I stand there watching this tremendous show then sit down and he keeps it right up and she goes on putting on that lipstick. A crazy little Irish girl named O'Toole.

"*Man,*" she finally says, and goes over and gets a stick of tea, and lights up. I cant believe it and finally in walks a three-year-old boy who says something extremely intelligent to his mother like "Mama, can I have a bathtub with baby eyes, man?" something like that, or, "Where's my baby toy I can go be a boy with," actually— Then her husband walks in, cat from the Cellar, that I saw there milling around and running around. I am supremely tested by this situation, and trying to get out of it I pick up a book (Zen Buddhism) and start reading. Cody doesnt care, but we're ready to go, we'll drive her right out to her photographer. They rush out and I follow them but the book in my hands, and have to run back and re-ring the bell (while Cody armarounds pretty Mizzus O'Toole) and her husband stares at me down the stairs and I say "I forgot the book" and run up and hand it to him, "I really did," and he yells down "I know you did, man," completely cool and perfect couple.

We drop her off and go on to get Raphael.

"Now aint that some little nice sweet something, dyou dig that little dress," and then instantly too he's mad. "Now all on account of this Raphael idea of yours we'll be late at the racetrack!"

"O Raphael's a great guy! I promise you I know!—What's the matter dont you like him?"

"He's one a those guys that dont dig—them Dagos—"

"Boy they got em rough and mean, too," I admit, "but Raphael is a great poet."

"Boy wiggle through that as you will but I cant understand him."

"Why? Because he keeps yelling? that's the way he talks!" (It's just as good as silence, just as good as gold, I coulda added.)

"It's not that— Sure I dig Raphael, man dont you know we been—" and he gets stony silent on the subject.

But I know I can (*I* can?) *Raphael* can prove he's a great cat—Cat, shmat, man, pan, dog is God spelled backwards—

"He's a good kid—and he's a *friend*."

"The Friends so-si-a-tay," says Cody in one of his rare instances of irony, which though when it comes, as in Dr. Samuel Johnson whom I also Boswelled in another lifetime, come so Irish Keltic Hard and final, it's like rock, receiving the crash of the sea, wont yield, but that slowly, but obdurately, irony meanwhile, iron in the rock, the nets the Keltic people spread on rock— Mostly in his tone of irony is the Irish Jesuit school, also to which Joyce belonged, not to mention hard Ned Gowdy back up there on that mountain, and besides Thomas Aquinas the ill-starred hard-begot Pope of Thought, the Jesuit Scholar— Cody had been to parochial school and was an altar boy— Priests had suffered at his neck as he twisted to break down buildings of heaven— But now he was back in the groove of his religion, believing on Jesus Christ, and in Him (as in Christian countries we'll use the "H")—

"Did you see the cross Raphael loaned me to wear? wanted to give me?"

"Yeah"

I dont think Cody approves of my wearing it—I leave it out, I'll go on—I get the strange feeling of it and then I forget it and everything takes care of itself— Same with anything, and everything is holy I said long ago—long ago before there appeared an I to say it—words to that effect anyway—

"All right we'll go to that damn Richmond and man it's a long way so let's hustle— You think he'll ever come down outa there?" peering now out the car window at Raphael's roof windows.

"I'll run up and get him, I'll ring." I jump out and ring and yell to Raphael up the stairs, opening the door, as a distinguished old lady makes her appearance—

"I'll be right down!"

I go out to the car and soon here comes Raphael dancing down the high porch steps and swinging as he goes and comes bashing into the car as I hold the door open for him, Cody starts us off, I slam the door and drape my elbow over the open window and here's Raphael, fingers up in little bunched fingerfists, "Yai, you guys, wow, you told me you'd be here at twelve o'clock sharp—"

"Midnight," mutters Cody.

"Midnight?!! You told me damn you Pomeray you waz gonna be—you ai, you, Oh I know you now, I see it all now, it's plots, everywhere it's plots, everybody wants to hit me over the head and deliver my body to the tomb— The last time I had a dream about you, Cody, and about you, Jack, it was much more with golden birds and all sweet fawns consoled me, I was the Consoler, I lifted my skirts of divinity to all the little children who needed it, I changed into Pan, I piped them a sweet green tune right out of a tree and *you were that tree! Pomeray you were that tree!*—I see it all now! You cant follow me!"

His hands all the time held up, gesturing with little snips, or mows, at the air, just like an Italian talking a long harangue in a bar to a whole brass-rail of listeners— Wow, I'm amazed by this sudden ring of sound, and the unimpeachable *delicatesse* of every Raphael's words and meanings, I *believe* him, he *means* it, Cody must *see* that he means, it's true, I look to see, he's just driving along listening sharply and also avoiding traffic—

Suddenly Cody says "It's that breach of time, when you see a pedestrian or a car or an upcoming crack-up you just crack right up like nothin's gonna happen and if it dont separate you got that extry breach of time to give em grace, because ordinarily ten times outa one them astral bodies'll separate, cat, and that's because it's all figured out in the hall up there where they make the Cee-ga-ree-los."

"Ach, Pomeray—I cant stand Pomeray—he gives me nothin but bullshit—he pulls my ears—it'll never end—I quit I give up— What time's the first race, man?" the latter spoken lowly and politely and with interest.

"Raphael's a *razzer!*" I yell out, "Raphael the Razzer"—(it was Cody had just said that, "One of them guys likes to razz the boys, you know" "Isn't that all right?" "It's awright"—)

"The time of the first race is well out of our reach now," says Cody bleak, "and naturally we cant play the daily double—"

"Who wants to play the daily double?" I yell. "The odds are never long enough. It's a hundred to one or fifty to one chance you got pickin two successive winners, shit."

"Daily Double?" says Raphael fingering his lip, and suddenly he's brooding into the road, and here we come in that little coupe with the old 1933 hardchug engine, and you see the vision of three faces in the glass, Raphael in the middle hearing nothing and seeing nothing but just looking straight ahead, like Buddha, and the driver of the Heavenly Vehicle (the full Oxcart Bullock White-as-Snow Number One Team) talking earnestly about numbers, waving with one hand, and the third person or angel listening with surprise. Because he's just then telling me that a secondchoice horse paid six dollars to show, then five dollars to show twice, then four three times, then a little under four (bout twenty forty cents) twice, and came in the money all day, first, second, or third all day—

"Numbers," says Raphael from far away. But he's got his little wallet of about thirty dollars with him and maybe he can make a hundred and get drunk and buy a typewriter.

"What we should do, insmuch you dont believe me, but I beg you to see and understand, but I'll tell ya what, I'll play him to win all day, 'cordin to Lazy Willy's system— Now Lazy Willy now you realize Raphael he was an old hand at bettin that system and when he died they found him dead out there in that clubhouse with $45,000 in his pocket—which means that by that time he was plankin real heavy and affectin the odds hisself—"

"But I only got 30 dollars!" yells Raphael.

"This'll come in time—" Cody was going to become a millionaire with Lazy Willy's system and go out building monasteries and Samarian retreats and hand out "fi-dollar-bills" to deserving bums in Skid Row and in fact even people in trolleys— Then he's going to get a Mercedes and go spinning down to Mexico City on that El Paso Highway, "doin 165 on the straightaways and boy you *know* that's gotta be in low gear because when you come to that curve and gotta make it at 80 or 100, and gotta swash the car through it's a matter of sideswipin that curve with your brakes—" He demonstrates a little by gunning up the motor and simultaneously going into low to ease us up at a convenient red stoplight (which he can tell is

red because the cars are stopped, tho colorblind)— What hazish gray vistas doth bold noble Cody see? This is a question I
could ask Raphael, and he'd answer me from his horse:

"Some hoar immaculate mystery."

87 "WHAT WE'LL DO," SAYS CODY ARM AROUND BOTH
OF US at the flag-whipping race track as we edge
right into the mob of bettors under the grandstand, "I'll play
to win, Raphael play to place, Jack play to show, all day, on
that second choice" (tapping his program at the second race
and at the horse-number now, he sees craning over heads, is
running second choice on the tote board)—Raphael doesnt understand any of it but at first we dont realize.

"No I wont bet," I say, "I never bet— Let's get a beer—
It's beer and baseball and hotdogs."

Because finally Raphael announces his horse to our immediate joint consternation as it shows he's understood nothing
whatever of what "second choice in the betting" meant—"I'm
gonna bet on number nine, it's a mystical number"

"It's Dante's mystical number!" I yell—

"Nine—*nine?*" says Cody, looking, wondering, "Why that
dog's goin off at thirty-to-one?"

I look to Cody to see if he understands, all of a sudden
nobody understands anything.

"Where's my beer?" I say, as though an attendant was
standing behind me with it. "Let's get a beer and you bet."

Raphael has his money out and is nodding seriously.

"Natcherly," says Cody, "I'll go with my secondchoice
horse and bet him to win— You understand? that's number
five."

"No!" laughs and shouts Raphael. "My horse is number
nine. Dont you under*stand?*"

"Yes I understand," concedes Cody and off we go to bet, I
wait at a beer counter as they merge into long panicky lines of

waiting bettors as the horses are nearing the six furlong pole
now for the dash and soon there'll be (there it is!) the warning
buzzer and they all hustle and push, the line is slow, and nobody's even once looked out at the actual horses out on that
physical field—it's all astral numbers and cigarsmoke and shuffling feet.—I look out over the crowd and over the field and
the distant Golden Gate Bridge across the water far away, it's
Golden Gate Fields Racetrack in Richmond California but it's
definitely an ant-heap in Nirvana, I can tell by the little cars far
away— They're smaller than you can believe— It's a vast
space trick— With what a particular reverence do the little
jockeys out there pat their horses into the starting-gate but we
cant see that far too well, I can just see the silk reverend jockeys
bending-bodied over their horses' necks, and nathless the fact
there are more horses' necks than horses in the world, the
horsenecks are strapping beautiful things— Brrang! They're
off— We haven't even bought a program so I dont know what
silks Cody's 5 is wearing, or Raff's 9, all we can do (like all the
other downtrodden bettors of Karma world) is wait till the pack
drives on down the 70-yard-pole and see which way the number sets, in that diamond heaving pack, and as for the announcer his announcings disappear under the roar of the crowd
at the far turn salience, which leaves us with upjumping looks
to see just numbers coming by—passing through—as soon as
the jockeys ease up around the clubhouse turn when the race is
over, fans are already clobbering the statistics on the third race
—Cody's 5 comes in third, Raphael's 9 is out, near last, a tired
horse of Dante—they'll be bringin him in by lamplight in my
dreams—Cody proudly advises us to recall and announces:
"Good, when the second choice comes in third, naturally that's
almost as it should be, right? Seeing as how he's third choice,
he should third choice it to the public's satisfaction, good good,
just let him lose all he wants, the more he loses the stronger I
get"

"How's that?" asks Raphael in astonishment and wants to know.

"As the second choice repeatedly loses my bets increase, so that, when he does come in, I gain by the large bet, back, all I lost, and gain more."

"It's all in the numbers," I say.

"It's amazing!" says Raphael. Inwardly he's mulling: "Some mystical number should come to me again. Probably nine again. It's like roulette, the gambler. Dolgoruky kept putting all he had on one thing and broke the house. I shall be like Dolgoruky! I dont care! If I lose it's because I'm a shit and if I'm a shit it's because the moon shines on shit! *Shine* on shit!" — "*Eat* my babies!"

Every day, according to Simon, "a poem creeps up into Raphael's head and become a high Poem." That's just the way Simon said it.

88 AS WE'RE GETTING READY TO BET ON THE THIRD RACE an old woman comes up to us, with big blank blue eyes and spinsterish, in fact with tight bunned pioneer hair (she looks exactly like a Grant Wood portrait, you expect to see Gothic barns in back of her), sincere as all get-out, says to Cody (who's known her from before at all the tracks):— "Bet on 3, and if you win give me half—I have no money— Just be two dollars"

"*Three?*" Cody glances at the program. "That dog, he wont win—"

"What is he?" I look. He's about Seventh Choice in a 12-horse field.

"Of course seventh choice often comes in twice a day," concedes Cody out loud, and Raphael is staring at the old dignified lady, who could very well be Cody's mother from Arkansaw, with amazement and private worry ("What are all these mad-people?") So Cody bets on her horse for her, plus his own, plus finally another hunch he has, scattering his money all over, so when his regular system horse does win the third race his profits arent enough to cover the speculation and the insanity— Meanwhile Raphael's played 9 again, mystic, who runs out— "Raphael if you wanta win some money today you better follow me," says Cody. "Now for obvious reasons the horse in this fourth race is as clear a cleancut second choice as I've ever seen, all alone there at 9-to-2, Number Ten"

"Number Two! That's my favorite number!" decides Raphael looking at us with a little child smile—

"Why not only is he a dog that Prokner that's ridin him keeps falling off—"

"The jockeys!" I yell. "Look Raphael the jockeys! Look at their beautiful silks!" They're coming out of the paddock, Raphael doesn't even look. "Think what weird little—what strange little dancers they are"

Number Two for sure is in Raphael's head—

This time, the fourth race, the starting gate is drawn right before our eyes by six big Budweiser Team horses each weighing a thousand pounds, beautiful big nags, with reverent old handlers, slow, they take their time moving that gate half-mile down to the front of the grandstand, nobody (except little children who play by the wire fence in the sun while their parents bet, little odd assortments of whites and blacks) nobody digs them, looks, or anything, it's all numbers, all heads are bent in the bright sunshine over gray form sheets, the *Daily Racing Form*, the *Chronicle* entries in green—some just pick mystical figures off the program, I myself keep scanning the program which I've finally appropriated off the ground for strange hints like the horse "Classic Face" is sired by Irwin Champion and his dam is Ursory—or I look for stranger hints, like "Grandpa Jack," or "Dreamer," or "Night Clerk" (which means the old man in the Bell Hotel may be bending his kindly astral head over our pitiful futile endeavors on the plain of racing)— In his first days of horseplaying Cody was unbelievable, he was actually the trainman assigned to snip tickets on the Bay Meadows Racing Special, and would come out all complete with blue brakeman's uniform with visored cap and all, black tie, white shirt, vest, proud, erect, neat, with his girl of that time (Rosemarie) and start out the first race with his program neat in his side pocket standing proudly in shambling lines of bettors to wait for his turn at the window, losing, till by the seventh race he'd be all disheveled, would have by now stashed his cap back on the train (parked at the gates with engine and all ready for the city-back-run) and because losing money his interest would have switched to women, "Look at that broad over there with her old daddy ah hum," even sometimes (running out of money) he'd try to con old ladies who liked his blue eyes to bet for him—the day ending always so sadly as he'd get back on the train, brush his uniform in the toilet (have me brush the back) and come out all neat to work the train (of disgruntled bettors) back across the lonesome red sunsets of the Bay Area— Now today he's just wearing off-day jeans, faded and tight, and a flimsy sports T-shirt and I say to Raphael "Looka that old Oklahoma hombre tiptoein to make his bet there, that's all Cody is, a rough hombre of the West"—and Raphael grins weakly seeing it.

Raphael wants to win money, never mind the poems—

We end up just sitting in benches in the upper grandstand and cant see the starting gate even tho it's right down there, I wanta go on the fence and explain racing to Raphael— "See the starter in his box—he'll press a button that rings the bell and bats open the bat cages and out they lunge— Watch those jockeys, every one of em's got hand a steel—"

Johnny Longden is among the great jockeys today, and Ishmael Valenzuela, and the very good Mexican called Pulido who seems to be so observant watching the crowd from his horse, actually interested, while the other jockeys brood and bite— "Cody had a dream last year that Pulido was riding a railroad train around the track the wrong way and when he came around the final clubhouse turn the whole train exploded and all's left is Pulido in the little horse-engine, winning alone—I said 'Wow, Pulido *won*'—so Cody gives me an extra $40 to play on him on every race and he doesn't hit once!"—I tell this to Raphael, who bites his fingernails—

"I think I'll go back to Number Nine"

"Folly the system, man!" pleads Cody—"I told you about Lazy Willy how they found him dead with $45,000 worth of uncashed win-tickets—"

"Listen Raphael," I put in, "Lazy Willy just sat around sipping coffee between races, with a pince nez probably, and came out at last minute odds and saw the score and went and made his bet and went and took a piss while that race was on— It's all in the numbers— The second choice's the consensus of the multitude reduced to a second degree which has been mathematically figured to come in so many percent times so if you keep jivin your bets according to the losses you've suffered you're bound to win, unless a tragic streak of losses—"

"That's right, *tragic*, now listen Raphael and you'll make some money—"

"Okay okay!"—"I'll try it!"—

Suddenly the crowd oohs as a horse rears in the starting gate and gets all tangled up and throws his man, Raphael gasps with astonished horror— "Look, the poor horse is caught!"

The grooms rush up and straddle and work and get the horse out, which is immediately scratched from the race, all bets off— "They can get hurt!" yells Raphael painfully— This doesn't concern Cody so much for some reason, maybe because he was a cowboy in Colorado and takes horses for granted, as once we'd seen a horse spill and thrash in the backstretch and nobody cared, everybody yelled for the oncoming far turn, there's the horse with broken leg (doomed to be shot) and the inert jockey a little white spot on the track, maybe dead, certainly injured, but all eyes are on the race, how these mad angels do race to their Karma disbenefaction— "What about the horse?" I'd yelled as the roar surged up down the homestretch and as penance I'd kept my eye on the scene of the accident, completely ignoring the outcome of the race, which Cody won— The horse was destroyed, the jockey ambulanced to the hospital— and not by Simon— The world's too big— It's only money, it is only life, the crowds roar, the numbers flash, the numbers are forgotten, the earth is forgotten—memory is forgotten—the diamond of silence seems to go on without going on—

The horses break and whang out by the rail, you hear the riding crops of the jocks planking the flanks, you hear boots and whistles, "Yah!" and off they mill around the first turn and everybody turns eyes back to the form sheets to see the numbers representing the symbol of what's happening around the Nirvana track—Cody's and Raphael's horse is well in front—

"I think he'll stay in front," I say, from experience, a good $2^1/_2$ lengths lead and loping and preserved by the rider's restraining hand— Around the far turn and in they come, you see that pathetic flash of spindly thoroughbred legs so breakable, then the dust cloud as they strightaway home, the jocks are wild— Our horse stays right in front and holds out from a contender and wins—

"Ah! Aye!" they rush to collect a pittance—

"See? Just stick with your old buddy Cody and you cant lose!"

Meanwhile we take trips around to the men's room, the beer counter, the coffee counter, hotdogs, and finally when the last race is coming up the skies have grown late-afternoon gold and long lines of bettors sweat for the buzzer—the characters of the track who looked so confident and fresh in the first race are all now disheveled-looking, heads down, crazed, some of them scour the floor for lost tickets or odd programs or dropped dollars— And it's also the time for Cody to begin to notice the girls, we have to trail several around the track and stand around peeking at them. Raphael says "Ah never mind the women, who's the horse now? Pomeray you're a sex fiend!"

"Look Cody you'd a won the first race that we missed," I say pointing at the big blackboard—

"Ah"—

We get sorta sick of one another and take separate leaks at urinals but we're all in it together— The final race is run— "Ah let's go back to the sweet city," I think, which is showing across the bay, full of promise that never takes place except in the mind—I keep getting the feeling too, as Cody wins he really loses, as he loses he really wins, it's all ephemeral and cant be grabbed by the hand—the money, yes, but the facts of patience and eternity, no— *Eternity!* Meaning more than all time and beyond all that little crap and on forever! "Cody you cant win, you cant lose, all's ephemeral, all is hurt," are my feelings— But while I am a sly non-gambler who wont even gamble on heaven, he is the earnest Christ whose imitation of Christ is in the flesh before you sweating to believe that all does really good-and-bad matter— All shining and shaking to believe it—a priest of life.

He ends up with a highly successful day, every horse came in the money, "Jack you sonumbitch if you'd a squeezed two little measly dollars outa those jeans each race and done what I said, you'd have a nice forty-dollar bill tonight," which is true but I aint sorry—except for the money— Meanwhile Raphael has come out just about even and still has his thirty dollars— Cody wins forty and pockets it all proud in neat little arrangements with the small bills on the outside—

It's one of his happy days—

We come walking out of the racetrack and past the parking-lot to where the little coupe is free-parked by a railroad spur-track, and I say, "There's your parking place, you just park there every day," because now he's won you wont stop him from coming every day—

"Yes, m'boy, and besides what you're seeing there will be a Mercedes-Benz in six months—or at first at least a Nash Rambler Stationwagon"

89   AH LAKE A DREAMS, EVERYTHING IS CHANGED—
We get in the little car and go back and as I see
the little reddened city on that white Pacific, I remember the
sight of Jack Mountain in high mountain dusks how the redness
hoared the topmost peak-wall till the sun all went down, and
still a little was left from the height and the curve of the earth,
and there's a little dog being led by a leash across super-traffics
and I say "The little pups of Mexico are so happy—"

"—as I live and breathe and I didnt keep it up didnt stay
with didnt nothing, I just let my system run away from me and
played other horses and not enough and lost five thousand dollars last year—dont you see what I'm in for this?"

"Solid!" yells Raphael. "We'll make it together! You and me!
You make it back and I make it on!" and Raphael gives me one
of his rare halfhearted grins. "But I see you now, I know you
now, Pomeray, you're *sincere*—you really wanta win—I believe you—I *know* you're Jesus Christ's contemporary frightening brother, I just dont want to be hun-gup on the wrong bets,
it's like being hun-gup on the wrong poetry, the wrong people,
the wrong side!"

"Everything's right side," I say.

"Maybe but I dont want crash—I dont wanta be no Fallen
Angel man," he says, piercingly sorrowful and serious. "You!
Duluoz! I see you your ideas goin down Skid Row drink with
the bums, agh, I've never even thought of doing such a thing,
why bring misery on yourself? Let the dog lie.—I wanta make
money, I dont wanta say Oh Ah Ogh I've lost my way, Oh Ah
Gold Honey I've lost my way, I *havent* lost my way yet—I'm
going to ask the Archangel to let me win. Hark!—the Bright
Herald hears me! I hear his trumpet! Hey Cody it's ta ta tara
tara the cat with the long trombone at the start of every race.
Do you dig that?"

He and Cody are completely in agreement on everything, I

suddenly realize I've succeeded in my wait to see them patch up and be friends— It's happened— There is very little vestige of doubt in either one, now— As for me, I'm in an excited state because I've been in an airy dungeon for two months and everything pleases and penetrates me, my snowy view of light-particles that permeate throughout the essence of things, passes right on through—I feel the Wall of the Emptiness— Naturally it's perfectly within my interests to see Cody and Raphael glad of each other, it has all to do with the nothing that is all, I have no reason to quibble with the absence of judgment placed in Things by the Absent Judge who builded the world without building it.

Without building it.

Cody lets us off in Chinatown all gleaming to go home and tell his wife he's won, and Raphael and I go walking down Grant Street in the dusk, bound for different destinations as soon as we see a monster movie on Market Street. "I dig what you meant Jack about Cody at the races. It was real funny, we'll go again Friday. Listen! I'm writing a real great new poem—" then suddenly he sees chickens in crates in the inside dark Chinese store, "look, look, they're all gonna die!" He stops in the street. "How can God make a world like that?"

"And look inside," I say, at back boxes full of white, "the thrashing doves—all the little doves'll die."

"I dont want a world like that from God."

"I dont blame you."

"That's what I mean, I dont want it— What a way to die!" indicating the animals.

("*All creatures tremble from fear of punishment,*" said *Buddha.*)

"They cut their necks over barrel," I say, omitting the "s" in a typical frequent French way of slipping s'ses, which Simon also does as a Russian, both of us stutter a bit—Raphael never stutters—

He just opes his mouth and blasts "It's all the little doves'll die my eye would have opened a long time ago. I dont like it anyway. I dont care— Oh Jack," suddenly he really grimaces to see the birds, standing in the dark street store sidewalk, I dont know if it ever happened before that somebody almost cried in front of Chinatown poultry storewindows, who else coulda done it but some silent saint like David D'Angeli (coming up)— And Raphael's grimace meaks me a leak-tear right quick, I see it, I suffer, we all suffer, people die in your arms, it's too much to bear yet you've got to go on as though nothing was happening, right? right, readers?

Poor Raphael, who's seen his father die in images of the rope-line, the buzz of his old home, "We had red peppers drying in the cellar on strings, my mother leaned against the furnace, my sister made crazy" (he describes it himself) — The moon shining on his youth and here's this Death of Doves looking him in the face, as you and me, but sweet Raphael it's too much— He is just a little child, I see the way he falls off and sleeps in our midst, leave the baby alone, I'm the old guard of a tender gang—Raphael will sleep in the fleece of the angels and all that black death instead of being a thing of the past I prophesy will be a blank— No sighs, Raphael, no cries?—the poet's got to cry— "Them little animals will have their necks chopped off by birds," says he—

"Birds with long sharp knives that shine in the afternoon sun."

"Yeah"

"And old Zing Twing Tong he lives up there in that pad and smokes opium of the world—opiums of Persia—all he's got is a mattress on the floor, a Travler portable radio, and his works are under the mattress— It's described as wretched mean hovels in the San Francisco *Chronicle*"

"Ah Duluoz, you're mad"

(Earlier in the day Raphael had said, after that outburst of hands-in-the-air speech, "Jack you're a giant," meaning a giant

of literature, tho earlier in the day I'd told Irwin I felt like a
cloud, from watching them all summer of Desolation, I'd become a cloud.)

"Just I—"

"I'm not gonna think about it, I'm goin home and sleep, I
dont wanta dream about wilted pigs and dead chickens in a
barrel—"

"You're right"

We fall to striding straight for Market. There we hike to the
Monster movie and first dig the pictures on the wall. "It's a
nowhere picture, we cant go see it," says Raphael. "There's no
monsters, all it is is a moonman with a suit on, I wanta see
monstrous dinosaurs and mammals of the other worlds. Who
wants to pay fifty cents to see guys with machines and panels—
and a girl in a monstrous lifebelt skirt. Ah, let's cut out. I'm
going home." We wait for his bus and he takes it. Tomorrow
night we'll meet at that dinner party.

I go happy down Third Street, dont know why— It's been
a great day. It's an even greater night but I dont know why.
The sidewalk is soft as I unroll out of under me. I pass old juke
joints where I used to go in and play Lester on the box and
drink beers and talk with the cats, "Hey! Whatcha doin down
here?" "In from New York," pronouncing it New Yahk, "The
Apple!" "Precisely the Apple" *"Down* City" *"Bebop* City"
"Bebop City" "Yeah!"—and Lester is playing "In a Little
Spanish Town," lazy afternoons I'd spent on Third Street sittin
in sunny alleys drinkin wine—sometimes talking— all the same
old most eccentric bo's in America come cuttin by, in long
white beards and broken coats, carrying little pittance paper-
bags of lemons—I walk past my old hotel, the Cameo, where
Skid Row drunks moan all night, you hear them in dark carpeted halls—it's creaky—it's the end of world where nobody
cares—I wrote big poems on the wall saying:—

> The Holy Light is all there is to see,
> The Holy Silence is all there is to hear,

The Holy Odor is all there is to smell,
The Holy Emptiness is all there is to touch,
The Holy Honey is all there is to taste,
The Holy Ecstasy is all there is to think . . .

it's silly—I dont understand the night—I'm afraid of people—I walk along happy— Nothing else to do— If I were pacing in my mountain yard I'd be just as bad off as I am walking down the city street— Or as well off— What's the difference?

And there's the old clock and the neons of the printing equipment building that remind me of my father and I say "Poor Pa" really feeling him and remembering him right there, as tho he could appear, to influence— Tho the influence one way or the other makes no difference, it's only history.

In the house Simon is out but Irwin is in the bed brooding, also talking quietly to Lazarus who sits on the edge of the other bed. I come in and open the window wide to the starry night and get my sleepingbag ready to sleep for the night.

"What the hell's you sad about, Irwin?" I ask.

"I'm just thinking Donald and McLear hate us. And Raphael hates me. And he doesnt like Simon."

"*Sure* he does—dont try to—" and he interrupts me with a big moan and arms to the ceiling from his disheveled bed:—

"Oh it's all this beast!—"

Brutish division was taking place in his idea-friends, some who were close and some not, but something beyond my non-political intelligence was percolating in Irwin's brain. His eyes are dark and smoldery with suspicion, and fears, and silent wrath. His eyes bulge to show it, his mouth is set in a determined Path. He's going to make it at great cost to his gentle heart.

"I dont *want* all this fighting!" he shouts.

"Right"

"I just want classical angels"—he'd often said that, his vision of everybody hand in hand in paradise and no bullshit. "Hand in *hand* it's got to be!"

Sullen compromises were sullying his air, his Heaven— He had seen the God of Moloch and all the other gods including Bel-Marduk— Irwin had begun in Africa, in the center of it, pouting with sullen lips, and walked on past to Egypt and Babylon and Elam and founded empire, the original Black Semite who cannot be separated from the White Hamite by words or deductions. He'd seen Moloch's face of Hate in the Babylonian night. In Yucatan he'd seen the Rain Gods, glooming by a kerosene lamp in the jungle rocks. He broods off into space.

"Well I'm going to sleep good tonight," I say. "Had a great day—Raphael and I just saw the thrashing doves"—and I tell him the whole day.

"Also I've been a little envious of you being a cloud," says Irwin seriously.

"*Envious?* Wow!— A giant cloud, that's all I am, a giant cloud, leaning on its side, all vapors—yep."

"I wish I was a giant cloud," sighs Irwin utterly seriously and yet tho he poke fun at me he wont laugh about it, he's too serious and concerned about the outcome of everything, if it's gonna be giant clouds he just wants to know it, that's all.

"Have you been telling Lazarus about the green faces in your window?" I ask, but I dont know what they've been discussing and go to bed, and wake up in the middle of night briefly to see Raphael come in and sleep on the floor, and I turn over and sleep on.

Sweet rest!

In the morning Raphael's on the bed and Irwin's gone but Simon's there, his day off, "Jack I'll go with you today to the Buddhist Academy." I've been planning to go there for days, have mentioned it to Simon.

"Yah but it might bore you. I'll go alone."

"Na, I'll stay with you—I wanta add to the beauty of the world"—

"How will that happen?"

"Just by I do the things you do, to help you, and I learn all about beauty and I grow strong in beauty." Perfectly serious.

"That's wonderful, Simon. Okay, good, we'll go— We'll walk—"

"No! No! There's a bus! See?" pointing away, jumping, dancing, trying to imitate Cody.

"Okay okay we'll take the bus."

Raphael has to go somewhere else, so we eat and comb (and take off) but before I stand on my head in the bathroom three minutes to ease my nerves and heal my sorrow veins and I keep worrying someone'll crash into the bathroom and knock me over on the sink . . . in the bathtub Lazarus' got big shirts soaking.

90 IT OFTEN HAPPENS I FOLLOW UP with a fit of ecstasy such as I'd had walking home on Third Street, with a day of despair, owing to which fact I cannot appreciate the really great new day that has broken, also sunny with blue skies, with goodhearted Simon all eager to make me glad, I fail to appreciate it till much later in reflection— We take a bus to Polk and walk up Broadway hill among flowers and fresh air and Simon is dancing along talking all his ideas—I see every point he makes but I keep gloomily reminding him it doesnt matter— Finally I end up snapping "I'm too old for young idealisms like that, I ben through all that!—all over again I gotta go through all that?"

"But it's real, it's truth!" yells Simon. "The world is a place of infinite charm! Give everybody love and they'll give it right back! I seen it!"

"I know it's true but I'm bored"

"But you cant be bored, if you get bored we all get bored, if we all get bored and tired we all give it up, then the world falls down and dies!"

"And it's as it should be!"

"No! it should be life!"

"That's no difference!"

"Ah, Jacky-boy dont give me that, life is life and blood and pulling and ticking" (and he starts tickling my ribs to prove it) "See? you jump away, you tickle, you life, you have living beauty in your brain and living joy in your hort and living orgasm in your body, all you gotta do is do it! *Do it!* Everybody loves to join arm-in-arms in the walk," and I can see he's been talking to Irwin—

"Ah lousy me I'hse tired," I have to admit—

"*Dont!* Wake up! Be happy! Where are we going now?"

"Right up this hill to the big Buddhist Academy, we'll go in Paul's cellar—"

Paul is a big blond Buddhist who is janitor of the Academy, he grins in the basement, in the Cellar nightclub when there's jazz he'll stand there eyes closed laughing and bouncing on both feet so glad to hear the jazz and crazytalk— Then he'll slowly light a big serious pipe and raise big serious eyes through the smoke and look right at you and smile around his pipe, a great guy— Many's the time he'd come to the shack on the horse-hill and slept in the old abandoned room in back, on a sleeping-bag, and when big gangs of us would bring him wine in the morning he'd sit up and take a slug anyway then go walking among the flowers, thinking, and come back to us with a new idea— "Just as you say, Jack, it takes a long tail to make a kite reach the infinite, I just thought now, I'm a fish— I go swimming through the trackless sea—just water, no ways, no directions and avenues—by flapping my tail however I move right along—but my head seems to have nothing to do with my tail—s'long as I can" (he squats to demonstrate) "flap those backfins, aimless like, I can just go on ahead without worryin— It's all in my tail and my head's just thoughts—my head's flounderin in thoughts but my tail's wigglin me right along"— Long explanations—a strange silent serious cat—I was coming to see about a lost manuscript, that might be in his room, as I'd left it in crates for anybody, in fact with the instructions: *If you dont understand this Scripture, throw it away. If you do understand this Scripture, throw it away. I insist on your freedom*—and now I realize Paul might have done just that, and I laugh to think and that's right—Paul had been a physicist, a student of mathematics, an engineering student, then a philosopher, now a Buddhist with no philosophy, "Just my fish-tail."

"See?" says Simon. "How great a day it is? The sun shining everywhere, pretty girls on the street, what more do you want? Old Jack!"

"Okay Simon, let's be angel birds."

"Be just angel birds here step aside m'boy angel birds."

We come into the basement entrance of the gloomy building and come to Paul's room, the door is ajar— Nobody in— We go in the kitchen, there's a big colored girl who says she's from Ceylon, real svelte and pretty, tho a little plump—

"Are you a Buddhist?" says Simon.

"Well I wouldnt be here—I'm goin back to Ceylon next week."

"Isnt that wonderful!" Simon keeps looking at me to appreciate her— He wants to make her, go to one of the upstairs bedrooms of this religious university and bang in beds—I think she senses that to some extent and cuts out politely— We go down the hall and look in a room and there's a Hindu young woman lying on a mattress on the floor with her baby and big shawls and books— She doesnt even rise as we talk to her—

"Paul's gone to Chicago," she says— "Look in his room for thee manuscript, it may be there."

"Wow," says Simon staring at her—

"And then you can go ask Mr. Aums in his office upstairs."

We tiptoe back down the hall, almost giggling, run up to use the toilet, comb, talk, come down to Paul's bedroom and search around his things— He has left a gallon jug of burgundy which we pour drinks from into delicate Japanese tea cups thin as wafers—

"Dont break these cups"

I sit leisurely at Paul's desk and spin him a note—I try to think up little funny Zen jokes and mysterious haikus—

"There's Paul's meditation mat—on rainy nights after he's stoked the furnace and et he sits there in the dark thinking."

"What does he think about?"

"Nothing"

"Let's go upstairs see what they're doon up there. Come on, Jack, dont give up, go on!"

"Go on where?"

"Go on with it, dont stop—"

Simon goes dancing his crazy play-act of the "Simon-in-the-World" routine with hands shushing and tiptoeing and Oops and exploration of the wonders ahead in the Forest of Arden— Just like I used to do myself—

A surly secretarial woman wants to know who wants to see Mr. Aums which enrages me, I just want to talk to him in the door, I start downstairs angrily, Simon calls me back, the woman is perplexed, Simon is dancing around and it's all as if his hands are held out supporting the woman and me in an elaborate play— Finally the door opens and out comes Alex Aums in a sharp blue suit, like a hepcat, cigarette in mouth, squinting at us narrow-eyed, "O there you are," to me, "how've you been? Wont you come in?" indicating the office.

"No, no, I just want to know, did Paul leave a manuscript with you, of mine, to hold or do you know of—"

Simon is looking back and forth at the two of us with per-plexity—

"No. Not at all. Nothing. It might be in his room. By the way," he says extremely friendly, "did you happen to see the article in the New York *Times* about Irwin Garden—it doesnt mention you in it but it's all about—"

"Oh yes I saw that."

"Well it's been nice seeing you again," finally, he says, and sees, and Simon nods approvingly, and I say "Same here, see you later Alex," and run down the stairs and out on the street Simon cries:—

"But why didnt you go up to him and shake hands and pat him on the back and be friends—why were you talking to each other across the hall and running away?"

"Well there was nothing to talk about?"

"But there was everything to talk about, the flowers, the trees—"

We hurry down the street arguing about it and finally sit down on a stone wall under a park tree, on the sidewalk, and here comes a gentleman with a bag of groceries. "Let's tell the whole world, beginning with him!—Hey Mister! See here! look this man is a Buddhist and can tell you all about the paradise of the love and the trees . . ." The man takes one quick glance and hurries on— "Here we are sitting under the blue sky —and nobody will listen to us!"

"That's awright Simon, they all know."

"You should have sat in Alex Aums' office and touched knees sitting in laughin chairs and talked about old times but all you did was be scared—"

I can see now if I'm going to know Simon for the next five years I'll have to go all this again, as I had done his age, but I see I'd better go through than not— Words that we have to use to describe words— Besides I wouldnt want to disappoint Simon or cast a pall on his young idealisms—Simon is sustained by a definite belief in the brotherhood of man but how long that will last before other issues cloud it out . . . or never . . . I feel sheepish anyway not being able to keep up with him.

"Fruit! That's what we need!" he calls out seeing a fruit store— We buy cantaloupes and grapes and split and walk down across the Broadway Tunnel yelling in loud voices to make the echo, munching on grapes and slobbering at canta-loupes and throwing them away— We come right out on North

Beach and head up to the Bagel Shop to see if we can find Cody.

"Keep it up! Keep it up!" yells Simon behind me pushing me as we walk fast down the narrow-walk-lane—I dont waste a grape, I eat every one of em.

91 PRETTY SOON, AFTER COFFEE, IT'S ALREADY TIME AND ALMOST LATE, to go to Rose Wise Lazuli's dinner party where Irwin and Raphael and Lazarus will meet us—

We're late, get involved in long walks up hills, laughing I am because of the crazy comments Simon makes, like "Look over there that dog—he has a bite up his tail—he's been in a fight and the gnashing mad teeth got im"—"that'll teach him a good lesson—that'll show him respect not to fight." And to ask directions, of a couple in an MG sports car, "How do we get to t-la t-la what's the name Tebsterton?"

"Oh Hepperston! Yes. Right up four blocks to the right."

I never know what right up four blocks to the right ever means, I'm like Rainey, who walked along with a map in his hands, drawn by his boss in the bakery, "walk to so and so street," Rainey wearing the uniform of the firm simply walks off from the job altogether because he doesnt know where they want him to go anyway— (a whole book about Rainey, Mr. *Caritas,* as David D'Angeli says, whom we're destined to meet tonight at the wild party in the rich house after the poetry reading—)

There's the house, we go in, the lady opens the door, such a sweet face, I like those serious woman eyes that get all liquid and bedroom eyes even in middle age, it denotes a lover-soul— Here I go, Simon's corrupted me or proselytized, one—Cody the Preacher's losing ground— Such a sweet woman with her elegant glasses, I think with a thin ribbon depending somewhere on her head-makeup, I think ear-rings, I cant remember — Very elegant lady in a splendid old house in San Francisco's

svelte district, on thick-rubbery-foliage hills, among wild
hedges of red flowers and granite walls leading up to parks of
abandoned Barbary Coast mansions, turned into ruinous old-
coat clubs at last, where the topers of Montgomery Street's
leading firms warm their behinds to cracking fires in big fireplaces and drinks are rolled up to em on wheels, over rugs—
Fog blows in, Mrs. Rose must shiver in the silence of her house
sometimes— Oh, and what must she do night-a-times, in her
"bright nightgown," as W. C. Fields'd say, and sits up a-bed
to listen to a strange noise downstairs then falls off to plotting
her fate her brooding plan of defeat every day— "Singing to
while away the mattick hay," is all I can hear— So sweet, and
so sad that she has to get up in the morning to her canary in
the bright yellow kitchen and know that he will die.—Reminds
me of my Aunt Clementine but not like her at all— "Who does
she remind me of?" I keep asking myself—she reminds me of
an ancient lover I had in some other place— We'd had pleasant
evenings together already, escorting them elaborately (she and
her poetess friend Bernice Whalen) down the stairs of The
Place, on a particularly mad night in there when a mad fool lay
on the piano on his back, on top, blowing the trumpet loud and
clear silly New Orleans riffs—which I had to admit were rather
good, as brocaded popoffs to hear down a street— Then we'd
(Simon and Irwin and I) taken the ladies to a wild jazz joint
with red and white tablecloths, and beer, great, the wild little
cats who were swingin in there that night (and had peyotl with
me) and one new cat from Las Vegas dressed loose and perfect,
with shoes like perfect elaborate sandals for Las Vegas wear,
for gambling places, and gets on the drums and washes up a
mad beat with a ruff of his sticks on cymbals and the bass
booms and falls in and so amazes the drummer he leans far back
almost falling and drumming that beat with his head at the bass
fiddler's heart—Rose Wise Lazuli had dug all these things with
me, and there'd been elegant conversations in cabs (clop clop
the Washington Square James), and I'd done one final thing

probably Rose, who is 56, never forgot:—at a cocktail party, in her house, escorting her best friend out into the night and to her bus 2½ blocks down (Raphael's Sonya's house is right near), the old lady finally taking a cab— "Why Jack," back at the party, "how *nice* of you to be so kind to Mrs. James. She is utterly the finest person you'll ever know!"

And here at the door now she greets:—"I'm so glad you could come!"

"I'm sorry we're late—we took the wrong bus—"

"I'm *so* glad you could come," she repeats, closing the door, so I realize she feels I'll hold up an impossible situation going on in the dining room, or, irony— "So glad you came," she says even once more and I realize it's just simple littlegirl logic, just keep repeating the kind amenities and your graciousness will not fall down— She in fact inspires an innocent atmosphere in a party otherwise bristling with antagonistic vibrations. I can see Geoffrey Donald laughing charmed, so I know all's okay, I go in and sit down and okay. Simon sits down at his place, with a "oo" of sincere respect on his lips. Lazarus is there, grinning like Mona Lisa just about, hands on each side of his plate to denote etiquette, a big napkin on his lap. Raphael is lounging low in his chair occasionally snapping at a piece of ham on his fork, with elegant lazy hands hanging, shouting, sometimes completely silent. Irwin is bearded and serious but laughing inside (from charmed happiness) so his eyes cant help twinkling. His eyes swivel from face to face, big serious brown eyes that if you choose to stare at them he'll stare right back and one time we challenged each other to a stare and stared for 20 minutes, or 10, I forget, and his eyes kept getting more crazy to come out, mine got tired— The Prophet of the Eyes—

Donald is delicate in a gray suit, laughing, beside a girl with expensive clothes and talks about Venice and what to see. Beside me is a pretty young girl who has just come to live in one of Rose's extra rooms, to study in San Francisco, aye, and then I think: "Did Rose invite me to meet her? Or did she know all

the poets and Lazarusses would follow me anyway?" The girl
gets up and does the serving, for Rose, which I like, but she
puts on an apron, a kind of servant's apron which for awhile
confuses me, in my crudeness.

Ah how elegant and wonderful is Donald, Fife of Fain, sitting next to Rose, making appropriate remarks not one of which
I remember they were so idly perfect, like, "Not as red as a
tomato, I hope," or, the crashing way he laughed suddenly
when everyone else did same as I made my boner *faux pas,*
which went recognized as a joke, starting out: "I *always* ride
freight trains."

"Who wants to ride freight trains!"—Gregory— "I dont
dig all this crap where you ride freight trains and have to exchange butts with bums— Why do you go to all that,
Duluoz?"— "Really no kiddin!"

"But this is a first-class freight train," and everybody guffaws
and I look to Irwin under the laughter and tell him: "It really
is, the Midnight Ghost is a first-class train, no stops on that
right-o-way," which Irwin knows from knowing about the railroad from Cody and myself— But the laughter is genuine, and
I console myself with the reminder, embodied in the Tao of
my rememberance. "The Sage who provokes laughter is more
valuable than a well." So I well at the wink of that brimming
wine welkin glass and pour out decanters of wine (red burgundy) in my glass. It's almost unmannerly the way I wail at
that wine— but everybody else starts imitating me—in fact I
keep refilling the hostess's glass then my own— When in
Rome, I always say—

The perfect devolvement of the party runs around the theme
how we gonna run the revolution. I supply my little bit by
saying to Rose: "I read about you in the New York *Times*
being the vital moving spirit behind the San Francisco poetry
movement— That's what you are, hey?" and she winks at me.
I feel like adding "You naughty girl" but I'm not out to be

witty, it's one of my fine relaxed nights, I like good food and good wine and good talk, as what beggar doesnt.

So Raphael and Irwin take up the theme: "We'll go all the way out! We'll take our clothes off to read our poems!"

They're shouting this at this polite table yet all seems natural and I look at Rose and again she winks, Ah she knows me— At a thank-God moment when Rose is on the phone and the others are getting coats in the hall, just us boys at the table, Raphael yells "That's what we'll do, we'll have to open their eyes, we'll have to *bomb* them! With *bombs!* we'll have to do it, Irwin, I'm sorry—it's true—it's all too true" and here he is standing up taking off his pants at the lace tablecloth. He goes right through with it pulling out his knees but it's only a joke and swiftly ties up again as Rose comes back: "Boys, we'll have to make it snappy now! It's almost time for the reading!"

"We're all gonna drive in separate cars!" she calls.

I who've been laughing all this time hurry to finish my ham, my wine, hurry to talk to the maiden girl who keeps whisking off dishes silently—

"We'll all be naked and *Time* Magazine *wont* take our pitcher! That's the true glory! Face it!"

"I'll jack off right in front of em!" yells Simon pounding the table, with big serious eyes like Lenin.

Lazarus is leaning forward eagerly in his chair to hear it all, but at the same time he's drumming on his chair, or swaying, Rose stands surveying us with a "tsk-tsk" but winks and lets us off—that's the way *she* is— All these crazy little poets eating and yelling in her house, thank God they never brought Ronnie Taker up there who'd-a walked off with the silver—he was a poet too—

"Let's start a revolution against me!" I yell.

"We'll start a revolution against Thomas the Doubter! We'll institute paradise gardens in the states of our empire! We'll plague the middleclass with naked nude babies growing up running across the earth!"

"We'll wave our pants from stretchers!" yells Irwin.

"We'll leap in the air and grab babies!" I yell.

"That's good," says Irwin.

"We'll bark at all mad dogs!" screams Raphael triumphantly. *Bang* on the table. "It'll be—"

"We'll bounce babies in our lap," says Simon direct at me.

"Babies, shmabies, we'll be like death, we'll kneel down to drink from soundless streams." (Raphael).

"Wow"

"Whatuz that mean?"

Raphael shrugs. He opens his mouth:—"We'll bang hammers in their mouth! They'll be hammers of fire! The hammers themselves'll be on fire! It'll *pound* and *pound* into their power brains!" And the way he says *brains,* it all sinks through us, the funny way of the "r's" . . . thick, sincere "r's" . . . "brwains . . ."

"When do I get to be a space ship commander?" says Lazarus who wants that out of our revolution.

"Lazarus! We'll provide you with imaginary golden turtle doves to take the place of your motor! We'll hang St. Francis in effigy! We'll kill all the babies in our brains! We'll pour wine down the throats of decaying horses!!! We'll bring parachutes to the poetry reading!"

(Irwin is holding his head.)

These are sample attempts at what he was really saying—

And we're all chargin in, like, Irwin charges in with: "We'll have assholes showing on the screens of Hollywood."

Or I say: "We'll attract attention from the bad mobsters!"

Or Simon: "We'll show them the golden brain of our cocks."

The way these people talk—Cody says: "We all go to Heaven leaning on the arm of someone we helped."

92

PASS THROUGH AS DOES THE VANISHING LIGHTNING, and dont worry—

We all pile in the two different cars, Donald driving in front, and go off to the poetry reading which I'm not going to enjoy or in fact bear, I've already got it in my mind (wine and all) to sneak out to a bar and meet everybody later— "Who is this Merrill Randall?" I ask—the poet who'll read his work.

"He's a thin elegant guy with hornrimmed glasses and nice ties that you met in New York in the Remo but you don't remember," says Irwin. "One of the Hartzjohn crowd—"

The high tea cups—it might be interesting to hear him converse spontaneously but I will not sit thru his crafty productions on a typewriter dedicated as they are usually to the imitation of the best poetry hitherto written, or at least the approximation— I'd rather hear Raphael's new bombs of words, in fact I'd rather hear Lazarus write a poem—

Rose is slowly anxiously wheeling her car to downtown San Francisco traffic, I cant help thinking "If old Cody was driving we'd be there and back by now"— Funny how Cody never comes to poetry readings or any of these formalities, he only came once, to honor Irwin's first reading, and when Irwin had finished howling the last poem and there was a dead silence in the hall it was Cody, dressed in his Sunday suit, who stepped up and offered his hand to the poet (his buddy Irwin with whom he'd hitch hiked thru the Texases and Apocalypses of 1947)—I always remember that as a typical humble beautiful act of friendship and good taste— Touching knees in the car and all upsidedown we all crane around as Rose strives to park in her slot, slowly— "Okay, okay, a little more, cut your wheel." And she sighs "Well that's that—" I feel like saying "O Rosey why dont you just stay home and eat chocolate bars and read Boswell, all this society-izing will bring you nothing

but lines of anxiety in your face—and a sociable smile is nothing but teeth."

But the hall of the reading is crowded with early arrivers,
and there's the ticket girl, and programs, and we sit around
talking and finally Irwin and I cut out to buy a fifth of sauterne
to loosen tongues— It's actually charming, Donald is there
alone now, the girl is gone, and he speaks fluid little charming
jokes—Lazarus stands in the background, I squat with the bottle—Rose has driven us and her work is done, she goes and
sits down, she has been the Mother driving the Vehicle Machine
to Heaven, with all her little children who wouldnt believe that
the house was on fire—

All that interests me is that there's going to be a party in a
big house afterwards, with punch bowl, but now in walks David
D'Angeli, gliding like an Arab, grinning, with a beautiful
French girl called Yvette on his arm and O my he's like some
elegant hero of Proust, *The Priest,* if Cody is the Preacher
David is the Priest but he's always got some beautiful chick in
chow, in fact I'm certain of the fact that the only thing may
prevent David from taking his Vow in the Catholic Orders is
he might want to get married (been married once already)
again, and raise children—of all of us David is the most beautiful man, he has perfect features, like Tyrone Power, yet more
subtle and esoteric, and that accent he talks in I do not know
where he picked it up— It's like a Moor educated at Oxford,
something distinctly Arabic or Aramaean about David (or Carthaginian, like Augustine) tho he's the son of a now-dead well-
to-do Italian wholesaler and his mother lives in a beautiful
apartment with expensive mahogany furniture and silver and
cellar full of Italian ham and cheese and wines—home-made—
David is like a Saint, he looks like a Saint, he is that fascinating
kind of figure who begins his youth as an evil-seeker ("Try
some of these pills," he'd said the first time Cody met him,
"it'll really give you the *final* kick" so that Cody never dared
take them) — There was David, that night, lying elegantly on

a white fur cover on a bed, with a black cat, reading the Egyptian Book of the Dead and passing joints around, talking strangely, "But how marvel-l-l-ous, real-ll-y," he'd say then, but since that time "the Angel knocked him off the chair," he saw a vision of the books of the Fathers of the Church, all of them in an instant, and he was *commanded* to return to the Catholic faith of his birth so instead of growing up an elegant and slightly effete hipster poet now suddenly he's a dazzling St. Augustine figure of past evils dedicated to the Vision of the Cross— Next month he's going into a Trappist Monastery for a spell and a try-out— At home he plays Gabrielli fullblast before going to communion— He is kind, just, brilliant, eager to explain, wont take no for an answer, "Your Buddhism is nothing but the vestiges of Manichaeism J-a-a-ck, face it—after *oll* you've been baptized and there's no *queshtion*, you see," holding out his thin white delicate priest-hand to gesture— Yet now he comes gliding into the poetry reading completely urbane, there's been gossip that he's decided to cease proselytizing and has entered upon the stage of urbane regularity silence on the subject, perfectly natural to have that gorgeous Yvette on his arm, and him all dolled to perfection in a simple suit and simple tie and a new crew cut that gives his sweet face a new virile look, tho his face in a year has changed from boyish sweetness to manly sweetness and gravity—

"You look more virile this year!" is the first thing I say.

"What do you mean *virile!*" he cries, stamping his foot and laughing— The way he sweeps right up on Arab glides and presents you his limp white earnest gentle hand— But as he talks and at all stages in his development all I can do is laugh, he really is very funny, he keeps his smile going beyond the bounds of reason and you realize his smile is a subtle joke (a big joke) that he expects you to realize anyway and he goes on shining white madness in that mask till all you can do then is hear his inner words that he's not speaking at all (undoubtedly funny words) and it's too much— "What are you *laughing* at,

J-a-a-ck!" he calls out— He pronounces his "a's" broad, it's a distinctly flavored accent made up of (apparently) American Italian second-generation but with strong Britishified overlays upon his Mediterranean elegance, which creates an excellent and strange new form of English I've never heard anywhere— Charity David, Civility David, who'd worn (at my urging) my poncho Capuchin rain-cape at my shack and gone out in it to meditate under the trees at night and had prayed on his knees probably, and come back to the lamplit shack where I'm reading "Manichaean" sutras and removed the cape only after letting me see how he did look in it, and he looked like a monk— David who'd taken me to church on Sunday morning and after communion here he comes down the aisle with the host melting underneath his tongue, eyes piously yet somehow humorously or at least engagingly lowered, hands clasped, for all the ladies to see, the perfect image of a priest— Everybody constantly telling him: "David write the confession of your life like St. Augustine!" which amuses him: "But *everybody!*" he laughs— But that's because they all know he's a tremendous hepcat who's been through hell and's headed now for heaven, which has no earthly use, and everybody really senses that he knows something that's been forgotten and that's been excluded from the experience of St. Augustine or of Francis or Loyola or the others— Now he shakes my hand, introduces me to blue-eyed perfect beauty Yvette, and squats with me for a slug of sauterne—

"What are you doing *now?*" he laughs.

"Will you be at the party later?—good—I'm cuttin out and goin to a bar—"

"Well dont get *drunk!*" he laughs, he always laughs, in fact when he and Irwin get together it's just one giggle after another, they exchange esoteric mysteries under the common Byzantium dome of their empty heads—mosaic tile by mosaic tile, the atoms are empty— "The tables are empty, everybody's gone over," I sing, to Sinatra's "You're Learning the Blues"—

"O that empty business," laughs David. "Really Jack, I expect you to make a better show of what you really do know, than all these Buddhist negatives—"

"O I'm not a Buddhist anymore—I'm not anything anymore!" I yell and he laughs and slaps me gently. He'd told me before: "You've been baptized, the mystery of the water has touched you, thank God for that—" . . . "otherwise I dont know what would have happened to you—" It's David's theory, or belief, that "Christ crashed through from Heaven to bring us deliverance"—and the simple rules laid down by St. Paul are as good as gold, inasmuch as they are all born of the Christ-Epic, the Son sent by the Father to open our eyes, by the supreme sacrifice of giving His life— But when I tell him Buddha didnt have to die in blood but just sat in peaceful ecstasy under the Tree of Eternity, "But J-a-a-c-k, that's not outside the *natural order*"— All events except the event of Christ are in the natural order, subordinate to the commandments of the Supernatural Order— How often in fact I'd feared to meet David, he really dented my brain with his enthusiastic, passionate and brilliant expositions of the Universal Orthodoxy— He'd been to Mexico and prowled among cathedrals, and made close friends with monks in monasteries—David also a poet, a strange refined poet, some of his earlier pre-conversion (pre-re) poems had been weird peyotl visions and such—and more than I ever saw— But I had never succeeded in bringing David and *Cody* together for a big long talk about Christ—

But now the reading is getting underway, there's Merrill Randall the poet arranging his manuscripts at the front desk so after we kill the fifth in the toilet I whisper to Irwin that I'm cutting out to a bar and Simon whispers "And I'm comin with you!" and Irwin really wants to come too but he has to stay and make a show of poetic interest— As for Raphael he's seated and ready to listen, saying:—

"I know it will be nowhere but it's the unexpected potry I

wanta hear," that little cat, so Simon and I hurry out just as Randall's begun his first line:

> "The duodenal abyss that brings me to the margin
> consuming my flesh"

and such, some line that I hear, and dont want to hear more, because in it I hear the craft of his carefully arranged thoughts and not the uncontrollable involuntary thoughts themselves, dig— Altho myself in those days I wouldnt have the nerve to stand up there and read even the Diamond Sutra.

Simon and I miraculously find a bar where two girls are sitting at a table waiting to be picked up, and in the middle of the room is a kid singing and playing jazz on the piano, and at the bar thirty men milling over beers— We immediately sit with the girls, after a little come-on, but I see right away they dont approve of either Simon or myself, and besides it's the jazz I wanta hear, not their complaints, at least jazz is new, and I go over and stand at the piano— The kid I'd seen before on Television (in Frisco) tremendously naïve and excited with a guitar yelling and singing, dancing, but now he's quieted down and's trying to make a living as a cocktail pianist— On TV he'd reminded me of Cody, a younger musical Cody, in his Old Midnight Ghost guitar (chug chugalug chugchug chugalug) I'd heard that Old *Road* poetry, and in his face I'd seen belief and love— Now he looks as if the City's finally brought him down and he idly picks on a few tunes— Finally I start singing a little and he starts playing "The Thrill Is Gone" and asks me to sing it, formally, which I do, not loud, and loose, imitating to a certain extent the style of June Christie, which is the coming man-style in jazz singing, the slur, the loose dont-care slides— the pathetic Hollywood Boulevard Loneliness— Meanwhile Simon wont give up and keeps jazzing at the girls— "Let's all go to my place . . ."

Time flies as we enjoy and suddenly in comes Irwin, every-where he appears with those big staring eyes, like a ghost, somehow he knew we'd come here (coupla blocks around), you cant evade him, "There you are, the reading is over, we're *all* going to a *big* party, what have you been doing?" and behind him in fact is Lazarus—

Lazarus amazes me at the party— It's in a regular mansion somewhere, with a paneled library containing a grand piano and leather easy chairs, and a large room with chandelier and oils, fireplace with creamy marble, and andirons of pure brass, and on a table a vast punch bowl and paper cups— In all the talking and yelling of a typical late-night cocktail party here's Lazarus all by himself in the library staring at an oil-portrait of a girl of 14, asking elegant queers at his side, "Who is she, where is she? Can I meet her?"

Meanwhile Raphael slouches on the couch and shouts out a reading of his own poems, "Buddha-fish" etc. which he has in his coat—I jump from Yvette to David to another girl back to Yvette, in fact finally Penny shows up again, escorted by the painter Levesque, and the party gets noisier—I even chat awhile with the poet Randall, exchanging views about New York—I end up upending the punch bowl into my cup, a tremendous task—Lazarus amazes me also the cool way he's passed thru the whole night, you turn around and he's got a drink in his hand, and smiling, but he's not drunk and not saying a word—

The dialogue of such parties is always one vast hubbub that rises to the ceiling and seems to clash and thunder there, the effect when you close your eyes and listen, is "Bwash bwash crash" as everybody is trying to *emphasize* their conversation at the risk of interruption or drown-out, finally it gets louder, the drinks keep coming, the hors d'oeuvres are destroyed and the punch is slaked in by hungry talking tongues, finally it degenerates into a shoutfest and always the host begins to worry about the neighbors and his last hour is spent in politely closing up the party— There are always late loud stragglers, *i.e.*, us,—the last partyers are always gently pushed out—as in my case, I go to the punch bowl to dump it in my cup but the host's best friend gently removes the bowl from my hand, saying "It's empty—besides the party's over"—the last horrible scene shows the bohemian cramming his pockets with free cigarettes that have been generously left in open boxes made of teakwood— It's Levesque the painter who does that, with an evil leer, a penniless painter, a crazy man, all his hair shaved off to a bare minimum fuzz and pucks and bruises all over him where he got drunk and fell down the night before— Yet the best painter in San Francisco—

The hosts nod and assure us out to the garden path and we all go shouting away in a drunken singing gang consisting of: Raphael, me, Irwin, Simon, Lazarus, David D'Angeli and Levesque the painter. The night's only begun.

93 WE ALL SIT ON A CURBSTONE and Raphael collapses sitting crosslegged in the road facing us and begins talking and gesturing in the air those hands— Some of us are sitting crosslegged— It's a long speech he makes which has drunken triumph in it, we're all drunk, but it's also got that bird-pure triumph of Raphael's anyway but here come the cops, and pull up in a cruiser. I get up and say "Let's go, we're making too much noise" and everybody's following me but the cops walk in on us and want to know who we are.

"We just came from that big party over there."

"Well you been makin too much noise— We got three calls from the neighbors"

"We're leaving," I say, and start off, and besides now the cops dig the big bearded Irwin Abraham and the suave gentlemanly David and the crazy dignified painter and then they see Lazarus and Simon, and they decide it would be too much in the station-house, which it surely would have been—I wanta instruct my bhikkhus to avoid the authorities, it's written in the Tao, it's the only way— It's the only straight line, right through—

Now we own the world, we buy wine on Market Street and jump all eight in buses and drink in the back and get off and go shouting down the middle of streets big long conversations— We climb a hill and go over a long path and up to a grass sidewalk top overlooking the lights of Frisco— We sit in the grass and drink wine— All talking— Then up to a man's pad, a house with a yard, a big Hi-Fi electromagnetic poo-bah big phonograph and they boom big numbers, organ masses— Levesque the painter falls down and thinks Simon's hit him, and comes crying to tell us—I start crying because Simon hit somebody, it's all drunk and sentimental, David finally leaves— But Lazarus "seen it," saw Levesque fall and hurt himself, and turns out next morning nobody hit nobody— An evening somewhat silly but filled with a triumph that was surely a drunken triumph.

In the morning Levesque comes with notebook and I tell him "Nobody hit you!"

"Well I'm glad to hear *that!*" he bellows—I'd once said to him "You must be my brother that died in 1926 and was a great painter and drawer at nine, when were you born?" but now I realize it's not the same person at all—if so, Karma has twisted. Levesque is earnest with big blue eyes and eager to help and very humble but suddenly too he'll go mad before your eyes and do a mad dance in the street that scares me. Also he laughs "Mwee hee hee ha ha" and hovers behind you . . .

I study his notebook, sit on the porch looking at the city, spend a quiet day, sketch pictures with him (one picture I sketch of Raphael asleep, Levesque says "O that's the Raphael-waist all right")— Then Lazarus and I dribble ghosts into his notebook with our crazy cartoon pencils. I'd like to see them again, especially Lazarus' strange wandering ghost-lines, which he draws with a radiantly bemused smile . . . Then by God we buy porkchops, all the store, Raphael and I discuss James Dean

in front of the movie rack, "What necrophilia!" he yells, meaning the girls adore a dead actor but what actor isnt, what actor
is— We cook porkchops in the kitchen and it's already dark.
We take a short walk up that same strange trail through a cliff-
grass empty lot, as we come down again Raphael is striding
thru the moonlit night exactly like an opium-pipe Chinaman,
his hands are in his sleeves and his head is bowed and he walks
right along, real dark and strange and bent to sorrowful re-
gards, his eyes raising and sweeping the scene, he looks lost
like little Richard Barthelmess in an old picture about London
opium smokers under lamps, in fact Raphael comes right under
the lamp and walks across to the other dark—hands in sleeves
he looks moody and Sicilian, Levesque says to me "Oh I wish
I could paint him walking like that."

"Draw it first with a pencil," I say, because all day I've been
drawing unsuccessfully with his ink—

We come in and I go to bed, in my sleepingbag, windows
open to the cool stars— And I sleep with my cross.

94   IN THE MORNING "ME AND RAPHAEL AND SIMON"
       walk off through the hot morning through big ce-
ment factories and ironworks and yards, I wanta walk and
show them things— At first they complain but then they get
interested in the big electromagnets that lift piles of pounded
scrap, and dumps em into hoppers, blam, "just by releasing the
juice at the switch, the power goes off, the mass drops," I explain to them. "And mass equals energy—and mass plus energy
equals emptiness."

"Yeah but look at that god-d-a-m ting," says Simon, mouth
open.

"It's *great!*" yells Raphael pounding his fist at me.—

We march on— We're going to see if Cody's at the railroad
station— We walk right in the trainman's lockers and I even
see if I got any mail there, from two years before when I was a

brakeman too, then we cut out to meet Cody in the Beach—the coffee joint— We take a bus the rest of the way—Raphael grabs the back seat and talks loudly, the maniac he wants the whole bus to hear, if he feels like talking— Meanwhile Simon has a banana he just bought and he wants to know if ours are just as big.

"Bigger," says Raphael.

"*Bigger?*" yells Simon.

"That's right."

Simon receives this information with complete serious consideration and reconsideration, I can see him moving his lips and counting—

Sure enough there's Cody, in the road, backing the little coupe 40 miles an hour up the steep hill, to swerve backwards into a slot and jump out—door wide open he leans out with big laughing red face hollering a sentence to us boys in the street and at the same time warning off impending motorists—

We rush up to a beautiful girl's pad, a beautiful pad, she's got a short haircut, she's in bed, under blankets, she's sick, she has big sad eyes, she has me play Sinatra louder on the phonograph, she has a whole album spinning— Yes, we can use her car—Raphael wants to move his stuff, from Sonya's, to the new pad of the party where the organ music was and Levesque cried, okay, Cody's car is too small— And then we'll slip to the races—

"No you cant go to the races in my car!" she yells—

"Okay—" "We'll be back"— We all stand around admiring her, sit awhile, even have long silences during which then she'll turn and start looking at us, and finally addresses us:

"What are you cats up to"—"anyway"—snuffing— "Wow," she says—"Relax"—"I mean it, you know?"— "*Like,* you know?"—

Yeah, we all agree but we cant get in at the same time so off we go to the races but Raphael's moving takes up all our time and finally Cody begins to see we'll be late for the first race

again—"I'll miss the daily double again!" he cries frantically—
showing his mouth open and his teeth—he really means it.

Raphael is fishing all his socks and things and Sonya is saying, "Listen, I dont want all them old biddies to know about
my life—I'm *living*, see—"

"That's great," I say, and to myself: a completely serious
little girl seriously in love— She's got a new boyfriend already
and that's what she means—Simon and I lift big albums of
records and books and bring them down to the car where Cody
is sulking—

"Hey Cody," I say, "come up and see the pretty girl—" He
doesnt want to—finally I say "We need your muscles to carry
that stuff" then he does come but when we're all settled and
back in the car ready to go, and Raphael says "Phew! that's
that!" Cody says:

"Hmf, muscles"

We have to drive to the new pad, and there I notice for the
first time a beautiful piano. The host, Ehrman, is not even up.
Levesque also lives here. Raphael will at least leave his stuff
here. It's already too late for the second race so finally I per-
suade Cody not to go to the races at all but go next time, check
the results tomorrow (turns out later he woulda lost), and just
enjoy an afternoon of doing nothing in particular.

So he pulls out his chessboard and plays chess with Raphael
to clobber him in revenge— His anger has already subsided
from a point where he was belting Raphael with his elbows as
he turned the car and Raphael'd yelled "Hey why you hittin
me? How come you dont think—"

"He's hittin you because he's sore cause you conned him
into moving your stuff and now he's late at the races. He's
chastisin you!" I add, shrugging— Now Cody, having heard us
talk this way, seems apparently contented and they play big evil
games of chess where Cody yells *"I got ya!"* while I play the
big loud records, Honegger, and Raphael plays Bach— What

we'll do is just goof, and in fact I make a run for two carry-cartons of beer.

Meanwhile the host, Ehrman, who's been sleeping in his room, comes out, watches us awhile, and goes back to bed— He doesnt care, he's got all that music blasting for him— It's Raphael's records, Requiems, Wagner, I jump and play Thelonious Monk—

"It's ridiculous!" yells Raphael examining his hopeless chess position— Then later: "Pomeray you wont let me finish the end game, you keep pulling the checks off the set, put em back, wa—" and Cody is plunging chesspieces on and off the board so fast I suddenly wonder if he is Melville's Confidence Man playing fabulously secretive earnest chess.

95 THEN CODY GOES TO THE BATHROOM AND SHAVES, AND RAPHAEL SITS DOWN AT THE PIANO slumped with one finger on the keys.

He starts hitting one note then two and back to one—

Finally he starts to play a melody, a beautiful melody that nobody heard before—tho Cody, razor to chin, claimed it was "Isle of Capri"—Raphael starts to lay down brooding fingers on chords— Pretty soon he's got his whole sonatal étude going so perfectly he's got bridges and choruses, returns to his choruses with fresh new themes, amazing how he'll suddenly plink up the perfect note-cry to resume his Italian Lovebird Song—Sinatra, Mario Lanza, Caruso, all sing that bird-pure note of cello-like sadness as is seen in the sad Madonnas—their appeal—Raphael's appeal is like Chopin, soft understanding fingers laid intelligently to a keyboard, I turn from the window where I'm standing and stare at Raphael playing, thinking "This is his first sonata—" I notice everybody quietly is listening, Cody in the bathroom and old John Ehrman in the bed, staring at the ceiling—Raphael plays only the white keys, as tho in a previous lifetime maybe (beside Chopin) he might have

been an obscure organist in a belfry playing an early Gothic
organ without minor notes— Because he does whatever he
wants with his major (white) notes, and produces indescribably
beautiful melodies that keep getting more tragic and heartbreaking, he's a pure bird singing, he said it himself, "I felt like
a little bird singing," and he said it so shiningly. Finally by the
window as I listen, every note perfect and it's the first time in
his life on the piano before serious listeners like the music master in the bedroom, it gets so sad, the songs too beautiful, as
pure as his utterances, showing his mouth's as clean as his
hand—his tongue as pure as his hand so that his hand knows
where to go for song—a Troubadour, an early Renaissance
Troubadour, playing a guitar for the ladies, making them
weep— He has me weep too . . . tears come into my eyes to
hear it.

And I think "How long ago it was I stood by a window,
when I was a music master in Pierluigi, and discovered a new
genius of music," I really have such grandiose thoughts—
meaning in previous rebirth, I was I and Raphael the new pianist genius—behind the drapes of all Italy wept the rose, and the
moon shined on the love bird.

Then I picture him playing like this, with candles, like
Chopin, even like Liberace, to gangs of women like Rose, making them cry—I picture it, the beginning of the spontaneous
virtuoso composer, whose works are taken down on a tape re-
corder, then written, and who therefore "writes" the first free
melodies and harmonies of the world, which should be pristine
music—I see, in fact, he's possibly even a greater musician than
a poet and he is a great poet. Then I think: "So Chopin got his
Urso, and now the poet blows both on piano and language—"
I tell all this to Raphael, who doesnt hardly believe it— He
plays another tune just as beautiful as the first anyway. Then I
know he can do it every time.

Tonight is the night we're going to have our pictures taken

by the magazine so Raphael yells at me "Dont comb your hair—leave your hair uncombed!"

96 AND AS I STAND BY THE WINDOW, one foot out like a Parisian Dandy, I realize the greatness of Raphael—the greatness of his purity, and the purity of his regard for me—and letting me wear the Cross. It had been his girl Sonya had just said, "Arent you wearing the Cross anymore?" and in such a nastified tone of voice as to indicate, *it was wearing the weary cross living with me?*—"Don't you comb your hair," says Raphael to me, and he has no money— "I dont believe in money."—The man on the bed in the bedroom hardly knows him, and he's moved in, and's playing his piano— The music master does agree and I see next day, as Raphael begins to play again to perfection, after a slower start than the day before owing to my perhaps rash mentioning of his musical talent—his musical genius—then Ehrman comes out of his sick room and strolls up in bathrobe, and as Raphael hits a perfect pure melodic note, I look at Ehrman and he's looking at me and both of us seem to nod agreement— Then he stands watching Raphael a few minutes.

In between those two sonatas we'd had our bloody pictures taken and had got drunk all as who would stay sober to have his picture taken and to be called "Flaming-Cool Poets"— Irwin and I'd put Raphael between us, at my suggestion, my saying "Raphael is the shortest, should be in the middle" and thus arm in arm all three we'd posed for the world of American Literature, someone saying as the shutters pop: "What a threesome!" like talking 'bout one of the Million Dollar Outfields— There I am the left fielder, fast, brilliant runner, baserunner, bagger of long flies, some over my shoulder, in fact I'm a wall-crasher like Pete Reiser and am all bruised up, I'm Ty Cobb, I hit and run and steal and flape them bases with sincere fury, they call me The Peach— But I'm crazy, nobody's ever liked my personality, I'm no Babe Ruth Beloved— In centerfield is Raphael the fair haired DiMag who can play faultless ball without appearing to try or strain, that's Raphael—the rightfielder is serious Lou Gehrig, Irwin, who hits long homeruns left-handed in the windows of the Harlem River Bronx— Later on we pose with the greatest catcher of all time, Ben Fagan, squat-legged ole Mickey Cochrane is what he is, Hank Gowdy, he dont have no trouble putting on and removing those shin guards and mask between innings—

I'd wanted to make it to his cottage in Berkeley, which has a little yard and a tree I slept under in the Fall starry nights, leaves falling on me in my sleep— In that cottage Ben and I had a big wrestling match which ended up me putting a splinter in my arm and him hurt in the back, two huge thudding rhinos we'd been wrassling for fun, like I'd done last in New York in a loft with Bob Cream, after which we played French Movies at a table, with berets and dialog—Ben Fagan with red serious face, blue eyes and big glasses, who'd been Lookout on ole Sourdough Mountain the year before me and knew the mountains too— "Wake up!" he yells, a Buddhist— "Dont step on the aardvark!" The aardvark is an ant-eater—"Buddha say:—dont bend over backwards." I say to Ben Fagan: "Why is the sun shining through the leaves?"—"It's your fault"—I say: "What is the meaning of this you meditated that your roof flew off?"—"It means horse burps in China and cow moos in Japan."—He sits and meditates with big broken pants—I had a vision of him sitting in empty space like that, but leaning forward with a big smile— He writes big poems about how he changes into a 32-foot Giant made of gold— He is very strange— He is a pillar of strength— The world will be better because of him— The world's *got* to get better— And it will take effort—

I take effort and say "Aw come on Cody you've got to like Raphael"—and so it's I'll bring Raphael to his house for the weekend. I will buy beers for everybody even tho I'll drink most of it— So I'll buy more— Till I go broke— It's all in the cards— We, *We? I* dont know what to do— But we're all the same thing— Now I see it, we're all the same thing and it will all work out okay if we just leave each other alone— Stop hating— Stop mistrusting— What's the point, sad dyer?

Arent you going to die?

Then why assassinate your friend and enemy—

We're all friends and enemies, now stop it, stop fighting, wake up, it's all a dream, look around, you dream, it's not really the golden earth that hurts us when you think it's the golden earth that hurts us, it's only the golden eternity of blissful safety— Bless the little fly— Dont kill anymore— Dont work in slaughterhouses— We can grow greens and invent synthetic factories finally run by atomic energy that will plop out loaves of bread and unbearably delicious chemical chops and butter in cans—why not?—our clothes will last forever, perfect plastic—we'll have perfect medicine and drugs to carry us through anything short of death—and we'll all agree that death is our reward.

Will anybody stand up and agree with me? Then good, all you have to do in my employ, is bless and sit down.

97 SO WE GO OUT AND GET DRUNK and dig the session in the Cellar where Brue Moore is blowing on tenor saxophone, which he holds mouthpieced in the side of his mouth, his cheek distended in a round ball like Harry James and Dizzy Gillespie, and he plays perfect harmony to any tune they bring up— He pays little attention to anyone, he drinks his beer, he gets loaded and eye-heavy, but he never misses a beat or a note, because music is his heart, and in music he has found that pure message to give to the world— The only trouble is, they dont understand.

For example: I'm sitting there on the edge of the bandstand right at Brue's feet, facing the bar, but head down to my beer, for modesty of course, yet I see they dont hear it— There are blondes and brunettes with their men and they're making eyes at other men and almost-fights seethe in the atmosphere— Wars'll break out over women's eyes—and the harmony will be missed—Brue is blowing right on them, "Birth of the Blues," down jazzy, and when his turn comes to enter the tune he comes up with a perfect beautiful new idea that announces the glory of the future world, the piano blongs that with a chord of understanding (blond Bill), the holy drummer with eyes to Heaven is lilting and sending in the angel-rhythms that hold everybody fixed to their work— Of course the bass is thronging to the finger that both throbs to pluck and the other one that slides the strings for the exact harmonic key-sound— Of course the musicians in the place are listening, hordes of colored kids with dark faces shining in the dimness, white eyes round and sincere, holding drinks just to be in there to hear— It augurs something good in men that they'll listen to the truth of harmony— Brue has nevertheless to carry the message along for several chorus-chapters, his ideas get tireder than at first, he does give up at the right time—besides he wants to play a new tune—I do just that, tap him on the shoe-top to acknowledge he's right— In between the sets he sits beside me and Gia and doesnt say much and appears to pretend not to be able to say much— He'll say it on his horn—

But even Heaven's time-worm eats at Brue's vitals, as mine, as yours, it's hard enough to live in a world where you grow old and die, why be dis-harmonious?

98 LET'S BE LIKE DAVID D'ANGELI, let's pray on our knees in privacy— Let's say "O Thinker of all this, be kind"— Let's entreat him, or it, to be kind in those thoughts— All he has to do is think kind thoughts, God, and the world is saved— And every one of us is God— What else? And what else when we're praying on our knees in privacy?

I've said my peace.

We've been to Mal's too (Mal the Namer, Mal Damlette), after the session, and there he is with his neat little cloth cap and neat sports shirt and checkered vest—but poor Baby his wife is sick on Milltowns, and all anxious when he comes out with us for a drink— It was I had said to Mal the year before, hearing him argue and fight with Baby, "Kiss her belly, just love her, dont fight"— And it had worked for a year—Mal only working all day as a Western Union telegram deliverer, walking around the streets of San Francisco with quiet eyes— Mal politely walks with me now to where I've got a bottle hidden in a Chinese grocery discarded box, and we toast a bit as of yore— He doesnt drink anymore but I tell him "These few shots shouldnt bother you"— Oh Mal was the big drinker! We'd lain on the floor, the radio fullblast, while Baby worked, with Rob Donnelly we'd lain there in the cold foggy day only to wake up to go get another jug—another fifth of Tokay—to drink it on a new outburst of talk, then the three of us falling asleep on the floor again— The worst binge I ever was on— three days of that and you live no more— And there's no need for that—

Lord be merciful, Lord be kind, whatever your name is, be kind—bless and watch.

Watch those thoughts, God!

We'd ended up like that, drunk, our picture taking, and slept at Simon's and in the morning it was Irwin and Raphael and me now inseparably entwined in our literary destinies— Taking it to be an important thing—

I stood on my head in the bathroom to cure my legs, from all the drinking-smoking, and Raphael opes the bathroom window and yells "Look! he's standing on his head!" and everybody runs over to peek, including Lazarus, and I say "O shit."

So Irwin later in the day says to Penny "O go stand on your head on the streetcorner" when she'd asked him "O what can I do in this mad city and you mad guys"— Fair enough answer but children shouldnt fight. Because the world is on fire—the eye is on fire, what it sees is on fire, the very seeing of the eye is on fire—this only means it will all end pure energy and not even that. It will be blissful.

I promise.

I know because you know.

Up to Ehrman's, up that strange hill, we'd gone, and Raphael played his second sonata for Irwin, who didnt quite understand— But Irwin has to understand so many things about the heart, the sayings of the heart, he has no time to understand harmony— He does understand melody, and climactic Requiems which he conducts for me, like Leonard Bernstein with a beard, in huge arm-raising finales— In fact I say "Irwin, you'd make a good conductor!"—But when Beethoven listened to the light, and the little cross was on the horizon of his town, his bony sorrow-head understood harmony, divine harmonic peace, and there was no need ever to conduct a Beethoven Symphony— Or to conduct his fingers on his sonatas—

But these are all different forms of the same thing.

I know it's inexcusable to interrupt a tale with such talk—but I've got to get it off my chest or I will die—I will die hopelessly—

And tho dying hopelessly is not really dying hopelessly, and it's only the golden eternity, it's not kind.

Poor Ehrman by now is supine with a fever, I go out and call his doctor for him, who says, "There's nothing we can do—tell him to drink a lot of juices and rest."

And Raphael yells "Ehrman you're gonna have to show me music, how to play the piano!"

"As soon as I get better"

It's a sad afternoon— In the waning wildsun street Levesque the painter does that mad baldheaded dance that scared me, as tho the devil were dancing— How can these painters take it? He yells something derisive it seems— The three, Irwin, Raff, me, wend down that lonesome trail— "I smell a dead cat," says

Irwin—"I smella dead sweet Chinaman," says Raphael, like before with hands in sleeves striding in the dusk down the steep trail—"I smell a dead rose," I say—"I smell a sweet tat," says Irwin—"I smell Power," says Raphael—"I smell sadness," I say—"I smell cold rose salmons," I add—"I smell the lonesome bittersweet," says Irwin—

Poor Irwin—I look at him— Fifteen years we've known each other and stared at each other worried in the void, now it's coming to an end—it will be dark—we must have courage—we'll make it by hook or crook in the happy sun of our thoughts. In a week it'll be all forgotten. Why die?

We come sadly to the house with a ticket to the opera, given us by Ehrman who cant go, we tell Lazarus to doll up for his first night at the opera in life— We tie his tie, select his shirt— We comb his hair— "Whatto I do?" he asks—

"Just dig the people and the music—it will be Verdi, let me tell you all about Verdi!" yells Raphael, and explains, ending up with a long explanation about the Roman Empire— "You gotta know history! You gotta read books! I'll tell you the books to read!"

Simon is there, okay, we'll all take a cab to the opera and drop Lazarus there and go on to see McLear in the bar—Patrick McLear the poet, our "enemy," has agreed to meet us in a bar— We drop Lazarus among pigeons and people, there are lights inside, opera club, private locker, boxes, drapes, masques, it will be Verdi opera—Lazarus will see it all downed in thunder— Poor kid, he's afraid to go in alone— He's worried what people will say about him— "Maybe you'll meet some girls!" urges Simon, and pushes him. "Go head, enjoy now. Kiss them and pinch them and dream of their love."

"Okay," agrees Lazarus and we see him bouncing into the opera in his put-together suit, his tie flying—a whole lifetime for "Goodlooking" (as his schoolteacher'd called him) of bouncing into operas of death—operas of hope—to wait—to watch— A whole lifetime of dreaming of the lost moon.

We go on—the cabdriver is a polite Negro who listens with sincere interest as Raphael tells him all about poetry— "You've gotta read poetry! You've gotta dig beauty and truth! Dont you know about beauty and truth? Keats said it, beauty is truth and truth is beauty and you're a beautiful man, you should know these things."

"Where do I get these books—in the library I suppose . . ."

"Shore! Or go down to the bookshops in North Beach, buy the little booklets of poems, read what the tortured and the hungry say about the tortured and the hungry."

"It is a tortured and a hungry world," he admits intelligently. I'm wearing dark glasses, I have my rucksack all packed ready to hop that freight Monday, I listen attentively. It's good. We fly thru the blue streets talking sincerely, like citizens of Athens. Raphael is Socrates, he will show; the cabdriver is Alcibiades, he will buy. Irwin is Zeus watching. Simon is Achilles grown tender everywhere. I am Priam, lamenting my burned city and my slain son, and the waste of history. I'm not Timon of Athens, I'm Croesus crying the truth on a burning bier.

"Okay," the cabdriver agrees, "I'll read poetry," and says good night to us pleasantly and counts his change and we run into the bar, to dark tables in the back, like back rooms of Dublin, and here Raphael surprises me by attacking McLear:

"McLear! you dont know about truth and beauty! You write poems and you're a sham! You live a cruel heartless life of the bougeois entrepreneur!"

"What?"

"It's as bad as killing Octavian with a broken bench! You're a mean senator!"

"Why are you saying all this—"

"Because you hate me and think I'm a shit!"

"You're a no good dago from New York, Raphael," I yell and smile, to indicate "Now we know Raphael's only hurt, stop the argument."

But crewcutted McLear wont be insulted, or bested in talk

anyway and fights back, and says: "Besides none of you know anything about language—except Jack."

Okay then if I know all about language let's not use it to fight.

Raphael is delivering his invective Demosthenean speech with those little plicks of fingertips in the air, but every now and then he has to smile to realize—and McLear smiles—it's all a misunderstanding based on the secret worries of poets in pants, as distinguished from poets in robes, like Homer who blindly chanted and wasn't interrupted or edited or put down by listeners one and all— Hoodlums at the front of the bar are attracted by the yells and the quality of the conversation, "Potry," and we almost get in a fight as we leave but I swear to myself "If I have to fight with the cross to defend the cross I'll fight but O I'd rather go away and let it blow over," which it does, thank God we go off free in the streets—

But then Simon disappoints me by pissing right in the street in full sight of whole blocks of people, to the point where a man comes and says "Why do you do a thing like that?"

"Because I needed a pee," says Simon—I hurry along with my pack, they follow laughing— In the cafeteria where we go for coffee Raphael instead bursts into a big loud speech to the whole audience and naturally they wont serve us— It's all about poetry and truth but they think it's mad anarchy (and to judge from the looks of us)— Me with my cross, my rucksack—Irwin with his beard—Simon with his crazy look— Anything Raphael does, Simon'll watch with ecstasy— He notices nothing else, the people horrified, "They've got to learn about beauty," says Simon to himself decisively.

And in the bus Raphael addresses the whole bus, wa, wa, a big speech about politics now, "Vote for Stevenson!" he yells, (for no known reason), "vote for beauty! Vote for truth! Stand up for your rights!"

When we get off, the bus stops, my beer bottles we've drained roll loudly on the floor of the back of the bus, the

Negro driver addresses us a speech before opening our
door:—"And dont ever drink beer in my bus again . . . We
ordinary people have troubles in this world, and you just add
to it," he says to Raphael, which isnt entirely true except for
just now yes, yet no passenger has objected, it's just a show in
a bus—

"It's a dead bus going to death!" says Raphael in the street.
"And that driver knows it and wont let it change!"

We rush to meet Cody at the station— Poor Cody, casually
entering the station bar to make a phonecall, all attired in uniform, is set upon and backslapped and howled by the gang of
crazy poets—Cody looks to me as tho to say: "Cant you quiet
them down?"

"What can I do?" I say. "Except advise kindness."

"O kindness be damned!" yells the world. "Let us have
order!" Once order comes, the orders come—I say "Let us
have forgiveness everywhere—try as hard as you can—
forgive—forget— Yes, pray on your knees for the power to
forgive and forget—then all will be snowy Heaven."

Cody hates the thought of taking Raphael and the gang on
the train— Says to me "At least comb your hair, I'll tell the
conductor who you are" (ex-trainman)— So I comb my hair for
Cody. For the sense of order. Just as well. I just wanta pass
through, Lord, to you—I'd rather be in your arms than the arms
of Cleopatra . . . till the night when those arms are the same.

So we say goodbye to Simon and Irwin, the train pulls south
into the darkness— It's actually the first leg of my three-
thousand-mile trip to Mexico and I'm leaving San Francisco.

99   RAPHAEL, AT CODY'S INSTIGATION, TALKS ALL
      ABOUT TRUTH AND BEAUTY TO A BLONDE, who
gets off at Millbrae leaving us no address, then he sleeps in his
seat— We're chaggling over rails down into the night.

There goes old brakey Cody with his lamp in the dark—
He's got a special little lantern used by all conductors and trainmen and switchmen a lot of em use em (that's language,
brother), instead of the big cumbersome regular— It fits into
the blue coat pocket, but for this move they're making, which
I go out on the ground to watch as Raphael sleeps lostchild in
the passenger seat (smoke, yards, it's like old dreams of when
you're with your father in a railroad train in a big town full of
lions)—Cody trots up to the engine and dislocates her air-hoses
for her then gives the sign "Go ahead" and they go Dieseling
down to the switch pulling the flower car for the morning, Sunday morning—Cody jumps out and throws the switch, in his
work I see the furious and believing earnestness of his moves,
he wants the men working with him to have complete confidence in him, and that's because he believes in God (God bless
him—)—the engineer and fireman watch as his light jiggles in
the dark as he's jumping off the front footboard and lighting up
to the switch, all on little rocks that turn under your shoes, he
unlocks and throws the old mainline switch and in they go to
the house (—) track—the track has a special name—which is
perfectly logical to all the railroad men, and means nothing to
anyone else—but that's their work—and Cody is the Champeen Brakeman on that railroad—I've huddled over the Obispo
Bump under boards, I know— The trainmen who are all
watching anxiously and staring at their watches will know that
Cody wont waste time and foul up the main, he sets out his
flower car and that will deliver Bodhisattva to Papa in flowers—his little children will turn over and sigh in their cribs—
'Cause Cody comes from the land where they let the children
cry—"Passing through!" he says waving his big palm—"Stand
aside, apricot tree!"—He comes running back to his footboard
and we're off to tie up—I watch, in the cold vaguely fruit-
scented night—the stars break your heart, what are they doon
there?—Over there is the hill with the bleary lights of side-
streets—

We tie up, Cody rubs and dries his hands in the toilet of the coach and says to me "Boy dont you know that I'm headed for Innisfree! Yessir boy with those horses I'm finally gonna learn to *smile* again. Man I'll just be smilin all the time I'll be so *rich*— You dont believe? Didnt you see what happened the other day?"

"Yeh but that's not important."

"*What's* not important, mo-ney?" he shows his teeth yelling at me, mad at his brother for bein so Innisfree—

"All right, you'll be a millionaire. Get me no yacht with blondes and champagne, all I want is a shack in the woods. A shack on Desolation Peak."

"And a chance" tapping me, leaping forward "to play the system with the money I'll send you by Western Union soon's we're ready to expand our business across the country— You cover the New York tracks, I'll stick to the rail here and cover these tracks and we'll set Old Sleepyhead Raphael there a-sailin for them Tropical Park Isles—he can cover Florida—and Irwin New Orleans—"

"And Marlon Brando Santa Anita," I say—

"And Marl that's right and the whole gang—"

"Simon at Setabustaposk Park in Sardine Russia"

"Semopalae Russia for Lazarus so dear m'boy it's in the bag a dead sure fire headbang *cinch*" whacking his fist, "except I gotta brush the back a my suit, here's the brush, get those specks off the back of me willya?"

And I proudly like an old New Orleans movie porter in old trains, brush his back clean of specks—

"That's fine, me boy," says Cody, placing the *Racing Form* neatly in the side of his uniform, and now we march on to Sunnyvale—"there's old Sunnyvale out there" says Cody looking out as we clank into a station, and he goes out calling "Sunny-Vale" to the passengers, twice, and some of em yawn and get up—Sunnyvale where Cody and I'd worked together, and the conductor said he talked too much tho Cody did show me how not to get on a diesel footboard— (If you get on the wrong way you're ground under, sometimes it isnt noticed in the dark) (You stand there in the dark on a track and wont see nothing because a low flatcar's sneakin up to ya like a snake)— So Cody is the Conductor of the Heavenly Train, and we'll all get our tickets pinched by him because we were all good lambs believed in roses and lamps and eyes of the moon—

> Water from the moon
> Comes all too soon

100

BUT HE'S MAD AT ME FOR BRINGING RAPHAEL TO HIS HOUSE for the weekend, tho he doesnt care, he figures Evelyn wont like him, or it— We get off the train at San Jose, wake up Raphael, and get into his new family car, a Rambler Stationwagon, and off we go, he's mad, he slams the car around with vicious twists and yet doesnt make a sound with his tires, he's learned that old trick before— "All right," he seems to say, "we'll go to the pad and sleep. *And*," he says out loud, "you two guys enjoy yourselves tomorrow watching the big Pro Football game Packers and Lions, I'll be back bout six, and drive you in Monday dawn to the first train back—that I'm working in, you see, so you dont have to worry about getting on— Now chillun, here's the pad," turning into a narrow country road, and another, and into a driveway and a garage— "There's the Spanish Mansion Pad and first thing is sleep."

"Where do I sleep?" says Raphael.

"You sleep on the sofa in the parlor," I say, "and I'll sleep in the grass in my sleepingbag. I've got my spot out there in the backyard."

Okay, we get out and I go in the back of the huge yard among bushes, and spread out my sack, from the rucksack, on dewy grass, and the stars are cold— But that star air hits me and as I slip into my bag it's like a prayer— To sleep is like a prayer, but under the stars, if you wake up at night, at 3 A.M., you'll see what a big beautiful Heavenly Milky Way room you're sleeping in, cloudy-milk with a hundred thousand myriads of universes, and more, the number is unbelievably milky, no Univac Machine with the brainwash mind can measure that extent of our reward that we can see up there—

And the sleep is delicious under stars, even if the ground is humpy you adjust your limbs to it, and you feel the earth-damp but it only lulls you to sleep, it's the Palaeolithic Indian in all of us— The Cro-Magnon or Grimaldi Man, who slept on the ground, naturally, and often in the open, and looked at the stars on his back and tried to calculate the dipankara number of them, or the hoodoo oolagoo mystery of them blearing there— No doubt he asked "Why?" "Why, name?"— Lonely lips of Palaeolithic men under the stars, the nomad night—the crackle of his campfire—

Aye, and the zing of his bow—

Cupid Bow me, I just sleep there, tight— When I wake up it's dawn, and gray, and frosty, and I just burrow under and sleep on— In the house Raphael is having another sleeping experience, Cody another, Evelyn another, the three children another, even the doggy another— It will all dawn on tender paradise, though.

101   I WAKE UP TO THE DELICIOUS LITTLE VOICES OF TWO LITTLE GIRLS and a little boy, "Wake up Jack, *breakfast is ready*." They sorta chant "breakfast is ready" because they've been told to but then they explore around my bushes a minute then leave and I get up and leave my pack right there in the straw grass of Autumn and go into the house to wash up—Raphael is up brooding at the corner chair— Evelyn is all radiant blonde in the morning. We grin at each other and talk— She'll say "Why didn't you sleep in the

kitchen couch?" and I'll say "O I love to sleep out in that yard, I always get such good dreams"— She says "Well it's nice to have people who have good dreams nowadays." She brings me my coffee.

"Raphael what are you brooding about?"

"I'm brooding about your good dreams," he says absently gnawing his fingernail.

Cody is all a-bustle in the bedroom jumping around changing the Television set and lighting cigarettes and running to the toilet to do his morning toilet between programs and scenes— "Oh isnt she darling?" he'll say as a woman comes on to advertise soap, and from the kitchen Evelyn will hear him and say something, "She must be an old *hag*."

"Hag, shmag," 'll say Cody, "I'll let her climb into my bed any tam."—"Oh poo," she'll say, and let it go at that.

All day long nobody likes Raphael, he gets hungry and asks me for food, I ask Evelyn for some jelly sandwiches, which I make— The children and I go off on a magic walk through the little Kingdom of The Cats—it's all prune trees, that I eat out of, and we go through roads and fields to a magic tree with a magic little hut under it built by a boy—

"What does he do in there I say?"

"Oh," says Emily, 9, "he just sits and sings."

"What does he sing?"

"Anything he likes."

"And," says Gaby, 7, "he is a very nice boy. You should see him. He's very funny."

"Yes, tee hee, he's very funny," says Emily.

"He is *very* funny!" says Timmy, 5, and so low to the ground down there holding my hand I'd forgot all about him— All of a sudden I'm wandering around in desolation with little angels—

"We'll take the secret trail."

"The short trail."

"Tell us a story."

"Nah."

"Where does this path lead?"

"It leads to the Kings," I say.

"*Kings?* Humph."

"Trapdoors and ooboons," I say.

"O Emily," announces Gaby, "isnt Jack *funny?*"

"He sure is," almost sighs Emily, dead serious.

Timmy says: "I have fun with my hands," and he shows us mystic mudra birds—

"And there's a bird singing in the tree," I advise them.

"Oh I hear *him*," says Emily—"I'm going to explore further."

"Well dont get lost."

"I am the giant in the tree," says Timmy climbing the tree.

"Hang on tight," I say.

I sit down and meditate and relax— All's well—the sun is warm through the branches—

"I am real high," says Timmy, higher.

"You sure are."

We walk back and on the road a dog comes up and rubs Emily's leg and she says "O, he is just like a person."

"He *is* a person," I say ("more or less").

We come back to the house, eating prunes, all glad.

"Evelyn," I say, "it's wonderful when you have three children I cant tell the difference between one or the other—they're all uniformly sweet."

Cody and Raphael are yelling bets in the bedroom to the TV game—Evelyn and I sit in the parlor and have one of our long quiet talks about religion— "It's all different words and phrases to express the same thing," says Evelyn balancing sutras and readings in her hands— We always talk about God. She has resigned herself to Cody's wildness because it's as it should be— One day she even rejoiced in the opportunity to thank God when nasty children threw eggs in her window: "I was thanking Him for the opportunity to forgive." She's a very pretty little woman and a topnotch mother— She's not con-

cerned one way or the other, though, about anything in princi-
ple— She really has achieved that cold void truth we're all
yakking about, and in practice she displays warmth—what
more you need? On the wall is the strange gold-lamé Christ
she did at age 14, showing a squirt of blood coming out of His
pierced side, very Medieval—and over the mantelpiece two
good portraits of her daughters, simply painted— In the afternoon she comes out in her bathingsuit, blonde and like it's
lucky when you live in California, and takes sunbath, while
I demonstrate swan dives and jack knifes to her and to the
kids—Raphael watches the ball game, wont swim—Cody goes
off to work— Comes back— It's a quiet Sunday afternoon in
the country. What's to get excited?

"Very very quiet, children," says Cody removing his brakeman clothes and getting in his bathrobe. "Supper, Maw." . . .
"Dont we ever get anything to eat around here?" he adds.

"Yeah," says Raphael.

And Evelyn comes up with a beautiful tasty supper that we
all eat in candlelight preceded by Cody and the children reciting
a Little Lord's Prayer about supper—*"Bless the food we are
about to eat"*— It's no longer than that, but they've got to recite
it all together, while Evelyn watches, I close my eyes, and Raphael wonders—

"This is crazy, Pomeray," he says finally— "And you really
really truly *believe* in all this stuff?—Awright that's a one way
to do it—" Cody puts on Okie Revival Healers on Television
and Raphael says "It's *bull*shit!"

Cody refuses to agree—finally Cody prays a little with the
Television audience where the healer asks for attention to pray,
Raphael is out of his mind— And in the evening here comes a
woman being interviewed for the $64,000 Question, and an-
nounces she's a butcher in the Bronx and you see her simple
serious face, maybe mincing a little, maybe not, and Evelyn and
Cody agree and hold hands (at their end of the bed, on pillows,
as Raphael sits Buddha at their feet and then me on the door

with a beer). "Dont you see it's just a simple sincere woman Christian," says Evelyn, "just good oldfashioned folks—well-behaved Christians"—and Cody agrees "That's it precisely, darling" and Raphael yells: "WHO WANTS TO HEAR HER, SHE KILLS PIGS!" And Cody and Evelyn are shocked out of their faces, both stare at Raphael wide-eyed, besides he's said it so suddenly, and what he's saying, they cant help seeing that it's true but it's got to be true, she kills pigs—

Now Raphael starts razzing Cody and feels much better— It turns into a funny night, we all get high on the moving programs we see, Rosemary Clooney singing so prettily, and Million Dollar Movies that we cant see because Cody'll jump and click on the piece of a photographed sports game, then jump to a voice, a question, jump on, cowboys shooting toy guns in little dusty hills, then bang he hits a big worried face in a panel show or You Ask The Questions—

"How can we see the show?" yells Raphael and Evelyn all the same time—

"But it's all one show, Cody knows what he's doing, he knows everything— Looka there Raphael, you'll see."

Then I go in the hall to investigate a sound (King Cody: "Go see what that is") and it's a big bearded Patriarch of Constantinople with a black suede jacket and glasses and Irwin Garden, emerging from the gloom of Russia beyond— It *frights* me to see it!—I jump back into the room, half out of scared and half telling Cody "Irwin is here"— Behind Irwin are Simon and Gia—Simon takes his clothes off and jumps in the moonlight swimmingpool, just like an ambulance driver of a Lost Generation cocktail party in 1923—I bring them out to the deck chairs by the moonlight shining pool to let Evelyn and Cody sleep—Gia is standing beside me, laughs, and walks off with her hands in her pockets, she's wearing pants—for a minute I think she's a boy—she slouches and smokes like a boy—one of the gang—Simon pushes her at me: "She loves ya, Jack, she loves ya."

I put on Raphael's dark glasses as we sit in the booth in a restaurant ten blocks down the highway— We order a whole pot of coffee, in the Silex—Simon piles dishes and toasts and cigarette butts in a tall dirty tier of Babel— The management is concerned, I tell Simon to stop "It's high enough"—Irwin sings a little tune:

> "Silent night
> holy night"—

Smiling at Gia.

Raphael broods.

We go back to the house, where I'll sleep in the grass, and they say goodbye to me at the driveway, Irwin saying "We'll sit in the yard and have a farewell."

"No," I say, "if you're gonna go go."

Simon kisses me on the cheek like a brother—Raphael gives me his dark glasses as a gift, after I give him back the cross, which he still insisted I keep— It's sad—I hope they dont see my weary goodbye face—the blear of time in our eyes—Irwin nods, that little simple friendly sad persuasive and encouraging nod, "Okay, we'll see you in Mexico."

"Goodbye Gia"—and I go to my yard and sit awhile smoking in a beach chair as they drive away—I stare into the swimmingpool like a college director, a movie director—like a Madonna in the bright water—surrealistic swimmingpool— then I look towards the kitchen door, the darkness there, and I see materialize fast a vision of a gang of dark men wearing silver rosaries and silver trinkets and crosses around their dark chests—it comes very fast then it goes.

How glittering are those shining things in the dark!

102 THE NEXT NIGHT AFTER I'VE DONE KISSING MAW AND THE BABIES goodbye, Cody drives me to the San Jose railyards.

"Cody, I had a vision last night of a gang of dark men like Raphael and David D'Angeli and Irwin and me all standing in the gloom with glittering silver crucifixes and neck chains over our dark dingy breasts!—Cody, Christ *will* come again."

"Why shuah," he nods suavely, handling the brake apparatus, "S'why I say—"

We park by the yards and watch the smoky engine scene and the new thrumming diesels and the yard office with bright lights, where we'd worked together in our ragged brakeman days—I am very nervous and keep wanting to get out of the car and out to that track to catch the Ghost as she pulls out but he says "O man they're only switchin now—wait till the engine's tied on—you'll see it, a great big four-unit sonumbitch'll get you flyin down that Los Angeles no time but Jack be careful keep a good handhold and remember what I always told you boy we been buddies a long time in this lonesome world I love you more than ever and I dont want to lose you son—"

I have a half pint of whisky for my whistling trip on the flat, offer him a shot— "That's a man's business you're going into now," he says, seeing I drink whisky now instead of wine, and shakes his head— When he does swing the car out back of a string of deadhead passenger cars and sees me hoist on my old freight train jacket with the sleeves bulging over my hands and the doleful POW stain left on the armband from some Korean War pre-history (jacket bought in strange torn Indian stores in El Paso) he stares to see me out of my city uniform and in my night-hopping uniform—I wonder what he thinks of me— He's all instructions and care. He wants me to hop on from the fireman's side but I dont like the six or seven rails I have to cross to get to the main (where Ghost Zipper'll be flipping)

—"I might trip in that dark—let's get on the engineer's side."
We have oldtime arguments about railroad methods, his are
long involved razorsharp Okie logics based on imaginary fears,
mine are silly innocent green mistakes based on actual Canuck
safety-measures—

"But on the engineer side man they'll *see* you, that big spot'll
fall right on ya!"

"I'll hide between the deadheads."

"No—come inside."

And like oldtime carstealing days there he is, a renowned
employee of the company, sneaking into the empty cars, looking around whitefaced like a thief not to be seen, in absolute
darkness—I refuse to haul my pack inside for nothing and
stand between the cars and wait— He whispers from a dark
window:

"Keep out of sight whatever you do!"

Suddenly the herder's across from us with his green lamp,
giving the come-on sign, the engine's blasted her BAW BAW
hiball, and suddenly the big yellow glare is right on me and I
back up against the bucklers shivering, Cody's scared me—
And instead of joining him in a shot of my whisky I'd ab-
stained, boasting "Never drink on duty," seriously meaning the
duty of grabbing moving grabirons and heaving onto a difficult
flatcar with heavy pack, if I'd have drank a shot I wouldnt
now be shivering, shaking— The herder sees me, again Cody's
terrified whisper:

"Keep out of sight!"

and the herder yells:

"Having trouble?" which then instantly I take either to mean,
"money trouble so have to hop freights?" or "cop trouble so
have to hide out of sight?" but I just liltingly yell out without
thinking "Yeah— O kay?" and the herder instantly replies:

"T's awright"

Then as the big train slowly turns into the main with ever
blindinger glare I add and yell "I'll catch her right here" to

indicate to the herder I'm just a good old talkative simple boy
not out to wreck open box doors and bash panels—Cody is a
dead silent lump huddled in the dark coach window, for all I
know down on the floor—

He'd told me "Jack be sure and wait till twenty cars go by
because you dont wanta be too close up front that engyne when
you go through those tunnels at Margarita you can suffocate
from the diesel fumes" but as I wait for the twenty to pass I get
scared as the momentum picks up, they lumber faster, I strike
out from my hiding place as the sixth or seventh passes and
wait for two more, heart pounding, make a few experimental
taps at passing nightsteel rungs (O Lord of our fathers what a
cold show is the show of things!) and finally I move up, trot,
get level with a front grabiron, grab a hold, trot with it, fear,
breathing, and haul up on board in one graceful easy nothing-
to-it waking-from-a-dream laughable move and there I am
standing on my flat waving back at forever invisible Cody
somewhere there, wave many times to make sure he's seen me
make it and wave, and it's goodbye old Cody . . .

—And all our fears were in vain, a dream, just like the Lord
said—and that's the way we'll die—

It's all night down the Coast I drink my whisky and sing to
the stars, remembering previous lifetimes when I was a prisoner
in dungeons and now I'm in the open air—down, down, as
prophesied in my Desolation Song, through the tunnels of
smoke, where red bandana to nose covers that, down to Obispo
where I see cool Negro hoboes on the car next to mine calmly
smoking cigarettes in the cabs of lashed trucks and right in
front of everybody! Poor Cody! Poor me! To L.A., where, in
the morning after washing with drip water from melting reefers
and trudging into town, I finally buy a ticket and am the only
passenger on the bus and as we pull out for Arizona and my
desert sleep there and my coming Mexico, suddenly another bus
is alongside us and I look and it's twenty young men sitting

among armed guards, on their way to prison, a prison bus, and two of them turn and see me and all I do is slowly lift my hand and slowly wave hello and look away as they slowly smile—

Desolation Peak, what more do you want?

BOOK TWO

PASSING
THROUGH

PART ONE

PASSING THROUGH MEXICO

1 AND NOW, AFTER THE EXPERIENCE ON TOP OF THE
MOUNTAIN where I was alone for two months
without being questioned or looked at by any single human
being I began a complete turnabout in my feelings about life—I
now wanted a reproduction of that absolute peace in the world
of society but secretly greedy too for some of the pleasures of
society (such as shows, sex, comforts, fine foods & drink), no
such things on a mountain—I knew now that my life was a
search for peace as an artist, but not only as an artist— As a
man of contemplations rather than too many actions, in the old
Tao Chinese sense of "Do Nothing" (Wu Wei) which is a way
of life in itself more beautiful than any, a kind of cloistral fervor
in the midst of mad ranting action-seekers of this or any other
"modern" world—

It was to prove that I was able to "do nothing" even in the
midst of the most roisterous society that I had come down from
the mountain in Washington State to San Francisco, as you saw,
where I spent that week of drunken "carrasals" (as Cody once

said) with the desolation angels, the poets and characters of the San Francisco Renaissance— A week and no more, after which (with a big hangover and some misgivings of course) I hopped that freight down to L.A. and headed for Old Mexico and a resumption of my solitude in a hovel in the city.

It's easy enough to understand that as an artist I need solitude and a kind of "do-nothing" philosophy that does allow me to dream all day and work out chapters in forgotten reveries that emerge years later in story form— In this respect, it's impossible, since it's impossible for everybody to be artists, to recommend my way of life as a philosophy suitable for everyone else— In this respect I'm an oddball, like Rembrandt— Rembrandt could paint the busy burghers as they posed after lunch, but at midnight while they slept to rest for another day's work, Old Rembrandt was up in his study putting on light touches of darkness to his canvases— The burghers didnt expect Rembrandt to be anything else but an artist and therefore they didnt go knocking on his door at midnight and ask: "Why do you live like this, Rembrandt? Why are you alone tonight? What are you dreaming about?" So they didnt expect Rembrandt to turn around and say to them: "You must live like I do, in the philosophy of solitude, there's no other way."

So in the same way I was searching for a peaceful kind of life dedicated to contemplation and the delicacy of that, for the sake of my art (in my case prose, tales) (narrative rundowns of what I saw and how I saw) but I also searched for this as my way of life, that is, to see the world from the viewpoint of solitude and to meditate upon the world without being imbroglio'd in its actions, which have by now become famous for their horror & abomination—I wanted to be a Man of Tao, who watches the clouds and lets history rage beneath (something which is no longer allowed after Mao & Camus?) (that'll be the day)—

But I never dreamed, and even in spite of my great determination, my experience in the arts of solitude, and my poverty's freedom—I never dreamed I'd be taken in too by the world's action—I didnt think it possible that— . . .

Well, on with the details, which is the life of it—

2 IT WAS OKAY AT FIRST, after I saw that prison bus outside L.A., even when the cops stopped me in the Arizona desert that night when I was hiking out under a full moon at 2 A.M. to go spread my sleepingbag in the sand outside Tucson— When they found out I had enough money for a hotel they wanted to know why I sleep in the desert— You cant explain to the police, or go into a lecture—I was a hardy son of a sun in those days, only 165 pounds and would walk miles with a full pack on my back, and rolled my own cigarettes, and knew how to hide comfortably in riverbottoms or even how to live on dimes and quarters— Nowadays, after all the horror of my literary notoriety, the bathtubs of booze that have passed through my gullet, the years of hiding at home from hundreds of petitioners for my time (pebbles in my window at midnight, "Come on out get drunk Jack, all big wild parties everywhere!")—oi— As the circle closed in on this old independent renegade, I got to look like a Bourgeois, pot belly and all, that expression on my face of mistrust and affluence (they go hand in hand?)— So that (almost) if it was now the cops were stopping me on a 2 A.M. highway, I almost expect they'd tip their caps— But in those days, only five years ago, I looked wild and rough— They surrounded me with two squad cars.

They put spotlights on me standing there in the road in jeans and workclothes, with the big woeful rucksack a-back, and asked:—"Where are you going?" which is precisely what they asked me a year later under Television floodlights in New York, "Where are you going?"—Just as you cant explain to the police, you cant explain to society "Looking for peace."

Does it matter?

Wait and see.

P.S. Imagine telling one thousand raving Tokyo snake-dancers in the street that you're looking for peace though you wont join the parade!

3   MEXICO—A GREAT CITY FOR THE ARTIST, where he can get cheap lodgings, good food, lots of fun on Saturday nights (including girls for hire)— Where he can stroll streets and boulevards unimpeded and for that matter at all hours of the night while sweet little policemen look away minding their own business which is crime detection and prevention— In my mind's eye I always remember Mexico as gay, exciting (especially at 4 P.M. when the summer thundershowers make people hurry over glistening sidewalks which reflect blue and rose neons, the hurrying Indian feet, the buses, raincoats, little dank groceries and shoe repairs, the sweet glee of the voices of the women and children, the stern excitement of the men who still look like Aztecs)— Candlelight in a lonely room, and writing about the world.

But I always get surprised when I arrive in Mexico to see I'd forgotten a certain drear, even sad, darkness, like the sight of some Indian man in a brown rust suit, with open collared white shirt, waiting for a Circumvalacion bus with a package wrapt in newspaper (El Diario Universal), and the bus is loaded with sitters and strap hangers, dark green gloom inside, no lights, and will take him bouncing over mud hole backstreets for a half hour to the outskirts of the adobe slums where a smell of dead animals and of shit lingers forever— And to glory in any big description of the bleakness of that man is not fair, is, in sum, immature—I wont do it— His life is a horror— But suddenly you see a fat Indian old lady in a shawl holding a little girl by the hand, they're going into the *pasteleria* for bright pastries! The little girl is glad— It's only in Mexico, in the sweetness and innocence, birth and death seem at all worthwhile . . .

4   I CAME INTO TOWN ON THE BUS FROM NOGALES and immediately rented a rooftop adobe hut, fixed it up to my liking, lit a candle and started to write about the coming-down-from-the-mountain and the wild week in Frisco.

Meanwhile, downstairs in a dismal room, my old 60-year-old friend Bull Gaines provided me with companionship.

He too lived peacefully.

Slow doing of things, all the time, there he stands hunch-backed and skinny going through interminable searches through coat, drawer, suitcase, under rugs and newspapers for his endlessly hidden stashes of junk— He says to me "Yessir, I like to live peacefully too—I guess you got your art, as you say, altho I doubt it" (looking at me out of the corner of his glasses to see how I take the joke) "but I got my junk— As long as I got my junk I'm satisfied to stay home and read H. G. Wells' *Outline of History*, which I've re-read about a hunnerd times I guess— Satisfied with a little Nescafé at my side, an occasional ham sandwich, my newspaper and a good night's sleep with a few goofballs, hm-m-m-m-m"—

"Hm-m-m-m" is where, on finishing a sentence, Gaines always lets out that low junkey groan, tremulous and as though some kind of secret laughter or pleasure that he completed his sentence well, with a sock, in this case "with a few goofballs"— But even when he says "I think I'll go to bed" he adds that "Hm-m-m-m" so you realize it's just his way of singing his saying— Like, imagine an Indian Hindu singer doing just that to a beat of gourds and Dravidian tambourines. Old Guru Gaines, in fact, the first of many characters I was to know from that innocent time to now— There he goes poking through his bathrobe pockets looking for a lost *codeinetta*, forgetting he already ate it the night before— He has the typical bleak junkey dresser, with a full length mirror on each creaky door, inside of which hang battered coats from New York with the lints of the pockets strong enough to boil down in a spoon after 30 years of drug addiction—"In many ways," he says, "there's a great resemblance between the dope fiend so called and the artist so called, they like to be alone and comfortable provided they have what they want— They dont go mad running around looking for things to do 'cause they got it all inside, they can sit for hours without movin. They're sensitive, so called, and dont turn away from the study of good books. And look at those Orozcos I cut out of a Mexican magazine and put on my wall. I study those pictures all the time, I love em— M-m-m-m-m."

He turns, tall and wizardly, preparing to begin a sandwich. With long thin white fingers he plucks a slice of bread out with the dexterity you might expect from tweezers. He then puts ham on the bread in a meditation that takes almost two minutes, carefully arranged and rearranged. Then he puts the other bread over it and carries the sandwich to his bed, where he sits on the edge, eyes closed, wondering if he can eat it and going hm-m-m-m. "Yes sir," he says, starting to search in his bedside drawer again for an old cotton, "the dope fiend and the artist have lots in common."

5 HIS ROOM HAD WINDOWS OPENING ON THE VERY SIDE-WALK OF MEXICO with thousands of hepcats and children and yakking people going by— From the street you saw his pink drapes, looking like the drapes of a Persian pad, or like a Gypsy's room— Inside you saw the battered bed sinking in the middle, itself covered with a pink drape, and his easy chair (an old one but his long Daddy legs stuck out comfortably from it and rested almost level with the floor)— And then the "burner" which he used to heat water for his shaves, just an old electric heat lamp upside down or something (I really cant remember the outlandish, the perfect, the really simple arrangement only a junkey brain could figure out)— Then the sad pail, in which the old invalid pee'd, and had to go upstairs every day

to empty in the only toilet, a chore I did for him whenever I lived nearby, as I'd done twice now— Whenever I went upstairs with that pail as the women of the house watched I always remembered the marvelous Buddha saying: "I recall that during my five hundred previous rebirths, I had used life after life to practice humility and to look upon my life humbly as though it was some saintly being called upon to suffer patiently"— More direct than that, I knew that at my age, 34, it were better to help an old man than to gloat in lounges—I thought of my father, how I helped him to the toilet when he was dying in 1946. Not to say that I was a model sufferer, I've done more than my share of idiotic sinning and stupid boasting.

There was a Persian feeling in Bull's room, of an old Guruish Oriental Minister of the Court temporarily taking drugs in a distant city and knowing all the time that he is doomed to be poisoned eventually by the King's wife, for some old obscure evil reason he wont tell about except "Hm-m-m-m."

When the old Minister rode in cabs with me as he went downtown to connect for his morphine, he always sat right next to me and let his bony knees flop against mine— He never as much as laid a hand on my arm when we were in the room, even to make a point or make me listen, but in the backs of cabs he became mock senile (I think to fool the cabdrivers) and let his together-knees keel over on mine, and even slumped like a destitute old horseplayer low in the seat and against my elbow— Yet when we got out of the cab and went down the sidewalk, he'd walk six or seven feet away from me, a little behind, as though we were not together, which was another trick of his to fool watchers in his land of exile ("Man from Cincinnata," he said)— The cabdriver sees an invalid, the sidewalk populaces see an old hipster walking alone.

Gaines was the now fairly famous character who stole an expensive overcoat every day of his life for twenty years in New York and pawned it for junk, a great thief.

Said "When I got to Mexico the first time some bastard stole my watch—I went into a watch store and gestured with one hand while I picked (hooked) (wired) with the other and walked out with a watch, *even!*—I was so mad I took chances but the guy never saw me—I was bound to get my watch back— Aint nothin an old thief hates *worse*—"

"Takes some doing to steal a watch in a *Mexican store!*" I said.

"Hm-m-m-mm."

Then he'd send me on errands: to the corner store for boiled ham, sliced by machine by the Greekish proprietor who was a typical tightfisted middleclass Mexican merchant but sorta liked Old Bull Gaines, called him "Señor Gahr-va" (almost like Sanskrit)— Then I'd have to go traipsing to Sears Roebuck on Insurgentes Street for his weekly *News Report* and *Time* Magazine, which he read from cover to cover in his easy chair, high on morphine, sometimes falling asleep in the middle of a sentence in the Last Luce Style but waking up to finish it from right where he left off, only to fall asleep again right on the next sentence, sitting there nodding as I dreamed into space in the company of this excellent and quiet man— In his room, of exile, though dismal, like a monastery.

6   I'D ALSO HAVE TO GO TO THE SUPER MERCADO and buy his favorite candies, chocolate triangles full of cream, refrigerated— But when it came to going to the laundry he came with me just to josh the old Chinese laundryman. He'd always say: "Opium today?" and make the sign of the pipe. "No tellee me where."

And the little shriveled opium addict Chinaman would always say "No savvy. No no no."

"Them Chinese are the most tightlipped junkeys in the world," says Bull.

We get in a cab and go downtown again, he's leaning weakly with a weak grin against me— Says "Tell the driver to stop at every drugstore he sees and you run out and buy a tube of *codeinettas* in each one, here's fifty pesos." Which we do. "No sense burnin down lettin any of these druggists get wise. Then they cant put the finger on you." And on the way home he always tells the driver to stop at Cine So and So, the nearby movie house, and walks the extra block so no cabby ever knows where he lives. "When I go across the border nobody can put the finger on me because I put the finger up my ass."

What a strange vision, an old man walking across the border with his finger up his behind?

"I get a rubber finger that doctors use, I fill it with junk, I put it in— Nobody can put the finger on me because I got the finger up my ass. I always come back across the border at another town," he adds.

When we return from a cab trip the landladies greet him with respect, "*Señor* Garv-ha! Si?" He unlocks his padlock, unlocks the key lock under it, and pushes into his room, which is dank. No amount of smoky kerosene heat can help. "Jack, if you really wanted to help an old man you'd come with me to the West Coast of Mexico and we'd live in a grass hut and smoke the local opium in the sun and raise chickens. That's the way I'd like to end my days."

His face is thin, with white hair combed sleekly back with water like a teenager. He wears purple slippers when he sits in his easy chair, high on junk, and begins to re-read *The Outline of History*. He lectures me all day on all kinds of subjects. When it's time for me to go up to my hut on the roof and write he says "Hm-mmm, it's still early, why dont you stay around awhile—"

Outside the pink curtains the city hums and croons with cha-cha night. And there he is mumbling on: "Orphism is one subject should interest you, Jack—"

And I sit there with him, when he falls asleep for a minute I've got nothing to do but think, and often I thought: "Who on earth, claiming to be sound of mind, could call this gentle old

guy a *fiend*—thief or no thief, and where are the thieves . . .
as thievish . . . as your respectable day-by-day business . . .
thieves?"

7 EXCEPT FOR THE TIMES WHEN HE WAS VIOLENTLY ILL from
lack of his medicine, and I had to run errands for him
into the slums where connections like Tristessa or the Black
Bastard sat behind pink drapes of their own, I had a quiet time
on my roof. I especially joyed in the stars, the moon, the cool
air up there three flights from the musical street. I could sit on
the edge of the roof and look down and listen to the cha-chas
of the taco jukeboxes. I had my little wines, lesser drugs of my
own (for excitement, for sleep, or for contemplation, and when
in Rome) —and with the day done and all the washerwomen
sleeping I had the whole roof to myself. I paced up and down
in my soft desert boots. Or I went inside the hut and brewed
another pot of coffee or cocoa. And I went to sleep well, and
woke up to bright sun. I wrote a whole novel, finished another,
and wrote a whole book of poetry.

Once in a while poor old Bull struggled up the winding iron
stairs and I made him spaghetti and he'd fall asleep on my bed
a moment and burn a hole in it with his cigarette. He'd wake
up and start a lecture on Rimbaud or something. His longest
lectures were on Alexander the Great, the Epic of Gilganish,
Ancient Crete, Petronius, Mallarmé, Current Affairs such as the
Suez Crisis of that time (ah, the clouds didnt notice no Suez
Crisis!), old days in Boston Tallahassee Lexington and New
York, his favorite songs, and stories about his old buddy Eddy
Corporal. "Eddy Corporal walk into the same clothing store
every day, talk and joke with the salesmen and walk out with a
suit doubled up inside his belt buckle I dont know how he did
it, some weird trick he had. Man was an oil burner type junkey.
Bring him five grains and he shoots it up, *all*."

"What about Alexander the Great?"

"Only general I know of rode in front of his cavalry swinging a sword" and he's asleep again.

And that night I see the Moon, Citlapol in Aztec, and even draw a picture of it on the moonlit roof with house paint, blue and white.

8 AS AN EXAMPLE, THEREFORE, OF MY PEACE AT THE TIME. But events were brewing.

Take another look at me to get the story better (now I'm getting drunk):—I am a widow's son, at the time she is living with relatives, penniless. All I have is that summer's mountain lookout pay converted into pitiful $5 traveler's checks—and the big gooky rucksack full of old sweaters and wraps of peanuts and raisins in case I get caught starving and all such hoboish shifts—I'm 34, regular looking, but in my jeans and eerie outfits people are scared to look at me because I really look like an escaped mental patient with enough physical strength and innate dog-sense to manage outside of an institution to feed myself and go from place to place in a world growing gradually narrower in its views about eccentricity every day— Walking thru towns in the middle of America I got stared at weirdly—I was bound to live my own way— The expression "nonconformity" was something I'd vaguely heard about somewhere (Adler? Eric Fromm?)— But I was determined to be *glad!*—Dostoevsky said "Give man his Utopia and he will deliberately destroy it with a grin" and I was determined with the same grin to *disprove* Dostoevsky!—I was also a notorious wino who exploded anywhere anytime he got drunk— My friends in San Francisco said I was a Zen Lunatic, at least a Drunken Lunatic, yet sat with me in moonlight fields drinking and singing— At age 21 I had been discharged from the Navy as a "schizoid personality" after telling the Navy doctors I could not take discipline— Even I cant understand how to explain myself— When my books became notorious (*Beat Generation*) and interviewers tried to ask me questions, I just answered with everything I could think of—I had no guts to tell them to leave me alone, that, as Dave Wain later said (a great character at Big Sur) "Tell 'em you're busy interviewing yourself"— Clinically, at the time of the beginning of this story, on the roof over Gaines, I was an Ambitious Paranoid— Nothing could stop me from writing big books of prose and poetry for nothing, that is, with no hope of ever having them published—I was simply writing them because I was an "Idealist" and I believed in "Life" and was going about justifying it with my earnest scribblings— Strangely enough, these scribblings were the first of their kind in the world, I was originating (without knowing it, you say?) a new way of writing about life, no fiction, no craft, no revising afterthoughts, the heartbreaking discipline of the veritable fire ordeal where you cant go back but have made the vow of "speak now or forever hold your tongue" and all of it innocent go-ahead confession, the discipline of making the mind the slave of the tongue with no chance to lie or re-elaborate (in keeping not only with the dictums of Dichtung Warheit Goethe but those of the Catholic Church my childhood)—I wrote those manuscripts as I'm writing this one in cheap nickel notebooks by candlelight in poverty and fame— *Fame* of self— For I was Ti Jean, and the difficulty in explaining all this and "Ti Jean" too is that readers who havent read up to this point in the earlier works are not filled in on the background— The background being my brother Gerard who said things to me before he died, though I dont remember a word, or maybe I do remember a few (I was only four)— But said things to me about a *reverence* for life, no, at least a reverence of the *idea* of life, which I translated as meaning that life itself is the Holy Ghost—

That we all wander thru flesh, while the dove cries for us, back to the Dove of Heaven—

So I was writing to honor that, and had friends like Irwin Garden and Cody Pomeray who said I was doing okay and

encouraged me though I was really too sweetly insane to listen
to even them, I woulda done it anyway— What is the *Light*
that bears us down— The Light of *Falling*— The Angels are
still *Falling*— Some kind of explanation like that, hardly the
thing for an N.Y.U. Seminar, kept me up so I could *fall* with
man, with Lucifer, to Buddha's eccentric humility ideal—
(After all, why did Kafka write he was a Bug this big)—

And also dont think of me as a simple character— A lecher,
a ship-jumper, a loafer, a conner of older women, even of
queers, an idiot, nay a drunken baby Indian when drinking—
Got socked everywhere and never socked back (except when
young tough football player)— In fact, I dont even know *what*
I was— Some kind of fevered being different as a snowflake.
(Now talking like Simon, who comes up ahead.) In any case, a
wondrous mess of contradictions (good enough, said Whitman)
but more fit for Holy Russia of 19th Century than for this modern America of crew cuts and sullen faces in Pontiacs—

"Did I say all?" said Lord Richard Buckley before he died.

So the brew was this:—the boys were coming down to Mexico City to join me. The Desolation Angels again.

9 IRWIN GARDEN WAS AN ARTIST LIKE ME, the author of the
great original poem "Howling," but he never needed
solitude the way I did, was continually surrounded by friends
and sometimes dozens of acquaintances who would come to his
door in beards rapping softly in the night—Irwin was never
without his own immediate entourage, as you saw, beginning
with his companion and lover Simon Darlovsky.

Irwin was queer and said so in public, thus precipitating
tremors from Philadelphia to Stockholm in polite business suits
and football coach pants— In fact, on the way down to join me
(I am a non-queer) in Mexico Irwin had just removed all his
clothes at a poetry reading in Los Angeles when a heckler'd
yelled "Whattaya mean, *naked?*" (meaning the way he used

the expressions "naked beauty" or "naked confessions" in his poems)— So he undressed and stood there nekkid before men and women, but a pretty cool crowd of ex-Parisian expatriates and surrealists however—

He was coming down to join me in Mexico with Simon, the blond Russianblood boy of 19 who originally was not queer but had fallen in love with Irwin and Irwin's "soul" and poetry, so accommodated his Master—Irwin was herding two other boys before him to Mexico, one was Simon's kidbrother Lazarus (15½) and the other Raphael Urso of New York a great young poet (the same who wrote "Atom Bomb" later and *Time* Magazine reprinted a piece of it to show how ridiculous but everybody loved it)—

First off, by the way, the reader should know that as an author I'd got to know many homosexuals—60% or 70% of our best writers (if not 90%) are queers, for man sex, and you get to meet them all and converse and swap manuscripts, meet them at parties, readings, everywhere— This doesnt prevent the nonhomosexual writer from *being* a writer or from associating with homosexual writers— Same was the case with Raphael, who "knew everybody," as I did—I could give you a list a mile long of the homosexuals in the arts but there's no point in making a big *tzimis* about a relatively harmless and cool state of affairs— Each man to his own tastes.

Irwin wrote and said they were arriving within a week so I hurried up and finished my novel in a burst of energy just in time for the date of their arrival, but they were two weeks late because of a silly stopover en route in Guadalajara to visit a dull woman poetess. So I ended up sitting on the edge of my *tejado* rooftop looking down on the street for the Four Marx Brothers to come walking down Orizaba.

Meanwhile Old Gaines was also anxious for their arrival, years of exile (from family and law in U.S.A.) had made him lonely and besides he'd known Irwin very well in the old days on Times Square when (1945) Irwin and I and Hubbard and

Huck used to hang around the hustler bars picking up on drugs. In those days Gaines was in the height of his heyday as coat thief and used to lecture us on anthropology and archaeology sometimes in front of Father Duffy's statue, tho no one listened. (It was I who'd finally hit on the great idea of *listening* to Gaines, tho Irwin had too, even in the early days.)

You can see by now Irwin is a weird cat. In my days on the road with Cody he'd followed us to Denver and everywhere bringing his apocalyptic poems and eyes. Now that he was a famous poet he was mellower, doing the things he'd always wanted to do, traveling even more, writing less though, but pulling in the skeins of his purpose—you might almost say "Mother Garden."

I daydreamed of their arriving at night as I looked down from my roof edge, of what I'd do, throw a pebble, yell, mystify them somehow, but I never dreamed of their actual arrival in bleak reality.

10 I WAS SLEEPING, I'd been up all night scribbling poems and blues by candlelight. I usually slept till noon. The door scraped open and in walked Irwin alone. Back in Frisco old Ben Fagan the poet had told him: "Write to me when you get to Mexico and tell me the first thing you noticed about Jack's room." He wrote back: "Baggy pants hanging from nails on the wall." He stood there looking around the room. I rubbed my eyes and said "Damnit you're two weeks late."

"We slept at Guadalajara and dug Alise Nabokov the strange poet. How weird her parrots and her pad and her husband— How are you Jacky?" and he laid his hand tenderly on my shoulder.

It's strange what long trips people take in their lifetimes, Irwin and I who'd started as friends on the Columbia campus in New York now facing each other in a dobe hovel in Mexico

City, the histories of people oozing out like long worms across the plaza of the night— Back and forth, up and down, sick and well, it makes you wonder what the lives of our ancestors were also like. "What were the lives of our ancestors?"

Irwin says "Giggling in rooms. Come on, get up, at once. We're going downtown right away to dig Thieves' Market. Raphael has been writing big mad poems all the way down from Tijuana about the doom of Mexico and I wanta show him some real doom, for sale in the market. Did you ever see the broken armless dolls they sell? And old rickety wormeaten Aztec wooden statues you cant even carry—"

"Used can openers."

"Strange old shopping bags from 1910."

We were at it again, every time we got together the conversation became a poem swinging back and forth except when we had stories to tell. "Old curds of milk floating in pea soup."

"What about your pad?"

"The first thing, yah, we have to rent one, Gaines says we can get the one downstairs cheap and there's a kitchen."

"Where are the boys?"

"All in Gaines' room."

"And Gaines' talking."

"Gaines is talking and telling them all about Minoan Civilization. Let's go."

In Gaines' room Lazarus the 15-year-old weirdy who never speaks sat listening to Gaines with honest innocent eyes. Raphael was slumped in the old man's easy chair enjoying the lecture. Gaines lectured from the edge of the bed with a necktie between his teeth as he pulled tight to make a vein pop or make *something* happen to give himself a needle shot of morphine. Simon stood in the corner like a saint in Russia. It was a great occasion. There we were all in the same room.

Irwin received a shot from Gaines and lay down on the bed under the pink drapes and sighed. Laz the child received one of Gaines' soft drinks. Raphael thumbed thru *The Outline of His-*

tory and wanted to know Gaines' theory of Alexander the Great. "I wanta be like Alexander the Great," he yelled, he somehow always yelled, "I wanta dress in rich jeweled general outfits and swing my sword at India and go glimpsing at Samarkand!"

"Yeah," I said, "but you dont wanta have your first lieutenant buddy murdered or have a whole village of women and children killed!" The argument started. I remember now, the first thing we did was argue about Alexander the Great.

Raphael Urso I liked quite well, too, in spite or perhaps because of a previous New York hassle over a subterranean girl, as I say. He respected me tho he was always talking behind my back, in a way, tho he did that to everybody. For instance he whispered to me in the corner "That Gaines is a *grippling*."

"What you mean?"

"The day of the grippling is come, the hunchback creep . . ."

"But I thought you liked him!"

"Look at my *poems*—" He showed me a notebook full of scribblings in black ink and drawings, excellent eerie drawings of starved children drinking from a big fat Coca-Cola bottle with legs and teats and a hank of hair labeled "Mexico Doom." "There's *death* in Mexico—I saw a windmill turning death this way—I dont *like* it here—and your old Gaines is a *grippling*."

As an example. But I loved him too because of his utterdust broodings, the way he stands on a streetcorner looking down, at night, hand to brow, wondering where to go in the world. He dramatized the way we all felt. And his poems did that best of all. That kind of old invalid Gaines was a "grippling" was merely Raphael's cruel but honest horror.

As for Lazarus, when you ask him "Hey Laz, are you okay?" he just looks up with innocent level blue eyes and a slight almost cherubic hint of a smile, sad, and doesnt need to reply. If anything, he reminded me more of my brother Gerard than anyone in the world. He was a tall slumping teenager with pimples but a handsome profile, completely helpless if it hadnt been for the care and protection of his brother Simon. He couldnt count money too well, or ask directions without getting involved, and least of all get a job or even understand legal papers and even newspapers. He was on the verge of catatonia like an older brother now in an institution (an older brother who had been his idol, by the way). Without Simon and Irwin to herd him along and protect him and provide him with bed and board, the authorities would have netted him at once. Not that he was cretinous, or unintelligent. He was extremely brilliant in fact. I saw letters he wrote at age 14 before his recent spell of silence: they were perfectly normal and better than average writings, in fact sensitive and better than anything I could have written at 14 when I also was an innocent introverted monster. As for his hobby, drawing, he was better at that than most artists alive today and I always knew he was really a great young artist pretending to be withdrawn so people would leave him alone, also so people wouldnt ask him to get a job. Because often I've seen the strange side glance he gives me which is like the look of a fellow or a brother conspirator in a world of busybodies, say—

Like the look that says: "I know, Jack, that you know what I'm doing, and you're doing the same thing in your way." For Laz, like myself, also spent whole afternoons staring into space, doing nothing whatever, except maybe brush his hair, mostly just listening to his own mind as tho he too was alone with his Guardian Angel. Simon was usually busy, but during his semiannual "schizophrenic" spells he withdrew from everybody and also sat in his room doing nothing. (I'm telling you, these were real Russian brothers.) (Actually partly Polish.)

11 WHEN IRWIN HAD FIRST MET SIMON, Simon pointed to trees and said "See, they're waving at me and bowing hello." Besides all that weird interesting native mysticism, he was really an angelic kid and for instance now in Gaines' room

he immediately undertook to empty the old man's pail upstairs, even rinsed it, came down nodding and smiling at the curious landladies (the landladies hung out in the kitchen boiling pots of beans and heating tortillas)— He then cleaned up the room with broom and dustpan, moved us all sternly aside, wiped clean the wall table and asked Gaines if he wanted anything at the store (almost with a bow). His relation to me was, like he'd bring me two fried eggs on a plate (later) and say "Eat! Eat!" and I'd say no I wasn't hungry and he'd yell "Eat, you brat!! If you dont watch out we'll have a revolution and make you work in the mills!"

So between Simon, Laz, Raphael and Irwin there was plenty of fantastically funny action going on, especially when we all sat down with the head landlady to hassle over the rent of their new apartment which was to be on the ground floor with windows opening on the tile courtyard.

The landlady was actually a European lady, French I think, and since I'd told her the "poets" were coming she sat somewhat politely and ready to be impressed on the couch. But if her vision of poets was of some caped de Musset or elegant Mallarmé—just a bunch of hoods. And Irwin haggled her down 100 pesos or so with arguments about no hot water and not enough beds. She said to me in French: *"Monsieur Duluoz, est ce qu'ils sont des poètes vraiment ces gens?"*

"Oui madame," answered Irwin himself in his most elegant tone, assuming the role he called "the well groomed Hungarian," *"nous sommes des poètes dans la grande tradition de Whitman et Melville, et surtout, Blake."*

"Mais, ce jeune là." She indicated Laz. *"Il est un poète?"*

"Mais certainement, dans sa manière" (Irwin).

"Et bien, et vous n'avez pas l'argent pour louer à cinq cents pesos?"

"Comment?"

"Five hundret pesos—*cinquo ciente pesos.*"

"Ah," says Irwin leaping into Spanish, "*Sí, pero el departamiento n'est pas assez grande* for the whole lot."

She understood all three languages and had to give in. Meanwhile, that settled, we all rushed out to dig Thieves' Market downtown but as we emerged on the street some Mexican kids drinking Cokes gave out a long low whistle at us. I was enraged because not only I was subjected to this now in the company of my motley weirdy gang but I didnt think it was fair. Yet Irwin, that international hepcat, said "That's not a whistle addressed at queers or anything you're thinking in your paranoia—it's a whistle of admiration."

"Admiration?"

"Certainly" and several nights later sure enough the Mexicans rapped on our door with Mescals in their hands, wanting to drink and toast, a bunch of Mexican medical students in fact living two flights above us (more later).

We started off down Orizaba Street on our first walk in Mexico City. I walked with Irwin and Simon in front, talking; Raphael (like Gaines) walked far to the side alone, along the curb, brooding; and Lazarus stomped along in his slow monster walk a half a block behind us, sometimes staring at the centavos in his hand and wondering where he could get an ice cream soda. Finally we turned around and found him stepping into a fish store. We all had to go back and get him. He stood there before giggling Mexican girls holding out his hand with the centavos in it saying "Ice crim suda, I wanta ice crim suda" in his funny New York accent, muttering at them, looking at them innocently.

"Pero, señor, no comprendo."

"Ice crim suda."

When Irwin and Simon gently led him out, once again as we resumed our walk he fell behind half a block and (as Raphael now cried sadly) "Poor Lazarus—wondering about pesos!" "Lost in Mexico wondering about pesos! What will ever happen to poor Lazarus! So sad, so *sad*, life, life, who can ever *stand* it!"

But Irwin and Simon walked gaily ahead to new adventures.

12 SO MY PEACEFULNESS IN MEXICO CITY WAS AT AN END tho I didnt mind too much because my writing was done for awhile but it was really too much the next morning when I was sleeping sweetly on my solitary roof Irwin bursting in "Get up! We're going to Mexico City University!"

"What do I care about Mexico City University, let me go sleep!" I was dreaming of a mysterious world mountain where everybody and everything was, why bother?

"You fool," said Irwin in one of the rare instances when he let slip what he really thought of me, "how can you sleep all day and never see anything, what's the sense of being alive?"

"You invisible bastard I can see right thru you."

"Can you really?" suddenly interested sitting on my bed. "What does it look like?"

"It looks like a lot of little Gardens are going to travel prating to the grave, talking about wonders." It was our old argument about Samsara vs. Nirvana tho the highest Buddhist thinking (well, Mahayana) stresses that there is no difference between Samsara (this world) and Nirvana (the no-world) and maybe they're right. Heidegger and his "essents" and his "nothing." "And so if that's the case," says I, "I'm going back to sleep."

"But Samsara is just the X-mystery mark on the surface of Nirvana—how can you reject this world, ignore it like you try, poorly really, when it is the surface of what you want and you should study it?"

"So already I should go riding on bummy buses to a silly university with a heart-shaped stadium or something?"

"But it's a big international famous university full of ignus and anarchists with some of the students from Delhi and Moscow—"

"So screw Moscow!"

Meanwhile here comes Lazarus up on my roof carrying a chair and a big bundle of brand new books he'd had Simon buy for him yesterday (quite expensive) (books on drawing and art)— He sets up his chair near the roof's edge, in the sun, as the washerwomen giggle, and starts reading. But even as Irwin and I are still arguing about Nirvana in the cell he gets up and goes back downstairs, leaving the chair and the books right there—and never looked at them again.

"This is insane!" I yell. "I'll go with you to show you the Pyramids of Teotihuacan or something interesting, but dont drag me to this silly excursion—" But I end up going anyway because I want to see what they're all going to do next.

After all, the only reason for life *or* a story is "What Happened Next?"

13 IT WAS A MESS IN THEIR APARTMENT BELOW. Irwin and Simon slept in the doublebed in the only bedroom, Lazarus slept on a thin couch in the livingroom (in his usual manner, with just one white sheet drawn up and completely around and over him like a mummy), and Raphael across the room on a shorter couch, curled up with all his clothes on in a little sad dignified heap.

And the kitchen was already littered with all the mangoes, bananas, oranges, garbanzos, apples, cabbages and pots we'd bought yesterday in the markets of Mexico.

I always sat there with a beer in my hand watching them. Whenever I rolled a joint of pot they all smoked at it without a word, though.

"I want roastbeef!" yelled Raphael waking up on his couch. "Where's the meat around here? Is it all Mexico death meat?"

"We're going to the university first!"

"I want meat first! I want garlic!"

"Raphael," I yell, "when we come back from Irwin's university I'll take you to Kuku's where you can eat a huge T-bone steak and throw the bones over your shoulder like Alexander the Great!"

"I want a banana," says Lazarus.

"You ate em all last night, ya maniac" says Simon to his brother yet arranging his bed neatly and tucking in the sheet.

"Ah, charming," says Irwin emerging from the bedroom with Raphael's notebook. He quotes out loud: " 'Heap of fire, haylike universe sprinting towards the gaudy eradication of Swindleresque ink?' Wow, how great that is—do you realize how *fine* that is? The universe is on fire and a big swindler like Melville's confidence man is writing the history of it on inflammable gauze or something but in *self eradicating ink* on top of all that, a big hype fooling everybody, like magicians making worlds and letting them disappear by themselves."

"Do they teach that at the university?" I say. But we go anyway. We take a bus and go out for miles and nothing happens. We wander around a big Aztec campus talking. The only thing I clearly remember is my reading an article by Cocteau in a Paris newspaper in the reading room. The only thing that really happens therefore *is* that self eradicating magician of gauze.

Back in town I lead the boys to Kuku's restaurant and bar on Coahuila and Insurgentes. This restaurant had been recommended to me by Hubbard years ago (Hubbard up ahead in the story) as being a fairly interesting Viennese restaurant (in all the Indian city) run by a Viennese fellow of great vigor and ambition. They had a great 5-peso soup full of everything that could feed you for an entire day, and of course the enormous T-bone steaks with all the trimmings for 80 cents American money. You ate these huge steaks in candlelit dimness and drank mugs of good barrel beer. And at the time I'm writing about, the Viennese blond proprietor did indeed rush around eagerly and energetically to see that everything was just right. But only last night (now, in 1961) I went back there and he was asleep in a chair in the kitchen, my waiter spat in a corner of the diningroom, and there was no water in the restaurant bathroom. And they brought me an old sick steak badly cooked, with potato chips all over it—but in those days the steaks were still good and the boys dove in trying to cut them up with butter knives. I said "Like I say, like Alexander the Great, eat that steak with your hands" so after a few furtive looks around in the half darkness they all grabbed their steaks and tore at them with ronching teeth. Yet they all looked so humble because they were in a restaurant!

That night, back at their apartment, rain splattering in the courtyard, suddenly Laz had a fever and went to bed— Old Bull Gaines came over for his daily evening visit wearing his best stolen tweed jacket. Laz was suffering from a weird virus that many American tourists get when they come to Mexico, not exactly dysentery either but something undetermined. "Only one sure cure," says Bull, "a good shot of morphine." So Irwin and Simon discussed it anxiously and decided to try it, Laz was in misery. Sweat, cramps, nausea. Gaines sat on the edge of the sheeted bed and tied up his arm and popped a sixteenth of a grain in, and in the morning Lazarus jumped up completely well after a long sleep and rushed out to find an ice cream soda. Which makes you realize the restrictions on drugs (or, *medicine*) in America comes from doctors who dont want people to heal themselves—

Amen, Anslinger—

14   AND THAT WAS THE REALLY GREAT DAY when we all went to the Pyramids of Teotihuacan— First we had our picture taken by a photographer in the park downtown, the Prado— We all stand there proud, me and Irwin and Simon

standing (today I'm amazed to see I had broad shoulders then), and Raphael and Laz kneeling in front of us, like a Team.

Ah sad. Like the old photographs all brown now of my mother's father and his gang posing erect in 1890 New Hampshire— Their mustaches, the light on their heads—or like the old photographs you find in abandoned Connecticut farmhouse attics showing an 1860 child in a crib, and he's already dead, and *you're* really already dead— The old light of 1860 Connecticut enough to make Tom Wolfe cry shining on the little baby's proud be-bustled brown lost mother— But our picture really resembles the old Civil War Buddy Photographs of Thomas Brady, the proud captured Confederates glaring at the Yankees but so sweet there's hardly any anger there, just the old Whitman sweetness that made Whitman cry and be a nurse—

We hop a bus and go rattling to the Pyramids, about 30, 20 miles, the fields of pulque flash by—Lazarus stares at strange Mexican Lazaruses staring at him with the same divine innocence, but with brown eyes instead of blue.

When we reach there we start walking to the pyramids in the same straggling way, Irwin and Simon and me in front talking, Raphael off to the side musing, and Laz 50 yards behind clomping like Frankenstein. We start climbing the stone steps of the Pyramid of the Sun.

All fireworshipers worshiped the sun, and if they gave a person to the sun and ate the person's heart, they ate the Sun. This was the Pyramid of horrors where they bent the victim back over a stone sink and cut his beating heart out with one or two movements of a heart-clipper, raised the heart to the sun, and ate it. Monstrous priests not even hep to effigy. (Today in modern Mexico children eat candy hearts and skulls at Halloween.)

Your Indiana scarecrow is an old Thuringian phantasy . . .

When we got to the top of the Pyramid I lit up a marijuana cigarette so we could all examine our instincts about the place. Lazarus reached out his arms to the sun, straight up, altho we hadnt told him what it was up there, or what to do. Altho he looked goofy doing this I realized he knew more than any one of us.

Not to mention your Easter bunny . . .

He reached up his arms straight and actually clawed for the sun for thirty seconds. Me thinkin I'm beyond all this but a big *Buddha* sit crosslegged at the top, put my hand down, and immediately feel a biting sting. "My God I been bit by a scorpion at last!" but I look down at my bleeding hand and it's only tourist broken glass. So I wrap the hand up in my red neckerchief.

But sitting up there high and thoughtful I began to see something about Mexican history I'd never find in books. The runners come panting that all Texcoco is in warlike rouge again. You can see all Lake Texcoco like a warning glittering on the horizon south, and west of that the huddled monster hint of a greater kingdom inside the crater:—the Kingdom of Azteca. Ow. The Teotihuacan priests propitiate gods by the millions and invent them as they go along. Two monstrous empires only 30 miles away visible to the naked eye from the top of their own flimsy funeral pyre. They therefore in dread turn their eyes north to the perfect smooth mountain behind the pyramids with its perfect grassy top where no doubt (as I sat there realizing) lived in a hut an aged sage, the actual King of Teotihuacan. They climbed to his hut in the evening for advice. He waved a feather as tho the world meant nothing and said "Oh," or more likely "Oops!"

I told this to Raphael who thereupon framed his eyes with far seeing general's hand and looked at the blink of the Lake. "By God you're right, they musta shit in their pants up here." Then I told him of the mountain in back and that Sage but he said "Some goatherd eccentric Oedipus." Meanwhile Lazarus was still trying to grab the sun.

Little kids came up to sell us what they said were genuine relics found under the ground: little stone heads and bodies. Some craftsmen were making perfect raggedy looking imitations in the village below where, at dusk's *obscura*, boys played sad basketball. (Gee, just like Durrell and Lowry!)

"Let's investigate the caves!" yells Simon. Meanwhile an American tourist woman arrives at the top and tells us to sit still while she takes color photographs of us. I'm sitting cross-legged with a bandaged hand turning to look at waving Irwin and grinning others as she snaps it: she later sends the picture to us (address given) from Guadalajara.

We go down to investigate the caves, the alleys under the Pyramid, me and Simon hide in one dead-end cave giggling and when Irwin and Raphael come groping by we yell "Whoo!" Lazarus, tho, he's in his element stomping up and down silently. You couldnt scare him with a ten-foot sail in his bathroom. The last time I'd played ghosts was during the war at sea off the coast of Iceland.

We then emerge from the caves and cross a field near the Pyramid of the Moon that has hundreds of big ant villages each one clearly defined by a heap and a heap of activity all around it, Raphael deposits a small twig in one of the Spartas and all the warriors rush up and carry it away so's not to disturb the Senator and his broken bench. We put still another bigger twig and those crazy ants carry it away. For a whole hour, smoking pot, we lean over and examine these ant villages. We dont hurt one citizen. "Look that guy hurrying from the edge of town carrying that piece of dead scorpion meat to the hole—" Down the hole he goes for meat's winter. "Sposin we had a jar of honey, would they think it was Armageddon?"

"They'd have big Mormon prayers before doves."

"And build tabernacles and sprinkle em with ant piss."

"*Really* Jack—maybe they'd just store the honey and forget all about *you*" (Irwin).

"Are there ant hospitals underneath the mound?" The five of us leaned over the ant village wondering. When we built little mounds the ants immediately started the great state tax-paid task of removing them. "You could squash the whole village, make assemblies rage and pale! just with your foot!"

"While the Teo priests goofed up there these ants were just beginning to dig a real underground super market."

"It must be great by now."

"We could take a shovel and investigate all their corridors— What pity God must have not to step on them" but no sooner said than done, Lazarus in walking away from us back to the caves has left his monstrous shoe tracks in a straight absent-minded line across half a dozen earnest Roman villages.

We follow Lazarus walking around the ant villages carefully. I say: "Irwin, didnt Laz hear what we said about the ants—for an hour?"

"Oh *yah*," gaily, "but now he's thinking about something else."

"But he's walking right thru, right on their villages and heads—"

"Oh yah—"

"With his big huge shoes!"

"Yah, but he's thinking about something or other."

"What?"

"I dont know—if he had a bicycle it'd be worse."

We watched Laz stomping straight across the Moon Field to his goal, which was a rock to sit on.

"He's a monster!" I cried.

"Well you're a monster yourself when you eat meat—think of all the little happy bacterias have to take a gruesome trip thru the cave of your acid entrails."

"And they all turn into hairy knots!" adds Simon.

15 SO, AS LAZARUS WALKS THROUGH VILLAGES, so God walks thru our lives, and like the workers and the warriors we worry like worrywarts to straighten up the damage as fast as we can, tho the whole thing's hopeless in the end. For

God has a bigger foot than Lazarus and all the Texcocos and Texacos and Mañanas of tomorrow. We end up watching a dusk basketball game among Indian boys near the bus stop. We stand under an old tree at the dirtroad crossing, receiving dust as it's blown by the plains wind of the High Plateau of Mexico the likes of which none bleaker maybe than in Wyoming in October, late October . . .

p.s. The last time I was in Teotihuacan, Hubbard said to me "Wanta see a scorpion, boy?" and lifted up a rock— There sat a female scorpion beside the skeleton of its mate, which it had eaten— Yelling "Yaaaah!" Hubbard lifted a huge rock and smashed it down on the whole scene (and tho I'm not like Hubbard, I had to agree with him that time).

16 HOW UNBELIEVABLY BLEAK the actual world really is after you've dreamed of gay whore streets and gay dancing nightclubs but you end up as Irwin and Simon and I did, the one night we went out alone, staring among the cold and bony rubbles of the night— Tho there may be a neon at the end of the alley the alley is incredibly sad, in fact impossible— We'd started out in more or less sports attire, with Raphael in tow, to go dancing at the Club Bombay but the moment broody Raphael smelled those dead dog streets and saw the soiled uniforms of beat *mariachi* singers, heard the whine of the mess of insane horror which is your modern city street night he went home in a cab alone, saying "Shit on all this, I want Eurydice and Persephone's horn—I dont wanta go mudtrampling thru all this sickness—"

Irwin has a persevering grim gaiety which leads him on leading me and Simon to the soiled lights— In the Club Bombay are a dozen crazy Mexican girls dancing at a peso a throw with their pelvics tossed right into the men, sometimes holding the men by the pants, as an unbelievably melancholy orchestra trumpets out blue songs from the bandstand of sorrows— The trumpeters have no expression, the mambo drummer is bored, the singer thinks he's in Nogales serenading the stars but's only buried in the slums' slummiest hole agitating mud from our lips— Mudlipped whores just around the slimy corner of the Bombay are standing ranked against pockholed walls full of bedbugs and cockroaches calling out to parades of lechers who prowl up and down trying to see what the girls look like in the dark—Simon is wearing a bright tan sportcoat and goes dancing romantically with his pesos all over the floor, bowing to his black haired companions. "Doesnt he look romantic?" says Irwin sighing in the booth where we're drinking Dos Equis.

"Well he's not exactly the image of the gay American tourist living it up in Mexico—"

"Why *not?*" says Irwin annoyed.

"The world is so goofy everywhere—like you imagine that when you get to Paris with Simon there'll be raincoats and Arc de Triomphes of brilliant sadness and all the time you'll be yawning at bus stops."

"Well, Simon's having a good time." Yet Irwin cant entirely disagree with me as we roam up and down the dark whore street and he shudders to see the glimpses of filth inside the cribs, behind pink rags. He wont take a girl and go in. Simon and I are bound to make it. I find a whole group of whores sitting like a family on the doorstep, old ones protecting young ones. I motion for the youngest one, fourteen. We go in as she yells *"Agua caliente"* to a subsidiary hot water whore girl. In behind flimsy curtains you hear creaking platforms where a thin mattress's been laid on rotten boards. The walls leak oozy doom. As soon as a Mexican girl emerges from a curtain and you see the girl swinging her legs back to the floor in a flash of dark thighs and cheap silk, my little girl leads me in and starts washing unceremoniously in the squatting position. *"Tres peso,"* she says sternly, making sure to get her 24 cents before we start. When we do start she's so small you cant find her for at least a minute of probing. Then the rabbits run, like American high school kids going a mile a minute . . . the only way for the young, actually. But she is not particularly interested either. I find myself losing myself in her without one iota of trained responsibility holding me back, like, "Here I am completely free as an animal in a crazy Oriental barn!" and thus I go, nobody *cares*.

But Simon in his strange Russian eccentricity has meanwhile picked out a fat old whore battered from Juarez on down no doubt since the days of Diaz, he goes in the back with her and we actually (from the sidewalk) hear great giggles going on as Simon evidently is joking with all the ladies. Ikons of the Virgin Mary burning in holes in the wall. Trumpets around the corner, the awful smell of old fried sausages, brick smell, damp brick, mud, banana peels—and over a broken wall you see the stars.

A week later poor Simon had gonorrhea and had to get penicillin shots. He hadnt bothered to clean up with the special salve medicine, as I had.

17 HE DIDNT KNOW THAT NOW AS WE LEFT THE WHORE STREET and just strolled up the main drag of beat (poor) Mexican nightlife, Redondas Street. All of a sudden we saw an amazing sight. A little young swishy fairy of about 16 hurried past us holding the hand of a ragged barefoot Indian boy of 12. They kept looking over their shoulders. I looked back and noticed the police were watching them. They turned sharply and hid in a dark sidestreet door. Irwin was in ecstasy. "Did you *see* the older one, just like Charley Chaplin and the Kid twinkling down the street hand in hand in love, chased by the big butch fuzz— Let's *talk* to them!"

We approached the strange pair but they hurried away scared. Irwin had us cruise up and down the street till we bumped into them again. The cops were out of sight. The older kid saw something sympathetic in Irwin's eyes and stopped to talk, asking for cigarettes first. In Spanish, Irwin gleaned that they were lovers but homeless and the police were persecuting them specially for some bugged reason or one jealous cop. They slept in empty lots in newspapers or sometimes in paper posters torn from signs. The older one was just a swishy kid but with none of your American googly gushiness of such types, he was stern, simple, serious, with a dedicated sort of courtdancer professionalism about his queerness. The poor child of 12 was only an Indian boy with big brown eyes, an orphan probably. He just wanted Pichi to get him an occasional tortilla and show him where to sleep in safety. The older, Pichi, wore makeup, purple eyelids and all and quite gaudy but he kept looking more like a performer in a show than anything else. They hurried away down the blue worm alley as the cops reappeared—we saw them twinkling away, two pairs of feet, towards dark shacks of the closed garbagey market. They made Irwin and Simon look like ordinary people.

Meanwhile whole gangs of Mexican hipsters mill around, most of them with mustaches, all broke, quite a few of Italian and Cuban descent. Some of them even write poetry, as I found later, and have their regular Master-Disciple relationship just like in America or London: you see the head cat in his topcoat explaining some obscure point about history or philosophy as the others listen smoking. For smoking pot they go into rooms and sit till dawn wondering why they cant sleep. But unlike American hipsters they all have to go to work in the morning. They're all thieves but they seem to steal eccentric objects that strike their fancy unlike the professional thieves and pickpockets who also mill around Redondas. It's an awful street, a street of nausea, actually. The music of trumpets everywhere makes it even more awful somehow. In spite of the fact that the only definition of a "hipster" is that he is a person who can stand on certain street corners in any foreign big city in the world and connect for pot or junk without knowing the language, it all makes you want to go back to America to Harry Truman's face.

18

WHICH IS WHAT RAPHAEL ALREADY PAINFULLY WANTED TO DO, agonized more than any of us. "Oh God," he wept, "it's like a dirty old rag somebody finally used to wipe up spit in the men's room! I'm going to fly back to New York, *spit* on this! I'm going downtown and get me a rich room in a hotel and wait for my money! I aint going to spend my life studying garbanzos in a garbage can! I want a castle with a moat, a velvet hood over my Leonardo head. I want my old Benjamin Franklin rocking chair! I want velvet drapes! I wanta ring for the butler! I want moonlight in my hair! I want Shelley and Chatterton in my chair!"

We were back at the apartment listening to this as he packed. While we roamed the street he'd come back and chatted with poor old Bull all night and also received a taste of morphine. ("Raphael's the smartest of you all," said Old Bull the next day, pleased.) Meanwhile Lazarus had stayed home alone doing God knows what, listening, probably, staring and listening in the room. One look at that poor kid trapped in this crazy dirty world and you wondered what would happen to all of us, all, all thrown to the dogs of eternity in the end—

"I wanta die a better death than this," continued Raphael as we listened attentively. "Why aint I in a loft in an old church in Russia composing *hymns* on *organs!* Why do I have to be the grocer's boy? It's *creepy!*" He pronounced it New Yorkese almost *cweepy.* "I aint lost my way! I'm gonna get what I want! When I pee'd in beds when I was a kid and tried to hide the sheets from my mother I knew it was all gonna be creepy! The sheets fell in the creepy street! I looked at my poor sheets way down there over a creepy fire hydrant!" We were all laughing now. He was warming up to his evening's poem. "I want Moorish ceilings and roastbeefs! We havent even eaten in one fancy restaurant since we came here! Why cant we even go ring the Cathedral bells at Midnight!"

"All right," said Irwin, "let's go tomorrow to the Cathedral on the Zocalo and ask to ring the bells." (Which they did, the next day, the three of them, they got permission from the porter and grabbed big ropes and swung and dangled off big bonging songs I probably heard on my roof as I read alone the Diamond Sutra in the sun—but I wasnt there and dont know exactly what else happened.)

Now Raphael begins to write a poem, suddenly he's stopped talking as Irwin lit a candle and as we all sit relaxing in low tones you can hear the crazy scratchety scratch of Raphael's pen racing over the page. You can actually *hear* the poem for the first and last time in the world. The scratchings sound just like Raphael's yellings, with the same rhythm of expostulation and bombast booms of complaint. But in the scratchety scratch you also hear the somehow miraculous making of words into English from the head of an Italian who never spoke English in the Lower East Side till he was seven. He has a great mellifluous mind, deep, with amazing images that are like a daily shock to all of us when he reads us the daily poem. For instance, a night ago he'd read H. G. Wells' history and immediately sat down with all the names of a spate of history in mind and strung it off delightfully: something about Parthians and Scythian paws that made you *feel* history, paw and claw and all, instead of just understanding it. When he scratched out poems in our candlelight silence none of us ever spoke. I realized what a dopey crew we were, by dopey I mean so innocent of the way it's said by the authorities that life should be lived. Five grown American men and scratchety scratch in a candlelight room. But when he was through I'd say "All right now read what you wrote."

"Oh Hawthorne's baggy trousers, the unmendable hole . . ." And you see poor Hawthorne, even tho he wears that awkward crown, tailorless in a New England blizzard attic (or something), in any case, tho it may not amaze the reader, it amazed us, even Lazarus, and we did love Raphael. And we were all in the same boat, poor, in a foreign land, our art rejected more or less, crazy, ambitious, finally childlike. (It was only later we became famous and our childlikeness was insulted, but later.)

Upstairs, clearly down the court, you could hear the pretty hamonizing of the Mexican mad students who'd whistled at us, guitars and all, country campo love songs and then suddenly a dopey attempt at Rock n Roll probably for our benefit. In answer Irwin and I began singing Eli Eli, low soft and slow. Irwin is really a great Jewish cantor with a clear tremulous voice. His real name is Avrum. The Mexican guys were dead quiet listening. In Mexico people sing in big gangs even after midnight with the windows open.

19 THE NEXT DAY RAPHAEL MADE ONE LAST EFFORT to cheer himself up by buying a huge roastbeef in the Super Mercado, sticking it full of garlic cloves, and shoving it in the oven. It was delicious. Even Gaines came over and ate with us. But the Mexican students were all suddenly at the door with bottles of mescal (unrefined tequila) and Gaines and Raphael sneaked off while the rest of us bleakly entertained. The head man of the gang though was a stalwart handsome goodnatured Indian in a white shirt who insisted on everything being amenable and fun. He must have made a fine doctor. Some of the others had mustaches from middleclass *mestizo* homes, and one final student who would certainly never become a doctor, kept passing out on every drink, insisted on taking us to a whorehouse and when we got there they were too expensive and he was thrown out for drunkenness anyway. We stood in the street again, looking everywhichaway.

So we moved Raphael down to his fancy hotel. It had big vases, rugs, Moorish ceilings and American women tourists writing letters in the lobby. Poor Raphael sat there in a big oaken chair looking around for a benefactress who would take him home to her penthouse in Chicago. We left him musing

about the lobby. The next day he got a plane for Washington
D.C. where he was invited to stay at the home of the Poetry
Consultant of the Library of Congress, where I would see him
strangely soon.

I see that vision of Raphael, the dust is blowing across the
street corner, his deep brown eyes inside high cheekbones
under a crop of fawn hair, or like the hair of a satyr, really like
the hair of a regular American cornerstone kid of the cities . . .
which way is Shelley? which way Chatterton? how come there
are no funeral pyres, no Keats, no Adonaïs, no wreathéd
horse & cherubs? God knows *what* he's thinking. ("Fried
shoes," he however later told *Time* Magazine, but wasn't being
serious.)

20　IRWIN AND SIMON AND I ACCIDENTALLY WOUND UP
IN A CHARMING AFTERNOON at Lake Xochimilco,
the Floating Gardens of Paradise I'd say. A group of Mexicans
from the park took us there. First we lunched on turkey *molé*
at the waterside booth. Turkey *molé* is seasoned chocolate sauce
over turkey, very good. But the proprietor was also selling raw
pulque (unrefined mescal) and I got drunk. But there's no better
place in the world to get drunk than the Floating Gardens,
naturally. We hired a barge and got poled down dreamy canals
full of floating flowers and whole little islands moving
around— Other barges floated past us poled by the same grave
ferrymen with whole families celebrating weddings aboard, so
as I sat there crosslegged with the pulque at my shoes suddenly
a floating heaven music came and went at my side, complete
with pretty girls, children and old handlebar mustaches. Then
women in low kyak boats rowed up to sell flowers. You could
hardly see the boat for all the flowers. There were areas of
dreamy reeds where the women paused to rearrange bouquets.
All kinds of *mariachi* bands passed north and south mingling
several tunes at once in the soft sunny air. The boat itself felt

like a lotus. When you pole a boat there's smoothness you dont get with oars. Or motors. I was smashed drunk on the pulque (as I say, unrefined juice of the cactus, like green milk, awful, a penny a glass.) But I waved at passing families. For the most part I sat in ecstasy feeling I was in some Buddhaland of Flowers and Song. Xochimilco is what's left of the lake that was filled over to build Mexico City on. You could imagine what it was in Aztec times, the barges of courtesans and priests in the moonlight . . .

At dusk that day we played piggyback in the yard of a nearby church, tug of war. With Simon on my back we managed to topple over Pancho, who carried Irwin.

On the way back we watched the fireworks of November 16 at the Zocalo. When the Mexicans have fireworks everybody stands there yelling OOO! being showered finally by huge pieces of falling fire, it's insane. It's like war. Nobody cares. I saw a flaming wheel pirouetting down right on the crowd across the square. Men rushed away pushing baby carriages to safety. The Mexicans kept lighting madder and bigger stationary affairs that roared and hissed and exploded all over. Finally they sent up a barrage of final boombooms that were beautiful, ending with the great God finale Bomb, Plow! (& everybody goes home.)

21 ARRIVING AT MY ROOM ON THE ROOF after all these frantic days I'd go to bed with a sigh. "When they leave I'll get back on the beam again," quiet cocoas at midnight, long sleeps— Yet also I couldn't imagine what I was going to do anymore anyway. Irwin sensed it, has always directed me in some ways, said "Jack you've had all your peace in Mexico and on the mountain, why dont you come to New York with us now? Everybody's waiting for you. Your book'll be published eventually, within a year even, you can see Julien again, get a

pad or a room in the Y or anything. It's time for you to *make it!*" he yelled. "After all!"

"Make *what?*"

"Get published, meet everybody, make money, become a big international traveling author, sign autographs for old ladies from Ozone Park—"

"How you going to New York?"

"We'll simply check the paper for share the car rides— There's one in the paper today. Maybe we can even go thru New Orleans—"

"Who wants to see that dreary old New Orleans."

"Oh you're a fool—*I've never seen New Orleans!*" he yelled. "I *wanta* see it!"

"So you can tell people you saw it?"

"Never mind all that. Ah Jack," tenderly, putting his head against mine, "poor Jacky, tortured Jacky—all bugged and alone in an old maid's cell— Come with us to New York and visit museums, we'll even go back and walk over the Columbia campus and tweak old Schnappe in the ear— We'll present Van Doren with our plans for a new world literature— We'll camp on Trilling's doorstep till he gives us back that quarter." (Talking about college professors.)

"All that literary stuff is just a drag."

"Yes but it's also interesting in itself, a big charming camp we can dig— Where's your old Dostoevsky curiosity? You've become so *whiney!* You're coming on like an old sick junkey sitting in a room in nowhere. It's time for you to wear berets and suddenly amaze everybod' who's forgotten you're a big international author even celebrity— We can do anything we *want!*" he yelled. "Make movies! Go to Paris! Buy islands! Anything!"

"Raphael."

"'Yes but Raphael doesnt moan like you he's lost his way, he's *found* his way—imagine now he'll be hosted in Washington and meet Senators at cocktail parties. It's time for the poets to *influence* American Civilization!" Garden, like a contemporary

American novelist who claimed he was a two-fisted leftwing hipster leader and hired our Carnegie Hall to announce such, in fact like certain Harvard scholars in high places, was a scholar interested in *politics* eventually tho he made his mystic point about visions of eternity he'd seen—

"Irwin if you'd really seen a vision of eternity you wouldnt care about influencing American Civilization."

"But that's just the point, it's where I at least have some authority to speak instead of just stale ideas and sociological hangups out of handbooks—I have a Blakean message for the Iron Hound of America."

"Whoopee—and whattaya do next?"

"I become a big dignified poet people listen to—I spend quiet evenings with my friends in my smoking jacket, perhaps—I go out and buy everything I want in the supermarket—*I have a voice in the supermarket!*"

"Okay?"

"And you can come and have your publications arranged *at once,* those incompetents are stalling out of just stupid confusion. 'Road' is a big mad book that will change America! They can even make money with it. You'll be dancing naked on your fan mail. You can look Boisvert in the eye. Big Faulkners and Hemingways will grow thoughtful thinking of you. It's *time!* See?" He stood holding his arms out like a symphony conductor. His eyes were fixed on me hypnotically mad. (Once he'd said to me seriously, on pot, "I want you to listen to my speeches like across Red Square.") "The Lamb of America will be raised! How can the East have any respect for a country that has no prophetic Poets! The Lamb must be raised! Big trembling Oklahomas need poetry and nakedness! Airplanes must fly for a reason from one gentle heart to an open heart! Namby pamby dillydallyers in offices have to have somebody give them a rose! Wheat's got to be sent to India! New hip classical doll scenes can take place in bus stations, or in the Port Authority, or the Seventh Avenue toilet, or in Missus Rocco's parlor in East *Bend* or something" shaking his shoulder with his old New York hipster hunch, the neck convulsive . . .

"Well, maybe I'll go with ya."

"You might even get yourself a girlfriend in New York like you used to do—Duluoz, the trouble with you is you havent a girl in years. Why do you think that you have grimy black hands that shouldnt go on the white shiny flesh of chicks? They all wanta be loved, they're all human trembling souls scared of you because you glare at them because you're afraid of them."

"That's right Jack!" pipes in Simon. "Gotta give those girls a little workout boy, sonny boy, hey sonny boy!" coming over and rocking my knees.

"Is Lazarus going with us?" I ask.

"Sure. Lazarus can take big long walks up Second Avenue and look at the pumpernickel breads or help old men into the Library."

"He can read papers upsidedown in the Empire State Building" says Simon still laughing.

"I can gather firewood on the River," says Lazarus from his bed with the sheet up to his chin.

"What?" We all turn to hear him again, he hasnt spoken in 24 hours.

"I can gather firewood on the river," he concludes closing down the word "river" as tho it was a pronouncement that none of us need discuss anymore. But he repeats it one last time . . . "on the river." "Firewood," he adds, and suddenly there he is giving me that humorous side-glance meaning he's just pulling all our legs but wont say it's so.

PART TWO

PASSING THROUGH NEW YORK

22

IT WAS A HORRIBLE TRIP. We contacted, that is Irwin contacted in a perfect businesslike efficient way this Italian from New York who was a language teacher in Mexico but looked exactly like a Las Vegas gambler, a Mott Street hood, in fact I wondered what he was doing in Mexico really. He had an ad in the paper, a car, a Puerto Rican passenger already contracted, and the rest of us could fit all around with all the shebang's baggage on the roof of the car. Three in front and three in back, knee to knee in horror for three thousand miles! But no other way—

The morning we left (I forgot to mention that Gaines had been sick several times and sent us downtown on junk errands that were difficult and dangerous . . .) Gaines was sick the morning we left but we tried to rush away without being noticed. Actually of course I wanted to go in and say goodbye to him but the car was waiting and there was no doubt he wanted me to go downtown get his morphine (he was short again). We could hear him coughing as we passed the street window with the sad pink drape, 8 o'clock in the A.M. I couldn't resist just sticking my head against the hole in the window saying: "Hey Bull, we're going now. I'll see ya—when I come back—I'll be back soon—"

"No! No!" he cried in the trembling sick voice he had when he tried to convert his addiction withdrawal pain to barbiturate torpor, which left him a mess of tangled bathrobes and sheets and spilled piss. "No! I want you to go downtown do somethin for me— It wont take long—"

Irwin tried to assuage him thru the window but Gaines started crying. "An old man like me, you shouldnt leave me alone. Not like this especially not when I'm sick and cant raise my hand to find my cigarettes—"

"But you were all right before Jack and I got here, you'll be all right again."

"No, no, call Jack! Dont leave me like this! Dont you remember all the old days we had together and the times I fixed you up with those pawn tickets and laid money on ya— If you leave me like this this morning I'm goinna *die!*" he cried. We couldnt see him, just hear him from his pillow. Irwin called Simon to yell something at Gaines and together we actually ran away in shame and miserable horror, with our luggage, down the street—Simon looked at us whitefaced. We swirled around the sidewalk in confusion. But the cab we'd already hailed was waiting and the natural cowardly thing to do was just pile right in and head for New York. Simon came after, jumping in. It was a "Whoo" of relief but I never knew how Gaines got out of that particular day's sickness. But he did. But you'll see what happened, later . . .

The driver was Norman. When we were all seated in Norman's car he said the springs would bust before New York or even before Texas. Six men and a pile of bags and rucksacks on the roof tied all around with rope. A miserable American scene again. So Norman started the motor, raced it, and like those dynamite trucks in movies about South America he started rolling at one mile per hour, then 2, then 5, as we all held our breath of course, but he got her going to 20, then 30, then out on the hiway to 40 and 50 and we suddenly all realized it was just a long car ride and we'd just breeze on hiways in a good old American machine.

So we settled down to the trip beginning with the rolling of joints of pot, to which the young Puerto Rican passenger Tony didnt object—he was on his way to Harlem. Strangest of all suddenly this big gangster Norman starts singing arias in a piercing tenor voice as he drives along, the which goes on all the way all night to Monterey. Irwin joins him from beside me in the back singing arias I never knew he knew, or singing the notes of Bach's Toccata and Fugue. I'm so befoggled by all these years of traveling and suffering sadness I almost forget to realize Irwin and I used to listen to Bach's Toccata and Fugue with earphones in the Columbia Library.

Lazarus sits in front and the Puerto Rican gets interested in interviewing him, finally so does Norman realizing what a weird kid he is. By the time we get to New York three days and nights later he is sternly advising Lazarus to exercise a lot, drink milk, walk straight and join the Army.

But at first there's hostility in the car. Norman comes on rough with us thinking we're a bunch of faggy poets. As we hit the mountains at Zimapan we're all high and suspicious anyway on tea. But he makes it worse. "Now you all have to consider me the captain and absolute master of this ship. You just cant sit there lettin me do all the work. Cooperate! When we come to a left curve, we all together singing lean to the left, and vicie vercie with the right coives. You got that?" At first I laugh thinking it's funny (also very practical for the tires as he explained) but no sooner we hit the first mountain curve and we (the boys) lean over, Norman and Tony aint even leaning over at all but just laughing. "Now the right!" says Norman, and again the same silly thing.

"Hey how *come* you aint leaning!" I yell.

"I've got my *driving* to think about. Now you boys just do what I say and everything'll be fine and we'll get to New York," a little peevish now that someone had spoken out. I was scared of him at first. In my pot paranoia I suspected he and Tony were crooks who would just hold us up en route for whatever we had, which wasnt much though. As we went along and he grew more annoying it was Irwin (who never fights) finally saying:

"Oh shut up"

& all the car was cool thereon.

23   IT EVEN BECAME A GOOD TRIP and it was even almost fun at the border at Laredo to have to unpack all the incredible heap on the roof including Norman's bicycle and show it to guards in steel rimmed spectacles who saw they had no chance to check everything in such a hopeless clutter of junk.

The wind was whipping keen in the Rio Grande Valley, I felt great. We were in Texas again. You could smell it. The first thing I ordered was ice cream softies for all of us, nobody objecting at all. And we rolled to San Antonio in the night. It was Thanksgiving Day. Sad signs announced Turkey dinner in the cafés of San Antone. We didnt dare stop for that. The American road restless runners are terrified of relaxing even a minute. But outside San Antonio at 10 P.M. Norman was too exhausted to go on and stopped the car near a dry riverbottom to nap in the front seat while Irwin and I and Laz and Simon took out our sleepingbags and spread them on the 20° frosty ground. Tony slept in the backseat. Irwin and Simon slithered somehow into Irwin's new Mexican-bought blue French sleepingbag with the hood, a slim bag and not even long enough for their feet. Lazarus was to get into my Army sleepingbag with me. I let him get in first and then slithered in where I could work the zipper over my neck. There was no way of turning over without a signal.

The stars were cold and dry. Sagebrush with frost, the smell of cold winter cow dung. But that air, that divine Plains air, I actually fell asleep on it and in the middle of our sleep I made a motion to turn over and Laz went right over. It was strange. It was also uncomfortable because you couldnt move at all except to turn over en masse. But we were doing all right and it was Norman and Tony who couldnt stand the cold in the car who woke us all up at 3 A.M. to resume with the heater on the run.

Motley dawn in Fredericksburg or someplace which I'd crossed a thousand times like.

24   THOSE LONG DRONING RUNS ACROSS A STATE'S AFTERNOON with some of us sleeping, some of us talking, some of us eating sandwiches of despair. Whenever I ride like that I always wake up from a nap with the sensation that I'm being driven to Heaven by the Heavenly Driver, no matter who he is. There's something strange about one person guiding the car while all the others dream with their lives in his steady hand, something noble, something old in mankind, some old trust in the Good Old Man. You come out of a drowsy dream of sheets on a roof and there you are in the Arkansas piny barrens zipping along at 60, wondering why and looking at the driver, who is stern, who is still, who is lonesome at the controls.

We arrived at Memphis in the evening and ate a good meal at last in a restaurant. It was then Irwin got mad at Norman and I was afraid Norman would stop the car and fight him in the road: some argument about Norman being a pest all the way which was really no longer true: so I said "Irwin you cant talk to him like that, he has a right to get sore." So I established in the car that I was a big bumbling bullshitter who didnt want fights for any reason whatever. But Irwin wasnt mad at me either and Norman became silent on the subject. The only time

I ever really fought a man was when he was socking my dou-
bled-up buddy Steve Wadkovsky against the car at night,
beaten but kept beating him, a big guy. I rushed in and engaged
him across the road with rights and lefts some of which con-
nected but all light like taps, or slaps, to his back, where his
father dragged me off in dismay. I cant defend myself, only
friends. So I didnt want Irwin to fight Norman. Once I got mad
at Irwin (1953) and said I'd kick him in the pants but he said "I
can beat you up with my mystic strength," which scared me.
Anyway Irwin doesnt take any bull from anybody, while me,
I'm always sitting there with my Buddhist "vow of kindness"
(vowed alone in the woods) taking abuse with pent up resentment that never comes out. But a man, hearing the Buddha (my
hero) (my *other* hero, Christ is first) never answered abuse,
came up to the sighing Bhagavat and spit in his face. Buddha is
reported to have said: "Since I cant use your abuse, you may
have it back."

In Memphis Simon and Laz the brothers suddenly engaged
in horseplay at the gas station sidewalk. Annoyed, Lazarus gave
Simon one push and sent him skittering half way across the
street, strong as an ox. One big Russian Patriarch Push that
amazed me. Laz is six feet tall and wiry but as I say walks bent
over, like an old 1910 hipster, rather like a farmer in the city.
(The word "beat" comes from the old Southern countryside.)

In West Virginia at dawn Norman suddenly made me drive.
"You can do it, dont worry, just drive, I'll relax." And it was
that morning I really learned how to drive. With one hand on
the bottom of the steering wheel I somehow managed perfectly
all kinds of curves right and left with going-to-work cars
squeezing in on a narrow two lane. For the right curve the right
hand, for the left the left. I was amazed. Everybody in the back
seat was asleep, Norman talked to Tony.

I felt so proud of myself that I bought a quart of port wine
in Wheeling that evening. That was the night of nights on the
trip. We all got high and sang a million simultaneous arias as

Simon drove grimly (Simon the old ambulance driver) clear to Washington D.C. at dawn, over a superhiway thru the woods. When we rolled into town Irwin yelled and shook Lazarus to wake up to see the Nation's capital. "I wanta sleep."

"No wake up! you'll never see Washington again probably! Look! The White House that big white dome with the light! Washington's monument, that big needle in the sky—"

"Old mint," said I as we rolled by it.

"This is where the President of the U.S. lives and does all his thinking about what America's going to do next. Wake up—sit like this—look—big Justice Departments where they rule on censorship—" Lazarus looked out nodding.

"Big empty Negroes standing by mailboxes," I said.

"Where's the Empye State Building," says Laz. He thinks Washington is in New York. In fact he probably thinks Mexico is a circle around.

25 THEN WE GO BARRELING TO THE NEW JERSEY TURN-PIKE in the eye-dry morning of transcontinental automobile horror which is the history of America from pioneer wagon to Ford— In Washington Irwin has called the Poetry Consultant of the Library of Congress to ask about Raphael, who hasnt arrived yet (waking up the man's woman at dawn) (but poetry is poetry)— And as we drive the Turnpike Norman and Tony up front with Laz are both earnestly advising him about how to live now, how not to goof, how to get a hold of himself good— As for going in the Army Laz says "I dont wanta be told what to do" but Norman insists we all have to be told what to do, but I disagree because I'm just like Lazarus about the Army or the Navy too—(if I can get away with it, if *he* can, by diving into the night of the self and becoming obsessed with one's own solo Guardian Angel)— Meanwhile Irwin and Simon are now completely and finally exhausted and sit erect in the back seat with me (all's well, toot) but with their

heads fallen down sweaty and suffering on their breasts, the
mere sight of them, of their weariness-slicked unshaven sweaty
countenances with lips poofed in horror— Ah— It makes me
realize it was somehow worth it to leave the peace of my Mexican Moon Roof to go yungling and travailing across harsh folly
world with them, to some silly but divine destination in some
other part of the Holy Ghost— Tho I disagree with their ideas
about poetry and peace I cant help loving their suffering sweaty
faces and disheveled heads of hair like my father's hair when I
found him dead in the chair— In the chair of our home—
When I was absolutely incapable of believing there was such a
thing as the death of Papa let alone mine own— Two crazy
boys exhausted years later heads down like my dead father
(with whom I'd hotly argued also, O why? or why not, when
angels gotta yell about something)— Poor Irwin and Simon in
the world together, *compañeros* of a Spain of their own, bleak
parking lots in their brows, their noses broken with greasy . . .
restless philosophers with no bones . . . saints and angels of a
high assembly from the past in that post I held as Babe of
Heaven— Falling, falling with me and Lucifer and Norman
too, falling, falling in the car—

What will be the death of Irwin? My cat's death is a claw in
the earth. Irwin a toothbone? Simon a brow? Grinning skulls
in all the car? Lazarus has to join the Army for this? The mothers of all these men pining away in shaded livingrooms now?
The fathers horny handed buried with shovels on their breasts?
Or printer's ink fingers curled over rosary tomb? And their
ancestors? The aria singers gulping earth? Now? The Puerto
Rican with his cane reed where herons hay graves? The soft
dawn wind off Carib doth rustle Camacho's oil flutter? The
deep French faces of Canada staring forever in the ground?
The Singers of Dawn Mexico hung up on *corazón* (heart), no
more ope the high barred window serenade handkerchief girl
lips?

No.

Yes.

26 I WAS ABOUT TO COME ACROSS A BELLY OF WHEAT myself which would make me forget about death for a few months—her name was Ruth Heaper.

It happened like this: we arrived in Manhattan on a freezing November morning, Norman said goodbye and there we were on the sidewalk, the four of us, coughing like tuberculars from lack of sleep and too much resultant concomitative smoking. In fact I was sure I had T.B. And I was thinner than ever in my life, about 155 pounds (to my present 195), with hollowed cheeks and really sunken eyes in a cavernous eye bone. And it was *cold* in New York. It suddenly occurred to me we were all probably going to die, no money, coughing, on the sidewalk with bags, looking in all four directions of regular old sour Manhattan hurrying to work for pizza night comforts.

"Old Manhattoes"—"bound round by flashing tides"—the deep VEEP or VEEM of freighter stack whistles in the channel or at the dock. Hollow eyed coughing janitors in candy stores remembering the greater glory . . . somewhere . . . Anyway: "Irwin, what the hell are we gonna do now?"

"Dont worry, we'll ring Phillip Vaughan's doorbell just two blocks away on Fourteenth"—Phillip Vaughan aint in— "We could have camped on his wall-to-wall French translation rug till we found rooms. Let's try two girls I know down here."

That sounds good but I expect to see a couple of suspicious sandy uninterested Dikes with sand for us in their hearts— But when we stand there and yell up at cute Chelsea District Dickensian windows (our mouths blowing fog in the icy sun) they stick their two pretty brunette heads out and see the four bums below surrounded by the havoc of their inescapable sweatsmelling baggage.

"Who is that?"

"Irwin Garden!"

"Hello Irwin!"

"We just got back from Mexico where women are serenaded just like this from the street."

"Well sing a song, just dont stand there coughing."

"We'd like to come up and make a few phonecalls and rest a minute."

"Okay."

Minute indeed . . .

We puffed up four flights and came into the apartment which had a wooden creaky floor and a fireplace. The first girl, Ruth Erickson, stood greeting us, I suddenly remembered her:—Julien's old girlfriend before he got married, the one he said had Missouri River mud running thru her hair, meaning he loved her hair and loved Missouri (his home state) and loved brunettes. She had black eyes, white skin, black black hair and big breasts: what a doll! I think she'd grown taller since the night I got drunk with her and Julien and her roommate. But out of the other bedroom steps Ruth Heaper in her pajamas yet, brown sleek hair, black eyes, little pout and who are you and what for? And built. Or as Edgar Cayce says, builded.

But that's all right but when she throws herself in a chair in such a way I see her pajama bottom I go mad. There's also something about her face I never saw before:—a strange boyish mischievous or spoiled pucky face but with rosy woman lips and soft cheek of fairest apparel of morning.

"Ruth Heaper?" I say when introduced. "Ruth who heaped the heap of corn?"

"The same," she says (or I guess she said, I dont remember). And meanwhile Erickson has gone downstairs to fetch the Sunday papers and Irwin is washing in the bathroom, so we all read the paper but I cant keep my thoughts off the sweet thighs of Heaper in those pajamas right there in front of me.

Erickson is actually a girl of tremendous consequence in our Manhattan now who heaps lots of influence with phonecalls and dreams and plots over beers to cupid up people, and makes men guilty. Because (making men guilty) she is an irreproachably sensitive open lady tho I suspect her of evil motives right off. But as for Heaper, she has wicked eyes too, but that's only because she's been spoiled by her self made grandfather, who sends her like Television sets for Christmas for her apartment and she's not impressed at all— Only later I learned she also walked around Greenwich Village with boots on, carrying a whip. But I cant see that the reason is congenital.

All four of us are trying to make her, the four coughing ugly bums of their doorstep, but I can see I got the upper hand just by staring into her eyes with my hungry want-you campy "sexy" look which nevertheless is as genuine as my pants or yours, man or woman—I *want* her—I'm out of my mind with weariness & goop—Erickson brings me a darling beer—I'm going to make love to Heaper or die—She knows it—She however starts singing all the tunes from *My Fair Lady* perfectly, imitating Julie Andrews perfectly, the Cockney accent and all—I realize now this little Cockney was a boy in my previous lifetime as a Boy Pimp and Thief in London—She's come back to me.

Gradually, like always the case, the four of us boys get to use the bathroom and shower and clean up suitably somewhat, even shaves— We're all going to have a gay night now to find some old friend of Simon's in the Village, with the happy Ruths, walk around in cold lovely New York winds in love— Oh boy.

What a way to end that horrible trip up.

27 AND WHERE'S MY "PEACE"? Ah, there it is in that belly of pajama wheat. That naughty kid with shiny black eyes who knows I love her. We all go out to the Village streets, bang on windows, find "Henry," walk around Washington Square Park and at one point I demonstrate my best ballet leap to my Ruth who loves it— We go arm in arm

behind the gang—I think Simon is a little disappointed she hasnt chosen him— For God's sake Simon give me *something*— Suddenly Ruth says just the two of us oughta go up and hear the whole album of *My Fair Lady* again, meet the others later— Walking arm in arm I point to upstairs windows of my delirious Manhattan and say: "I wanta write about everything that happens behind every one of those windows"

"Great!"

On the floor of her bedroom as she starts the record player I just kiss her, down to the floor, like a foe—she responds foe-like by saying if she's gonna make love it aint gonna be on the floor. And now, for the sake of a 100% literature, I'll describe our loving.

28

IT'S LIKE A BIG SURREALISTIC DRAWING BY PICASSO with this and that reaching for this and that— even Picasso doesnt want to be too accurate. It's the Garden of Eden and anything goes. I cant think of anything more beautiful in my life (& aesthetic) than to hold a naked girl in my arms, sideways on a bed, in the first preliminary kiss. The velvet back. The hair, in which Obis, Parañas & Euphrates run. The nape of the neck the original person now turned into a serpentine Eve by the Fall of the Garden where you feel the actual animal soul personal muscles and there's no sex—but O the rest so soft and unlikely— If men were as soft I'd love them as so— To think that a soft woman desires a hard hairy man! The thought of it amazes me: where's the beauty? But Ruth explains to me (as I asked, for kicks) that because of her excessive softness and bellies of wheat she grew sick and tired of all that, and desired roughness—in which she saw beauty by contrast—and so like Picasso again, and like in a Jan Müller Garden, we mortified Mars with our exchanges of hard & soft— With a few extra tricks, politely in Vienna—that led to a breathless timeless night of sheer lovely delight, ending with sleep.

We ate each other and plowed each other hungrily.

The next day she told Erickson it was the first *extase* of her career and when Erickson told me that over coffee I was pleased but really didnt believe it. I went down to 14th Street and bought me a red zipper sweat jacket and that night Irwin and I and the kids had to go look for rooms. At one point I almost bought a double room in the Y.M.C.A. for me and Laz but I thought better of it realizing he'd be a weight on my few remaining dollars. We finally found a Puerto Rican rooming-house room, cold and dismal, for Laz, and left him there dismally. Irwin and Simon went to live with rich scholar Phillip Vaughan. That night Ruth Heaper said I could sleep with her, live with her, sleep with her in her bedroom every night, type all morning while she went to work in an agency and talk to Ruth Erickson all afternoon over coffee and beer, till she got back home at night, when I'd rub her new skin rash with unguents in the bathroom.

29 RUTH ERICKSON HAD A HUGE DOG in the apartment, Jim, who was a giant German Police Dog (or Shepherd) (or Wolf) who loved to wrassle with me on the varnished wooden floor, by fireplaces— He'd have eaten whole assemblies of hoodlums and poets at one command but he knew Ruth Erickson liked me—Ruth Erickson called him her lover. Once in a while I took him out on a leash (for Ruth) to run him up and down curbstones for his peepees and works, he was so strong he could drag you half a block in search of a scent. Once when he saw another dog I had to dig my heels into the sidewalk to hold him. I told Ruth Erickson it was cruel to keep such a big monstrous man on a leash in a house but it turned out he'd just almost recently died and it was Erickson who saved his life with 24-hour care, she really loved him. In her own bedroom was a fireplace and jewelry on her dresser. At one point she had a French Canadian from Montreal go in there

whom I didnt trust (he borrowed $5 from me and never paid it back) and did away with one of her expensive rings. She questioned me about who could have taken it. It wasnt Laz, it wasnt Simon, it wasnt Irwin, it wasnt me, for sure. "It's that crook from Montreal." She actually wanted me to be *her* lover in a way but loved Ruth Heaper so it was out of the question. We spent long afternoons talking and looking into each other's eyes. When Ruth Heaper came from work we made spaghetti and had big meals by candlelight. Every evening another potential lover came for Erickson but she rejected all of them (dozens) except the French Canadian, who never made it (except possibly with Ruth Heaper when I was away) and Tim McCaffrey, who did make it he said with my blessings. He himself (a young *Newsweek* staffer with big James Dean hair) came and asked me if it was okay, apparently Erickson had sent him, to pull my leg.

Who could think of anything better? Or worse?

30 WHY "WORSE"? Because by far the sweetest gift on earth, inseminating a woman, the feeling of that for a tortured man, leads to children who are torn out of the womb screaming for mercy as tho they were being thrown to the Crocodiles of Life—in the River of Lives—which is what birth is, O Ladies & Gentlemen of gentle Scotland— "Babies born screaming in this town are miserable examples of what happens everywhere," I once wrote— "Little girls make shadows on the sidewalk shorter than the Shadow of death in this town," I also wrote— Both the Ruths had been born screaming girls but at age 14 they suddenly got the urge sexily & snakily to make others cream & scream— It's awful— The essential teaching of the Lord Buddha was: "No More Rebirth" but this teaching was taken over, hidden, controverted, turned upside down and defamed into Zen, the invention of Mara the Tempter, Mara the Insane, Mara the Devil— Today

whole big intellectual books are being published about "Zen" which is nothing but the Devil's Personal war against the essential teaching of Buddha who said to his 1250 boys when the Courtesan Amra and her girls were approaching with gifts across the Bengali Meadow: "Tho she is beautiful, and gifted, 't were better for all of you to fall into a Tiger's mouth than to fall into her net of plans." *Oyes?* Meaning by that, for every Clark Gable or Gary Cooper born, with all the so called glory (or Hemingway) that goes with it, comes disease, decay, sorrow, lamentation, old age, death, decomposition— meaning, for every little sweet lump of baby born that women croon over, is one vast rotten meat burning slow worms in graves of this earth.

31

BUT NATURE HAS MADE WOMEN SO MADDENINGLY DESIRABLE for men, the unbelievable, the impossible-to-actually-believe wheel of birth and dying turns on and turns on, as tho some Devil was turning the Wheel himself hard and sweaty for suffering human horror to try to make an imprint somehow in the void of the sky— As tho anything, even a Pepsi Cola ad with jetplanes, could be printed up there, unless the Apocalypse— But Devilish nature has so worked it that men desire women and women scheme for men's babies— Something we were proud of when we were Lairds but which today makes us sick to think of it, whole supermarket electronic doors opening by themselves to admit pregnant women so they can buy food to feed death further— Bluepencil me that, U.P.I.—

But a man is invested with all this trembling tissue, the Hindus call it "Lila" (Flower), and there's nothing he can do with his tissue save get him to a monastery where however horrible male perverts sometimes wait for him anyway— So why not loll in the love of belly wheat? But I knew the end was coming.

Irwin was absolutely right about visiting the publishers and arranging for publication and money— They advanced me $1000 payable at $100 a month installments and the editors (without my knowledge) bent their wrenny heads over my faultless prose and prepared the book for publication with a million *faux pas* of human ogreishness (Oy?) —So I actually felt like marrying Ruth Heaper and moving to a country home in Connecticut.

Her skin rash, according to soulmate Erickson, was caused by my arrival and lovemaking.

32 RUTH ERICKSON AND I HAD DAYLONG TALKS during which she confided her love for Julien in me— (what?)— Julien my best friend, perhaps, with whom I'd been living in a loft on 23rd Street when first met Ruth Erickson— He was madly in love with her at the time but she did not reciprocate (as I knew she'd do, at the time)— But now that he was married to that most charming of earth's women, Vanessa von Salzburg, my witty buddy and confidante, O *now* she wanted Julien! He'd even telephoned her long distance in the Middle West but to no avail at the time—Missouri River in her hair indeed, Styx, or Mytilene more likely.

There's old Julien now, home from work at the office where he's a successful young executive in a necktie with a mustache tho in his early days he'd sat in puddles of rain with me pouring ink over our hair yelling Mexican Borracho Yahoos (or Missourian, *one*)— The moment he comes home from work he plumps into the splendid leather easy chair his Laird's wife's bought him first thing off, before cribs, and sits there before a crackling fire tweaking his mustache— "Nothing to do but raise kids and tweak your mustache," said Julien who told me he was the new Buddha *interested* in rebirth!—The new Buddha *dedicated* to Suffering!—

I'd often visited him in the office and watched him work, his office style ("Hey you fucker come 'ere!") and his speech clack

("Whatsamatter with you, any lil old West Virginia suicide is worth ten tons of coal or John L. Lewis!")—He saw to it that the most (to him) important and saddy-dolly stories got over the A.P. wire— He was the favorite of the very frigging President of the whole wire service, Two-Fisted So-and-So Joe— His apartment where I hung out in the afternoons except those afternoons when I kaffee-klatched with Erickson was the most beautiful apartment in Manhattan in its own Julien-like way, with small balcony overlooking all the neons and trees and traffics of Sheridan Square, and a kitchen refrigerator full of ice cubes and Cokes to go with ye old Partners Choice Whiskey-boo—I'd spend the day talking to Wife Nessa and the kids, who told us to shush when Mickey Mouse came on TV, then in'd walk Julien in his suit, open collar, tie, saying "Shit— imagine comin home from a hard day's work and finding this McCarthyite Duluoz here" and sometimes he'd be followed by one of his assistant editors like Joe Scribner or Tim Fawcett— Tim Fawcett who was deaf, had a hearing aid, was a suffering Catholic, and still loved suffering Julien— Plup, Julien falls in his leather easy chair before a Nessa-prepared fire, and tweaks his mustache— It was the theory of Irwin and Hubbard too that Julien grew that mustache to look older and uglier than he wasnt at all— "Anything to eat?" he says, and Nessa comes out with half a broiled chicken at which he picks desultorily, has a coffee, and wonders if I'll go down and get another pint of Partners Choice—

"I'll pay half."

"Ah you Kanooks are always payin half" so we go down together with Potchki the black spaniel on the leash, and before the liquor store we hit a bar and have a few rye and Cokes watching TV with all the other sadder New Yorkers.

"Bad blood, Duluoz, bad blood."

"Whattaya mean?"

He suddenly grabs me by the shirt and pulls it yanking two buttons off.

"Why are you always tearing my shirt?"

"Ah your mother aint here to sew em, hey?" and he pulls further, tearing my poor shirt, and looks at me sadly, Julien's sad look is a look that says:—

"Ah shit man, all *your* and *my* little tight ass schemes to make 24 hours a day run discipline the clock—when we all go to heaven we wont even know what the sighin was all about or what we looked like." Once I'd met a girl and told him: "A girl that's beautiful, sad" and he'd said "Ah everybody's beautiful and sad."

"Why?"

"You wouldnt know, you bad blooded Kanook—"

"Why do you keep sayin I've bad blood?"

"Cause you grow tails in your family."

He's the only man in the world who can insult my family, really, because he's insulting the family of earth.

"What about *your* family?"

He doesnt even hear to answer:—"If you had a crown on your head they'd have to hang you even sooner." Back upstairs at the apartment he starts exciting the female dog by stimulating her: "Oh what a black dribbling bottom . . ."

There's a December blizzard going on. Ruth Erickson comes over, as arranged, and she and Nessa talk and talk while me and Julien sneak out to his bedroom and go down the fire escape in the snow to hit the bar for some more rye and soda. I see him jump nimbly beneath me so I do the same nimble jump. But he's done it before. It's a ten-foot drop from that swinging fire escape to the sidewalk and as I fall I realize it but not soon enough, and turn over in my fall and fall right on my head. C r a c k ! Julien lifts me up with a bleeding head. "All that for just running out on the women? Duluoz you look better when you're bleeding."

"All that bad blood going out," he adds in the bar, but there's nothing cruel about Julien, just *just*. "They used to bleed nuts like you in old England" and when he begins to see the pained expression on my face he becomes commiserative.

"Ah poor Jack" (head against mine, like Irwin, for the same and yet not the same reasons), "you should have stayed wherever you were before you came here—" He calls the bartender for mercurochrome to fix my wound. "Old Jack," there are times too when he becomes absolutely humble in my presence and wants to know what I really think, or *he* really thinks. "Your opinions are now *valuable*." The first time I'd met him in 1944 I thought he was a mischievous young shit, and the only time I got high on pot in his presence I divined he was against me, but since we were always drunk . . . and yet. Julien with his slitted green eyes and Tyrone Power slender wiry masculinity punching me. "Let's go see your girl." We take a cab to Ruth Heaper's in the snow and as soon as we walk in and she sees me drunk she grabs a handful of my hair, pulls it, pulls several hairs out of my important combing spot and starts punching fists into my face. Julien sits there calling her "Slugger." So we leave again.

"Slugger dont like you, man," Julien says cheerfully in the cab. We go back to his wife and Erickson who are still talking. Gad, the greatest writer who ever lived will have to be a woman.

33   THEN IT'S TIME FOR THE LATE SHOW ON TV so me and Nessa make more ryes and Cokes in the kitchen, bring them out tinkly by the fire, and we all draw our chairs before the TV screen to watch Clark Gable and Jean Harlow in a picture about rubber plantations in the 1930's, the parrot cage, Jean Harlow is cleaning it out, says to the Parrot: "What *you* ben eatin, *cement?*" and we all roar with laughter.

"Boy they dont make pictures like *that* anymore" says Julien sipping his drink, tweaking his mustache.

On comes a Late Late film about Scotland Yard. Julien and I

are very quiet watching our old histories while Nessa laughs. All she had to deal with in *her* previous lifetime were baby carriages and daguerrotypes. We watch the Lloyds of London Werewolf crap out the door with a slanting leer:—

"That sonofabitch wouldnt a given you two cents for your own mother!" yells Julien.

"Even with a bedstead," adds I.

"'Avin 'is 'anging in Turkish Baths!" yells Julien.

"Or in Innisfree."

"Throw another log on the fire, Muzz," says Julien, "Dazz" to the kids, to Muzz Momma, which she does with great pleasure. Our movie reveries are interrupted by visitors from his office: Tim Fawcett yelling because he's deaf:—

"C a—*r i s t!* That U.P.I. dispatch told all about some mother who was a whore who had to do with all the little bastard's horror!"

"Well the little bastard's dead."

"Dead? He blew his head clean off in a hotel room in Harrisburg!"

Then we all get drunk and I end up sleeping in Julien's bedroom while he and Nessa sleep on the open-out couch, I open the window to the fresh air of the blizzard and fall asleep beneath the old oil portrait of Julien's grandfather Gareth Love who is buried next to Stonewall Jackson in Lexington Virginia— In the morning I wake up to two feet of snowdrifts over the floor and part of the bed. Julien is sitting in the livingroom pale and sick. He wont even touch a beer, he has to go to work. He has one softboiled egg and that's it. He puts on his necktie and shudders with horror to the office. I go downstairs, buy more beer, and spend the whole day with Nessa and the kids talking and playing their piggy back games— Come dark in comes Julien again, two hiballs stronger, and falls to drinking again. Nessa brings our asparagus, chops and wine. That night the whole gang (Irwin, Simon, Laz, Erickson and some writers from the Village some of them Italian) come in to watch TV with us. We see Perry Como and Guy Lombardo hugging each other on a Spectacular. "Shit," says Julien, drink in hand in the leather chair, not even tweaking his mustache, "them Dagos'll all go home and eat ravioli and die of puking."

I'm the only one who laughs (except Nessa secretly) because Julien is the only guy in New York who'll speak his mind whatever his mind is at the time it happens, no matter what, which is why I love him:—a Laird, sirs (Dagos excuse us).

34 I HAD ONCE SEEN A PHOTO OF JULIEN when he was 14, in his mother's house, and was amazed that any person could be so beautiful— Blond, with an actual halo of light around his hair, strong hard features, those Oriental eyes—I'd thought "Shit would *I* have liked Julien when he was 14 looking like that?" but no sooner I tell his sister what a great picture it was she hid it, so the next time (a year later) when we again accidentally visit her apartment on Park Avenue "Where's that great picture of Julien?" it's gone, she's hid it or destroyed it— Poor Julien, over whose blond head I see the stare of America's Parking Lots and Bleakest Glare—the Glare of "Who-are-you, Ass?"—A sad little boy finally, whom I understood, because I'd known many sad little boys in Oy French Canada as I'm sure Irwin had known in Oy New York Jews— The little boy too beautiful for the world but finally saved by a wife, good old Nessa, who said to me one time: "While you were passed out on the couch I noticed your pants were shining!"

Once I'd said to Julien "Nessa, I'm gonna call her 'Legs' because she has nice legs" and he answered:—

"If I catch you making any pass at Nessa I'll kill you" and he meant it.

His sons were Peter, Gareth and one was on the way who would be known as *Ezra*.

35

JULIEN WAS MAD AT ME because I'd made love to one of his old girlfriends, not Ruth Erickson— But meanwhile while we were having a party at the Ruths some rotten eggs were thrown up at Erickson's window and I went downstairs with Simon later to investigate. Only a week before Simon and Irwin had been stopped by a gang of juvenile delinquents with broken bottles at their throats, only because Simon had looked at the gang in front of the variety (variety indeed) store— Now I saw the kids and said "Who threw those rotten eggs?"

"Where's that dog?" said the kid stepping up with a sixfoot teenager.

"He wont harm you. Did you throw the eggs?"

"*What* eggs?"

As I stood there talking to them I noticed they wanted to pull out knives and stab me, I was scared. But they turned away and I saw the name "Power" on the back of the jacket of the younger kid, I said:—"Okay Johnny Power dont throw no more eggs." He turned around and looked at me. "That's a great name," I said, "Johnny Power." That was more or less the end of that.

But meanwhile Irwin and Simon had arranged an interview with Salvador Dali. But before that I have to tell you about my coat, but first Lazarus' brother Tony.

Simon and Lazarus had two brothers in the madhouse, as I say, one of them a hopeless catatonic who refused attention and probably looked at his attendants with the thought: "I hope those guys dont teach me to touch them, I'm full of hopeless electric snakes" but another brother who was only a schizoid (advanced) personality hoping to still make it in the world and consequently and no lie was helped to escape from the hospital in Long Island by Simon himself in some well worked scheme like the schemes of Rififi French Thieves— So now Tony was out and working (of all things, as I'd done as a kid) as a pinboy in a bowling alley, in the Bowery however, where we went to see him and where I saw him in the pit bending to set up the tenpins fast— Then later, the next night, while I was hanging around Phillip Vaughan's apartment reading Mallarmé and Proust and Courbière in French, Irwin rang the bell and I answered the door to see the three of them, Irwin, Simon and little short blond pimply Tony between them—"Tony, meet Jack." And as soon as Tony saw my face, or eyes, or body, or whatever it was, he turned abruptly and walked away from everybody and I never saw him again.

I think it was because I looked like the older catatonic brother, at least Laz told me so.

Later I went to visit my old friend Deni Bleu.

Deni Bleu is that fantastic character I lived with on the West Coast in my road days, who stole everything in sight but gave it away to widows sometimes (*Bon coeur*, good heart) and who was now living meanly I'd say in an apartment on 13th Street near the waterfront with an icebox (in which nevertheless he still stored his home made special recipe chicken consommé)— Who'd put on Chef hats and roast whole huge Turkeys on Thanksgiving for parties of Village hipsters and beatniks who only ended up sneaking out with drumsticks in their coats— Only because he wanted to meet a cool Greenwich Village chick— Poor Deni. Deni who had a telephone and a full icebox and bums who preyed on him, sometimes when he went away on weekends the bums'd leave all the lights on, all the water running and the doors to his apartment unlocked— Who was continually being betrayed, even by *me*, as he claimed. "Now Duluoz," says this big 220-pound blackhaired fat Frenchman (who'd stolen and now only *scrounged* for what was *due* him), "you have always messed me up no matter how you tried to do otherwise—I see you now and I feel pity for you." He whipped out some government bonds with photos of him pointing at the government bonds and in red ink is written: *I shall always be*

able to afford consommé and turkey. He lived only a block away
from the Ruths. "Now that I see you so scroungy, and sad, and
down on your luck, and lost, and cant even buy yourself a
drink, or even say 'Deni, you've fed me many times but will
you please lend me so and so?' because you've never, *never*
asked me to lend you money" (he was a seaman and a furniture
mover between trips, an old prepschool friend of mine my father'd met and *liked*) (but Julien'd said his hands and feet were
too small to go with his huge powerful body) (but who you
gonna listen to?) he now says to me: "So I'm giving you this
genuine vicuña coat as soon as with this razor blade I cut out
the very important fur lining—"

"Where'd you get the coat?"

"Never *mind* where I got the coat, but since you insist, since
you're angling for some way to mess me up, since *en effet vous
ne voulez pas me croire,* I got this coat in an empty warehouse
while I was moving out some furniture— It so happens that I
had information at the time that the owner of the coat was dead,
mort, so I took it, do you under*stand* Duluoz?"

"Yeah."

"Yeah he says" and looking up at his Angel-like Tom
Wolfe's brother. "All he's got to say is 'Yeah' and I'm about to
give him a two-hundred-dollar coat!" (It was only a year later
the Washington scandal about vicuña coats, unborn calf coats,
was about to start) (but first he took out the fur lining). The
coat was huge, long, hung to my shoes.

I said "Deni, do you expect me to walk around the streets of
New York with a coat hanging to my shoes?"

"Not only do I expect that," he said putting a woollen ski
cap on my head and yanking it down over my ears, "but I
expect you to keep stirring those eggs like I told you." He'd
mixed six scrambled eggs with a quarterpound of butter and
cheese and spices, turned on a low flame, and had me stir with
a tablespoon while he busied himself mashing buttered mashed
potatoes thru a strainer, for supper at midnight. It was delicious.

He showed me some infinitesimal ivory elephant figurines (about as big as a piece of dust) (from India) and explained to me how delicate they were and how some joker had blown them out of his hand in a bar last New Year's Eve. He also produced a bottle of Benedictine Liqueur which we drank all night. He wanted to be introduced to the Ruths. I knew it wouldnt work. He is an oldfashioned French *raconteur* and *bon vivant* who needs a French wife, and shouldnt be hanging around the Village trying to make those cold lonesome chicks. But as always he held me by the arm and told me all his latest stories, which he repeated the night I invited him to drinks at Julien's and Nessa's. For this occasion he sent a telegram to his favorite not-interested girl saying that we would have cocktails at the home of "*le grand journaliste,* Julien Love" but she never showed up. But after he told all his jokes Nessa got going on her own jokes and Deni laughed so hard he sheed in his pants, went to the bathroom (he'll kill me for this), washed out his shorts, hung them up, came back laughing, absentmindedly forgot them, and when Nessa and I and Julien woke up next morning bleary eyed and sad, we laughed to see the huge world wide shorts hanging from their bathroom shower— "Who could ever be so big to wash those?"

But Deni was no slob.

36 WEARING DENI'S HUGE VICUÑA COAT with the ski cap over my ears, in cold biting winds of December New York, Irwin and Simon led me up to the Russian Tea Room to meet Salvador Dali.

He was sitting with his chin on a finely decorated tile headed cane, blue and white, next to his wife at the café table. He had a little wax mustache, thin. When the waiter asked him what he wanted he said "One grapefruit . . . *peenk!*" and he had big blue eyes like a baby, a real *oro* Spaniard. He told us no artist was great unless he made money. Was he talking about Ucello,

Ghianondri, Franca? We didnt even know what money really was or what to do with it. Dali had already read an article about the "insurgent" "beats" and was interested. When Irwin told him (in Spanish) we wanted to meet Marlon Brando (who ate in this Russian Tea Room) he said, waving three fingers at me, "He is more beautiful than M. Brando."

I wondered why he said that but he probably had a tiff with old Marlon. But what he meant was my eyes, which were blue, like his, and my hair, which is black, like his, and when I looked into his eyes, and he looked into my eyes, we couldnt stand all that sadness. In fact, when Dali and I look in the mirror we cant stand all that sadness. To Dali sadness is beautiful. He said: "As a politician I'm a Royalist—I would like to see the Throne of Spain reborn, Franco and the others out— Last night I finished my latest painting using a pubic hair for the last final touch."

"Really?"

His wife paid absolutely no attention to this information like it was all natural, which it certainly is. When you're married to Dali with the pubic cane, ah Quoi? In fact I got very friendly with his wife while Dali himself spoke broken French-English-Spanish with crazy Garden who pretended to (and indeed did) understand his speech.

"*Pero, qu'est ce que vous penser de Franco?*"

"*C'est nes pas'd mon affaire, mon homme, entiendes?*"

Meanwhile, the next day, old Deni, no Dali himself but just as good, invites me to earn $4 lifting a gas stove six flights up— We bend our fingers, sinew our wrists, raise the stove and go up six flights to an apartment of queers, one of whom, seeing my wrist's bleeding, puts kindly mercurochrome upon it.

37 CHRISTMAS COMING UP, and Ruth Heaper bored by her grand-father's sending her a whole portable TV, I head south to see my mother again—Ruth kisses me and loves me goodbye. On the way down I plan to see Raphael at the home of Varnum Random the poetry consultant of the Library of Congress— What a mess! But how funny! Even Varnum must remember it with horrified glee. A cab from the railroad station takes me out to the suburbs of Washington D.C.

I see the swell house with dim night lights and ring the doorbell. It's Raphael answers saying "You shouldnt be here but I'm the one told you I was here so here you are."

"Well does Random mind?"

"No of course not—but he's asleep with his wife now."

"Is there any booze?"

"He has two beautiful grown daughters you'll see tomorrow— It's a real ball, it's not for you. We'll go to the Zoo in his Mercedes Benz—"

"You got pot?"

"Still got some from Mexico."

So we turn on in the big empty piano livingroom and Raphael sleeps on the livingroom couch so I can go down in the basement and sleep in the little draped-cubicle couch the Randoms have arranged for him.

Once down there high on pot, I see tubes of oil paint, and paper watercolor books, and paint me two pictures before I sleep . . . "The Angel" and "The Cat". . . .

And in the morning I see the real horror of it all, in fact I added to the horror by my really importunate presence (but I wanted to see Raphael). All I remember is that the incredible Raphael and incredible me were really imposing on this gentle and quiet family the head of which, Varnum, a bearded Kindly Jesuit I guess, bore everything with a manly aristocratic grace, as I was to do later? But Varnum really knew that Raphael was

a great poet and drove him off that afternoon to a cocktail
party in Cleopatra's Needle while I wheedled in the livingroom
writing poems and talking to the youngest daughter, 14, and
the oldest, 18, and wondering where the Jack Daniels bourbon
of the house was hidden—which I got to later—

There's Varnum Random the great American poet watching
the Mud Bowl on TV over his *London Literary Supplement,*
Jesuits always seem to be interested in football— He shows me
his poems which are as beautiful as Merton's and as technical as
Lowell's— Schools of writing limit men, even me. If there were
anything somber about holy airplanes during the war I would
add the last dark touch. If everybody in the world, when they
dream of roosters, died, as Hsieh An said, everybody would be
dead at sunrise in Mexico, Burma and the World. . . . (and
Indiana). But no such thing happens in the real world not even
in Montmartre when Apollinaire climbs the hill by the pile of
bricks to get to his drunken room, as winds of February blow.
Bless the ride.

38   AND THERE'S INSANE RAPHAEL with a huge nail and
a huge hammer actually banging into the smartly
decorated wall so he can hang his oil-on-wood painting of
Michelangelo's David—I see the housewife wince—Raphael
apparently thinks that painting will be held and revered there
on the wall forever right by the Baldwin grand piano and the
T'ang Tapestry— Furthermore, he then asks for breakfast—I
figure I'd better get going. But Varnum Random actually asks
me to stay one more day so I spend the whole afternoon writing
poems high on benny in the parlor and I call them the *Washington D.C. Blues*—Random and Urso argue with me about my
theory of absolute spontaneity— In the kitchen Random takes
out the Jack Daniels and says "How can you get any refined or
well gestated thoughts into a spontaneous flow as you call it? It

can all end up gibberish." And that was no Harvard lie. But I said:

"If it's gibberish, it's gibberish. There's a certain amount of control going on like a man telling a story in a bar without interruptions or even one pause."

"Well it'll probably become a popular gimmick but I prefer to look upon my poetry as a craft."

"Craft *is* craft."

"Yes? Meaning?"

"Meaning crafty. How can you confess your crafty soul in craft?"

Raphael took Random's side and yelled:—

"Shelley didnt care about theories about how he was to write 'The Skylark.' Duluoz you're full of theories like an old college perfesser, you think you know everything." ("You think you're the only one," he added to himself.) Triumphantly he swept off with Random in the Mercedes Benz to meet Carl Sandburg or somebody. This was the great "making it" scene Irwin had crowed about. I yelled after them:

"If I had a Poetry University you know what would be written over the entrance arch?"

"No, what?"

"Here Learn That Learning Is Ignorance! Gentlemen dont burn my ears! Poetry is lamb dust! I prophesy it! I'll lead schools in exile! I dont Care!" They werent bringing me to meet Carl Sandburg whom I'd known anyway seven years ago at several parties where he stood before the fireplace in a tuxedo and talked about freight trains in Illinois 1910. And actually threw his arms around me going "Ha ha ha! You're just like me!"

Why am I saying all this? I felt forlorn and lost, even when Raphael and I and Random's wife went to the Zoo and I saw a female monkey giving the male monkey some skull (or as we call it in the Lower East Side, Poontang) and I said "Did you see them practicing fellatio?" The woman blushed and Raphael said "Dont talk like that!"—where'd *they* ever hear the word *fellatio!*

But we had one fine dinner downtown, Washingtonians stared to see the bearded man wearing my huge vicuña coat (which I gave Random in exchange for an Air Force fur collared leather coat), to see the two pretty daughters with him, the elegant wife, the tousled bedraggled black haired Raphael carrying a Boito album and a Gabrielli album, and me (in jeans), all coming in to sit at a back table for beer and chicken. In fact all miraculously piling out of one tiny Mercedes Benz.

39   I FORESAW A NEW DREARINESS in all this literary success. That night I called a cab to take me to the bus station and downed half a bottle of Jack Daniels while waiting, sitting on a kitchen stool sketching the pretty older daughter who was on her way to Sarah Lawrence college to learn all about Erich Fromm in the pots and pans. I gave her the sketch, rather accurate, thinking she'd keep it forever like Raphael's Michelangelo. But when we were both back in New York a month later a big package came containing all our paintings and sketches and stray T-shirts, with no explanation, meaning "Thank God you've gone." And I dont blame them, I still feel ashamed about that uninvited visit and havent done such a thing since and never will.

I got down to the bus station with my rucksack and foolishly (high on Jack Daniels) began talking to some sailors who then got a guy with a car to drive out to the back streets of Washington in search of an afterhours bottle. A Negro connection was dickering with us when up walked a Negro cop who wanted to search us all, but was outnumbered. I simply walked away with my rucksack on my back, to the station, got on the bus and fell asleep with the pack by the driver's well. When I woke up in Roanoke Rapids at dawn it was gone. Somebody had taken it off at Richmond. I let my head fall on the seat in that harsh glare nowhere worse in the world than in America with a stupid guilty hangover. A whole new novel (*Angels of Desolation*), a whole book of poetry, and the finishing chapters of another novel (about Tristessa), together with all the paintings not to mention the only gear I had in the world (sleepingbag, poncho, sweater of holy favor, perfect simple equipments the result of years' thinking), gone, all gone. I started to cry. And I looked up and saw the bleak pines by the bleak mills of Roanoke Rapids with one final despair, like the despair of a man who has nothing left to do but leave the earth forever. Soldiers waited for the bus smoking. Fat old North Carolinians watched hands aback clasped. Sunday morning, I empty of my little tricks to make life livable. An empty orphan sitting nowhere, sick and crying. Like dying I saw all the years flash by, all the efforts my father had made to make living something to be interested about but only ending in death, blank death in the glare of automobile day, automobile cemeteries, whole parking lots of cemeteries everywhere. I saw the glum faces of my mother, of Irwin, of Julien, of Ruth, all trying to make it to go on believing without hope. Gay college students in the back of the bus making me even sicker to think of their purple plans all in time to end blind in an automobile cemetery insurance office for nothing. Where's yonder old mule buried in those piny barrens or did the buzzard just eat? Caca, all the world caca. I remembered the enormous despair of when I was 24 sitting in my mother's house all day while she worked in the shoe factory, in fact sitting in my father's death chair, staring like a bust of Goethe at nothing. Getting up once in a while to plunk sonatas on the piano, sonatas of my own spontaneous invention, then falling on the bed crying. Looking out the window at the glare of automobiles on Crossbay Boulevard. Bending my head over my first novel, too sick to go on. Wondering about Goldsmith and Johnson how they burped sorrow by their firesides in a life that was too long. That's what my father told me the night before he died, "Life is too long."

So wondering if God is a personal God who's actually personally concerned about what happens to us, every one. Putting us up to burdens? To Time? To the crying horror of birth and the impossible lostness of the promise of death? And why? Because we're fallen angels who said in Heaven "Heaven is great, *it better be* anyway" and off we fell? But do you or do I remember doing such a thing?

All I remember is that before I was born there was bliss. I actually remember the dark swarming bliss of 1917 altho I was born in 1922! New Years' Eves came and went and I was just blisshood. But when I was dragged out of my mother's womb, blue, a blue baby, they yelled at me to wake up, and slapped me, and ever since then I've been chastised and lost for good and all. Nobody slapped me in bliss! Is God *everything?* If God is everything then it's God who slapped me. For personal reasons? Do I have to carry this body around and call it mine own?

Yet in Raleigh a tall blue-eyed Southerner told me my bag was being shipped to my destination station in Winter Park. "God bless you," I said, and he did a calm double take.

40 AS FOR MY MOTHER, there's no other like her in the world, really. Did she bear me just to have a little child to bless her heart? She got her wish.

At this time she was retired from a lifetime (beginning at 14) of shoe skiving in shoe factories of New England and later New York, was collecting her social security pittance and living with my married sister as a kind of housemaid tho she didnt mind doing the housework at all, natural to her. A neat French Canadian born in St. Pacôme in 1895 while her pregnant mother was visiting Canada from New Hampshire. She was born a twin but the gleeful fleshly little twin died (O what would she have been like?) and the mother died too. So my mother's position in the world was immediately cut off. Then her father died at 38. She was housemaid for aunts and uncles till she met my father who was infuriated at the way she was being treated. My father dead, and I a bum, she was housemaid for relatives again tho in her prime (wartime New York), she used to make $120 a week sometimes at the shoe factories on Canal Street and in Brooklyn, those times when I was too sick or sad to be on my own with wives and friends, and I came home, she totally supported me while I however wrote my books (with no real hope of ever having them published, just an artist). In 1949 I earned about $1000 on my first novel (advance) but that never went far so now she was at my sister's, you saw her in the door, in the yard emptying the garbage, at the stove making roasts, at the sink washing dishes, at the ironing board, at the vacuum cleaner, all gleeful anyway. A suspicious paranoid who told me Irwin and Julien were devils and would ruin me (probably true), she nevertheless was gleeful as a child most of the time. Everybody loved her. The only time my father ever had any cause to complain about this pleasant peasant woman was when she'd let him have it fullblast for losing all his money gambling. When the old man died (age 57) he said to her, to Memère as my nephew now called her (short for *grandemère*):—"Angie, I never realized what a great women you are. Will you ever forgive me for all the wrong things I've done like those times I was away for days and the money I lost gambling, the few pitiful dollars I could've spent on you with some silly hat?—"

"Yes, Emil, but you always gave us the house money for food and rent."

"Yes, but I lost a lot more than that on the horses and playing cards and money I gave away to a lot of bums— Ah!—But now that I'm dying I guess, and here you are workin in the shoe factory, and Jacky's here to take care of me, and I aint worth it, *now* I realize what I lost—all those years—" One night he said he wished he had real old good Chinese food so Memère gave me five dollars and had me ride the subway all the way from Ozone Park to Chinatown New York to buy

Chinese food in cartons, and bring it back. Pa ate every bit of it but threw up (cancer of the liver).

When we buried him she insisted on an expensive coffin, which made me so goddamed mad, but not only that, though I wasnt mad on that score, she had his old sweet body ambulated to New Hampshire for funeral and burial there by the side of his first son, Gerard, my holy brother, so now as thunder breaks in Mexico City where I write, they're still there, side by side, 35 and 15 years there in the earth, but I never revisited their graves knowing that what's there is not really Papa Emil or Gerard, only dung. For if the soul cant escape the body give the world to Mao Tse-tung.

41 I KNOW BETTER than that—God must be a personal God because I've known a lot of things that werent in texts. In fact when I went to Columbia all they were trying to teach us was Marx, as if I cared. I cut classes and stayed in my room and slept in the arms of God. (This is what the dialectical materialists call "cherubim tendencies," or the psychiatrists call "schizoid tendencies.") Ask my brother and my father in their graves about tendencies.

I see them tending towards the golden eternity, where all is restored again forever, where actually whatever you loved is all compacted in One Essence— The Only One.

Now Christmas Eve we all sat around drinking Martinis in front of the TV. Poor little sweet Davey the gray cat who used to follow me into the North Carolina woods when I went there to meditate with the dogs, who therefore used to hide above my head in the tree, once throwing down a twig or leaf to make me notice him, he was now a ragged cat taken to carousal and fights and even got bitten by a snake. I tried to sit him on my lap but he didn't remember anymore. (Actually my brother-in-law kept throwing him out the door.) Old Bob the dog who used to lead me thru the woods down midnight paths, shining white somehow, he was now dead. I think Davey missed him.

I took out my sketchbook and sketched Ma as she dozed in her chair during midnight mass from New York. When I later showed the picture to a girl friend in New York she said it looked very Medieval—the strong arms, the stern sleeping face, the repose in faith.

Once I took home five teaheads in Mexico City who were selling me pot but they all turned out to be thieves, stealing my scout knife, flashlight, Murine and Noxzema while my back was turned, tho I noticed it and said nothing. At one point the leader stood behind me, as I sat, for a good thirty seconds of silence, during which time it occurred to me he was probably going to stab me with my own knife so they could search the apartment at leisure for my hidden money. I wasnt even scared, I just sat there not caring, high. When the thieves finally left at dawn one of them insisted I give him my $50 raincoat. I said *"Non"* distinctly, for sure, finally, saying that my mother would kill me: *"Mi madre,* pow!" pantomiming a punch to my own chin— To which the strange leader said in English: "So you *are* afraid of something."

On the porch of the house was my old rolltop desk with all the unpublished manuscripts in it, and the couch where I slept. To sit at my old desk and stare was sad. All the work I'd done at it, four novels and innumerable dreams and poems and notes. It made me realize suddenly I was working as hard as any man in the world so what did I have to reproach myself for, privately or otherwise? Saint Paul wrote (Corinthians 8:10): *"Therefore I write these things being absent, lest being present I should use sharpness, according to the power which the Lord hath given me to edification, and not to destruction."*

When I left, after Ma made a huge delicious turkey dinner for New Year's Day, I told her I'd be back in the Fall to move her out to a little house of her own, figuring I'd make enough money on the book that had just been accepted. She said, *"Oui,*

Jean, I *do* want a lil home of my own," almost crying, and I kissed her goodbye. "Don't let those bums in New York talk you into anything," she added, because she was convinced that Irwin Garden was out to get me, as my father had predicted for some reason, saying: "Angie, tell Jack that Irwin Garden is going to try to destroy him someday, and that Hubbard too— That Julien is all right— But Garden and Hubbard are going to *destroy* him." And it was weird to ignore it since he'd said it just before he died, in a quiet prophetic voice, as tho I were some kind of important Saint Paul or even a Jesus with foreordained Judases and enemies in the Kingdom of Heaven. "Stay away from them! Stick to your little girlfriend who sent you the cigars!" yelled my ma, meaning the box of cigars Ruth Heaper had mailed me for Christmas. "They'll *destroy* you if you let them! I dont like the funny look in their face!" Yet, strangely, I was on my way back to New York to borrow $225 from Irwin so I could sail to Tangiers Morocco to visit with Hubbard!

Wow.

42 AND MEANWHILE IN NEW YORK, in fact, Irwin and Raphael and Ruth Heaper posed for sinister photos in the Ruth Apartment showing Irwin in a black turtleneck sweater, Raphael in an evil cap (obviously making love to Ruth) and Ruth herself in her pajamas.

Raphael was always making time with my girls. Unfortunately my pa'd never known him.

On the train to New York I saw a pregnant woman pushing a baby carriage in front of a cemetery.

(That's a pome.)

The first thing on tap as I unpacked in Ruth Heaper's bedroom was *Life* Magazine was going to take all our pictures in Gerard Rose's print and frame shop in Greenwich Village, arranged by Irwin. Gerard Rose had never liked me and didn't

like this whole idea at all. Gerard was the original cool subterranean who was so bugged, so listless, yet so goodlooking like
Gerard Phillipe, yet so down, so bored, that when Hubbard
met him he said this to me in comment on Gerard:—"I can just
picture Gerard and me sittin in a bar when the Mongols invade
New York—Gerard's leaning his head on his hand sayin 'Tar-
tars Everywhere.'" But I liked Gerard of course and when I
finally published my book that Fall he yelled: "Ho ho! The
Playboy of the Beat Generation? Wanta buy a Mercedes?" (as
if I could afford it then or now.)

So, for the *Life* photographers I drank up, got high, combed
my hair and had them shoot me standing on my head: "Tell
everybody this is the way to keep the doctor away!" They didnt
even smile. They took other photos of Raphael and Irwin and
Simon and me sitting on the floor, interviewed us and wrote
notes, went away inviting us to a party, and never even published the pictures or the story. There's the saying around the
trade that the cutting room floor of *Life* Magazine is cluttered
a foot deep with "Lost Faces," or "The Face on the Cutting
Room Floor." It wasnt about to destroy my potentiality as an
artist, a writer, but it was an awful waste of energy and in a
way a grisly joke.

Meanwhile we went to the party indicated and heard a man
in a Brooks Brothers jacket say: "Who wants to be a party
pooper after all?" The moment we heard the word "pooper"
we all left, something somehow wrong with it, like the farts of
summer camp counselors.

43 YES, IT WAS ONLY THE BEGINNING. But things were
still horribly funny in those days, like Raphael
painting a mural with house paint on the wall of a bar on 14th
Street and 8th Avenue, for money, and the owners of the bar
were big Italian gangsters with gats. They stood around in
loose-fitting suits as Raphael painted huge monks on the wall.

"The more I look at it the more I like it," said a mobster, rushing to the phone as it rang, taking a bet and sticking it in his hat. The mobster bartender wasnt quite so sure:

"I don't know, I think Raphael dont know what he's up to."

Raphael whirls around with the brush, the other hand forefinger to thumb like an Italian, "Lissen you guys! You dont know anything about beauty! You're all a bunch of big mobsters wondering where beauty hides! Beauty hides in Raphael!"

"Why does beauty hide in Raphael?" they ask somewhat concerned, scratching their armpits, pushing back their hats, answering the phone to take more bets.

I sat there with a beer wondering what would happen. But Raphael *yelled* at them: I suddenly realized he would have made the most beautiful persuasive mobster in New York or in the whole entire Mafia: "Ech! All your lives eating popsicles on Kenmare Street then when you grow up you bring no popsicle beauty with you. Look at this painting! It's beauty!"

"Am I in it?" asks the bartender, Rocco, with an upward angelic look at the mural to make the other mobsters laugh.

"Of course you're in it, you're the monk on the end, the black monk— What you need is *white hair!*" yells Raphael dipping his brush in a bucket of white paint and suddenly daubing huge white waterfalls around the black monk's head.

"Hey!" yells Rocco seriously amazed. "I dont have white hair or even long white hair?"

"You do now because I've pronounced it, I've pronounced you *Beauty Hair!*" and Raphael dabs more white all over the whole mural, ruining it actually as everybody's laughing and he's grinning that thin Raphael grin as tho he had a throatful of laughter he doesnt want to let out. And it was then I really loved him because he wasnt afraid of any mobsters, in fact he was a mobster himself and the mobsters knew it. As we hurry from the bar back to Ruth's pad for spaghetti supper Raphael says to me angrily: "Ah, I think I'll quit the poetry racket. It's not gettin me nowhere. I want tiplet pigeons on my roof and a villa on Capri or in Crete. I dont wanta have to talk to those dopey gamblers and hoods, I wanta meet counts and princesas."

"You want a *moat!*"

"I want a *heartshaped* moat like in Dali— When I meet Kirk Douglas I dont wanta have to apolo*gize*." And at Ruth's he immediately plunges in and boils canned clams in a vat of oil, meanwhile boiling spaghettini, and pours it all out, mixes it, mixes a salad, lights a candle, and we all have a perfect Italian Clam Spaghetti supper with laughs. Avant garde opera singers rush in and start singing beautiful songs by Blow and Purcell with Ruth Erickson but Raphael says to me: "Who are all these creeps" (almost "cweeps")— "Gripplings, man." He wants to kiss Ruth Heaper but I'm there so he rushes out to find a girl in the bar on Minetta Lane, a colored and white mixed bar now closed.

And the next day Irwin carts me and Simon and Raphael off in a bus to Rutherford New Jersey to meet William Carlos Williams the old great poet of 20th Century America. Williams is a general practitioner all his life, his office is still there where he'd examined patients for 40 years and got his material for fine Thomas Hardy-like poems. He sits there staring out the window as we all read him our poems and prose. He's actually bored. Who wouldnt at 72? He's still thin and youthful and grand, tho, and at the end he goes down to the cellar and brings up a bottle of wine to cheer us all up. He tells me: "Keep writing like that." He loves Simon's poems and later writes in a review that Simon is actually the most interesting new poet in America (Simon will write lines like, "Does the fire hydrant weep as many tears as me?" or "I have a red star on my cigarette")— But of course Dr. Williams loves Irwin of nearby Paterson N.J. the best because of his huge, in a sense uncriticizable howling altogether sameness greatness (like Dizzy Gillespie on trumpet, Dizzy comes on in *waves* of thought, not in phrases)— Let Irwin or Dizzy get warmed up and the walls fall down, at least the walls of your ear-porch—Irwin writes about

tears with a big tearful moan, Dr. Williams is old enough to
understand— Actually a historic occasion and finally we dopey
poets ask him for the last advice, he stands there looking thru
the muslin curtains of his livingroom at the New Jersey traffic
outside and says:

"There's lots of bastards out there."

I've wondered about that ever since.

And I had spent most of the time talking to the doctor's
charming wife, 65, who described how handsome Bill had been
in his young days.

But there's a man for you.

44 IRWIN GARDEN'S FATHER Harry Garden comes to
Dr. Williams' house to drive us home, to his own
house in Paterson where we'll have a supper and a big talk
about poetry—Harry is a poet himself (appears on the editorial
page of the *Times* and *Tribune* several times a year with perfectly rhymed love and sadness lyrics)— But he's a bug on
puns and as soon as he walks into Dr. Williams' house he says
"Drinkin wine, hey? When your glass is always empty that's
when you're really sippin"—"Ha ha ha"—Rather a good pun,
even, but Irwin looks at me with consternation as tho it was
some impossible social scene in Dostoevsky. "How would you
like to buy a necktie with hand painted gravy stains?"

Harry Garden is a high school teacher of about 60 about to
retire. He has blue eyes and sandy hair like his eldest son Leonard Garden, now a lawyer, while Irwin has the black hair and
black eyes of his beautiful mother Rebecca, of whom he wrote,
now dead.

Harry gaily drives us all to his home exhibiting ten times
more energy than boys young enough to be his grandsons. In
his kitchen which has swirling wallpaper I go blind over wine
as he reads and puns over coffee. We retire to his study. I start
reading my silly far-out poem with just grunts or "g r r r r"

and "f r r r r t" in it to describe the sounds of Mexico City street traffic—

Raphael yells out "Ah that's not poetry!" and old man Harry looks at us with frank blue eyes and says:—

"You boys are fighting?" and I catch Irwin's quick glance. Simon is neutral in Heaven.

The fight with Raphael the Mobster carries over to when we're catching the Paterson bus to New York, I jump in, pay my fare, Simon pays his (Irwin stayed with his father) but Raphael yells out "I aint got no money, why dont you pay my fare Jack?" I refuse. Simon pays it with Irwin's money. Raphael starts to harangue me about what a coldblooded money-fisted Canook I am. By the time we get to Port Authority I'm practically crying. He keeps saying: "All you do is hide money in your beauty. It makes you ugly! You'll *die* with money in your hand and wonder why the Angels wont lift you up."

"The reason *you* havent got money is because you keep spending it."

"*Yes* I keep spending it! And why not? Money is a lie and poetry is truth— Could I pay my bus fare with truth? Would the driver understand? No! Because he's like you, Duluoz, a scared tightfisted and even tight-ass son of a bitch with money hidden in his 5 & 10 socks. All he wants to do is DIE!"

But tho I could have used a lot of arguments like why did Raphael blow his money on a *plane* from Mexico when he could have rode with us in the woesome car, I cant do anything but wipe the tears in my eyes. I dont know why, maybe because he's right when all is said and done and we've all given good money for all our funerals, yay— O all the funerals ahead of me, for which I'll have to wear ties! Julien's funeral, Irwin's funeral, Simon's funeral, Raphael's funeral, Ma's funeral, my sister's funeral, and I already wore a tie and bleaked at dirt for my *father's* funeral! Flowers and funerals, the loss of broad shoulders! No more the eager clack of shoes on the sidewalk to somewhere but a drear *fight* in a grave, like in a French movie,

the Cross cant even stand erect in such silk and mud— O Tal-
leyrand!

"Raphael I want you to know that I love you." (This information was imparted eagerly to Irwin the next day by Simon,
who saw its importance.) "But dont bug me about money.
You're always talkin about how you dont need money but it's
the only thing you want. You're trapped in ignorance. I at least
admit it. But I love you."

"You can *keep* your money, I'm going to Greece and have
visions— People will *give* me money and I'll throw it away—
I'll *sleep* on money—I'll turn over in my *dreams* on money."

It was snowing. Raphael accompanied me to Ruth Heaper's
where we were supposed to eat supper and tell her all about
our meeting with William Carlos Williams. I saw a funny look
in her eye, in Ruth Erickson's too. "What's the matter?"

In the bedroom my love Ruth tells me her psychoanalyst has
advised her to tell me to move out of her room and go get a
room of my own because it isnt good for her psyche or mine.

"This asshole wants to screw you himself!"

"Screw is just the right word. He said you were taking ad-
vantage of me, that you're irresponsible, do me no good, get
drunk, bring drunk friends—all hours of the night—I cant
rest."

I pack up all my gear and walk out with Raphael into the
increasing snowstorm. We go down Bleecker Street, or Bleaker
Street, one. Raphael is now sad for me. He kisses me on the
cheek as he leaves (to go have supper with a girl uptown), and
says, "Poor Jack, forgive me Jackie. I love you too."

I'm all alone in the snow so I go to Julien's and we get drunk
again in front of the TV, Julien finally getting mad and ripping
my shirt and even my T-shirt off my back and I sleep drunk on
the livingroom floor till noon.

The next day I get a room in the Marlton Hotel on 8th Street
and start typing what I wrote in Mexico, double space neatly

for the publishers, thousands of dollars hidden in that pack of mine.

45   WITH ONLY TEN DOLLARS LEFT I GO DOWN TO THE CORNER DRUGSTORE on 5th Avenue to buy a pack of butts, figuring I can buy a roast chicken that night and eat it over my typewriter (borrowed from Ruth Heaper). But in the drugstore the character says "How are things in Glacamora? You living around the corner or in Indiana? You know what the old bastard said when he kicked the bucket . . ." But later when I get back to my room I find he's only given me change for a five. He has pulled the shortchange hype on me. I go back to the store but he's off duty, gone, and the management is suspicious of me. "You've got a shortchange artist working in your store—I dont wanta put the finger on anybody but I want my money back—I'm *hungry!*" But I never got the money back and I shoulda stuck the finger up my ass. I went on typing on just coffee. Later I called Irwin and he told me to call Raphael's uptown girl because maybe I could live with her as she was already sick of Raphael.

"Why's she sick of Raphael?"

"Because he keeps laying around on the couch saying 'Feed Raphael'! *Really!* I think she'd like you. Just be cool nice Jack and call her." I called her, Alyce Newman by name, and told her I was starving and would she meet me in Howard Johnson's on 6th Avenue and buy me two frankfurts? She told me okay, she was a short blonde in a red coat. At 8 P.M. I saw her walk in.

She bought me the hotdogs and I gobbled them up. I'd already looked at her and said "Why dont you let me stay at your apartment, I've got a lot of typing to do and they cheated me out of my money in a drugstore today."

"If you wish."

46 BUT IT WAS THE BEGINNING of perhaps the best love affair I ever had because Alyce was an interesting young person, a Jewess, elegant middleclass sad and looking for something— She looked Polish as hell, with the peasant's legs, the bare low bottom, the *torque* of hair (blond) and the sad understanding eyes. In fact she sorta fell in love with me. But that was only because I really didnt impose on her. When I asked her for bacon and eggs and applesauce at two in the morning she did it gladly, because I asked it sincerely. Sincerely? What's insincere about "Feed Raphael"? Old Alyce (22) however said:

"I s'pose you're going to be a big literary god and everybody's going to eat you up, so you should let me protect you."

"How do they go about eating lit'ry gods?"

"By bothering them. They gnaw and gnaw till there's nothing left of you."

"How do you know about all this?"

"I've read books—I've met authors—I'm writing a novel myself—I think I'll call it *Fly Now, Pay Later* but the publishers think they'd get trouble from the airlines."

"Call it Pay Me The Penny After."

"That's nice— Shall I read you a chapter?" All of a sudden I was in a quiet home by lamplight with a quiet girl who would turn out to be passionate in bed, as I saw, but my God—*I dont like blondes*.

"I dont like blondes," I said.

"Maybe you'll like me. Would you like me to dye my hair?"

"Blondes have soft personalities—I've got whole future lifetimes left to deal with that softness—"

"Now you want hardness? Ruth Heaper actually isnt so great as you think, she's only after all a big awkward girl who doesnt know what to do."

I had me a companion there, and more so I saw it the night

I got drunk in the White Horse (Norman Mailer sitting in the back talking anarchy with a beer mug in his hand, my God will they give us beer in the Revolution? or Gall?)— Drunk, and in walks Ruth Heaper walking Erickson's dog and starts to talk to me persuading me to go home with her for the night.

"But I'm living with Alyce now—"

"But dont you still love me?"

"You said your doctor said—"

"Come on!" But Alyce somehow arrives at the White Horse and drags me out forcibly as if by the hair, to a cab to her home, from which I learn: Alyce Newman is not going to let anybody steal her man from her, no matter who he will be. And I was proud. I sang Sinatra's "I'm a Fool" all the way home in the cab. The cab flashed by oceangoing vessels docked at the North River piers.

47   AND ACTUALLY ALYCE AND I WERE WONDERFUL HEALTHY LOVERS— She only wanted me to make her happy and she did everything in her power to make me happy too, which was enough—"You should know more Jewish girls! They not only love you they bring you pumpernickel bread and sweet butter with your morning coffee."

"What's your father like?"

"He's a cigarsmoker—"

"And your mother?"

"Lace doilies in the livingroom—"

"And you?"

"I dont know."

"So you're going to be a big novelist— Who are your models?" But all her models were wrong, yet I knew she could do it, be the first great woman writer of the world, but I guess, I think, she wanted babies anyhow anyway— She was sweet and I still love her tonight.

We stayed together for an awful long time, too, *years*—

Julien called her Ecstasy Pie— Her best friend, the dark haired
Barbara Lipp, happened by circumstance to be in love with
Irwin Garden—Irwin had steered me to a haven. In this haven
I slept with her for lovemaking purposes but after we were
done I'd go to the outer bedroom, where I kept the winter
window constantly open and the radiator shut off, and slept
there in my sleepingbag. Eventually that way I finally got rid
of that tubercular Mexican cough— I'm not so dumb (as Ma
always said).

48

SO IRWIN WITH THAT $225 IN HIS POCKET first
takes me to Rockefeller Center for my passport
before we wander downtown talking about everything like we
used to do in our college days— "So now you're going to
Tangiers to see Hubbard."

"My mother says he's going to destroy me."

"Oh he'll probably try but he wont make it, like me," putting his head against my cheek and laughing. That Irwin.
"What about all the people who want to destroy *me* but I keep
on leaning my head against the bridge?"

"What bridge?"

"The Brooklyn Bridge. The bridge over the Passaic River
in Paterson. Even your bridge on the Merrimac full of mad
laughter. Any kinda bridge. I'll lean my head against *any* old
bridge any time. A spade in the Seventh Avenue toilet leaning
his head against toilets or something. I'm not fighting with
God."

"Who *is* God?"

"That big radar machine in the sky, I guess, or dead eyes
see." He was quoting one of his teenage poems, "Dead Eyes
See."

"What *do* dead eyes see?"

"Remember that big building we saw on 34th Street one

morning when we were high, and we said there was a giant in it?"

"Yeh—with his feet stuck out or something? That was a long time ago."

"Well dead eyes see that Giant, no less, unless the invisible ink is already invisible and even the Giant's gone."

"D'you like Alyce?"

"She's okay."

"She tells me this Barbara is in love with you."

"Yes I guess so." He couldnt be more bored. "I love Simon and I dont want no big Jewish wives yelling at me over the dishes— Look at that sickened face just went by." I turned to see a lady's back.

"Sickened? How?"

"Got the expression of sneers and hopelessness, gone forever, ugh."

"Doesnt God love her?"

"Oh read Shakespeare again or something, you're getting even almost maudlin." But he wasn't even interested in saying it. He looked about in the Rockefeller Building. "Look who's there." It was Barbara Lipp, who waved at us and came over.

And after a brief talk, and after we got my passport, we walked downtown just talking and just as we crossed Fourth Avenue and 12th there was Barbara again waving at us, but just by accident, really, a most strange circumstance.

"Yeh like it's the second time I've run into you today," says Barbara, who looks just like Irwin, black hairs, black eyes, same low voice.

Irwin says: "We were looking for the giant shot."

"What's the giant shot." (Barbara)

"Some big shit shot." And all of a sudden they go into a big Yiddishe controversy about shit shot I cant even understand, laughing in the street in front of me, giggling in fact. These lazy ladies of Manhattan. . . .

49

SO I GET MY BOAT TICKET AT A SEEDY YUGOSLAVIAN SHIPPING OFFICE on 14th Street and my sailing date is Sunday— The ship is the S.S. Slovenia, it's Friday.

Saturday morning I appear at Julien's apartment wearing dark glasses because of sore-eyed hangover and a scarf around my neck to kelp the cough—Alyce is with me, we've had our last taxi ride down the Hudson River piers seeing the huge thin shanked bows of Liberté's and Queen Elizabeths ready for the Le Havre anchor shot—Julien looks at me and cries: "Fernando!"

Fernando Lamas the Mexican actor he means. "Fernando the old international roué! Going to Tangiers to investigate Ay-rab girls, hey-y?" Nessa bundles up the kids, it's Julien's day off, and we all go to my pier in Brooklyn to have a farewell party in the cabin on my boat. I have a whole two-bed stateroom to myself since nobody ever sails with the Yugoslavian fleet except spies and *conspirateurs*. Alyce is delighted to see the masts of ships and the noonday sun on harbor water even tho she'd cast aside Wolfe for Trilling years ago. All Julien wants to do is climb around the housing with the kids. Meanwhile I'm mixing drinks in the stateroom which is already awry due to the fact they're loading on the port side first and the whole deck keels over. Sweet Nessa has a going-away present for me, *Danger à Tanger*, a cheap French novel about Arabs dropping bricks on the heads of the British Consulate. The men of the crew dont even speak English, just Yugoslav, tho they look Nessa and Alyce over with authoritative glances as tho they could speak any language at all. Me and Julien take his boys to the flying bridge to watch the loading operations.

Imagine having to travel thru time every day of your life carrying your own face and making it look like your own face! Fernando Lamas indeed! Poor Julien with his mustache doth carry his face grimly and interminably no matter what anybody say, philosopher or not. To weave that juice mask and let it look like yourself, while your liver gathers, your heart batters, t'would be enough to make God cry saying "All my children are martyrs and I want them back in perfect safety! Why did I emanate them in the first place, because I wanted to see a flesh movie?" Pregnant women who smile dont even dream about this. God Who is everything, the Already Thus, He Whom I saw on Desolation Peak, is also a smiling pregnant woman not even dreaming about this. And if I should complain about the way they manhandled Clark Gable in Shanghai or Gary Cooper in High Noon Town, or how I'm driven mad by old lost college roads in the moon, aye, moonlight, moonlight, moonlight me that, moonlight— Moonlight me some moonshine, adamantine you mine. Julien keeps stressing his lips, plurk, and Nessa holds high cheekboned flesh in escrow, and Alyce goes "Hum" in long-haired sadness and even the children die. Old Fernando the Philosopher wishes he could tell Julien something to tell everybody over the Universal Wire. But the Yugoslav Red Star stevedores dont care as long as they got bread, wine, and woman— Tho they may glare along stonewalls at Tito as he passes, yair— It's this business of holding your you-face to you every day, you might let it drop (like Irwin tries) but in the end an angelic question will fill you with surprise. Julien and I mix mad drinks, drink them, he and Nessa and the kids go off at dusk down the gangplank and Alyce and I lay passed out in my bunk, till eleven P.M., when the Yugoslav Steward knocks on my door, says "You stay on the ship? Okay?" and goes off into Brooklyn to get drunk with the crew—Alyce and I waking up, at one A.M., arm in arm in a dreadsome ship, agh— Only one watchman alone on the walk— Everybody drinking in bars of New York.

"Alyce" I say "let's get up and wash and take a subway to New York— We'll go to the West End and have a gay beer." But what's in the West End but death anyway?

Alyce only wants to sail to Africa with me. But we dress and go hand in hand down the gangplank, empty pier, and go cross-ing huge plazas of Brooklyn's hoodlum gangs with me with a bottle of wine in my hand like a weapon.

I've never seen a more dangerous neighborhood than those Brooklyn housing projects behind Bush Terminal pier.

We finally get to Borough Hall and dive into a subway, Van Cortlandt line, takes us all clear to 110th Street and Broadway and we go in the bar where my old favorite bartender Johnny is tending the beer.

I order bourbon and whiskey—I see the vision of haggard awful deathly faces passing one by one thru the bar of the world but my God they're all on a train, an endless train, and it end-lessly runs into the Graveyard. What to do? I try to tell Alyce:—

"Leecey, I see nothing but horror and terror everywhere—"

"That's because you're sick from drinking too much."

"But what'll I do with the horror and the terror I see?"

"Sleep it off, man—"

"But the bartender gave me the bleakest look—as tho I was dead."

"Maybe you are."

"Because I'm not staying with you?"

"That's right."

"But that's solipsistic stupid woman explanation of the hor-ror we share—"

"Share and share alike."

The endless train into the endless graveyard, all full of cock-roaches, kept running and running into Johnny the Bartender's hungry haggard eyes—I said "Johnny don't you see? We're all made at for perfidy?" and suddenly I realized I was making poems out of nothing at all, like always, so that if I were a Burroughs Adding Machine Computer I'd still make numbers dance to me. All, all, for tragedy.

And poor Leecie, she didnt understand Goyeshe me.

Go to Part Three.

PART THREE

PASSING THROUGH TANGIERS, FRANCE AND LONDON

50

WHAT A CRAZY PICTURE, maybe the picture of the typical American, sitting on a boat mulling over fingernails wondering where to really go, what to do next—I suddenly realized I had nowhere to turn at all.

But it was on this trip that the great change took place in my life which I called a "complete turningabout" on that earlier page, turning from a youthful brave sense of adventure to a complete nausea concerning experience in the world at large, a *revulsion* in all the six senses. And as I say the first sign of that revulsion had appeared during the dreamy solitary comfort of the two months on Desolation mountain, before Mexico, since which time I'd been melanged again with all my friends and old adventures, as you saw, and not so "sweetly," but now I was alone again. And the same feeling came to me: Avoid the World, it's just a lot of dust and drag and means nothing in the end. But what to do instead? And here I was relentlessly being carried to further "adventures" across the sea. But it was really in Tangiers after an overdose of opium the turningabout really clicked down and locked. In a minute—but meanwhile another experience, at sea, put the fear of the world in me, like an omen warning. This was a huge tempest that whacked at our C-4 from the North, from the Januaries and Pleniaries of Iceland and Baffin Bay. During wartime I'd actually sailed in those Northern seas of the Arctic but it was only in summertime: now, a thousand miles south of these in the void of January Seas, gloom, the cappers came glurring in gray spray as high as a house and plowed rivers all over our bow and down the washes. Furyiating howling Blakean glooms, thunders of thumping, washing waving sick manship diddling like a long cork for nothing in the mad waste. Some old Breton knowledge of the sea still in my blood now shuddered. When I saw those walls of water advancing one by one for miles in gray carnage I cried in my soul WHY DIDNT I STAY HOME!? But it was too late. When the third night came the ship was heaving from side to side so badly even the Yugoslavs went to bed and jammed themselves down between pillows and blankets. The kitchen was insane all night with crashing and toppling pots even tho they'd been secured. It scares a seaman to hear the Kitchen scream in fear. For eating at first the steward had placed dishes on a wet tablecloth, and of course no soup in soupbowls but in deep cups, but now it was too late for even that. The men chewed at biscuits as they staggered to their knees in their wet sou'westers. Out on deck where I went a minute the heel of the ship was enough to kick you over the gunwale straight *at* walls of water, sperash. Deck lashed trucks groaned and broke their cables and smashed around. It was a Biblical Tempest like an old dream. In the night I prayed with fear to God Who was now taking all of us, the souls on board, at this dread particular time, for reasons of His own, at last. In my semi delirium I thought I saw a snow white ladder being held down to us from the sky. I saw Stella Maris over the Sea like a statue of Liberty all in shining white. I thought of all the sailors that ever drowned and O the choking thought of it, from Phoenicians of 3000 years ago to poor little teenage sailors of America only last war (some of whom I'd sailed in safety with)— The carpets of sinking water all deep blue *green* in the middle of the ocean, with their damnable patterns of foam, the sickening choking *too-much* of it even tho you're only looking at the surface— beneath all that the upwell of cold miles of fathoms—swaying, rolling, smashing, the tonnages of Peligroso Roar beating, heaving, swirling—not a face in sight! Here comes more! Duck! The whole ship (only as long as a Village) ducks into it shuddering, the crazy screws furiously turn in nothingness, shaking the ship, slap, the bow's now up, thrown up, the screws are dreaming deep below, the ship hasnt gained ten feet—it's like that— It's like frost in your face, like the cold mouths of ancient fathers, like wood cracking in the sea. Not even a fish in sight. It's the thunderous jubilation of Neptune and his bloody wind god canceling men. "All I had to do was stay home, give it all up, get a little home for me and Ma, meditate, live quiet, read in the sun, drink wine in the moon in old clothes, pet my kitties, sleep good dreams—now look at this *petrain* I got me in, Oh dammit!" ("Petrain" is a 16th Century French word meaning "mess.") But God chose to let us live as at dawn the captain turned the ship the other way and gradually left the storm behind, then headed back east towards Africa and the stars.

51   I FEEL I DIDNT EXPLAIN THAT RIGHT, but it's too late, the moving finger crossed the storm and that's the storm.

I thereafter spent ten quiet days as that old freighter chugged and chugged across the calmest seas without seeming to get anywhere and I read a book on world history, wrote notes, and paced the deck at night. (How insouciantly they write about the sinking of the Spanish fleet in the storm off Ireland, ugh!) (Or even one little Galilean fisherman, drowned forever.) But even in so peaceful and simple an act as reading world history in a comfortable cabin on comfortable seas I felt that awful revulsion for everything—the insane things done in human history even before us, enough to make Apollo cry or Atlas drop his load, my God the massacres, purges, tithes stolen, thieves hanged, crooks imperatored, dubs praetorian'd, benches busted on people's heads, wolves attacked nomad campfires, Genghiz Khans ruining—testes smashed in battle, women raped in smoke, children belted, animals slaughtered, knives raised, bones thrown— Clacking big slurry meatjuiced lips the dub Kings crapping on everybody thru silk—The beggars crapping thru burlap— The mistakes everywhere the mistakes! The smell of old settlements and their cookpots and dungheaps— The Cardinals like "Silk stockings full of mud," the American congressmen who "shine and stink like rotten mackerel in the moonlight"— The scalpings from Dakota to Tamurlane— And the human eyes at Guillotine and burning stake at dawn, the glooms, bridges, mists, nets, raw hands and old dead vests of poor mankind in all these thousands of years of "history" (they call it) and all of it an awful mistake. Why did God do it? or is there really a Devil who led the Fall? Souls in Heaven said "We want to try mortal existence, O God, Lucifer said it's great!"— Bang, down we fall, to this, to concentration camps, gas ovens, barbed wire, atom bombs, television murders, Bolivian starvation, thieves in silk, thieves in neckties, thieves in office, paper shufflers, bureaucrats, insult, rage, dismay, horror, terrified nightmares, secret death of hangovers, cancer, ulcers, strangulation, pus, old age, old age homes, canes, puffed flesh, dropped teeth, stink, tears, and goodbye. Somebody else write it, I dont know how.

How to live with glee and peace therefore? By roaming around with your baggage from state to state each one worse deeper into the darkness of the fearful heart? And the heart only a thumping tube all delicately murderable with snips of artery and vein, with chambers that shut, finally someone eats it with the knife and fork of malice, laughing. (Laughing for awhile anyway.)

Ah but as Julien would say "There's nothing you can do about it, revel in it boy— Bottoms up in every way, Fernando." I think of Fernando his puffed alcoholic eyes like mine looking out on bleak palmettos at dawn, shivering in his scarf: beyond the last Frisian Hill a big scythe is cutting down the daisies of his hope tho he's urged to celebrate this each New Years Eve in Rio or in Bombay. In Hollywood they swiftly slide the old director in his crypt. Aldous Huxley half blind watches his house burn down, seventy years old and far from the happy walnut chair of Oxford. Nothing, nothing, nothing O but *nothing* could interest me any more for one god damned minute in anything in the *world*. But where else to go?

On the overdose of opium this was intensified to the point where I actually got up and packed to go back to America and find a *home*.

52   AT FIRST THE SEA FEAR SLEPT, I actually enjoyed the approach to Africa and of course I had a ball the first week in Africa.

It was sunny afternoon February 1957 when we first saw the pale motleys of yellow sand and green meadow which marked the vague little coast line of Africa far away. It grew bigger as the afternoon drowsed on till a white spot that had troubled me for hours turned out to be a gas tank in the hills. Then like seeing sudden slow files of Mohammedan women in white I saw the white roofs of the little port of Tangiers sitting right there in the elbow of the land, on the water. This dream of white robed Africa on the blue afternoon Sea, wow, who dreamed it? Rimbaud! Magellan! Delacroix! Napoleon! White sheets waving on the rooftop!

And suddenly a small Moroccan fishing boat with a motor

but a high balconied poop in carved Lebanese wood, with cats
in jalabas and pantaloons chattering on deck, came plopping by
turning south down the Coast for the evening's fishing beneath
the star (now) of Stella Maris, Mary of the Sea who protects all
fishermen by investing with grace of hope in the dangers of the
sea her own Archangelic prayer of Safety. And some Mahomet
Star of the Sea of their own to guide them. The wind ruffled
on their clothes, their hair, "their real hair of real Africa" I said
to myself amazed. (Why travel if not like a child?)

Now Tangiers grew, you saw sandy barrens of Spain on the
left, the hump leading to Gibraltar around the Horn of
Hesperid, the very amazing spot the entryway to the Mediterranean Atlantis of old flooded by the Ice Caps so celebrate in the
Book of Noah. Here's where Mister Hercules held the world up
groaning as "rough rocks groaning vegetate" (Blake). Here the
patch-eyed international gem smugglers sneaked up with blue
.45's to steal the Tangier harem. Here the crazy Scipios came to
trounce the blue eyed Carthage. Somewhere in that sand beyond the Atlas Range I saw my blue eyed Gary Cooper winning the "Beau Geste." And a night in Tangiers with Hubbard!

The ship anchored in the sweet little harbor and spun slowly
around giving me all kinds of views of city and headland from
my porthole as I packed to leave the ship. On the headland
around Tangiers Bay was a beacon turning in the blue dusk like
St. Mary assuring me port is made and all's all safe. The city
turns on magical little lights, the hill of the Casbah hums, I
wanta be out there in those narrow Medina alleys looking for
hasheesh. The first Arab I see is too ridiculous to believe: a
little bum boat puts out to our Jacob's Ladder, the motor men
ragged teenage Arabs in sweaters like the sweaters of Mexico,
but in the mid boat stands a fat Arab in a grimy red fez, in a
blue business suit, hands behind him, looking for to sell cigarettes or buy something or anything at all. Our handsome Yugo
captain shouts them away from the bridge. At about seven we
dock and I go ashore. Big Arabic Letterings are stamped on my

fresh innocent passport by clerks in dusty fezzes and baggy pants. In fact it's exactly like Mexico, the Fellaheen world, that is, the world that's not making History in the present: *making* History, manufacturing it, shooting it up in H bombs and Rockets, reaching for the grand conceptual finale of Highest Achievement (in our times the Faustian "West" of America, Britain and Germany high and low).

I get a cab to Hubbard's address on a narrow hilly street in the European quarter beneath the Medina twinkle hill.

Poor Bull has been on a health kick and is already asleep at 9:30 when I knock on his garden door. I'm amazed to see him strong and healthy, no longer skinny from drugs, all tanned and muscular and vigorous. He's six foot one, blue eyes, glasses, sandy hair, 44, a scion of a great American industrial family but they've only a-scioned him a $200 a month trust fund and are soon to cut that down to $120, finally two years later rejecting him completely from their interior decorated livingrooms in retirement Florida because of the mad book he's written and published in Paris (*Nude Supper*)—a book enough to make any mother turn pale (more anon). Bull grabs his hat and says "Come on, let's go dig the Medina" (after we turn on) and vigorously striding like an insane German Philologist in Exile he leads me thru the garden and out the gate to the little magic street. "Tomorrow morning first thing after I've had my simple breakfast of tea and bread, we'll go rowing in the Bay."

This is a command. This is the first time I've seen "Old Bull" (actually a friend of the "Old Bull" in Mexico) since the days in New Orleans when he was living with his wife and kids near the Levee (in Algiers Louisiana)— He doesnt seem any older except he doesnt seem to comb his hair as carefully any more, which I realize the next day is only because he's distraught and completely bemused in the midst of his writing, like a mad haired genius in a room. He's wearing American Chino pants and pocketed shirts, a fisherman's hat, and carries a huge clicking switchblade a foot long. "Yessir, without this switchblade I'd be dead now. Bunch of Ay-rabs surrounded me in an alley one night. I just let this old thing click out and said 'Come on ya buncha bastards' and they cut out."

"How do you *like* the Arabs?"

"Just push em aside like little pricks" and suddenly he walked right thru a bunch of Arabs on the sidewalk, making them split on both sides, muttering and swinging his arms with a vigorous unnatural pumping motion like an insane exaggerated Texas oil millionaire pushing his way thru the Swarms of Hong Kong.

"Come on Bull, you cant do that every day."

"*What?*" he barked, almost squeaking. "Just brush em aside, son, dont take no shit from them little pricks." But by next day I realized *everybody* was a little prick:—me, Irwin, himself, the Arabs, the women, the merchants, the President of the U.S.A. and Ali Baba himself; Ali Baba or whatever his name was, a child leading a flock of sheep in the field and carrying a baby lamb in his arms with a sweet expression like the expression of St. Joseph when he himself was a child:—"Little prick!" I realized it was just an expression, a sadness on Bull's part that he would never regain the innocence of the Shepherd or in fact of the little prick.

Suddenly as we climbed the hill of white street steps I remembered an old sleeping dream where I climbed such steps and came to a Holy City of Love. "Do you mean to tell me that my life is going to change after all that?" I say to myself, (high), but suddenly to the right there was a big Kaplow! (hammer into steel) ca blam! and I looked into the black inky maw of a Tangiers garage and the white dream died right there, for good, right in the greasy arm of a big Arab mechanic crashing furiously at the fenders and hems of Fords in the oil rag gloom under one Mexican lightbulb. I kept on climbing the holy steps with weariness, to the next horrible disappointment. Bull kept yelling back "Come on, step on it, young man like you cant even keep up with old man like me?"

"You *walk* too fast!"

"Lard assed hipsters, aint no good for nothing!" says Bull.

We walk almost running down a steep hill of grass and boulders, with a path, to a magical little street with African tenements and again I'm hit in the eye by an old magic dream: "I was born here: This is the street where I was born." I even look up at the exact tenement window to see if my crib's still there. (Man, that hasheesh in Bull's room—and it's amazing how American potsmokers have gone around the world by now with the most exaggerated phantasmagoria of gooey details, hallucinations actually, by which their machine-ridden brains though are actually given a little juice of the ancient life of man, so God bless pot.) ("If you were born on this street you musta drowned a long time ago," I add, thinking.)

Bull goes arm swinging and swaggering like a Nazi into the first queer bar, brushing Arabs aside and looking back at me with: "Hey what?" I cant see how he can have managed this except I learn later he's spent a whole year in the little town sitting in his room on huge overdoses of morfina and other drugs staring at the tip of his shoe too scared to take one shuddering bath in eight months. So the local Arabs remember him as a shuddering skinny ghost who's apparently recovered, and let him rant. Everybody seems to know him. Boys yell "Hi!" "Boorows!" "Hey!"

In the dim queer bar which is also the lunching spot of most of the queer Europeans and Americans of Tangiers with limited means, Hubbard introduces me to the big fat Dutch middleaged owner who threatens to return to Amsterdam if he dont find a good "poy" very soon, as I mentioned in an article elsewhere. He also complains about the declining peseta but I can surely see him moaning in his private bed at night for love or something in the sorry *internationale* of his night. Dozens of weird expatriates, coughing and lost on the cobbles of Moghreb—some of them sitting at the outdoor cafe tables with the glum look of foreigners reading zigzag newspapers over unwanted

Vermouth. Ex-smugglers with skipper hats straggling by. No joyful Moroccan tambourine anywhere. Dust in the street. The same old fish heads everywhere.

Hubbard also introduces me to his lover, a boy of 20 with a sweet sad smile just the type poor Bull has always loved, from Chicago to Here. We have a few drinks and go back to his room.

"Tomorrow the Frenchwoman who runs this pension will probably rent you that excellent room on the roof with bath and patio, my dear. I prefer being down here in the garden so I can play with the cats and I'm growing some roses." The cats, two, belong to the Chinese housekeeper who does the cleaning for the shady lady from Paris, who owns the apartment building on some old Roulette bet or some old rearview of the Bourse, or something—but later I find all the real work is done by the big Nubian Negress who lives in the cellar (I mean, if you wanted big romantic novels about Tangiers).

5 3   BUT NO TIME FOR THAT! Bull insists we go rowing. We pass whole cafes of sour Arab men on the waterfront, they're all drinking green mint tea in glasses and chain smoking pipes of kief (marijuana)— They watch us pass with those strange redrimmed eyes, as tho they were half Moorish and half Carthaginian (half Berber)— "God those guys must hate us, for some reason."

"No," says Bull, "they're just waiting for someone to run amok. D'jever see an amok trot? An amok occurs here periodically. He is a man who suddenly picks up a machete and starts trotting thru the market with a regular monotonous trot slashing people as he passes. He usually kills or maims about a dozen before these characters of the cafes get wind of it and get up and rush after him and tear him to bits. In between that they smoke their endless pipes of pot."

"What they think of you trottin down to the waterfront every morning to rent a boat?"

"Somewhere among them is the guy that gets the profits—" Some boys are tending rowboats at the quai. Bull gives them money and we get in and Bull rows off vigorously, standing facing forward, like a Venetian oarsman. "When I was in Venice I noticed that this is the only real way to row a boat, standing up, boom and bam, like this," rowing with forward motion. "Outside of that Venice is the dreariest town this side of Beeville Texas. Dont ever go to Beeville boy, or Venice either." (Beeville a sheriff'd caught him making love to his wife June in the car, parked on the highway, for which he spent two days in jail with a sinister deputy in steel rimmed spectacles.) "Venice—my God, on a clear night you can hear the shrieks of the fairies on St. Marks Plaza a mile away. You can see successful young novelists being rowed away into the night. In the middle of the Canal they suddenly assault the poor Italian Gondoleer. They have palazzos with people straight out of Princeton amortifyin' chauffeurs." The funny thing is that when Bull was in Venice he was invited to an elegant party in a Palace, and when he appeared at the door, with his old Harvard friend Irwin Swenson the hostess held out her hand to be kissed—Irwin Swenson said: "You see in these circles you must kiss the hand of the hostess, customarily"— But as everybody stared at the pause in the door Bull yelled out "Aw gee, I'd rather kiss her *cont!*" And that was the end of that.

There he is rowing energetically as I sit on the poop digging Tangiers Bay. Suddenly a boatload of Arab boys rows up and they yell in Spanish to Bull: *"Tu nuevo amigo Americano? Quieren muchachos?"*

"No, *quiere mucha*-CHAS."

"Por que?"

"Es macho por muchachas mucho!"

"Ah," they all wave their hands and row away, looking for money from visiting queers, they'd asked Hubbard if I was queer. Bull rowed on but suddenly he was tired and had me row. We were nearing the end of the harbor wall. The water got choppy. "Ah shit, I'm tired."

"Well for God's sake make a little effort to get us back a ways." Bull was already tired and wanted to go back to his room to make majoun and write his book.

54 MAJOUN IS A CANDY you make with honey, spices and raw marijuana (kief)— Kief is actually mostly stems with fewer leaves of the plant chemically known as Muscarine— Bull rolled it all up into edible balls and we ate it, chewing for hours, picking it out of our teeth with toothpicks, drinking it down with hot plain tea— In two hours our eyes' irises would get huge and black and off we'd go walking to the fields outside town— A tremendous high giving vent to many colored sensations like, "Notice the delicate white shade of those flowers under the tree." We stood under the tree overlooking the Bay of Tangiers. "I get many visions at this spot," says Bull, serious now, telling me about his book.

In fact I hung around his room several hours a day altho I now had a great room on the roof, but he wanted me to hang around about noon till two, then cocktails and dinner and most of the evening together (a very formal man) so I happened to be sitting on his bed reading when often, while typing out his story, he'd suddenly double up in laughter at what he done and sometimes roll on the floor. A strange compressed laugh came out of his stomach as he typed. But so wont no Truman Capote think he's only a typewriter, sometimes he'd whip out his pen and start scribbling on typewriter pages which he threw over his shoulder when he was through with them, like Doctor Mabuse, till the floor was littered with the strange Etruscan script of his handwriting. Meanwhile as I say his hair was all askew, but as that was the gist of my worries about him he twice or thrice looked up from his writing and said to me with frank blue eyes "You know you're the only person in the world who can sit in the room while I'm writing and I dont even know you're *there?*" A great compliment, too. The way I did it was to concentrate on my own thoughts and just dream away, mustn't disturb Bull. "All of a sudden I look up from this horrible pun and there you are reading a label on a bottle of Cognac."

I'll leave the book for the reader to see, *Nude Supper*, all about shirts turning blue at hangings, castration, and lime— Great horrific scenes with imaginary doctors of the future tending machine catatonics with negative drugs so they can wipe the world out of people but when that's accomplished the Mad Doctor is alone with a self operated self tape recording he can change or edit at will, but no one left, not even Chico the Albino Masturbator in a Tree, to notice— Whole legions of shitters patched up like bandaged scorpions, something like that, you'll have to read it yourself, but so horrible that when I undertook to start typing it neatly doublespace for his publishers the following week I had horrible nightmares in my roof room—like of pulling out endless bolognas from my mouth, from my very entrails, feet of it, pulling and pulling out all the horror of what Bull saw, and wrote.

You may talk to me about Sinclair Lewis the great American writer, or Wolfe, or Hemingway, or Faulkner, but none of them were as honest, unless you name . . . but it aint Thoreau either.

"Why are all these young boys in white shirts being hanged in limestone caves?"

"Dont ask me—I get these messages from other planets— I'm apparently some kind of agent from another planet but I havent got my orders clearly decoded yet."

"But why all the vile rheum—like r-h-e-u-m."

"I'm shitting out my educated Middlewest background for once and for all. It's a matter of catharsis where I say the most horrible thing I can think of— Realize that, the most *horrible* dirty slimy awful niggardliest posture possible— By the time I finish this book I'll be as pure as an angel, my dear. These great

existential anarchists and terrorists so-called never even their
own drippy fly *mentioneth*, dear— They should poke sticks thru
their shit and analyze *that* for social progress."

"But where'll all this shit get us?"

"Simply get us rid of shit, *really Jack*." He whips out (it's 4
P.M.) the afternoon's apéritif cognac bottle. We both sigh to see
it. Bull has suffered so much.

55   FOUR P.M. IS ABOUT TIME John Banks drops in. John
Banks is a handsome decadent chap from Birmingham England who used to be a gangster there (he says),
later turned to smuggling and in his prime sailed dashingly into
Tangiers Bay with a cargo of contrabands in a sloop. Maybe he
just worked the coal boats, I dont know, like it aint too far
from Newcastle to Birmingham. But he was a blue eyed spirited
dashing dog from England with a limey accent and Hubbard
just loved him. In fact every time I revisited Hubbard in New
York or Mexico City or Newark or someplace he always had
a favorite *raconteur* he'd found someplace to regale him with
marvelous stories at cocktail time. Hubbard was really the most
elegant Englishman in the world. In fact I have visions of him
in London sitting before a club fire with celebrated doctors,
brandy in hand, telling stories about the world and laughing
"Hm hm hm" from the pit of his stomach bending, such an
enormous Sherlock Holmes. In fact Irwin Garden that crazy
Seer once said to me quite seriously "Do you realize Hubbard
is somewhat like Sherlock Holmes' older brother?"

"Sherlock Holmes' older *brother?*"

"Havent you read all of Conan Doyle? Anytime Holmes was
stuck to solve a crime he took a cab to the Soho and hit up on
his older brother who was always an old drunk layin around
with a bottle of wine in a cheap room, O delightful! Just like
you in Frisco."

"*Then* what?"

"Older Holmes would always tell Sherlock how to solve the case— It seems he knew everything goin on in London."

"Didnt Sherlock Holmes' brother ever put on a tie and go to the Club?"

"Only to knaow mother" says Irwin sluffin me off but now I see Bull is actually Sherlock Holmes' older brother in London talking shop with the gangsters of Birmingham, to get the latest slang, as he's also a linguist and philologist interested not only in the local dialects of Shitshire and the other shires but all the latest *slang*. In the midst of a tale about his experiences in Burma John Banks, over window-darkening cognacs and kief, lets out with the amazing phrase "There she is jugglin me sweetbreads with her tongue!"

"*Sweet*breads?"

"Not pumpernickel, ducks."

"Then what?" laughs Bull holding his belly and by now his eyes are shining sweet blue tho at the next moment he may aim a rifle over us and say:—"I always wanted to take this one to the Amazon, if it could only decimate *piranha*."

"But I havent finished my story about Burma!" And it was always cognac, stories, and I'd step out to the garden now and then and marvel at that purple sunset bay. Then when John or the other raconteurs left Bull and I would stride to the very best restaurant in town for a supper, usually steak with pepper sauce à la Auvergne, or Pascal pollito à la Yay, or anything good, with a gibbering dipper of good French wine, Hubbard throwing chicken bones over his shoulder whether or not the basement of El Paname currently contained women or not.

"Hey Bull, there's some long necked Parisiennes with pearls at the table behind you."

"*La belle gashe,*" flup, chicken bone, "what?"

"But they're all drinkin out of long stemmed glasses."

"Ah dont bore me with your New England dreams" but he never did just throw the whole plate over his shoulder like

Julien done in 1944, crash. Suavely he lights up however a long joint of marijuana.

"Can you light up marijuana in here?"

He orders Benedictine with dessert. By *God* he's bored. "When will Irwin get here?" Irwin's on his way with Simon in another Yugoslavian freighter but a freighter in April with no storms. Back at my room he whips out his binoculars and stares to sea. "When will he get here?" Suddenly he starts crying on my shoulder.

"What's the matter?"

"I just don't know"—he's really crying and he really means it. He's been in love with Irwin for years but if you ask me in the strangest way. Like the time I showed him a picture Irwin drew of two hearts being pierced by Cupid's arrow but by mistake he'd drawn the arrow's shaft only thru one heart and Hubbard's yelling "That's it! That's what I mean!"

"What *do* you mean?"

"This autocratic person can only fall in love with the image of himself."

"What's all this *love* business between grownup men." This was on the occasion in 1954 when I was sitting home with my mother and all of a sudden the doorbell rings, Hubbard pushes the door in, asks for a dollar to complete the cab fare (which my mother actually pays) and then sits there with us distractedly writing a long letter. And my mother'd only just about then been saying "Stay away from Hubbard, he'll destroy you." I never saw a stranger scene. Suddenly Ma said:—

"Will you have a sandwich, Mister Hubbard?" but he only shook his head and went on writing and he was writing a big involved love letter to Irwin in California. The reason he'd come to my house, he admitted in Tangiers in his bored but suffering tones, was, "Because the only connection I had at that agonized time with Irwin was thru *you,* you'd been getting long letters from him about what he was doing in Frisco. Laborsome human prose but I had to have some connection with him, like you were this great bore getting big letters from my rare angel and I had to see you as secondbest to *nothing*." But this didnt insult me because I knew what he meant having read *Of Human Bondage* and Shakespeare's will, and Dmitri Karamazov too. We'd gone from Ma's house (sheepishly) to a bar on the corner, where he went on writing while this secondbest ghost kept ordering drinks and watching in silence. I loved Hubbard so for just his big stupid soul. Not that Irwin wasnt worthy of him but how on earth could they consummate this great romantic love with Vaseline and K.Y.?

If the Idiot had molested Ippolit, which he didnt, there'd have been no counterfeiter Uncle Edouard for sweet crazy Bernard to gnash on. But Hubbard wrote on and on this huge letter in the bar while the Chinese Laundryman watched him from across the street nodding. Irwin had just gotten himself a chick in Frisco and Hubbard says "I can just see this great Christian whore" though he neednt worry on that point, Irwin soon met Simon after that.

"What's Simon like?" he says now crying on my shoulder in Tangiers. (O what would my mother have said to see Sherlock Holmes' older brother crying on my shoulder in Tangiers?) I drew a picture of Simon in pencil to show him. The crazy eyes and face. He didnt really believe it. "Let's go down to my room and kick the gong around." This is Cab Calloway's old expression for "smoking the opium pipe." We'd just picked it up over desultory coffees in the Zoco Chico from a man in a red fez whom Hubbard confidentially accused (to me) of causing hepatitis throughout Tangerx (real spelling). With an old olive oil can, a hole in it, another hole for the mouth, we stuffed raw red opium in the well hole and got it lit and inhaled huge blue gobs of opium smoke. Meanwhile an American acquaintance of ours showed up and said he'd found the whores I'd been asking for. While Bull and John Banks smoked me and Jim found the girls striding in long jalabas under neon cigarette signs, took em to my room, took turns with the trick-turners,

and went down again to smoke more Opium. (The amazing
thing about the Arab prostitute is to see her remove her veil
from over her nose and then the long Biblical robes, suddenly
leaving nothing but a peachy wench with a lascivious leer and
high heels and nothing else—yet on the street they look so
mournfully holy, those eyes, those dark eyes alone in all that
chastest cloth . . .)

Bull looked at me funnily later and said: "I dont feel this, do
you?"

"No. We must be so *saturated!*"

"Let's try eating it" and so we sprinkled pinches of raw O
mud in hot cups of tea and drank up. In a minute we were
stoned cold blue death. I went upstairs with a pinchful and
sprinkled more into my tea, which I brewed on the little kerosene heater Bull had kindly bought me in exchange for typing
up the first sections of his book. On my back for twenty-four
hours thence I stared at the ceiling, as that Virgin Mary head-
light turning across the Bay headland sent streamer after
streamer of salvation light over the picaresque of my ceiling
with all its talking mouths— Its Aztec faces— Its cracks thru
which heaven you can see— My candlelight— Gone out on
Holy Opium— Experiencing as I say that "Turning-about"
which said: "Jack, this is the end of your world travel— Go
home— Make a home in America— Tho this be that, and that
be this, it's not for you— The holy little old roof cats of silly
old home town are *cry*ing for you, Ti Jean— These fellas dont
understand you, and Arabs beat their mules—" (Earlier that
day when I saw an Arab beat his mule I almost rushed up to
grab the stick from his hand, and beat *him* with it, which would
have precipitated riots on Radio Cairo or in Jaffa or anywhere
where idiots beat their loving animals, or *mules,* or mortal suffering actors who are doomed to carry other people's burdens)— The fact that the sweet little box bent back is only a
fact for come. Come comes, and's done. Print that in Pravda.
But I lay there for twenty-four or maybe thirty-six hours star-

ing at the ceiling, puking in the hall toilet, on that awful old opium mud whilst meanwhile a nextdoor apartment featured the creaks of pederast love which didnt bother me except at dawn the sweet smiling sad Latin boy went into my bathroom and laid a huge dung in the bidet, which I saw in the morning horrified, how could anybody but a Nubian Princessa stoop down to clean it? *Mira?*

Always Gaines had told me in Mexico City that the Chinese said that Opium was for sleep but for me it wasnt sleep but this horrible turning and turning in horror in bed (people who poison themselves moan), and realizing "Opium is for Horror—De Quincey O my—" and I realized my mother was waiting for me to take her home, my mother, my mother who smiled in her womb when she bore me— Though every time I sang "Why Was I Born?" (by the Gershwins) she snapped "Why are you singing that?"—I slurp up the final cup of O.

Happy priests who play basketball in the Catholic church behind, are up at dawn ringing the Benedict Bell, for me, as Stella the star of the Sea shines hopeless on waters of millions of drowned babies still smiling in the womb of the sea. Bong! I go out on the roof and glare gloomily at everybody, the priests are looking up at me. We just stare. All my olden friends are ringing bells in monasteries everywhere. There's a conspiracy going on. What would Hubbard say? There's no hope even in the cassocks of Sacristy. To never see the Bridge at Orleans again is not perfect safety. The best thing to do is be like a baby.

56 AND I HAD REALLY LIKED TANGIERS, the fine Arabs who never even looked at me in the street but minded their eyes to themselves (unlike Mexico which is *all* eyes), the great roof room with tile patio looking down on the little dreamy Spanish Moroccan tenements with an empty lot hill that had a shackled goat grazing— The view over those

roofs to the Magic Bay with its sweep to the Headland Ultimo, on clear days the distant shadow mump of Gibraltar far away— The sunny mornings I'd sit on the patio enjoying my books, my kief and the Catholic churchbells— Even the kids' basketball games I could see by leaning far over and around and—or down straight I'd look to Bull's garden, see his cats, himself mulling a minute in the sun— And on heavenly starlit nights just to lean on the roof rail (concrete) and look to sea till sometimes often I saw glittering boats putting in from Casablanca I felt the trip had been worthwhile. But now on the opium overdose I felt snarling dreary thoughts about all Africa, all Europe, the world—all I wanted somehow now was Wheaties by a pine breeze kitchen window in America, that is, I guess a vision of my childhood in America— Many Americans suddenly sick in foreign lands must get the same childlike yen, like Wolfe suddenly remembering the lonely milkman's bottle clink at dawn in North Carolina as he lies there tormented in an Oxford room, or Hemingway suddenly seeing the autumn leaves of Ann Arbor in a Berlin brothel. Scott Fitz tears coming into his eyes in Spain to think of his father's old shoes in the farmhouse door. Johnny Smith the Tourist wakes up drunk in a cracked Istanbul room crying for ice cream sodas of Sunday Afternoon in Richmond Hill Center.

So by the time Irwin and Simon finally arrived for their big triumphant reunion with us in Africa, it was too late. I was spending more and more time on my roof and now actually reading Van Wyck Brooks' books (all about the lives of Whitman, Bret Harte, even Charles Nimrod of South Carolina) to get the feel of home, forgetting entirely how bleak and grim it had been only a short while ago like in Roanoke Rapids the lost tears— But it *has* been ever since then that I've lost my yen for any further outside searching. Like Archbishop of Canterbury says "A constant detachment, a will to go apart and wait upon God in quiet and silence," which more or less describes his own feeling (he being Dr. Ramsey the scholar) about retirement in this gadfly world. At the time I sincerely believed that the only decent activity in the world was to pray for everyone, in solitude. I had many mystic joys on my roof, even while Bull or Irwin were waiting for me downstairs, like the morning I felt the whole living world ripple joyfully and all the dead things rejoice. Sometimes when I saw the priests watching me from seminary windows, where they too leaned looking to sea, I thought they knew about me already (happy paranoia). I thought they rang the bells with special fervor. The best moment of the day was to slip in bed with bedlamp over book, and read facing the open patio windows, the stars and the sea. I could also hear it sighing out there.

57 MEANWHILE THE BIG LOVELY ARRIVAL was strange with Hubbard suddenly getting drunk and waving his machete at Irwin who told him to stop frightening everybody— Bull had waited so long, in such torment, and now he realized probably in an opium turningabout of his own that it was all nonsense anyway— Once when he'd mentioned a very pretty girl he met in London, daughter of a doctor, and I'd said "Why dont you marry a girl like that someday?" he said: "O dear I'm a bachelor, I want to live alone." He didnt particularly want to live with anybody, ever. He spent hours staring in his room like Lazarus, like me. But now Irwin wanted to do everything right. Dinners, walks around the Medina, a proposed railroad trip to Fez, circuses, cafes, swims in the ocean, hikes, I could see Hubbard grabbing his head in dismay. All he went on doing were the same thing: his 4 P.M. apéritifs signalled the new excitement of the day. While John Banks and the other raconteurs swarmed around the room laughing with Bull, drinks in their hands, poor Irwin bent to the kerosene burner cooking big fishes he'd bought in the market that afternoon. Once in a while Bull bought us all dinner at the Paname but it was too expensive. I was waiting for my next advance install-

ment from the publishers so I could start back for home via Paris and London.

It was a little sad. Bull would be too tired to go out so Irwin and Simon would call up to me from the garden just like little kids calling at your childhood window, "Jack-Kee!" which would bring tears to my eyes almost and force me to go down and join them. "Why are you so with*drawn* all of a sudden!" cried Simon. I couldnt explain it without telling them they bored me as well as everything else, a strange thing to have to say to people you've spent years with, all the *lacrimae rerum* of sweet association across the hopeless world dark, so dont say anything.

We explored Tangiers together, the funny thing too was that Bull had explicitly written to them in New York *never* to go into a Mohammedan establishment like a tea shop or anything where you sat down socially, they would not be wanted, but Irwin and Simon had come to Tangiers via Casablanca where they'd already strolled into Mohammedan cafés and smoked pot with the Arabs and bought some even to take away. So now we strolled into a strange hall with benches and tables where teenagers sat either sleeping or playing checkers and drinking green mint tea in glasses. The eldest boy was a young hobo in flowing rags and bandages for a hurt foot, barefooted, the robe's hood over his head like St. Joseph, bearded, 22 or so, Mohammed Mayé by name, who invited us to his table and produced a bag of marijuana which he thumbed into a long-stemmed pipe and lighted and passed around. Out of his tattered robes he pulled out a worn newspaper picture of his hero, Sultan Mohammed. A radio was blaring the endless yellings of Radio Cairo. Irwin told Mohammed Mayé he was Jewish and that was alright with Mohammed and everyone else in the joint, absolutely cool bunch of hipsters and urchins probably of a new "beat" east— "Beat" in the original true sense of mind-your-own-business— Because we did see gangs of bluejeaned Arab teenagers playing rock n roll records in a crazy jukebox hangout full of pinball machines, just like Albuquerque New Mexico or anywhere, and when we went to the circus a big gang of them cheered and applauded Simon when they heard him laugh at the juggler, all turning around, a dozen of them, "Yay! Yay!" like hepcats at a Bronx dance. (Later Irwin traveled further and saw the same thing in all countries of Europe and heard about it going on in Russia and Korea.) Old mournful Holy Men of the Mohammedan world called "Men Who Pray" (*Hombres Que Rison*), who walked the streets in white robes and long beards, were said to be the only last remaining individuals who could cause gangs of Arab hipsters to disperse with just one look. Cops made no difference, we saw a riot in the Zoco Grande that flared up over an argument between Spanish cops and Moroccan soldiers. Bull was there with us. All of a sudden a seething yelling mass of cops and soldiers and robed oldsters and bluejeaned hoodlums came piling up the alley from wall to wall, we all turned and ran. I myself ran alone down one particular alley accompanied by two Arab boys of ten who laughed with me as we ran. I ducked into a Spanish wine shop just as the proprietor dragged down the sliding iron door, bang. I ordered a Malaga as the riot boomed on by and down the street. Later I met the gang at café tables. "Riots every day," said Bull proudly.

But the "ferment" in the Middle East we could all see was not as simple as our passports indicated, where officials (1957) had forbidden us to visit Israel for instance, which had made Irwin mad and for good reasons judging from the fact that the Arabs didnt care if he was Jewish or whichever as long as he came on cool the way he always does anyway. That "international hepness" I mentioned.

One look at the officials in the American Consulate where we went for dreary paper routines was enough to make you realize what was wrong with American "diplomacy" throughout the Fellaheen world:—stiff officious squares with contempt even for their own Americans who happened not to wear neck-

ties, as tho a necktie or whatever it stands for meant anything
to the hungry Berbers who came into Tangiers every Saturday
morning on meek asses, like Christ, carrying baskets of pitiful
fruit or dates, and returned at dusk in silhouetted parades along
the hill by the railroad track. The railroad track where barefooted prophets still walked and taught the Koran to children
along the way. Why didnt the American consul ever walk into
the urchin hall where Mohammed Mayé sat smoking? or squat
in behind empty buildings with old Arabs who talked with their
hands? or *any* thing? Instead it's all private limousines, hotel
restaurants, parties in the suburbs, an endless phoney rejection
in the name of "democracy" of all that's pith and moment of
every land.

The beggar boys slept with their heads on tables as Mohammed Mayé passed us pipe after pipe of strong kief and hasheesh,
explaining his city. He pointed out the window down a parapet:
"The sea used to be right here." Like an old memory of the
flood still there at the gates of the flood.

The circus was a fantastic North African jumble of phenome-
nally agile acrobats, mysterious fire eaters from India, white
doves walking up silver ladders, crazy comedians we didnt understand, and bicyclists Ed Sullivan never saw and should see.
It was like "Mario and the Magician," a night of torments and
applause ending with sinister magicians nobody liked.

58   MY MONEY CAME and it was time to go but there's
        poor Irwin at midnight calling up to me from the
garden "Come on down Jack-Kee, there's a big bunch of
hipsters and chicks from Paris in Bull's room." And just like in
New York or Frisco or anywhere there they are all hunching
around in marijuana smoke, talking, the cool girls with long
thin legs in slacks, the men with goatees, all an enormous drag
after all and at the time (1957) not even started yet officially
with the name of "Beat Generation." To think that I had so

much to do with it, too, in fact at that very moment the manuscript of *Road* was being linotyped for imminent publication and I was already sick of the whole subject. Nothing can be more dreary than "coolness" (not Irwin's cool, or Bull's or Simon's, which is natural quietness) but postured, actually secretly *rigid* coolness that covers up the fact that the character is unable to convey anything of force or interest, a kind of sociological coolness soon to become a fad up into the mass of middleclass youth for awhile. There's even a kind of insultingness, probably unintentional, like when I said to the Paris girl just fresh she said from visiting a Persian Shah for Tiger hunt "Did you actually shoot the tiger yourself?" she gave me a cold look as tho I'd just tried to kiss her at the window of a Drama School. Or tried to trip the Huntress. Or *something*. But all I could do was sit on the edge of the bed in despair like Lazarus listening to their awful "likes" and "like you know" and "wow crazy" and "a wig, man" "a real gas"— All this was about to sprout out all over America even down to High School level and be attributed in part to my doing! But Irwin paid no attention to all that and just wanted to know what they were thinking anyway.

Lying on the bed stretched out as tho gone forever was Joe Portman son of a famous travel writer who said to me "I hear you're going to Europe. How about traveling with me on the Packet? We'll get tickets this week."

"Okay."

Meanwhile the Parisian jazz musician was explaining that Charley Parker wasnt disciplined enough, that jazz needed European classical patterns to give it depth, which sent me upstairs whistling "Scrapple," "Au Privave" and "I Get a Kick."

59

AFTER ONE LONG HIKE ALONG THE SURF and up into the Berber foothills, where I saw Moghreb itself, I finally packed and got my ticket. Moghreb is the Arab name of the country. The French call it *La Marocaine*. It was a little shoeshine boy on the beach who pronounced the name for me by spitting it out and giving me a fierce look then trying to sell me dirty pictures then rushing off to play soccer in the beach sand. Some of his older buddies told me they couldnt get me any of the young girls on the beach because they hated "Christians." But did I want a boy? The shoeshine boy and I watched an American queer angrily tearing up dirty pictures and throwing the pieces to the wind as he hurried from the beach, crying.

Poor old Hubbard was in bed when I left and actually looked sad when he gripped my hand and said "Take care of yourself, Jack" with that upward lilt on my name which tries to ease the seriousness of goodbye. Irwin and Simon waved from the dock as the Packet eased off. Both of them wearing glasses finally lost sight of my own waves as the ship turned about and headed for the waters off Gibraltar in a sudden heaving mass of smooth glassy groundswells. "Good, God, Atlantis is still yelling underneath."

I saw little of the kid Portman on the trip. We were both miserably gloomy on our backs on burlap covered bunks amidst the French Army. Next to my bunk was a young French soldier who said not a word to me for days and nights, just lay there staring at the bunk springs overhead, never got up with all of us to line up for beans, never did anything, not even sleep. He was coming home from duty in Casablanca or maybe even war in Algeria. I suddenly realized he must've gotten a drug habit. He had no interest in anything at all but his own thoughts, even when the three Mohammedan passengers who happened to be bunked up with us French troops suddenly leaped up in the middle of the night and jabbered at gay lunches out of paper bags:—Ramadan. Can't eat till a certain time. And I realized again how stereotyped is the "world history" given us by newspapers and officials. Here were three miserable skinny Arabs disturbing the sleep of one hundred and sixty-five French troops, armed at that, in the middle of the night, yet not one bucko or first lieutenant yelled out *"Tranquille!"* They all bore the noise and discomfort in silence that was well nigh respectful for the religion and the personal integrity of these three Arab men. Then what was the war about?

Out on deck in the daytime the troops sang on the deck eating beans out of their ration pots. The Balearic Islands passed by. It seemed for a moment the troops were actually looking forward to something gay and exciting and *home,* in France, in Paris especially, girls, thrills, homecomings, delights and new futures, or perfect happy love, or something, or maybe just the Arc de Triomphe. Whatever visions an American has of France or Paris who's never been there, I had for them:—even of Jean Gabin sitting smoking on a wrecked fender in a dump with that Gallic heroic lip-pressing *"Ça me navre"* which had made me trill as a teenager to think of all that smoky France of realistic honesty, or even just the baggy pants of Louis Jouvet going up the stairs of a cheap hotel, or the obvious dream of long night streets of Paris full of gay troubles good enough for a movie, or the sudden great beauty in a wet overcoat and beret, all such nonsense and all of it completely evaporating away when the next morning I saw the awful white chalk cliffs of Marseilles in the fog and a gloomy cathedral on a cliff making me bite my lip as if I'd forgotten my own stupid memory. Even the soldiers were glum filing off the ship down into sheds of customs guards after we'd negotiated several dull canals to our slip. Sunday morning in Marseilles, now where? One to a lace livingroom, one to a pool hall, one to an upstairs apartment in a suburban cottage on the highway? One to a third floor tenement. One to a pastry shop. One to a woodyard (as dismal as the woodyards on rue Papineau in Montreal).

(That suburban cottage has a dentist living downstairs.) One even to a long hot wall in mid-Bourgogne leading to aunts in black in the parlor glaring? One to Paris? One to sell flowers in Les Halles on howling winter mornings? One to be black-smith off rue St. Denis and its black coated whores? One to lounge with nothing to do before the afternoon movie marquees of rue Clignancourt? One to be big sneering telephoner from Pigalle nightclub, as it sleets outside? One to be porter in the dark cellars of rue Rochechouart? Actually I dont know.

I went off by myself, with my big rucksack, towards America, my home, my own bleak France.

60 IN PARIS I SAT AT THE OUTDOOR CHAIRS OF CAFÉ BONAPARTE talking to young artists and girls, in the sun, drunk, only four hours in town, and here comes Raphael swinging across Place St. Germain seeing me from a mile away and yelling "*Jack! There* you are! Millions of girls surround you! What are you *gloomy* about? I will show you Paris! There's love everywhere! I've just written a new poem called Peru!" (Pewu!) "I have a girl for you!" But even he knew he was kidding but the sun was warm and we felt good drinking together again. The "girls" were snippy students from England and Holland looking for a chance to make me feel bad by calling me a jerk as soon as I gave no indication I would court them a whole season with flowered notes and writhings of agony. I just wanted them to spread their legs in a human bed and forget it. My God you cant do that since Sartre in romantic existential Paris! Later these very girls would be sitting around in other world capitals saying wearily to their escort of Latins, "I'm just waiting for Godot, man." There are some really ravishing beauties going up and down the streets but they're all going somewhere else—to where a really fine young Frenchman with burning hopes awaits them, however. It took a long time for Baudelaire's ennui to come back waving

from America, but it did, starting in the Twenties. Jaded Raphael and I rush off to buy a big bottle of cognac and drag a redhaired Irishman and two girls to Bois de Boulogne to drink and yak in the sun. Through muzzled drunk eyes, tho, I do see the gentle park and the women and children, like in Proust, all gay as flowers in their town. I notice how the Paris policemen hang around in groups admiring women: any trouble comes up they have a gang there and of course their famous capes with built in crowbars. Actually I feel like digging Paris life that way, by myself, personal noticings, but I'm doomed to several days of exactly what you would find in Greenwich Village. For Raphael later takes me to meet disagreeable American beatniks in apartments and bars and all that "cool" comes on again, only it's Easter and the fantastic candy stores of Paris have chocolate fishes in their windows three feet long. But it's all a big ambulation around St. Michel, St. Germain, around and around till Raphael and I end up in streets of night like in New York looking around for where to go. "Couldnt we find Celine someplace micturating in the Seine or blow up a few rabbit hutches?"

"We'll go see my girl Nanette! I'll give her to you." But when I see her I know he'll never give her to me, she's an absolute trembling beauty and loves Raphael to death. We all go off gaily to shishkabob and bop. I spend the entire night translating her French to him, how much she loves him, then have to translate his English to her, how he knows that *but*.

"Raphael dit qu'il t'aime mais il veux vraiment faire l'amour avec les étoiles! C'est ça qu'il dit. Il fait l'amour avec toi dans sa manière drôle." ("Raphael says he loves you but he really wants to make love to the stars, that's what he says, he makes love to you in his funny way.")

Pretty Nanette says in my ear in the noisy Arab cocktail lounge: *"Dit lui que ma soeur vas m'donner d'l'argent demain."* ("Tell him my sister'll give me money tomorrow.")

"Raphael why dont you just give her to me! She has no money!"

"What'd she say just then?" Raphael has made a girl fall in love with him without even being able to talk to her. It all ends up a man is tapping me on the shoulder as I wake up with my head on a bar where they're playing cool jazz. "Five thousand francs, please." That's five of my eight, my Paris money's all gone, three thousand francs left comes to $7.50 (then)—just enough to go to London and get my English publisher money and sail home. I'm mad as hell at Raphael for making me spend all that money and there he is yelling at me again how greedy and nowhere I am. Not only that as I lay there on his floor he makes love to Nanette all night, as she whimpers. In the morning I sneak out with the excuse a girl is waiting for me at a café, and never come back. I just walk all over Paris with the bag on my back looking so strange even the whores of St. Denis dont look at me. I buy my ticket to London and eventually go.

But I did see finally the Parisian woman of my dreams in an empty bar where I sipped coffee. There was only one man on duty, a nice looking guy, and in walks a pretty Parisienne with that slow tantalizing nowhere-to-go walk, hands in pockets, saying, simply *"ça va? La vie?"* Apparently ex-lovers.

"Oui. Comme ci comme ça." And she flashes him that languid smile worth more than her whole naked body, a really philosophic smile, lazy and amorous and ready for anything, even rainy afternoons, or bonnets on the Quai, a Renoir woman with nothing to do but come revisit her old lover and taunt him with questions about life. Like you can see even in Oshkosh though, or Forest Hills, but what a walk, what a lazy grace as tho her lover was chasing her on a bicycle from the railyards and she didnt care. Edith Piaf's songs express that type of Parisian woman, whole afternoons of fondling hair, actually boredom, ending in sudden disputes over coat money which run out the window so loud even the sad old Sûreté will come in eventually to shrug at tragedy and at beauty, knowing all the time it's

neither tragic nor beautiful just boredom in Paris and love for nothing else to do, really—Paris lovers wipe the sweat off and crack long loaves of bread a million miles from Gotterdammer-ung across the Marne (I guess) (never having met Marlene Die-trich in a Berlin Street)—

I arrive in London in the evening, Victoria Station, and go at once to a bar called "Shakespeare." But I might as well've walked into Schrafft's:—white table cloths, quiet clinking bar-tenders, oak paneling among Stout ads, waiters in tuxedos, ugh, I walk out of there as fast as I can and go roaming the nighttime streets of London with that pack still on my back as bobbies watch me pass with that strange still grin I remember so well, and which says: "There 'e is, clear as your nose, it's Jack the Ripper come back to the scene of 'is crimes. Keep an eye on 'im whilst I call the Hinspector."

61 MAYBE YOU COULD HARDLY BLAME THEM either be-cause as I walked thru the fogs of Chelsea looking for fish n chips a bobby walked in front of me half a block, just vaguely I could see his back and the tall bobby hat, and the shuddering poem occurred to me: *"Who will strangle the bobby in the fog?"* (for some reason I dont know, just because it was foggy and his back was turned to me and my shoes were silent soft soled desert boots like the shoes of *footpads*)— And at the border, that is at the customs of the English Channel (Newha-ven) they'd all given me strange looks as tho they knew me and since I only had fifteen shillings in my pocket ($2) they'd almost barred me from entering England altogether, only relenting when I showed proof I was an American writer. Even then, though, the Bobbies were standing watching me with that faint evil halfsmile, rubbing their jaws wisely, even nodding, as tho to say "We seen the likes a *im* before" although if I'd been with John Banks I'd be in the gaol house now.

From Chelsea I carried that woesome pack of mine clear

around downtown London in the foggy night, ending exhausted at Fleet Street where by God I saw old 55-year-old Julien of the future a bowlegged blondy Scotsman emerging from the Glasgow Times *tweaking his mustache* just like Julien (who is of Scot descent), hurrying on twinkling newspaperman feet to the nearest pub, the King Lud, to foam at beers of Britain's barrels— Under the streetlamp right where Johnson and Boswell strolled, there he goes, in tweed suit, "knaows mothah" and all that, bemused with the news of Edinborough, Falklands and the Lyre.

I managed to borrow five pounds from my English agent at his home and hurried thru the Soho (Saturday Midnight) looking for a room. As I was standing before a record store staring at an album cover of Jerry Mulligan's big goofy American hipster face a bunch of Teddy Boys spilling out with thousands of others from Soho boites approached me, like the bluejeaned Moroccan hipsters but all beautifully dressed however in vests and ironed pants and shiny shoes, saying "I say, do you knaow Jerry Mulligan?" How they spotted me in those rags and rucksack I'll never know. Soho is the Greenwich Village of London full of sad Greek and Italian restaurants with checkered tablecloths by candlelight, and jazz hangouts, nightclubs, strip joints and the like, with dozens of blondes and brunettes cruising for money: "I sye, ducks" but none of them even looking at me because I was dressed so awful. (I'd come to Europe in rags expecting to sleep in haystacks with bread and wine, no such haystack anywhere.) "Teddy Boys" are the English equivalent of our hipsters and have absolutely nothing to do with the "Angry Young Men" who are not street characters twirling keychains on corners but university trained middleclass intellectual gentlemen most of them effete, or when not effete, political instead of artistic. Teddy Boys are dandies on street corners (like our own brand of special zooty well-dressed or at least "sharp" hipsters with lapel-less jackets or soft Hollywood-Las Vegas sports shirts). The Teddy Boys have not yet started *writ-*

ing or at least publishing and when they do they'll make the Angry Young Men look like academic poseurs. The usual bearded Bohemians also roam around the Soho but they've been there since well before Dowson or De Quincey.

Piccadilly Circus, where I got my cheap hotel room, is the Times Square of London except there are charming street performers who dance and play and sing for pennies thrown at them, some of them sad violinists recalling the pathos of Dickens' London.

What amazed me as much as anything were the fat calm tabby cats of London some of whom slept peacefully right in the doorway of butcher shops as people stepped over them carefully, right there in the sawdust sun but a nose away from the roaring traffic of drams and buses and cars. England must be the land of cats, they abide peacefully all over the back fences of St. John's Wood. Elderly ladies feed them lovingly just like Ma feeds my cats. In Tangiers or Mexico City you hardly ever see a cat, if so late at night, because the poor often catch them and eat them. I felt London was blessed by its kind regard for cats. If Paris is a woman who was penetrated by the Nazi invasion, London is a man who was never penetrated but only smoked his pipe, drank his stout or half n half, and blessed his cat on the purring head.

In Paris on cold nights the apartment houses along the Seine look bleak like the apartment houses of New York on Riverside Drive on January nights when all the inhospitable blasts of the Hudson hit men in spats rounding the corner to their foyer, but on the banks of the Thames at night there seems to be a kind of hope in the twinkle of the river, of East End across the way, something bustlingly Englishy hopeful. During the war I'd also seen the interior of England, those incredibly green countrysides of haunted mead, the bicyclists waiting at the railroad crossing to get home to thatched house and hearth—I loved it. But I had no time and no desire to hang around, I wanted to go *home*.

As I walked down Baker Street one night I actually looked for Sherlock Holmes' address forgetting completely he'd been just a fiction in Conan Doyle's mind!

I got my money in the agency office on the Strand and bought a ticket to New York on the Dutch ship S.S. *Nieuw Amsterdam* sailing from Southampton that night.

PART FOUR

PASSING THROUGH
AMERICA AGAIN

62 SO I'D MADE THAT BIG TRIP TO EUROPE at just the wrong time in my life, just when I became disgusted with any new experience of any kind, so I'd rushed through and here I was already going back, May 1957, shamefaced, dull-hearted, scowling, ragged and nuts.

And as the *Nieuw Amsterdam* pulls out to sea from the Southampton dock that night I waltz into the thirdclass diningroom hungry for my supper but here are two hundred and fifty fastidiously dressed tourists sitting at glittering cutleries and white tablecloths being served by anxious tuxedo'd waiters under grand chandeliers. The waiters do a doubletake when they see me in my jeans (my only pants) and open collared flannel shirt. I walk across their gantlet line to my assigned table which is right in the middle of the diningroom and has four table partners in impeccable suits and gowns, ow. A German laughing girl in a party dress: a German in a suit, severe and neat: and two Dutch young businessmen headed for Lu-chow's in Export New York. But I have to sit there. And strangely enough the German is polite to me, even seeming to like me (Germans always like me for some reason), so that when the ratty waiter gets impatient with me when I scan the incredibly luxurious menu with mixed up thoughts ("Wow will it be almondine salmon with wine sauce or roast beef au jus with petites pommes de terres de printemps or omelette speciale with avocado salad or filet mignon smothered in mushrooms, *mon doux*, what'll I do?") and he says nastily tapping his wrist: "Well make up your mind!" the German youth stares at him indignantly. And when the waiter's gone to bring me roasted brains and asperge hollandaise he says, "I voud not take dat from a vaiter if I vere you!" He snaps this out at me like a Nazi, actually like a well bred German or continental gentleman in any case, but with sympathy for me, but I say:—

"I dont care."

He points out that somebody's got to care or "Dis peoples vill get atrocious und forgetting deir place!" I cant explain to him that I dont care because I'm a French Canadian Iroquois American aristocrat Breton Cornish democrat or even a beat hipster but when the waiter comes back the German makes sure to make the waiter run back for extras. Meanwhile the German girl is gaily enjoying herself foreseeing her voyage of six days with three handsome young Europeans and even looking at me with a straight human smile. (I'd already run into official European snobbery when strolling Saville Row or Threadneedle Street or even Downing Street being stared at by government fops in wescots, who'd have done better with lorgnettes, as brief as that.) But next morning I was unceremoniously moved to a corner table where I wouldnt be so conspicuous. As far as I was concerned I would have preferred to eat in the galley with my elbows on the table anyway. But now I was trapped with three elderly Hollander schoolteachers, a girl of 8, and an American girl of 22 with dark rings of dissipation under her eyes which didnt bother me except that she traded her German sleeping pills for my Moroccan ones (soneryls) but her sleeping pills were actually pep pills of some terrifying variety that kept you awake.

So three times a day I sneaked to my corner in the diningroom and faced these women with a bleak smile. Roaring gay laughter came from my original German table.

My stateroom had one other old man in it, a fine old Hollander who smoked a pipe, but the horrible thing was that his old wife came in constantly to hold his hand and talk, so that I was reluctant to even wash at the sink. I had the upper bunk where I read day and night. I noticed that the old Dutch lady had that same almost breakable delicate white forehead skin with pale blue veins in it you sometimes see in a Rembrandt portrait. . . . Meanwhile, our third class quarters being in the stern of the ship, we rolled and pitched sickeningly all the way to Nantucket Lightship. The original crowd in the diningroom diminished every day as everybody got sea sick. On the first night at a nearby table a whole clan of Dutchmen had started out laughing and eating, all brothers and sisters and in-laws going to live or visit in America, but by the time we were two days out of Southampton only one gaunt brother remained eating grimly everything that was brought to him, like myself afraid to waste all that good food that went with his fare ($225), even ordering extras and grimly eating that. I myself had my new young waiter rushing around for extra desserts. I wasnt going to miss one whipcream, nauseous or not.

At night the gay stewards always arranged dances with fun hats but that was when I'd put on my zippered windbreaker and scarf up and pace the decks, sometimes sneaking up to the first class deck and walking swiftly around and around the empty wind howling promenade, nobody there. I missed my old lonesome quiet Yugo freighter, though, because in the day time you saw all these sick people bundled up in deck chairs staring at nothing.

For breakfast I always had cold roast beef with Dutch sugar

powdered raisin bread followed by the usual bacon and eggs and pot of coffee.

At one point the American girl and her blond English girlfriend insisted I visit the gymnasium with them, which was always empty, it was only later I realized they probably wanted to sex. They kept eyeing the handsome sailors wistfully, I guess they'd read novels about "shipboard love affairs" and were trying desperately to get it done before New York. Some help *I* was dreaming of my veal and ham baked in foil. One morning in the fog the waters were calm and glassy and there was the Nantucket Lightship followed a few hours later by floating garbage from New York including one empty carton reading CAMPBELL'S PORK AND BEANS making me almost cry with joy remembering America and all the pork n beans from Boston to Seattle . . . and maybe those pine trees in a homestead window in the morning.

63

SO I RACED OUT OF NEW YORK and down South to get my mother, loaded with another publisher's installment ($100)— Just stopping long enough to spend two days with Alyce who was now soft and pretty in a Springtime dress and glad to see me— A few beers, a few lovings, a few whispered words in ear, and off I was to my "new life" promising I'd see her soon.

My mother and I packed all the pitiful junks of life and called the movers giving them the only California address I knew, Ben Fagan's cottage in Berkeley—I figured we'd go there by bus, all three thousand awful miles of it, rent an apartment in Berkeley and have plenty of time to re-route the movers to our new home which I promised myself would be my final glad sanctuary (hoping for pine trees).

Our "junk" consisted of old clothes I never would wear again, cartons of old manuscripts of mine some from 1939 with the paper already yellowed, pitiful heat lamps and *overshoes* of all things (overshoes of old New England), bottles of shaving lotion and holy water, even lightbulbs saved from years ago, old smoking pipes of mine, a basketball, a baseball glove, my God even a bat, old curtains that had never been put up for lack of a home, rolled-up useless rag rugs, books weighing a ton (even old editions of Rabelais with no covers) and all kinds of inconceivable pots and pans and sad shifts that people some- how need to keep to go on— Because I still remember the America when men traveled with nothing but a paperbag for luggage, always tied with string—I still remember the America of people waiting in line for coffee and donuts— The America of 1932 when people foraged in riverside dumps looking for junk to sell— When my father sold neckties or dug ditches for the W.P.A.— When old men with burlap bags at night fished thru garbage cans or collected rare horse dung in the streets— When yams were something to joy about. But here it was 1957 prosperous America and people laughing at all our junk in the center of which nevertheless my mother'd hidden her essential sewing basket, her essential crucifix, and her essen- tial family photo album— Not to mention her essential salt shaker, pepper shaker, sugar shaker (all full) and her essential bar of soap already half used, all wrapped in the essential sheets and blankets of beds not yet seen.

64 HERE NOW I'm telling about the most important person in this whole story and the best. I've no- ticed how most of my fellow writers all seem to "hate" their mothers and make big Freudian or sociological philosophies around that, in fact using it as the straight theme of their fanta- sies, or at least saying as much—I often wonder if they've ever slept till four in the afternoon and woke up to see their mother darning their socks in a sad window light, or come back from revolutionary horrors of weekends to see her mending the rips in a bloody shirt with quiet eternal bowed head over needle—

And not with martyred pose of resentment, either, but actually seriously bemused over *mending*, the mending of torture and folly and all loss, mending the very days of your life with almost glad purposeful gravity— And when it's cold she puts on that shawl, and mends on, and on the stove potatoes are burbling forever— Making some neurotics go mad to see such sanity in a room— Making *me* mad sometimes because I'd been so foolish tearing shirts and losing shoes and losing and tearing hope to tatters in that silly thing called *wild*— "You've got to have an escape valve!" Julien'd often yelled at me, "let out that steam or go mad!" tearing my shirt, only to have Memère two days later sitting in her chair mending that very shirt just because it was a shirt and it was mine, her son's— Not to make me feel guilty but to fix the shirt— Though it always made me feel guilty to hear her say: "It was such a nice shirt, I paid $3.25 for it in Woolworth's, why do you let those nuts tear at your shirt like that. *Ça pas d'bon sens.*" And if the shirt was beyond repair she'd always wash it and put it away "for patching" or to make a rag rug with. In one of her rag rugs I recognized three decades of tortured life not only by myself but herself, my father, my sister. She'd have sewn up the grave and used it if possible. As for food, nothing went wasted: an odd potato half eaten ends up delightfully tidbit fried by a piece of later meat, or a quarter of an onion finds its way into a jar of home-pickled onions, or old corners of roastbeef into a delicious homey burbling fricassee. Even a torn old handkerchief is washed and mended and better to blow your nose in than ten thousand crinkly new Brooks Brothers Handkerchiefs with idle monogram. Any stray toy I bought for her "doodad" shelf (little Mexican burros in plastic, or piggy banks or vaselets) remained on that shelf for years and years, duly dusted and arranged according to her taste esthetically. A minor cigarette hole in old jeans is suddenly patched with pieces of 1940 jean. Her sewing basket contains a wooden darner (like a small bowling duckpin) older than I am. Her needles some of them come from Nashua 1910. As the years go by her family write her increasingly loving letters realizing what they lost when they took her orphan money and spent it. At the TV which I bought her with my pitiful 1950 money she stares believingly, only a battered old 1949 Motorola set. She watches the commercials where the women primp or the men boast and doesnt even know I'm in the room. It's all a show for her eyes. I have nightmares of her and I finding pastrami slabs in old junkyards of New Jersey on a Saturday morning, or of the top drawer of her dresser open in the road of America showing silk bloomers, rosaries, tin cans full of buttons, rolls of ribbon, needle hassocks, powder pouffes, old berets and boxes of cotton saved from old medicine bottles. Who could put down a woman like that? Whenever I need something she has it somewhere:—an aspirin, an ice bag, a bandage, a can of cheap spaghetti in the cupboard (cheap but good). Even a candle when the big civilized power blows out.

For the bathtub, the toilet and the sink she has big cans of deterring powder and disinfectants. She has a dry mop and twice a week is reaching under my bed for gobs of dust which are rapped out the window sill, "*Tiens!* Your room is clean!" Wrapped somewhere in the moving carton is a big basket of clothespins to hang out the wash wherever she goes—I see her with basket of wet wash going out with clothespin in mouth, and when we have no yard, *right in the kitchen!* Duck under the wash and get your beer in the icebox. Like the mother of Hui Neng, I'd bet, enough to enlighten anybody with the actual true "Zen" of how to live in any time and just right.

Tao say, in more words than one, that a woman who takes care of her home has equalized Heaven and Earth.

Then on Saturday nights she's ironing on the battered ironing board bought by her a lifetime ago, the cloth all brown with burns, the creaky wooden legs, but all the wash comes out ironed and white and to be folded away in perfect paper-lined cupboards for use.

At night when she sleeps I bow my head in shame. And I know that in the morning when I wake up (maybe noon) she'll already have walked to the store on her strong "peasant" legs and brought back all the food towering in bags with the lettuce at the top, my cigarettes at the top, the hotdogs and hamburgs and tomatos and grocery slips to "show me," the pitiful nylon stockings on the bottom apologetically admitted to my sight— Ah me, and all the girls I'd known in America who dabbled at blue cheese and let it harden on the sill! Who'd spent hours before the mirror with blue eye shade! Who'd wanted taxis for their milk! Who'd groaned on Sunday without roasts! Who'd left me because I complained!

The trend nowadays is to say that mothers stand in the way of your sex life, as tho my sex life in the apartments of girls in New York or San Francisco had anything to do with my quiet Sunday nights reading or writing in the privacy of my clean homey bed room, when breezes riffle the curtain and cars shirsh by— When the cat meows at the icebox and already there's a can of Nine Lives for my baby, bought by Ma on Saturday morning (writing her lists)— As tho sex was the be-all of my love for the woman.

65 MY MOTHER PROVIDED ME WITH THE MEANS FOR PEACE and good sense— She didnt tear at her slip and rant I didnt love her and knock over dressers of makeup— She didnt harpy at me or croon at me for thinking my own thoughts— She only yawned at eleven and went to bed with her rosary, like living in a monastery with the Reverend Mother O'Shay—I might lie there in my clean sheets and think of running out to find a raunchy wild whore with stockings in her hair but it had nothing to do with my mother—I was free to do so— Because any man who's loved a friend and therefore made the vow to leave him and his wife alone, can do the same

for his friend his father— To each his own, and she belonged to my father.

But wretched leering thieves of life say no: say, "if a man lives with his mother he's *frustrated*": and even Genêt the divine knower of Flowers said a man who loves his mother is the worst scoundrel of them all: or psychiatrists with hairy wrists like Ruth Heaper's psychiatrists trembling for the snowy thighs of young patients: or sick married men with no peace in their eyes ranting at the bachelor's hole: or deadly chemists with no thought of hope: all say to me: "Duluoz you liar! Go out and live with a woman and fight and suffer with her! Go swarming in your bliss hair! Go ratcheting after fury! Find the furies! Be historical!" and all the time I'm sitting there enjoying and *in-joying* the sweet silly peace of my mother, a lady the likes of which you wont find any more unless you travel to Sinkiang, Tibet or Lampore.

66   BUT HERE WE ARE IN FLORIDA with two tickets to California waiting standing for the bus to New Orleans where we'll change for El Paso and L.A.— It's hot in May in Florida—I long to get out and go west beyond the East Texas Plain to that High Plateau and on over the Divide to dry Arizonies and beyond— Poor Ma is standing there absolutely dependent on me, foolish as I've been as you see. I wonder what my father is saying in Heaven? "That crazy Ti Jean is carting her three thousand miles in wretched buses just for a dream about a holy pine tree." But a kid is talking to us waiting in line at our side, when I say that I wonder if we'll ever get there or the bus will ever come he says:—

"Dont worry, you'll get there." I wonder how he knows we'll get there. "You'll not only get there, you'll come back and go elsewhere. Ha ha ha!"

Yet there's hardly anything in the world or at least in America more miserable than a transcontinental bus trip with limited means— More than three days and three nights wearing the same clothes, bouncing around into town after town, even at three o'clock in the morning when you've finally fallen asleep there you are being bounced over the railroad tracks of Oshkosh and all the lights are turned on bright to reveal your raggedness and weariness in the seat— To do that, as I'd done so often, as a strong young man, bad enough, but to have to do that when you're a 62-year-old lady . . . I really wondered quite often what my father was thinking in Heaven and prayed for him to give my mother strength to make it without too much horror— Yet was she more cheerful than I was— And she devised a terrific trick to keep us in fairly good shape, aspirins with Coke three times a day to calm the nerves.

From mid-Florida we rolled in the late afternoon over orange grove hills towards the panhandle Tallahassees and Mobile Alabamas of morning, no prospect of New Orleans till noon and already fair exhausted. Such an enormous country you realize when you cross it on buses, the dreadful stretches between equally dreadful cities all of them looking the same when seen from the bus of woes, the inescapable bus of never-get-there stopping everywhere (the joke about Greyhound stopping at every post) and worst of all the string of fresh enthusiastic drivers at every two or three hundred miles warning everyone to relax and be happy.

Sometimes during the night I'd look at my poor sleeping mother cruelly *crucified* there in the American night because of no-money, no-hope-of-money, no family, no nothing, just myself the stupid son of plans all of them compacted of eventual darkness. God how right Hemingway was when he said there was no remedy for life—and to think that negative little paper-shuffling prissies should write condescending obituaries about a man who told the truth, nay who drew breath in pain to tell a tale like that! . . . No remedy but in my mind I raise a fist to High Heaven promising that I shall bull whip the first bastard who makes fun of human hopelessness anyway—I know it's ridiculous to pray to my father that hunk of dung in a grave yet I pray to him anyway, what else shall I do? sneer? shuffle paper on a desk and burp with rationality? Ah thank God for all the Rationalists the worms and vermin got. Thank God for all the hate mongering political pamphleteers with no left or right to yell about in the Grave of Space. I say that we shall all be reborn with The Only One, that we will not be ourselves any more but simply the Companion of The Only One, and that's what makes me go on, and my mother too. She has her rosary in the bus, dont deny her that, that's *her* way of stating the fact. If there cant be love among men let there be love at least between men and God. Human courage is an opiate but opiates are human too. If God is an opiate so am I. Therefore *eat me. Eat* the night, the long desolate America between Sanford and Shlamford and Blamford and Crapford, eat the hematodes that hang parasitically from dreary southern trees, eat the blood in the ground, the dead Indians, the dead pioneers, the dead Fords and Pontiacs, the dead Mississippis, the dead arms of forlorn hopelessness washing underneath— Who are men, that they can insult men? Who are these people who wear pants and dresses and sneer? What am I talking about? I'm talking about human helplessness and unbelievable loneliness in the darkness of birth and death and asking "What is there to laugh about in that?" "How can you be *clever* in a meatgrinder?" "Who makes fun of misery?" There's my mother a hunk of flesh that didnt ask to be born, sleeping restlessly, dreaming hopefully, beside her son who also didnt ask to be born, thinking desperately, praying hopelessly, in a bouncing earthly vehicle going from nowhere to nowhere, all in the night, worst of all for that matter all in noonday glare of bestial Gulf Coast roads— Where is the rock that will sustain us? Why are we here? What kind of crazy college would feature a seminar where people talk about hopelessness, forever?

And when Ma wakes up in the middle of the night and groans, my heart breaks— The bus goes belumping over back lots of Shittown to go pick up one package in a dawn station. Groans everywhere, all the way to the back seats where black sufferers suffer no less because their skin is black. Yes, "Freedom Riders" indeed, just because you've got "white" skin and ride in the front dont make you suffer less—

And there's just no hope anywhere because we're all disunited and ashamed: if Joe says life is sad Jim will say that Joe is silly because it doesnt matter. Or if Joe says we need help Jim will say that Joe's a sniveler. Or if Joe says Jim is mean Jim'll bust down crying in the night. Or something. It's just awful. The only thing to do is be like my mother: patient, believing, careful, bleak, self-protective, glad for little favors, suspicious of great favors, beware of Greeks bearing Fish, make it your own way, hurt no one, mind your own business, and make your compact with God. For God is our Guardian Angel and this is a fact that's only proven when proof exists no more.

Eternity, and the Here-and-Now, are the same thing.

Send that message back to Mao, or Schlesinger at Harvard, or Herbert Hoover too.

67

AS I SAY, the bus arrives in New Orleans at noon and we have to disembark with all our tangled luggage and wait four hours for the El Paso express so me and Ma decide to investigate New Orleans and stretch our legs. In my mind I imagine a big glorious lunch in a Latin Quarter Abalone restaurant among grilleworked balconies and palms but as soon as we find such a restaurant near Bourbon Street the prices on the menu are so high we have to walk out sheepishly as gay businessmen and councilmen and tax collectors dine on. At 3 P.M. they'll be back at their office desks shuffling quintuplicates of onionskinned news concerning negative formalities and shoving them thru further paper machines that will multiply them ten times to be sent out to be done in triplicate to end up in wastebaskets when their salaries are in. For all the strong food and drink they get they give back triplicates of paper, signed, tho I cant understand it how it's done when I see sweating arms digging ditches in the streets in the Gulf shattering sun—

Just for the hell of it Ma and I just decide to walk into a New Orleans saloon that has an oyster bar. And there by God she has the time of her life drinking wine, eating oysters on the half shell with *piquante*, and yelling crazy conversations with the old Italian oyster man. "Are you married, ey?" (She's always asking old men if they're married, it's amazing how women are looking for husbands right up to the end.) No, he's not married, and would she like some clams now, maybe steamed? and they exchanged names and addresses but later never write. Meanwhile Ma is all excited to be in famous New Orleans at last and when we walk around she buys pickaninny dolls and praline candies all excited in stores and packs them in our luggage to send back by mail as presents to my sister in Florida. A relentless hope. Just like my father she just wont let anything discourage her. I walk sheepishly by her side. And she's been doing this for 62 years: at the age of 14 there she was, at dawn, walking to the shoe factory to work till six that evening, till Saturday evening, 72-hour workweek, all gleeful in anticipation of that pitiful Saturday night and Sunday when there'd be popcorn and swings and singing. How can you beat people like that? When Feudal tithe-barons made their grab, did they feel sheepish before the glee of their peasants? (surrounded as they were by all those dull knights all yearning to be buggered by masterful sadists from another burgh).

So we get back on the El Paso bus after an hour standing in line in blue bus fumes, loaded with presents and luggage, talking to everybody, and off we roar up the river and then across the Louisiana plains, sitting in front again, feeling gay and rested now and also because I've bought a little pint of booze to nip us along.

"I dont care what anybody say," says Ma pouring a nip into

her ladylike portable shot container, "a little drink never hurt nobody!" and I agree ducking down beneath the driver's rear vision seat and gulping up a snort. Off we go to Lafayette. Where to our amazement we hear the local people talking French exactly as we do in Quebecois, the *Cajuns* are only *Acadians* but there's no time, the bus is leaving for Texas now.

68

IN REDDISH DUSK we're rolling across the Texas plains talking and drinking but soon the pint runs out and poor Ma's sleeping again, just a hopeless baby in the world, and all that distance yet to go, and when we get there *what?* Corrigan, and Crockett, and Palestine, the dull bus stops, the sighs, the endlessness of it, only half way across the continent, another night of sleeplessness ahead and another one later, and still another one— Oh me—

Exactly 24 hours and then six more after arriving in New Orleans we are finally bashing down the Rio Grande Valley into the wink of El Paso night, all nine hundred *miserere* miles of Texas behind us, both of us completely doped and numb with tiredness, I realize there's nothing to do but get off the bus and get a hotel suite and get a good night's sleep before goin on to California more than another thousand bumpy miles—

And at the same time I will show my mother Mexico across the little bridge to Juarez.

69

EVERYBODY KNOWS WHAT IT FEELS LIKE after two days of vibration on wheels to suddenly lie in still beds on still ground and sleep— Right next to the bus station I got a suite and went out to buy chicken-in-the-basket while Ma washed up— As I look back on it now I realize she was having a big adventurous trip visiting New Orleans and staying in hotel suites ($4.50) and now going to Mexico for the first time tomorrow— We drank another half pint and ate the chicken and slept like logs.

In the morning, with eight hours till bus time, we sallied forth strong with all our luggage repacked and stored in 25¢ bus station lockers—I even made her walk the one mile to the Mexico bridge for exercise— At the bridge we paid three cents each and went over.

Immediately we were in Mexico, that is, among Indians in an Indian earth—among the smells of mud, chickens, including that Chihuahua dust, lime peels, horses, straw, Indian weariness— The strong smell of cantinas, beer, dank— The smell of the market—and the sight of beautiful old Spanish churches rising in the sun with all their woeful majestical Maria Guadalupes and Crosses and cracks in the wall— "O Ti Jean! I want to go in that church and light a candle to Papa!"

"Okay." And when we go in we see an old man kneeling in the aisle with his arms outstretched in penitence, a *penitente*, hours like that he kneels, old serape over his shoulder, old shoes, hat on the church floor, raggedy old white beard. "O Ti Jean, what's he done that he's so sad for? I cant believe that old man has ever done anything really bad!"

"He's a *penitente*," I tell her in French. "He's a sinner and he doesnt want God to forget him."

"Pauvre bonhomme!" and I see a woman turn and look at Ma thinking she said *"Pobrecito"* which is exactly what she said anyway. But the most pitiful sight suddenly in the old Juarez church is a shawled woman all dressed in black, barefooted, with a baby in her arms advancing slowly on her knees up the aisle to the altar. "What has happened *there?*" cries my mother amazed. "That poor lil mother has done no wrong! Is it her husband who's in prison? She's carrying that leetle baby!" I'm glad now I took Ma on this trip for her to see the real church of America if nothing else. "Is *she* a penitente *too?* Dat little baby is a penitente? She's got him all wrapped up in a leetle ball in her shawl!"

"I dont know why."

"Where's the priest that he dont bless her? There's nobody here but that poor leetle mother and that poor old man! This is the Church of Mary?"

"This is the church of Maria de Guadalupe. A peasant found a shawl in Guadalupe Mexico with Her Face imprinted on it like the cloth the women had at the cross of Jesus."

"It happened in Mexico?"

"*Si.*"

"And they pray to Marie? But that poor young mother is only half way to the altar— She comes slow slow slow on her knees all quiet. Aw but these are good people the *Indians* you say?"

"*Oui*—Indians just like the American Indians but here the Spaniards did not destroy them" (in French). "*Içi les espanols sont marié avec les Indiens.*"

"*Pauvre monde!* They believe in God just like us! I didnt know that, Ti Jean! I never saw anything like this!" We creeped up to the altar and lighted candles and put dimes in the church box to pay for the wax. Ma made a prayer to God and did the sign of the cross. The Chihuahua desert blew dust into the church. The little mother was still advancing on her knees with the infant quietly asleep in her arms. Memère's eyes blurred with tears. Now she understood Mexico and why I had come there so often even tho I'd get sick of dysentery or lose weight or get pale. "*C'est du monde qu'il on du coeur,*" she whispered, "these are people who have *heart!*"

"*Oui.*"

She put a dollar in the church machine hoping it would do some good somehow. She never forgot that afternoon: in fact even today, five years later, she still adds a prayer for the little mother with the child crawling to the altar on her knees: "There was something was wrong in her life. Her husband, or maybe her *baby* was sick— We'll never know— But I shall always pray for that leetle woman. Ti Jean when you took me there you showed me something I'd never believed I'd ever *ever* see—"

Years later, when I met the Reverend Mother in the Bethlehem Benedictine Monastery talking to her thru wooden nunnery bars, and told her this, she cried . . .

And meanwhile the old man *Penitente* still kneeled there arms outspread, all your Zapatas and Castros come and go but the Old Penitence is still there and will always be there, like Coyotl Old Man in the Navajo Mountains and Mescalero Foothills up north:—

Chief Crazy Horse looks north	*	Geronimo weeps—
with tearful eyes—	*	no pony
The first snow flurries.	*	With a blanket.

70 IT WAS ALSO VERY FUNNY to be in Mexico with my mother for when we came out of the church of Santa Maria we sat in the park to rest and enjoy the sun, and next to us sat an old Indian in his shawl, with his wife, saying nothing, looking straight ahead on their big visit to Juarez from the hills of the desert out beyond— Come by bus or burro— And Ma offered them a cigarette. At first the old Indian was afraid but finally he took a cigarette, but she offered him one for his wife, in French, in Quebecois Iroquois French, *"Vas il, ai paw 'onte, un pour ta famme"* so he took it, puzzled— The old lady never looked at Memère— They knew we were American tourists but never tourists like these— The old man slowly lighted his cigarette and looked straight ahead— Ma said to me: "They're afraid to talk?"

"They dont know what to do. They never meet anybody. They come from the desert. They dont even speak Spanish just Indian. Say Tarahumare."

"How's anybody can say dat?"

"Say Chihuahua."

Ma says "Chihuahua" and the old man grins at her and the old lady smiles. "Goodbye" says Memère as we leave. We go wandering across the sweet little park full of children and people and ice cream and balloons and come to a strange man with birds in a cage, who catches our eye and yells for our attention (I had taken my mother around to the back streets of Juarez). "What does he want?"

"Fortune! His birds will tell your fortune! We give him one peso and his little bird grabs a slip of paper and your fortune's written on it!"

"Okay! *Seenyor!*" The little bird beaks up a clip of paper from a pile of papers and hands it to the man. The man with his little mustache and gleeful eyes opens it. It reads as follows:—

"You will have goods fortuna with one who is your son who love you. Say the bird."

He gives the little paper to us laughing. It's amazing.

71 "NOW," SAYS MEMÈRE as we walk arm in arm thru the streets of Old Juarez, "how could that little silly bird know I have a son or *any*thing about me— Phew there's a lot of dust around here!" as that million million grained desert blows dust along the doors. "Can you explain me that? What is one peso, *eight cents?* And the little bird knew all dat? Hah?" Like Thomas Wolfe's Esther, "Hah?," only a longer lasting love. "Dat guy with the mustache doesnt know us. His little bird knew everything." She had the bird's slip of paper securely in her purse.

"A little bird that knew Gerard."

"And the little bird picked out the paper with his crazy face! Ah but the people are poor here, eh?"

"Yeh—but the government is taking care of that a lot. Used to be there were families sleeping on the sidewalk wrapped in newspapers and bullfight posters. And girls sold themselves for twenty cents. They have a good government since Aleman, Cardenas, Cortines—"

"The poor little bird of Mexica! And the little mother! I can always say I've seen Mexica." She pronounced it "Mexica."

So I bought a pint of Juarez Bourbon in a store and back we went to the American bus station in El Paso, got on a big doubledecker Greyhound that said "Los Angeles" on it, and roared off in a red desert dusk drinking from the pint in our front seats yakking with American sailors who knew nothing about Santa Maria de Guadalupe or the Little Bird but were good old boys nevertheless.

And as the bus rammed down that empty road among desert buttes and lava humps like the landscape of the moon, miles and miles of desolation towards that last faint Chihuahuan Mountain to the South or New Mexico dry rock range to the North, Memère drink-in-hand said: "I'm afraid of those mountains—they're trying to say something to us—they might fall right over us any minute!" And she leaned over to tell the sailors that, who laughed, and she offered them a drink and even kissed their polite cheeks, and they enjoyed it, such a crazy mother— Nobody in America was ever going to understand again what she'd try to tell them about what she saw in Mexico or in the Universe Entire. "Those mountains aint out there for nothing! They're there to tell us something! They're just sweet boys," and she fell asleep, and that was it, and the bus droned on to Arizona.

72   BUT WE'RE IN AMERICA NOW and at dawn it's the city called Los Angeles tho nobody can see what it can possibly have to do with angels as we stash our gear in lockers to wait for the 10 A.M. San Francisco bus and go out in gray streets to find a place for coffee and toast— It's 5 A.M. even too early for anything and all we get to see are the night's remnants of horrified hoodlums and bloody drunks staggering

around—I'd wanted to show her the bright happy L.A. of Art Linkletter Television shows or glimpses of Hollywood but all we saw was horror of Gruesome's end, the battered junkies and whores and suitcases tied with string, the empty traffic lights, no birds here, no Maria here—but dirt and death yes. Tho a few miles beyond these embittered awful paves were the soft shiny shores of a Kim Novak Pacific she'd never see, where *hors d'oeuvres* are thrown away to the dogs of sea— Where Producers mingle with their wives in a movie they never made— But all poor Memère ever saw of L.A. was dawn batteredness, hoodlums, some of them Indians of America, dead sidewalks, crops of cop cars, doom, early morning whistles like the early morning whistles of Marseilles, haggard ugly awful California City I-cant-go-on-what-am-I-doing-here *mierda*— Oh, who ever hath lived and suffered in America knows what I mean! Whoever rode coal cars out of Cleveland or stared at mailboxes in Washington D. C. knows! Whoever bled again in Seattle or bled again in Montana! Or peeled in Minneapolis! Or died in Denver! Or cried in Chicago or said "Sorry I'm burning" in Newark! Or sold shoes in Winchendon! Or flared out in Philadelphia? Or pruned in Toonerville? But I tell you there's nothing more awful than empty dawn streets of an American city unless it's being thrown to the Crocodiles in the Nile for nothing as catpriests smile. Slaves in every toilet, thieves in every hole, pimps in every dive, Governors signing redlight warrants— Gangs of ducktailed blackjacketed hoods on every corner some of them Pachucos, I pray in fact to my Papa "Forgive me for dragging Memère thru all this in search of a cup of coffee"— The same streets I've known before but not with *her*— But every evil dog in evildom understands it when he sees a man with his mother, so bless you all.

73 AFTER A WHOLE DAY RIDING thru the green fields and orchards of beautiful San Joaquin Valley, even my mother impressed tho she mentions the dry furze on those distant hills (and has already complained and rightly so about the caney wastes of Tucson and Mojave deserts)—as we sit there stoned to death with tiredness, of course, but almost there, only five hundred miles of valley up to north and the City—a long complicated way of telling you that we arrive at Fresno at dusk, walk around a little, get back on now with a fantastically vigorous Indian driver (some Mexican kid from Madera) off we go bashing to Oakland as the driver bears down on everything in that two way Valley lane (99) making whole populations of oncoming cars quake and revert into line— He'll just ram em right down.

So we arrive in Oakland at night, Saturday, (me finishing the last sip of my California rotgut port mixed with bus station ice) bang, we first thing see a battered drunkard all covered with blood staggering thru the bus station for emergency aid— My mother cant even see anymore, she's been sleeping all the way from Fresno, but she does see that sight and sighs wondering what next, New York? maybe Hell's Kitchen or Lower East Side East? I promise myself I'm going to show her something, a good little home and some quiet and trees, just like my father must've promised when he moved her from New England to New York—I get all the bags and hail a Berkeley bus.

Pretty soon we're out of Oakland downtown streets of empty movie marquees and dull fountains and we're rolling thru little long streets full of old 1910 white cottages and palms. But mostly other trees, your California northern trees, walnut and oak and cypress, and finally we come to near the University of California where I lead her down a leafy little street with all our gear towards the dull dimlamp of old Bhikku Ben Fagan studying in his backyard cabin. He's going to show us where to get a hotel room and help us find an apartment tomorrow either the upstairs or downstairs of a cottage. He's my only connection in Berkeley. By God as we come walking across his tall grass there we see him in a rose covered window with his head bent over the Lankavatara Scripture, and he's *smiling!* I cant understand what he's smiling about, *maya?* Buddha laughing on Mount Lanka or something? But here comes woesome old me and my maw down the yard with battered suitcases arriving almost like phantoms dripping from the sea. He's *smiling!*

For a moment, in fact, I hold my mother back and shush so I can watch him (the Mexicans call me an "adventurer") and by God he's just alone in the night smiling over old Bodhisattva truths of India. You cant go wrong with him. He's smiling *happily*, in fact, it's really a crime to disturb him—but it's got to be done, besides he'll be pleased and maybe even shocked into Seeing Maya but I have to clomp on his porch and say "Ben, it's Jack, I'm with my mother." Poor Memère is standing behind me with her poor eyes half closed from inhuman weariness, and despair too, wondering *now what* as big old Ben comes clomping to the little rose covered door with pipe in mouth and says "Well, well, well, whaddaya know?" Ben is too smart and really too nice to say anything like "Well hello there, when did you get in?" I'd already written ahead to him but had rather expected to arrive somehow in the daytime and find a room before dropping in on him, maybe alone while Memère could read a *Life* Magazine or eat sandwiches in her hotel room. But here it was 2 A.M., I was utterly stupefied, I'd seen no hotels or rooms to rent from the bus—I wanted to lean my shoulder on Ben somehow. He had to work in the morning too. But that smile, in the flowery silence, everybody in Berkeley asleep, and over such a text as the Lankavatara Scripture which says things like *Behold the hairnet, it is real, say the fools,* or like *Life is like the reflection of the moon on the water, which one is the true moon?*

meaning: Is reality the unreal part of unreality? or vice versa, when you open the door does anyone enter or is it you?

74 AND SMILING OVER THAT IN THE WESTERN NIGHT, stars waterfalling over his roof like drunkards stumbling downstairs with lanterns in their asses, the whole cool dew night I loved so much of northern California (that rainforest freshness), that smell of fresh green mint growing among tangled rubbery weeds and flowers.

The little cottage had quite a history, too, as I've shown earlier, had been the haven of Dharma Bums in the past where we'd had big tea discussions on Zen or sex orgies and yabyum with girls, where we'd played phonograph music and drank loudly in the night like Gay Mexicans in that quiet collegiate neighborhood, no one complaining somehow— The same old battered rocking chair was still on the little Walt Whitman rosey porch of vines and flowerpots and warped wood— In the back were still the little God-leak pots of Irwin Garden, his tomato plants, maybe some of our lost dimes or quarters or snapshots—Ben (a California poet from Oregon) had inherited this sweet little spot after everybody'd dispersed east some as far east as Japan (like old Dharma Bum Jarry Wagner)— So he sat there smiling over the Lankavatara Scripture in the quiet California night a strange and sweet sight to see after all those three thousand miles from Florida, for me— He was still smiling as he invited us to sit down.

"What now?" sighs poor Memère. "Jacky drag me all the way from my daughter's house in Florida with no plans, no money."

"There's lots of nice apartments around here for fifty dollars a month," I say, "and besides Ben can show us where to get a room tonight." Smoking and smiling and carrying most of our bags good old Ben leads us to a hotel five blocks away on University and Shattuck where we hire two rooms and go to sleep. That is, while Memère sleeps I walk back to the cottage with Ben to rehash old times. For us it was a strange quiet time between the era of our Zen Lunatic days of 1955 when we read our new poems to big audiences in San Francisco (tho I never read, just conducted sort of with a jug of wine) and the upcoming era of the paper and critics writing about it and calling it the "San Francisco Beat Generation Poetry Renaissance"— So Ben sat crosslegged sighing and said: "Oh nothing much happening around here. Think I'll go back to Oregon pretty soon." Ben is a big pink fellow with glasses and great calm blue eyes like the eyes of a Moon Professor or really of a Nun. (Or of Pat O'Brien, but he almost killed me when I asked him if he was an Irishman the first time I met him.) Nothing ever surprises him not even my strange arrival in the night with my mother; the moon'll shine on the water anyway and chickens'll lay more eggs and nobody'll know the origin of the limitless chicken without the egg. "What were you *smiling* about when I saw you in the window?" He goes into the tiny kitchen and brews a pot of tea. "I hate to disturb your hermitage."

"I was probably smiling because a butterfly got caught in the pages. When I extricated it, the black cat and the white cat both chased it."

"And a flower chased the cats?"

"No, Jack Duluoz arrived with a long face worrying about something, at 2 A.M. not even carrying a candle."

"You'll like my mother, she's a *real* Bodhisattva."

"I like her already. I like the way she puts up with you, you and your crazy three-thousand-mile ideas."

"She'll take care of everything . . ."

Funny thing about Ben, the first night me and Irwin had met him he cried all night face down on the floor, nothing we could do to console him. Finally he ended up never crying ever since. He had just come down from a summer on a mountain (Sourdough Mountain) just like me later, and had a whole book of new poems he hated, and cried: "Poetry is a lotta bunk. Who wants to bother with all that mental discrimination in a world already dead, already gone to the other shore? There's just nothin to do." But now he felt better, with that *smile,* saying: "It doesnt matter any more. I dreamed I was a Tathagata twelve feet long with gold toes and I didnt even care any more." There he sits crosslegged, leaning slightly to the left, flying softly thru the night with a Mount Malaya smile. He appears as blue mist in the huts of poets five thousand miles away. He's a strange mystic living alone smiling over books, my mother says next morning in the hotel "What kind of fella is that Benny? No wife, no family, nothing to do? Does he have a job?"

"He has a part time job inspecting eggs in the university laboratory up the hill. He earns just enough for his beans and wine. He's a *Buddhist!*"

"You and your Buddhists! Why dont you stick to your own religion?" But we go forth at nine in the morning and immediately miraculously find a fine apartment, groundfloor with a flowery yard, and pay a month's rent in advance and move our suitcases in. At 1943 Berkeley Way right near all the stores and from my bedroom window I can actually see the Golden Gate Bridge over the waters beyond the rooftops ten miles away. There's even a fireplace. When Ben gets home from work I go get him at his cottage and we go buy a whole frying chicken, a quart of whiskey, cheese and bread and accessories, and that night by firelight as we all get drunk in the new apartment I fry the chicken in the rucksack cookpots right on the logs and we have a great feast. Ben has already bought me a present, a tamper to tamp down the tobacco in my pipe, and we sit smoking by the fire with Memère.

But too much whiskey and we all get woozy and pass out. There are already two beds in the apartment and in the middle of the night I wake up to hear Memère's groan from the whiskey and somehow I realize our new home is already cursed thereby.

75

AND BESIDES MEMÈRE IS ALREADY SAYING that the mountains of Berkeley are going to topple over on us in an earthquake— Also she cant stand the morning fog— When she goes to the fine supermarkets down the street she hasnt got enough money anyway to buy anything she really wants—I rush out and buy a twelve-dollar radio and all the newspapers to make her feel good but she just doesnt like it— She says "California is sinister. I wanta spend my social security checks in Florida." (We're living on my $100 a month and her $84 a month.) I begin to see that she will never be able to live anywhere but near my sister, who is her great pal, or around New York City, which was her great dream once. Memère liked me too but I dont woman-chatter with her, spend most of my time reading and writing. Good old Ben comes over once in a while to cheer us up somehow tho he just depresses her. ("He's like an old Grandpaw! Where did you meet people like that? He's just a good old Grandpaw he's not a young man!") With my supply of Moroccan pep pills I write and write by candle-light in my room, the ravings of old angel midnight, nothing else to do, or I walk around the leafy streets noticing the difference between the yellow streetlamps and the white moon and coming home and painting it with house paint on cheap paper, drinking cheap wine meanwhile. Memère has nothing to do. Our furniture will come soon from Florida, that harried mass I told about. I therefore realize that I am an imbecile poet trapped in America with a dissatisfied mother in poverty and shame. It makes me mad I'm not a renowned man of letters living in a Vermont farmhouse with lobsters to broil and a wife to go downy with, or even my own woods to meditate in. I write and write absurdities as poor Memère mends my old pants in the other room. Ben Fagan sees the sadness of it all and puts his arm around my shoulders chuckling.

76   AND ONE NIGHT, IN FACT, I go to the nearby movie and lose myself for three hours in tragic stories about other people (Jack Carson, Jeff Chandler) and just as I step out of the theater at midnight I look down the street towards San Francisco Bay completely forgetting where I am and I see the Golden Gate Bridge shining in the night, and I *shudder with horror*. The bottom drops out of my soul. Something about that bridge, something *sinister* like Ma says, something like the forgotten details of a vague secanol nightmare. Come three thousand miles to shudder—and back home Memère is hiding in her shawl wondering what to do. It's really too much to believe. And like for instance we have a swell little bathroom but with slanted eaves but when I take joyous bubble baths every night, of hot water and Joy liquid soap, Memère complains she's afraid of that bathtub! She wont take a bath because she'll fall, she says. She's writing letters back to my sister and our furniture hasnt even arrived from Florida!

God! Who asked to be born anyway? What do with the bleak faces of pedestrians? What do with Ben Fagan's smoking pipe?

77   BUT HERE ON A FOGGY MORNING comes crazy old Alex Fairbrother in Bermuda shorts of all things and carrying a *bookcase* to leave with me, and not even really a bookcase but boards and redbricks— Old Alex Fairbrother who climbed the Mountain with me and Jarry when we were Dharma Bums who didnt care about anything— Time has caught up with us— Also he wants to pay me a day's wages to help him clean out a house in Buena Vista he owns— Instead of smiling at Memère and saying hello he starts right in talking to me the way he did in 1955, completely ignoring her even when she brings him a cup of coffee: "Well Duluoz, I see

you've made your way back to the West Coast. Speaking of
Virginia gentry did you know that they do go back to England— Fox trips— The mayor of London entertained about
fifty at the time of the 350th anniversary celebration and Elizabeth II let them have Elizabeth the First's wig (I think) to ex-
hibit and lots of things never lent out of the tower of London
before. You see I had a Virginia girl once . . . What kind of
Indians are Mescaleros? Library is closed today . . ." and Memère's in the kitchen saying to herself that all my friends are
insane. But actually I needed to earn that day's wages from
Alex. I'd already been down to a factory where I thought of
getting a job but just one glimpse of two kids pushing a bunch
of boxes around to the orders of a dull looking foreman who
probably questioned them about their private lives during lunch
hour, and I left—I'd even walked into the employment office
and right out again like a Dostoevsky character. When you're
young you work because you think you need the money: when
you're old you already know you dont need anything but death,
so why work? And besides, "work" always means somebody
else's work, you push another man's boxes around wondering
"Why doesnt he push his own boxes around?" And in Russia
probably the worker thinks, "Why doesnt the Peoples' Repub-
lic push their own goddam boxes around?" At least, by working for Fairbrother, I was working for a friend: he would have
me saw bushes so I could at least think "Well I'm sawing a
bush for old Alex Fairbrother who's very funny and climbed a
mountain with me two years ago." But anyway we set off for
work next morning on foot and just as we were crossing a small
side street a cop came over and gave us two tickets fining us $3
each for jaywalking, which was half my day's wages already. I
stared at the bleak California face of the cop in amazement.
"We were talking, we didnt notice no red light," I said, "besides it's eight o'clock in the morning there's no traffic!" and
on top of that he could see we had shovels on our shoulders
and were going to work someplace.

"I'm just doing my job," he says, "just like you're doing." I promised myself I'd never do another day's "work" at a "job" in America ever again come hell or high water. But of course it wasn't as easy as that with Memère to protect somehow— All the way from sleepy Tangiers of blue romance to the empty blue eyes of an American traffic cop somewhat sentimental like the eyes of Junior High School superintendents, rather, somewhat *un*sentimental like the eyes of Salvation Army mistresses beating tambourines on Christmas Eve. "It's my job to see that the laws are obeyed," he says absently: they never say anything about keeping law and order any more, there are so many silly laws including the ultimate imminent law against flatulating it's all too confused to even be called "order" anymore. While giving us this sermon some nut is holding up a warehouse two blocks away wearing a Halloween mask, or, worse, some councilman is tabling a new law in the legislature demanding stiffer penalties for "Jaywalking"—I can see George Washington crossing against the light, bareheaded and bemused, wondering about Republics like Lazarus, bumping into a cop at Market and Polk—

Anyway Alex Fairbrother knows about all this and is a big analytical satirist of the whole scene, laughs at it in his strange humorless way, and we actually have fun the rest of the day altho I cheat a little when he tells me to dispose of some piled underbrush I just dump it over the stone wall into the next lot, knowing he cant see me because he's on his hands and knees in the mud in the cellar taking it out by the handfuls and having me bring the buckets out. He's a very strange nut who's always moving furniture around and re-fixing things and houses: if he rents a small house on a Mill Valley hill he'll spend all his time building a small terrace by hand, but then move out suddenly, to another place, where he'll tear out the wallpaper. It is not at all surprising to see him suddenly coming down the street carrying two piano stools, or four empty art frames, or a dozen books on ferns, in fact I dont understand him but I like him.

He once sent me a box of Boy Scout cookies that came all crumbled in the mail from three thousand miles away. In fact there's something crumbly about *him*. He moves around the U.S.A. crumbling from job to job as a librarian where he apparently confuses the women librarians. He's very learned but it's on so many different and unconnected subjects nobody understands. He's very sad, actually. He wipes his glasses and sighs and says "It's disconcerting to see the population explosion is going to weaken American aid—maybe we should send them vaginal jelly in Shell Oil barrels? It would be a new kind of Tide Gamble made in America." (Here he actually refers to what is printed on cartons of Tide soap sent overseas, so he knows what he's talking about, it's only that no one else can connect why he said it.) Hard enough, even, in this vague world to know why anybody *exists* let alone *come on* like they do. Like Bull Hubbard has always said, I guess, life is "insufferably dull." "Fairbrother I'm bored!" I finally say—

Removing his glasses, sighing, "Try Suave. The Aztecs used Eagle oil. Had some long name starting with a 'Q' and ended with 'oil.' Quetzlacoatl. Then they could always wipe the extra goo off with a feathered serpent. Maybe they even tickled your heart before they tore it out. You cant always tell from the American Press, they have such long mustaches in the Pen & Pencil Set."

I suddenly realized he was just a crazy lonely poet speaking out an endless muttering monologue of poems to himself or anyone who listened day or night.

"Hey Alex, you mispronounced Quetzalcoatl: it goes Kwet-*sa*-kwatay. Like coyotl goes co-*yo*-tay, and peotl goes pey-*o*-tay, and Popocatepetl the volcano goes Popo-ca-*tep*-atay."

"Well you spit your pits out at the walking wounded there, I'm just giving it the old Mount Sinai Observation pronunciation . . . Like after all, how do you pronounce D.O.M. when you live in a cave?"

"I dont know, I'm only a Celtic Cornishman."

"Name of Cornish language is Kernuak. Cymeric group. If Celt and Cymry were pronounced as if with soft C's we'd have to call Cornwall Sornwall and then what would happen to all that corn we've eaten. When you go to Bude beware of the undertow. Even worse to haunt Padstow if you're good looking. Best thing to do is go in a pub and raise your glass to Mr. Penhagard, Mr. Ventongimps, Mr. Maranzanvose, Mr. Trevisquite and Mr. Tregeargate or go around digging for kistvaens and cromlechs. Or pray to Earth in the names of St. Teath, St. Erth, St. Breock, St. Gorran and St. Kew and it's not too far from derelict tin mine chimneys. Hail the Black Prince!" As he was saying this we were carrying our shoevels back at sunset eating ice cream cones (you cant blame me for misspelling "shovels" there).

He adds: "Clearly Jack what you need is a Land Rover and go camping in Inner Mongolia unless you wanta bring a bed lamp." All I could do, all anybody can ever do is *shrug* at all this, helplessly, but he goes on and on like that.

When we get back to my house the furniture has just come in from Florida and Ma and Ben are gleefully drinking wine and unpacking. Good old Ben has brought her some wine that night, and as tho he knew she didnt really want to unpack at all but just move back to Florida, which we finally did three weeks later anyway in this tangled year of my life.

78   BEN AND I GOT DRUNK one last time, sitting in his grass in the moonlight drinking whiskey from the bottle, whooee and wahoo like old times, crosslegged facing each other, yelling Zen questions: "Under the quiet tree somebody's blown my pussywillow apart?"

"Was it you?"

"Why do sages always sleep with their mouths open?"

"Because they want more booze?"

"Why do Sages kneel in the dark?"

"Because they're creaky?"

"Which direction did the fire go?"

"To the right."

"How do you know?"

"Because it burned me."

"How do you know?"

"I didnt know."

And such nonsense, and also telling long stories about our childhoods and pasts:—"Pretty soon Ben do you realize there'll be so many additional childhoods and pasts with everybody writing about them everybody'll give up reading in despair— There'll be an Explosion of childhoods and pasts, they'll have to have a Giant Brain print them out microscopically on film to be stored in a warehouse on Mars to give Heaven Seventy Kotis to catch up on all that reading— Seventy Million *Million* Kotis!—Whoopee!—Everything is free!—"

"Nobody has to care any more, we can even leave the whole scene to itself with Japanese fornicating machines fornicating chemical dolls on and on, with Robot Hospitals and Calculator Machine Crematories and just go off and be free in the universe!"

"In the freedom of eternity! We can just float around like Khans on a cloud watching the Samapatti T.V."

"We're doing that already."

One night we even got high on peotl, the Chihuahuan Mexican cactus button that gives you visions after three preliminary hours of empty nausea— It was the day that Ben had received a set of Buddhist monk robes in the mail from Japan (from friend Jarry) and the day I was determined to paint great pictures with my pitiful set of housepaints. Picture this for the insanity yet the harmlessness of a couple of goofballs who study poetry in solitude:—The sun is setting, ordinary people of Berkeley are eating their supper (in Spain, "supper" bears the mournful humble title of "La Cena," with all its connotations of earthly sorrowful simple food for the living beings who cannot live without it), but Ben and I have a gob of green cactus glup stuck in our stomachs, our eyes are iris-wide and wild, and here he is in those mad robes sitting absolutely motionless on his cottage floor, staring in the dark, upheld thumbs touching, refusing to answer me when I yell from the yard, actually sincerely seeing the old Pre-Heaven Heaven of Old in his quiet eyeballs waving like kaleidoscopes all deep blue and rose glory— And there *I* am kneeling in the grass in the half dark pouring enamel paint onto paper and *blowing* on it till it blossoms out and mixes up, and's going to be a great masterpiece until suddenly a poor little bug lands on it and gets stuck— So I spend the last thirty minutes of twilight trying to extricate the little bug from my sticky masterpiece without hurting it or pulling off a leg, but no go— So I lie there looking at the struggling little bug in the paint and realize I should never have painted at all for the sake of that little bug's life, whatever it is, or will be— And such a strange *dragon*-like little bug with noble forehead and features—I almost cry— The next day the painting is dry and the little bug is there, dead— In a few months his dust just vanishes away from the painting altogether— Or was it Fagan sent that little bug from his magic Samapatti revery to show me that art so sure and art so pure is not so sure and pure as all that? (Putting me in mind of the time I was writing so swiftly I killed a bug with the rash of my pencil deed, ugh—)

79 SO WHAT DO WE ALL DO in this life which comes on so much like an empty voidness yet warns us that we will die in pain, decay, old age, horror—? Hemingway called it a dirty trick. It might even be an ancient Ordeal laid down on us by an evil Inquisitor in Space, like the ordeal of the sieve and scissors, or even the water ordeal where they dump you in the water with toes tied to thumbs, O God— Only Lucifer could be so mean and *I am Lucifer* and I'm not that mean, in fact Lucifer Goes to Heaven— The warm lips against warm necks in beds all over the world trying to get out of the dirty Ordeal by Death—

When Ben and I sober up I say "How goes it with all that horror everywhere?"

"It's Mother Kali dancing around to eat up everything she gave birth to, eats it right back— She wears dazzling dancing jewels and covered all over with silks and decorations and feathers, her dance maddens men, the only part of her aint covered is her vagina which is surrounded with a Mandala Crown of jade, lapis lazuli, cornelean, red pearls and mother of pearl."

"No diamonds."

"No, that's beyond . . ."

I ask my own mother what's with all our horror and unhappiness, dont mention Mother Kali to scare her, she goes beyond Mother Kali by saying: "People's got to do right— Let's you and me get out of this lousy California with the cops wont let you walk, and the fog, and those damn hills about to fall on our back, and go *home*."

"But where's home?"

"Home is with your family— You've only got one sister— I've only got one grandson— And one son, *you*— Let's all get together and live *quiet*. People like your Ben Fagan, your Alex Poorbrother, your Irwin Gazootsky, they dont *know* how to live!—You gotta have *fun*, good food, good beds, nothing more— *La tranquillité qui compte!*—Never mind all the fuss about you worry this and that, make yourself a *haven* in this world and Heaven comes after."

Actually, there can be no haven for the living lamb but plenty haven for the dead lamb, okay, soon enough, but I'll follow Memère because she speaks of *tranquillity*. In fact she didnt realize it was I myself who'd wrecked all Ben Fagan's tranquillity by coming here in the first place, but okay. We already start packing to go back. She has her social security checks every month as I say and my book is coming out in a month. What she is really delivering to me is a message about quietude: in a previous lifetime she must surely (if there is such a thing as a previous lifetime possible to an individual soul-entity)—she must surely have been a Head Nun in a remote Andalusian or even Grecian nunnery. When she goes to bed at night I hear her rosary beads rattle. "Who cares about Eternity! we want the Here and Now!" yell the snakedancers of streets and riots and Guerneca hand grenades and airplane bombs. When sweetly waking in the night on her pillow my mother opens her tired pious eyes, she must be thinking: "Eternity? Here and Now? Wat they talkin about?"

Mozart on his death bed must have known this—

And Blaise de Pascal most of all.

80   THE ONLY ANSWER ALEX FAIRBROTHER HAS for my question about horror is with his eyes, his words are hopelessly entangled in a Joycean stream of learning like: "Horror Everywhere? That sounds like a nice idea for a new Tourist Bureau? You could have Coxie's Armies laid out in Arizona canyons buying tortillas and ice cream from the shy Navajos only the ice cream is really peyote ice cream green like pistachio and everybody goes back home singing Adios Muchachos Companéros de la Vida—"

Or something. It's only in his sighing eyes you see it, in his *crumbling* eyes, his disillusioned Boy Scout Leader eyes . . .

And then to top it all off one day Cody is rushing across our porch and into the house dying to borrow ten dollars from me for an urgent pot connection. I've practically *come* to California to be near old buddy Cody but his wife has refused to help this time, probably because I have Memère with me, probably because she's afraid he'll go mad with me again like he did on the road years ago— To him it makes no difference, he hasnt changed, he just wants to borrow ten dollars. He says he'll be back. Meanwhile he also borrows Ben's tendollar *Tibetan Book of the Dead* and rushes off, all muscular as usual in T-shirt and frayed jeans, crazy Cody. "Any girls around here?" he cries anxiously as he drives off.

But a week later I take Memère into San Francisco to let her ride the cable cars and eat in Chinatown and buy toys in Chinatown and I have her wait for me in the big Catholic church on Columbus while I rush to the Place, Cody's hangout, to see if I can recoup that $10 from him. By God there he is sipping a beer, playing chess with "The Beard." He looks surprised but he knows I want my ten bucks. He cashes a twenty at the bar and pays me and then even comes with me to meet Memère in the church. As we walk in he kneels and does the sign of the Cross, as I do, and Memère turns to see us do that. She realizes Cody and I are fatal lovely friends who are not bad boys at all.

So three days later as I'm kneeling on the floor unpacking a crate of advance copies of my novel *Road* which is all about Cody and me and Joanna and big Slim Buckle, and Memère's at the store so I'm alone in the house, I look up as a golden light appears in the porch door silently: and there stands Cody, Joanna (golden blonde beauty), big tall Slim Buckle, and behind them the midget 4:2 inch Jimmy Low (known not as a "midget" at all but simply Jimmy, or as Deni Bleu calls him, "A Little Man"). We all stare at one another in the golden light. Not a sound. I'm also caught red handed (as we all grin) with a copy of *Road* in my hands *even before I've looked at it for the first time!* I automatically hand one to Cody who is after all the hero of the poor crazy sad book. It's one of the several occasions in my life when a meeting with Cody seems to be suffused with a silent golden light, as I'll show another later, altho I dont even know what it means, unless it means that Cody is actually some kind of angel or archangel come down to this world and I recognize it. A fine thing to say in this day and age! And especially with the wild life he was now leading that was going to end in tragedy in six months, as I'll tell in a minute— A fine thing to be talking about angels in this day when common thieves smash the holy rosaries of their victims in the street . . . When the highest ideals on earth are based on the month and the day of some cruel bloody revolution, nay when the highest ideals are simply new *reasons* for murdering and despoiling people— And Angels? Since we've never seen an angel what angel do you mean? But it was Christ said "Since you've never seen my Father then how can you know my Father?"

81 AH YES, MAYBE I'M WRONG and all the Christian, Islamic, Neo Platonist, Buddhist, Hindu, and Zen Mystics of the world were wrong about the transcendental mystery of existence but I dont think so— Like the thirty birds who reached God and saw themselves reflected in His Mirror. The thirty Dirty Birds, those 970 of us birds who never made it across the Valley of Divine Illumination did really make it anyway in Perfection— So now let me explain about poor Cody, even tho I've already told most of his story. He is a *believer* in life and he *wants* to go to Heaven but because he loves life so he embraces it so much he thinks he sins and will never see Heaven— He was a Catholic altar boy as I say even when he was bumming dimes for his hopeless father hiding in alleys. You could have ten thousand cold eyed Materialistic officials claim they love life too but can never embrace it so near sin and also never see Heaven— They will contemn the hot-blooded lifelover with their cold papers on a desk because they have no blood and therefore have no sin? No! They sin by lifelessness! They are the ogres of Law entering the Holy Realm of Sin! Ah, I've got to explain myself without essays and poems—Cody had a wife whom he really loved, and three kids he really loved, and a good job on the railroad. But when the sun went down his blood got hot:—hot for old lovers like Joanna, for old pleasure like marijuana and talk, for jazz, for the gayety that any respectable American wants in a life growing more arid by the year in Law Ridden America. But he did not

hide his desire and cry *Dry!* He went all out. He filled his car
with friends and booze and pot and batted around looking for
ecstasy like some fieldworker on a Saturday night in Georgia
when the moon cools the still and guitars are twangin down the
hill. He came from sturdy Missouri stock that walked on strong
feet. We've all seen him kneel *sweating* praying to God! When
we went to San Francisco that day whole cordons of police
were surrounding the streets of North Beach looking for crazy
people like him. Somehow by some miracle we walked with
pockets full of bottles and pot right thru them, laughing with
girls, with little Jimmy, to parties, to bars, to jazz cellars. I
couldnt understand what the cops were doing! Why werent
they looking for murderers and robbers? When I once sug-
gested this to a policeman who stopped us because I was flag-
ging my buddy's car back with a railroad lamp so there'd be no
accidents anywhere the policeman said "You've got quite an
imagination, havent you?" (meaning I might be a murderer or
robber myself.) I'm no such thing and neither is Cody, you
have to be DRY to be those things! You have to HATE life to
kill it and rob it!

82   BUT ENOUGH ABOUT CALIFORNIA FOR NOW—I
later had adventures in Big Sur down there that
were really horrible and only as horrible as you get when you
get older and your last moment impels you to test *all*, to go
mad, just to see what the Void'll do— Suffice it to say that
when Cody said goodbye to all of us that day he for the first
time in our lives failed to look me a goodbye in the eye but
looked away shiftylike—I couldnt understand it and still
dont—I knew something was bound to be wrong and it turned
out very wrong, he was arrested a few months later for posses-
sion of pot and spent two years sweeping out the cotton room
in San Quentin tho I happen to know the real reason for this
horrible ordeal in the real world is not because of having two

cigarettes in his pocket (two bearded bluejeaned beatniks in a car saying "What's the hurry kid?" and Cody says "Drive me down to the station real quick I'll be late for my train") (his driving license taken away for speeding) ("and I'll give ya some pot for your trouble") and they turn out to be disguised cops— The real reason aside from he didnt look in my eyes, was, I once saw him belt his daughter across the room in a chastising crying scene and that's why his Karma devolved that way— Tit for Tat, and Jot for Tittle— Tho in two years Cody was about to become a greater man than ever as maybe he realizes all this— But, and, according to the laws of tit-for-tat what do I deserve myself?

83 WHY, JUST A LITTLE OLE EARTH QUAKE—Memère and me ride Greyhound bus all the way back to Florida the same wretched way, the furniture behind us, and find a backporch apartment for a low rent and move in— The late afternoon sun beats mercilessly on the tin porch roof as I take a dozen cold baths a day sweating and dying— And also I get mad because my poor little nephew Lil Luke keeps eating my Pecan Sandy Cookies (as Kookie a reason for one of the great foggy mistakes of my life) so I ragingly crazy angry go and actually take a bus *back* to Mexico, to Brownsville, across at Matamoros, and down a day and a half to Mexico City again— But at least Memère is well because at least she's only two blocks away from my sister and sorta likes her porch apartment because it has a kitchen bar which she calls "Gabe's Place"— And all you hearts who love life realize now that to love is to love— Tho I'm lost in the unutterable mental glooms of the 20th Century Scrivener of Soul Stories going down again to Gloom Mexico for no particular good reason—I always wanted to write a book to defend someone because it's hard to defend myself, it's an indefensible trip but maybe I'll get to see old Gaines again— He's not even there.

Ah you meerschaum merry thinking sad gentlemen in the London fog, and how'd it befall to you?—Gallows at dawn for a mean Magistrate with Wig of Doom?—I went to the old address to find Old Bull, the hole in his window was repaired, I climbed up the roof stairs to see my old room cell and the washer ladies— A young clean Spanish Woman had moved into my house and painted the walls whitewash new and sat there among laces talking to my old landlady to whom I said "Where is Mister Gaines?"—And in my inconceivable French head when she said *"Señor Gaines se murio"* I heard "Mister Gaines deathed himself"— But she means he'd died since I left— It's a terrible thing to hear from the lips of human beings that a fellow sufferer has finally died, ogred time with his rash deed, ploughed space with his Dare and Died in spite of all logically spiritual injunctions— Has cut out for good— Has taken that Honey-&-Milk Body out to God and didnt even write and tell you— Even the Greek cornerstore man said it, *"Señor Gahr-va se murio"*— He'd died up himself— He who cried to me and Irwin and Simon on the last day when we were running away to America and the World and for what?—So never again old Deathly Gaines riding cabs with me to Nowhere— And never instruct me again in the arts of Living and Dying—

84 SO I GO DOWNTOWN AND GET AN EXPENSIVE HOTEL ROOM to make up for it— But a sinister Marble Hotel it is— Now that Gaines' gone away all Mexico City is a sinister Marble Hive— How we continue in this endless Gloom I'll never know— Love, Suffer, and Work is the motto of my family (Lebris de Keroack) but seems I suffer more than the rest— Old Honeyboy Bill's in Heaven for sure anyway— Only thing now is Where's Jack Going?—Back to Florida or New York?—For further emptiness?—Old Thinker's thought his last thought—I go to bed in my new hotel room and soon fall asleep anyway, what can I do to bring Gaines back to the dubious privilege of living?—He's trying his best to bless me anyway but that night a Buddha's born to Gina Lollobrigida and I hear the room creak, the door on the dresser creaks back and forth slowly, the walls groan, my whole bed weaves like I say "Where am I, at sea?" but I realize I'm not at sea but in Mexico City— Yet the hotel room is rocking like a ship— It's a giant earthquake rocking Mexico— And how was dying, old buddy?—Easy?—I yell to myself *"Encore un autre petrain!"* (like the sea storm) and jump under the bed to protect myself against falling ceilings if any— *Hurracan* is whipping up to hit the Louisiana coast— The entire apartment building across the street from the post office on Calle Obregon is falling in killing everybody— Graves leer under Moon pines— It's all over.

Later I'm back in New York sitting around with Irwin and Simon and Raphael and Lazarus, and now we're famous writers more or less, but they wonder why I'm so sunk now, so unexcited as we sit among all our published books and poems, tho at least, since I live with Memère in a house of her own miles from the city, it's a peaceful sorrow. A peaceful sorrow at home is the best I'll ever be able to offer the world, in the end, and so I told my Desolation Angels goodbye. A new life for me.